ALSO BY HELEN HOWE

The Whole Heart
We Happy Few
The Circle of the Day

The Success

a novel by

HELEN HOWE

SIMON AND SCHUSTER

New York : 1956

PUBLISHED BY SIMON AND SCHUSTER, INC.
ROCKEFELLER CENTER, 630 FIFTH AVENUE
NEW YORK 20, N. Y.

LIBRARY OF CONGRESS CATALOG CARD NUMBER: 56-9919
MANUFACTURED IN THE UNITED STATES OF AMERICA
BY H. WOLFF, NEW YORK

To Quincy and Mark

Par nobile fratrum

Who can decide offhand which is absolutely better, to live or to understand life? We must do both alternately, and a man can no more limit himself to either than a pair of scissors can cut with a single one of its blades.

—William James, *Some Problems of Philosophy*

CONTENTS

—I—

Maggie

1

Maggie Fraser, ever since she could remember, had determined to be a success. Impatient by nature, when she found that she had not achieved fame during her first year out of college she decided that she might as well get married. As Maggie Bradfield she might do better.

Advancing up the aisle of Boston's Trinity Church as a bride on her father's arm, she was greeted by the expectant rustle of a large number of people rising from their seats. Heads were turned and eyes directed to follow her progress. In her everyday sweater and skirt Maggie suggested an overgrown filly; her long, skinny legs had not yet caught up to the fine figure of a woman whose weight they were rather awkward about supporting. Her motions were generally as unco-ordinated as her emotions were unfocused. Today she was transformed. Under the long flowing lines of her ivory-satin wedding dress she gave the appearance of being all of a piece, her head held high, the firm line of her arched nose duplicating Dr. Fraser's. A sparkle just short of a glitter flashed in her narrow turquoise-blue eyes as she surveyed her waiting bridegroom. She moved toward him, stopping to sway on the ball of each foot in time to the music, as a queen might have moved toward the throne on which she was about to seat herself, and reign.

A few minutes' preamble—"Dearly beloved, we are gathered together here in the sight of God"—and the clergyman was asking, "Dexter, wilt thou have this Woman to thy wedded wife, to live together after God's ordinance in the holy estate of Matrimony? Wilt thou love her, comfort her, honour, and keep her in sickness and in health; and, forsaking all others, keep thee only unto her, so long as ye both shall live?"

"I will," Dexter Bradfield answered. The public use of his voice heretofore had been confined to barking out football signals in the Harvard backfield. Now, though the aggressive squaring of his shoulders bespoke iron determination, his voice was so low that he was not heard beyond the chancel. Maggie, at the rehearsal the day before, had told him that he must be sure to "throw" his voice. He had failed to do so; at this rate it was obvious that she must bear the brunt of the performance.

"Margaret, wilt thou have this Man to thy wedded husband, to live together after God's ordinance in the holy estate of Matrimony? Wilt thou obey him, and serve him, love, honour, and keep him in sickness and in health; and, forsaking all others, keep thee only unto him, so long as ye both shall live?"

"I will!" Maggie's answer rang with a fine resonance. She had not played the part of James Madison for nothing in Vassar's Philaletheis production of *The First Lady of the Land*.

Five minutes more and the words rang out, "I pronounce that they are man and wife."

Down the aisle, on her husband's arm, walked Maggie. Passing the pew that contained her parents, she flashed them a perfect smile. Mrs. Bent, who had come on from New York for the wedding, and knew *everything*, had told her to be careful about not showing her gums. So many brides did when they smiled, and it could simply ruin the effect. Maggie flashed another flawless specimen toward the opposite pew, containing the Bradfields.

Her bridesmaids were less assured. Caroline Spafford, the maid of honor, known at college as Spaff, looked fixedly before her, unaware of the existence of the usher at her side. Spaff, of the very stuff of which "college material" is made, always stiffened in the presence of the opposite sex. The sheaf of delphinium and roses held by Kitten, Maggie's sister-in-law, the matron of honor, quivered in the crook of her elbow. Kitten was the most fragile and the gentlest of the three girls who were known to Vassar '22 as the Triumvirate. Indeed today she was the only member of the wedding party whose face recorded some of the emotions associated with the plighting of true love. Perhaps she was reliving her own wedding to Maggie's brother Roger that had taken place in the Unitarian church in Milton only a few months before.

The night before that wedding Dexter had driven Maggie home to Boston following the bridesmaids' and ushers' dinner at the Milton Hill House. She had already refused to marry him at least four times that winter, murmuring, "My career" and "I can't imagine not living in New York." But the painful fact was that a winter's study at a dramatic school had not secured her a job in summer stock. Moreover, Spaff, her roommate on West Tenth Street, was going away for the summer; solitude and boredom were as unthinkable to Maggie as returning home to her parents in Boston.

When Dexter deliberately stopped his car and turned off the ignition under a tree at the foot of Blue Hill and took Maggie in his arms, she, who—for all her ebullient spirits and popularity with other girls—was still what the Triumvirate called "inexperienced," learned what it was to be kissed and what it was to thrill to the kindling of passion, roused and returned. As maid of honor the next day, her arm tucked into Dexter's, as best man, Maggie had seen in a flash that they were a more striking couple than the bride and groom. Exquisite as Kitten was in her great-grandmother's seed pearls and white lace, with a bouquet of white lilac, she was almost too ethereal to suggest real flesh and blood. Roger, too, was dimmed by the pallor of stark fright. Maggie had had only to look in the mirror to see that her own appearance was brilliant: her skin glowed with the golden sheen of an apricot, her cheeks were splashed with as rosy a red as the American Beauties she carried, her dilated nostrils breathed life and fire. Dexter's six feet two and masculine good looks were worthy of her. She had learned deliciously, moreover, the emotion they could rouse in her. Suddenly, as Kitten's Mendelssohn "Recessional" pealed out, the color of her cheeks intensified in response to the quickening of her pulse. She turned, beaming, to whisper in Dexter's ear, under the triumphant notes of the organ, "Dexter, I'll marry you! Let's tell them at the reception!"

It had all happened in such a seething excitement that Maggie herself could not remember afterward any clear sequence of events. There were hurried whisperings with her mother and father, both of whom urged her not to do anything impulsive; there was more whispering and hugging, and even a little crying with Kitten in the pantry, while a bottleneck of guests jammed the living room, waiting to kiss the bride. And then came the moment when Kitten stood up to cut her cake and, lifting a glass of raspberry shrub, proposed a toast to the next Fraser-Bradfield bride and groom. There was at first a silent lack of comprehension, then a gasp of incredulity, and, finally, shrieks and squeals of pleasure and congratulation. If Maggie had failed to take Broadway by storm, she had certainly succeeded in stealing the show from the bride on her wedding day.

Today, Maggie's own wedding reception was held in the Frasers' house on the Charles River side of Brimmer Street. The guests could be sure of not being disappointed in Dr. Fraser's hospitality; they knew that the toasts would not be drunk in raspberry shrub.

The Bradfields, huddling in one corner of the living room, were living up to Dr. Fraser's description of them as being like the sociable weavers, South African members of the finch family, who live in a communal nest and move abroad only in a solid phalanx. In their case the genus was identifiable to inhabitants of Boston and its vicinity —a vicinity bounded on the south by Milton, where the family spent its winters, and on the north by Dunster, where it spent its summers— through its plumage of a towheaded crest. At the moment they seemed to fear the danger of sipping pollution as Dr. Fraser advanced on them, extending a glass of Pol Roget. In his pin-striped trousers and morning coat, with a white carnation in the buttonhole, he could hardly have made a greater contrast with Pa Brad, as awkward in his brown boots and blue serge suit as he was wretched in the stiff collar, around whose inner edge he kept passing a surreptitious finger. It was very hard for Dr. Fraser to believe that the Bradfields lived on the income of their income.

"Won't you break down your principles just for today, Mr. Bradfield?" Dr. Fraser asked genially.

"It is not a question of principles." Pa Brad spoke with an air of authority unusual for him. "It's just that we aren't *interested* in alcohol."

"Dear me," answered Dr. Fraser. Then, speaking over his shoulder, "Lulie, do come and meet my children's high-thinking in-laws. Probably Kitten has told you about Mrs. Bent." He turned back to Ma Brad. "She is our dearest friend and nearest neighbor in summer at Northeast Harbor."

"Oh, yes—" Ma Brad's spine visibly stiffened—"we know she lives in New York." A gasp of panic shivered through the family, as though they had scented a hawk upwind.

The older woman, with hair as white as her long glacé-kid gloves, and a large mohair hat of the same gray blue as her eyes, its ample brim tilting downward, carried in one hand a soft gold-mesh bag and in the other, with the glove rolled back to the wrist, held a glass of champagne. To most observers Mrs. Bent suggested charm as well as distinction; but the Bradfields were suspicious of "dressy" women, and downright terrified of anybody who could think of things to talk about with perfect strangers.

"What a delightful occasion this is!" she was saying with alarming ease. "The Bradfields and the Frasers seem to have a fatal attraction for one another! I always think that a brother and sister marrying a brother and sister makes one feel so *sure* about the future. As I consider myself the closest friend in the world of the Fraser family, naturally I have loved Maggie and Roger since they were children. And now I'm going to love your Kitten and Dexter too. Though Kitten looks like a little Dresden shepherdess, she gives the impression of being extremely *wise*. And Dexter—such a splendid young man! I hope that we shall see them both often at Northeast Harbor."

Ma Brad assumed the role of spokesman for the flock around her.

"The Bradfields have been going to Dunster since the land at Far Fields was deeded to them by the Indians. I'm sure that neither Kitten nor Dexter will ever be interested in going anywhere else."

Dr. Fraser opened his mouth to comment on the Bradfields' use of the word *interested* but, perhaps fortunately, was interrupted by the pressure of Mrs. Fraser's hand on his sleeve.

"Malcolm, dear, Maggie's going to cut the cake in the dining room. Won't you bring Mr. and Mrs. Bradfield along to watch? The young people look so happy, it's really fun just to stand on the sidelines."

The Bradfields seemed as grateful for the suggested diversion as shy children at a birthday party. They fell obediently into line behind their host and hostess, jostling their way through the crowds that flowed from library to living room, some coming down from the bedrooms above where wedding presents were on display, to join the stream that flowed downstairs to the large dark paneled dining room looking out on the Charles River.

Maggie stood at the head of the white-clothed table, before her wedding cake, brandishing a knife. Its point was directed toward her bridegroom's heart.

"She *is* lovely," Mrs. Bent murmured to both parents.

"She looks happy," said Mrs. Fraser with a grateful sigh.

"She looks as though she means business," said her father, adding genially to his new son-in-law, "Though she slay you, yet will you trust in her, Dexter?"

Dexter Bradfield, sublimely unaware that Scripture was being quoted at him, beamed down rapturously at Maggie. "Sure, I trust her," he said.

"Whenever I see Maggie looking like that—" Dr. Fraser chose Mrs. Bent as the recipient of his observation—"I remember Roger, when he was a little tyke at the *lycée* in Paris, comparing her to a picture of François *premier* in his history book."

It was a picture the family had often referred to since, showing the King of France wearing what looked like a tam-o'-shanter rakishly to one side and a blouse with a "bateau" neckline, broken by a long chain on which hung a locket. His nose was excessively long and its high arch pronounced; his lips were slender, with a smile that promised gaiety in its upturned corners. It was not only in appearance that Maggie made her family think of royalty; there was something no less than regal in her conviction of her own divine right to serve as a lightning conductor to bring heaven down to earth on demand. She welcomed each new person as corroboration of her own sense that life was a party to be enjoyed. That she herself considered herself the guest of honor was inevitable. In any gathering where she found herself she took up room in more than a merely physical sense. As a bride, at her own wedding reception, radiance flashed from her, as from a Fourth-of-July sparkler.

At the moment, she was about to stab her knife into the soft heart of the cake when Dexter put his hand on her wrist. "Wait, darling," he admonished. "Aren't you going to figure out how to make the slices the same size before you start?"

"The scientific approach! Typical!" Maggie called on the assembled guests for confirmation. "If all the slices aren't the same size, what's the dif?" She turned back to the snowy edifice, and the towering ramparts crumbled under her onslaught. "Come on now, bridesmaids, you get first whack. Put a piece under your pillow tonight, and whatever you dream will come true. Kitten's got her wish, so, Spaff, here you are."

Dr. Fraser moved alongside. "Would it be impertinent for me to ask what you're going to wish for, Spaff?" he asked.

"Heck, *I* don't know." Spaff knitted her solemn brow. "So far my wish is pretty general. I guess I just wish to function."

"Entirely natural. Every woman should," agreed the head of a gynecological service at Boston's Massachusetts General Hospital.

"I mean function in the group," answered Vassar's sociology major with disdain.

Mrs. Fraser, seeing that all the guests had a piece of cake, plucked at the bride's white-satin sleeve. "Maggie, dear, I'm afraid you should be going upstairs to change. People will be thinking of leaving."

There was a scramble, a clatter, and a chatter, and Maggie was racing up the big stairway with her bridesmaids at her heels.

Upstairs in her bedroom the girls gathered round the central figure, some helping to detach the veil and others to unhook the satin dress, leaving her standing in her camisole, petticoat, and the heavy bra that flattened out her naturally ample curves. Others extended a lime-green pleated crepe-de-Chine dress, into which, with arms held straight above her head, she wiggled.

Her friends assumed that Maggie must be suffering from stage fright. After all, they were getting her ready to be carried away from themselves forever—by a husband. The laughter and chatter rose in a crescendo to cover up a mounting sense of embarrassment.

"Honestly, Maggie, you looked divine! Most brides are generally so *sappy*."

"Dexter really is the best-looking thing! Anyone can tell just by looking at him that he simply worships the ground you walk on."

"Maggie, I just *adore* my bar pin. You were such a peach to give them to us."

The admiring chorus of maidens about her was silently echoed in the cloud of witnesses that surrounded Maggie in her bedroom. Photographs of college classmates sprouted on every side—on the bureau, on the desk, and from the edge of the mirror. They all testified to the qualities that made Maggie's hold on her friends unique—qualities that spelled excitement and daring enterprise. It was Maggie who goaded them into dotting their "i's" with small circles, putting a dab of Dorine on their cheeks, and dyeing their nightgowns black. The messages scrawled across the pictures testified to the place that Maggie held in the hearts of her classmates. "To the most likely to succeed—the one and only Maggie." "Laugh? I thought I'd split my stitches. To Maggie, the world's best cure for the dumps." "You show 'em, kiddo!"

Maggie, before her mirror, adjusting the cloche that hugged her forehead, with its curling feather over one ear, could see Kitten's reflection as well as her own. Kitten had pulled off her large mohair hat and was mopping her forehead with a folded handkerchief. "It's too tight," she murmured.

A friend at her elbow said, "The trouble is you've got too much hair."

Maggie wheeled. "If I were you, do you know what I'd do, Kitten?"

"No. What?" asked Kitten, looking at Maggie as a rabbit might have looked at a boa constrictor that he happened to admire and love as well as fear.

"I'd bob my hair!"

Spaff intervened. "But you're not Kitten. Kitten's hair suits her just the way it is."

"Pooh! Kitten's got curly hair, and if it were short she would look like a little cherub. That figure eight on the back of her head makes her look so respectable," Maggie pronounced disgustedly.

"But you have one yourself," ventured Kitten.

"That's entirely different. I'm tall and can carry it off." Maggie tossed her head as though to illustrate its capacity for coping with any responsibility, particularly if it belonged to somebody else. "If you're afraid to do it, I'll do it for you."

"Not *now*!" Kitten quavered. "You can't cut my hair now, Maggie!"

"Who says I can't?" An awe-struck gasp rippled through the circle that drew close. "Give me a pair of scissors, someone! Here, wait a jiffy. Here's an old newspaper." Spreading out sheets of it on the floor, she stepped on Tut-ankh-amen's face with one foot and with the other on the features of Ben Turpin as the Shriek of Araby. "Now, sit still," she commanded.

The girls were giggling. "Maggie, you're the limit!" "I never thought you'd dare!" "Honestly, doesn't she beat the Dutch!" "Whoever heard of a bride, at her own wedding, stopping to cut somebody else's hair? Dexter's probably pacing the front hall, wondering where you are, right this minute."

"Here we go, girls! More darned fun! More people killed! More blood spilled!" Maggie twirled a huge pair of scissors in her hand with the gesture of a dangerous barber; then, without waiting to draw breath or take soundings of any kind, she simply began to hack. Chop, chop, chop. In a flash, half of Kitten's head was shorn in a stiff, straight, ugly line. There was no sign of a curl.

Kitten herself, unaware of the massacre being performed, held her head forward over her lap and wiggled. "You tickle!" she brought out in a smothered voice and began to laugh.

"Look, Spaff!" Maggie shrieked, suddenly confronting her own handiwork. "Isn't it horrible! What's wrong?" And she began to laugh.

"Oh, Kitten," wailed Spaff, "you're ruined! You'll have to become a nun and take the veil!" And Spaff began to laugh.

Then the tornado struck. Starting with the Triumvirate as storm center, it picked up the girls, one by one, shaking them helpless. They were tossed to and fro under the wild, unreasoning cyclone—the giggles. Just as it seemed about to subside, fresh shrieks, squeals, howls, and whoops of laughter ricocheted back and forth, Maggie's high soprano pealing above all the others.

From under the whirlwind, more and more urgent, first softly, then louder, and then very loud, came the sound of knocking and her mother's voice on the other side of the closed door.

"Maggie! Girls! Please! I can't make myself heard."

Maggie called out, "We're doing something very important, Mother!" There was a wild burst of hysteria by way of assent.

"Maggie—" her mother spoke with unaccustomed severity—"it really is very rude to keep all the guests waiting. And poor Dexter. Don't forget, the only place we could find for him to change his clothes that wasn't occupied was the broom closet. He's still in there, waiting for you to come downstairs."

The words *broom closet* set up another stifled snicker. "All right, Mother, I'm coming. Just a jiffy! I just have to get my cape and gloves." She turned back to the bridesmaids. "Kitten, ram your hat down on your head, and nobody will notice. Spaff can fix it up for you later. Now you all go down ahead of me. As I run downstairs I'm going to toss my bouquet to one of you!" In consultation with Dexter she had already decided to throw it to his sister Marcia.

There was more clatter and more chatter, and the bridesmaids were downstairs ahead of her. Maggie leaned over to the upstretched arms and tossed her bouquet of lilies of the valley, white satin ribbons flying, toward Marsh. With the agility that had won her fame as a basketball forward on the Vassar varsity, Spaff intercepted the pass.

Twirling her white gloves over her head, Maggie tripped down the stairs to the hall where Dexter, on cue, had popped out of his stifling hideaway to take his place at her side.

The guests were lined along the hall, rose petals and rice in their hands. Maggie bolted, head down, under the barrage they let fly, hesitating just long enough at the threshold to be enfolded by her mother. "My darling child," whispered Mrs. Fraser.

The quaver in her mother's voice steadied Maggie. "Mother! Don't, please. It's contagious! Good-by, Father." Maggie suddenly stood before her father, stripped of the power to rule and charm that had held her up all day. The two meager words might have been spoken by a penniless waif shoved out into a cruel world. She felt a huge lump rise in her throat.

Dexter stepped forward to extend his hand to his father-in-law. "I'll take good care of her, Dr. Fraser," he said.

"Good-by, child." Dr. Fraser kissed Maggie abruptly and, pulling out a silk handkerchief, blew suddenly and loud. After Dexter's retreating back he called out, "Maggie will always take good care of herself. It's you I'm worried about, my boy!"

2

"LET's do something really *romantic* this afternoon!"

Maggie's voice was of the sort that could generally set reverberating sensations of warmth and pleasure. Bradfields, however, resisted on principle any assault of easy charm.

"That's a fine thing to say the last day of our honeymoon," said Dexter. "Haven't we done something romantic every day?" Holding a cyanide jar in his hand, the bridegroom peered into it with an expression of rapturous satisfaction at a hummingbird hawk moth he had just captured in the garden.

"Of course we have, darling. It's been wonderful, but—you know what I mean—let's do something extra special and wind it up with a bang."

The bride of two weeks suppressed a sigh as she looked out through the screened-in porch at the marshes of Dunster; the tide was dead low, and the mud flats beyond were clearly discernible. She had tried so hard to persuade Dexter to take her to Hawaii for their honeymoon. He might not get a holiday again for years—and it would be wonderful to know that at least once in their lives they had had a whiff of something really exotic. Dexter's mother had explained to her. "I'm sure Dexter wouldn't be happy in a place he couldn't put his teeth into. You're going to have to learn to love Far Fields, so you might as well begin now."

Far Fields was the name of the Bradfields' sixty acres at Dunster in Essex County, some thirty miles north of Boston. The land had belonged to the family for nearly three hundred years, although the half-dozen cottages scattered across it had been christened in homage to Gilbert and Sullivan in more recent times. Ma Brad had given Titipu, sacrosanct to family honeymooners, as an outright wedding present to Dexter and Maggie. Maggie was trying hard to see with the eyes of her husband not only the unpainted clapboard walls of the ugly little late-Victorian cottage but the surrounding countryside as well. Only occasionally, so far, had she yielded to the temptation of saying, "Wait till *you* see Northeast Harbor!"

"I know what we'll do. We'll go up the inlet in the canoe." Dexter spoke decisively and with as much apparent satisfaction as though he were offering Maggie a peep down the crater of Mauna Loa. "It's low tide, and we can walk along the dunes to the sandspit to get to the boathouse."

Presently, with her hand in his, Maggie was plodding through the deep sand as Fetch and Carrie, Dexter's Labrador retrievers, circled around them and then sloshed back into the slow-rolling waves to bark at sea gulls.

Dexter turned to ask her, "You're not really sorry, are you, Maggie, that we came to Dunster?"

"Of course I'm not, darling! It's been part of getting to know you. I don't know where one leaves off and the other begins."

It was true that each day she had looked at her husband against the backdrop of dunes and marshes, sea and sky, telling herself how handsome he was—the line from his straight, low brow to the tip of his nose "just like a Greek god"—and thinking how perfectly his protective family coloring was adapted to this native habitat. The blue eyes, the same color as his faded, shrunken blue jeans, might have been bleached by the white salt which seemed to cling to his eyelashes, just as his hair might have taken on its pale sand color from the endless beaches, blown by the unceasing southwest wind.

"I still can't believe you're my husband," Maggie said abruptly, and was surprised by the unaccountable drop in her spirits as she spoke the word.

Husband was the last word, Maggie thought, that had been in her mind when she met Dexter for the first time. Living in New York with Spaff, like Maggie just out of Vassar, she had come on to Boston for a week end in October to be greeted by an effusive hug from Kitten and a whisper in her ear, "We're going to be sisters!" Maggie had forthwith accompanied Roger to Milton the next day to meet his in-laws-to-be.

Kitten had warned her that after Sunday dinner the family would resort to its customary activity of touch football. It was from this scrimmage that Dexter extricated her to take her for a walk through the autumn woods of Blue Hill. There was something massive and foursquare about the tall, solid, all but stolid figure that strode before her under the falling leaves that made it all too easy for Maggie to put him down as "worthy"—in her lexicon no compliment. When Maggie told her father of the meeting, however, the way in which Dr. Fraser spoke of the younger man strengthened a stirring of attraction that, in spite of herself, she had felt during the afternoon.

"He's a fellow to watch," said Dr. Fraser. "The Mass General is lucky to have the caliber of radiological research going on in its laboratory that Bradfield is doing. Mark my words, you'll hear from that young man one of these days."

When Maggie did hear from him, asking her to come on from New York to go with him to the Harvard-Yale football game, she accepted forthwith. As she swung across the Larz Anderson Bridge on the way to the Stadium, her cheeks tingled to more than the icy November afternoon. She was delighted with her own appearance in a crimson duvetyn turban and enjoyed the feel of the raccoon-coated arm through which her own was tucked. If her feet barely touched the ground, peeping out from under her ankle-length coat trimmed with a large beaver collar, it was not only because they were being squeezed off it by the pressure of the surging crowd around her but because she felt elevated to a quickening state of excitement; the thrill of a Broadway opening dimmed, compared to it. This world of pretty girls and handsome young men, pennants and flowers, brass bands and cheering, had its idols too. And one of them—one of Harvard's most famous ex-football captains—was walking at her side.

On her next Sunday in Boston Dexter called for Maggie in Brimmer Street to walk her firmly around the Charles River Basin, stopping off at the Massachusetts General Hospital before returning her home. Opening a door marked *Forbidden,* he led her into the darkness of the developing room. "Just wait there," he said peremptorily, pointing to a shadowy corner, and appeared to forget her as he might a superfluous package. She shifted from one foot to another, watching, by the dim glow of a red light, his large bulk moving about. He seemed to be peering at the contents of a succession of stone tanks. There was an acrid smell of vinegar in her nostrils. Maggie felt diminished and ignored, but in direct ratio to her own sense of unimportance she was piqued and impressed by the stature of the man who took for granted such docile passivity on her part.

Maggie decided today, walking along the Dunster dunes, that what she already missed was the excitement of the time during which she wrote letters announcing her engagement. *My father says that my fiancé will be one of the really big research physicists in the country.* The very words *engaged* and *fiancé* had been part of a vocabulary as thrilling as the flurry in which she lived: congratulations pouring in, and presents, presents, presents. *Engaged!* She had not enjoyed her few short hours as bride more. But—*wife* . . .

She looked up to see that Dexter was scrutinizing her closely.

"I hope you're glad that I'm your husband," he said, looking questioningly into her eyes, as though he were aware of some veil that dimmed their vision. The fine lines at the corners of his eyes spoke his overflowing happiness; Maggie was beginning to learn that it did not occur to Dexter or to any Bradfield to put emotions both deep and obvious into words. If you loved a person you didn't have to tell him so twenty times a day. That, roughly, was their philosophy.

"I wouldn't be here if I weren't glad, darling," she said, "but don't you keep wondering what's ahead?"

"Certainly not. Why should I?"

"Because! Aren't you *curious*? It's like eating a wonderful dinner. We've only had a sip of our first cocktail, but I'm dying to know what the soup will be, let alone the roast and salad—*and* dessert!" She stopped before his rather sober gaze. "Oh, heavens, I can hear it coming! You're going to tell me, just like Father, not to be so greedy, to savor the flavors of life, and learn to be a gourmet."

"All I want is another sip of that cocktail." Dexter, almost brusquely, drew her to him. The very taste of his lips and feel of his skin, fresh as the wind that whipped about them, was enough to rouse Maggie's senses. At the insistent pressure of his huge frame conversational impulses oozed deliciously from her. As though she had been knocked down by one of the heavy rollers thundering in beside her, she could only yield to its power and, when it was over, right herself as best she could, shake the water out of nose and eyes, and gasp for breath.

On this last afternoon of their honeymoon dusk was falling gently when Dexter finally paddled Maggie through the inlet and out into its still headwaters in a secluded cove. Leaning against a back rest in the bottom of the canoe, facing him, she saw Dexter framed against the tall eel grass on the shore that seemed to have closed behind them; she could hear Fetch and Carrie squelching along the muddy bottom.

"Here we are," said Dexter, smiling contentedly. "Turn around, and you'll see where Sarge and I come in the fall for ducks. There's our hideout."

Maggie turned to inspect a small, round, nondescript island with one scrubby wind-swept pine tree in its center. Dexter was explaining further: "We keep our decoys in that shack there. You ought to see it, Maggie, before sunrise. Kitten often comes with us."

"*Kitten*! She can't bear to kill a fly. I can't imagine Kitten shooting."

"Oh, she doesn't even bring a gun. She comes just to 'drink in all the beauty,' she says. It looks swell on the marshes when the sun comes up, especially when they're red and brown in the autumn."

He put his dripping paddle down across the gunwales and, throw-

ing his head back, drew in a deep breath, letting it out in a sonorous, happy wheeze.

"You sound like a hippopotamus, darling."

Dexter seemed not to have heard. "This is all right," he said. "I guess this is just about my favorite place in the whole world." He looked lovingly over the peaceful marshes, then back to his bride in unhurried content. "When I was growing up and used to come here with Sarge, sometimes I'd wonder to myself if I'd ever bring my wife here. I used to imagine what she'd be like and how I'd show it all to her. Of course I never said so to Sarge. For all I know maybe he was thinking the same thing himself."

Maggie shifted her position. Speaking of Sarge, that reminded her. . . . Dexter's brother was as huge as he was, and now she wondered suddenly if she were planning a big enough meal for him on Sunday night. She was preparing her first party for the family, and she was determined to make a success of it.

"I've had a brilliant idea!" she declared. Her voice sounded surprisingly loud in the stillness. Dexter was still surveying his little island, his eyes narrowed by the last brilliant rays of the setting sun. "Would you like to know what it is?" she asked with a hint of impatience, as he appeared not to hear her.

"Well, *I* think," Maggie said, "that although my recipe for chowder is terribly hearty and really is a meal in itself—Mother never gives us anything for dessert after it except fruit—*I* think that maybe Sarge would enjoy it more if I had for dessert—"

Dexter lifted his hand. "Shhh!" he whispered. "Listen."

Silently, without taking his paddle out of the water, he maneuvered the canoe close to the shore. Maggie put her head to one side, just as he was doing, and, yes, sure enough, she did seem to catch a faint wet, whishing whisper from the roots of the nearby eel grass.

Dexter barely moved his lips as he mouthed the one word for Maggie. "Fiddlers," he said.

"Oh," said Maggie, peering inshore, where she could see an army of tiny crabs on the march. Each had appeared, as though on cue,

out of a little round hole, identical to his neighbor's, with the identical mound of wet sand piled close by. Each was carrying his top-heavy claw aloft as though it were a cumbersome musical instrument; they might have been hurrying off sideways to some clandestine orchestra rehearsal, set for a time and place that they alone knew.

Maggie and Dexter sat speechless, almost without breathing, for five minutes. Then, as her husband appeared totally unaware of her existence, she reached forward to touch him. "What are they going to do?" she asked in a whisper.

"They're not going to do anything," he whispered back.

"Then what are we waiting for?" she asked in her natural voice. At its sound the fiddlers scurried, each to the hole nearest at hand, out of sight, and the parade was over, the mud flat emptied of life.

"I thought they were going to *do* something," Maggie said apologetically. "I thought that's why you were so interested, and what we were waiting for."

"Living things don't have to *do* anything to interest me," Dexter said with a forbearance that was lost on his wife.

"Not even people?"

"I'm interested in all forms of life—except people," Dexter said placidly as he turned the canoe toward home.

It was the next afternoon, Saturday, that marked the official end of the honeymoon, when the rest of the Bradfields arrived for the summer in their annual migration from Milton.

Aunt Katta led the procession, bouncing along the bumpy driveway in her Ford, with the top down, the back seat filled with three Shetland sheepdogs. "Here we are," she called out heartily, "the whole fam dambly!"

Next came Pa and Ma Bradfield, well supplied with cocker spaniels, in the Franklin, the dust of its rear wheels blowing into the eager faces of Sarge and Marsh in their model-T Ford.

Hearing Sargent address his sister Marcia—"Ma'sh, I'll pahk the cah in the bahn"—Maggie smiled to herself, wishing her father could

have heard it. He enjoyed saying that, by using his ears, a stranger, hearing the Bradfields talk, could take his bearings as surely as any navigator from a bellbuoy, and know that he was not far from Boston.

Maggie went forward to kiss her mother-in-law. Because it was never natural to her to proceed with caution or to exert either control or tact, this was the moment she had chosen for the attempt Dexter had told her was doomed to fail. She was determined to prove she could carry it through to success. Maggie's reliance on her own power to charm rarely proved to be misplaced.

She was wearing a fresh pink linen dress and knew she looked her prettiest and freshest. "I'm so thrilled to see you!" she said with that ring of enthusiasm which convinced the person addressed that she meant what she said, for the very simple reason that she did—at that moment. "I know how sticky and tired you must feel this evening, and I promise to leave you alone. But, Ma Brad, *please*, tomorrow evening, Dexter and I want you all—the whole family—to have dinner with us at Titipu." Maggie smiled engagingly. There was no sound except for the scuffling of dogs underfoot. "At Titipu," she said a little louder, as though she were speaking to the deaf. "As a sort of housewarming!" The smile this time did not flash quite so brightly, although, inevitably, it was there. Maggie's fullest, dimple-accompanied, smile generally carried something conspiratorial with it. *You and I understand*, it seemed to say. And when it returned to her, reflected on the features of her interlocutor, the secret they shared appeared to be simply the affirmation of Maggie's own remarkable identity.

Her mother-in-law withheld the customary affirmation as she answered gently but firmly, "Dexter can't have thought we'd leave Castle Adamant on Sunday evening, Magpie." There was her new nickname. Maggie had forgotten it till this moment. She did not care for it at all; it seemed to carry somewhere an implicit reproof.

"But we'd just adore to come over some other Sunday evening!" Maggie heard herself exclaim too enthusiastically. "I thought what fun it would be this year if your first daughter-in-law were the one to give the first party to the whole family, to show how happy I am to be part of it. Father's clam chowder at Northeast is famous, and I'm using his recipe, and everything's all set, so do say you'll come. *Please!*"

"It isn't a question of 'another' Sunday evening. We *always* have the family, just as Ganny Bradfield always had them, at Castle Adamant. You and Dexter must be with us on Sunday evenings," Ma Brad said, looking off to the fields almost vaguely, as though it were a situation over which she had no more control than the rising of the sun. The subject appeared to be closed. "We'd love to come to you on Monday." She pointed to a shabby old straw valise, tied about with a peeling leather strap. "Dexter, dear, will you carry my dress suitcase into the house, please?" As Ma Brad swept past Maggie with the authority of a queen she tossed kindly in Maggie's direction, "I've always understood that in other parts of the country they serve what *we* call tomato soup, and call it chowder. It will be most interesting to taste your father's soup, Magpie, dear."

Magpie, indeed! Maggie Fraser had been used to having her own way all her life. It had not yet occurred to Maggie Bradfield that there could be any change in this natural order of the universe. As the glimmering of such an unthinkable idea flickered for an instant across her horizon the turquoise-blue eyes, only a few moments before full of the delight of self-assurance, flashed and narrowed.

3

It was not until Maggie crossed the threshold of Castle Adamant on Sunday evening that she had a chance to inspect fully the citadel of her new family.

She was only beginning to suspect how ill at ease they were in the outer world, how their only way of feeling able to meet that world on home ground was to affirm a sense of humor which, actually, they totally lacked. Over the walls of the house, inside and out, signs were strategically placed which, if they did not instantly convulse the reader, at least served to offer the Bradfields themselves a topic of conversation at which they could clutch during the first five minutes of any visit—always the hardest for the hosts.

The first sign, over the front door, declared THIS HOUSE IS UNDER MA-TIAL LAW. On the other side of the veranda were a few words by W. S. Gilbert: *There are one or two rules that all family fools Must observe, if they love their profession.* Upstairs the nautical tang to the family wit was made manifest in lettering on the doors of the two bathrooms, one reading NUNS, the other BUOYS.

On this first Sunday evening Maggie stood outside the doorway that proclaimed ma-tial law, eager to be pleased and to please. Her inherent good nature and bubbling belief that life was bound to be fun had washed away any sense of pique left from her mother-in-law's repudiation of her hospitality; she was ready for the evening in a mood which, if she had been given to self-analysis, would have declared her both unsnubbed and unsnubbable.

The moment she was across the threshold she was greeted by a whoop from Aunt Katta. "Magpie! How spiffy! All dressed up!"

Maggie could feel her face flame red, as it did when she was angry. "But I'm not dressed up. It's a perfectly simple pongee." She gave a nervous tug to the belt that encircled her at the line of her hipbone.

"But you've got on stockings! And made of *silk*!" Her sister-in-law, Marsh, eyed Maggie's finery suspiciously.

Dexter moved quietly forward to take his place beside her. "Ma wants us to eat," he said.

They filed into the dining room, through the golden-oak sliding doors.

"Magpie, my dear, will you, as our newest Bradfield, sit beside me?" Pa Bradfield rather shyly indicated the seat at his right.

"And I'm going to sit on Maggie's other side." Down beside her thumped Aunt Katta. Aunt Katta had close-cropped gray hair, the same light Bradfield eyes, and a tough leathery skin. Her hands and arms were covered with abrasions and contusions incurred in chopping wood and carpentry, and with scars administered in her hive of what she called her "bumblies." Dressed in a white-duck middy blouse, with navy-blue collar, she turned to Maggie, all joviality. "Well, here we are, lock, stock, and barrel, and love's young dream is over, chilluns! Has Dexter taught you your ABCs about who lives where at Far Fields? It's easy as rolling off a log. Castle Adamant, pay-ree-eye-ents and all unhatched chicks. You and Dexter are the Titiputies. Barataria, Rah-Rah and Kitten. Tower Green, Yours Truly." She gave a tweak to her sailor's black silk tie.

She turned back to a lusty ladling of fish chowder. The tableful was dedicated happily to the same task; one could almost hear the soup—a Sunday-night staple, winter and summer, made as only the Bradfields' Bridie could make it—slop from side to side in the willow-pattern plates. The low, happy buzz of talk might have been made by Aunt Katta's bees.

Maggie looked across at her brother and his wife, sitting side by side, talking quietly to each other. She longed to kick Roger under the table and all but point at their joint in-laws and say, "Different from our Sunday nights, isn't it?"

Presently Ma Brad struck her glass with a fork. "The Bradfield family may consider itself called to order, and proceed with the entertainment of the evening. My dear . . ." Mrs. Bradfield gestured to her mate, who rose. Beaming along the length of the table at each other, Ma and Pa Brad looked like two nice twin boys (they were, in fact, first cousins). The family imprint was on the gleaming, innocent faces of both—straight noses, low foreheads, and eyebrows and eyelashes too pale to be visible. Ma Brad's straw-colored hair was parted straight down the middle and looped back on each side to meet in a knot high on the back of her head. Pa Brad's head was quite bald, but his coloring testified to the fact that the crop that had once sprouted from above had been also of palest wheat.

Without further preamble he began to hum, clear and loud. He touched the first, third, fifth, and eighth notes of an octave in a key which must have found its perfect pitch in his head. "Mm . . . mmm . . . mmmm . . . mmmmm." Then in a sweet tenor voice he began to sing:

"On yonder hill there stands a creature;
Who she is I do not know.
I'll go and court her for her beauty;
She must answer Yes or No."

And from the other end of the table in a clear, if rather faint, soprano came

"O No, John! No, John! No-o, John! No!"

The family put down their spoons. Like interested spectators at a tennis match, they turned from one end of the table to the other as the interplay unfolded. The course of the sweet old ballad went on, sedately, deliberately, until the climax appeared in sight.

"Madam, I have vowed to love you;
Would you have me change my mind?"

Ma Brad, with a coquettish toss of her head that unloosed the hairpins in her slippery, uncurled hair, unhinging the moorings of her hairnet, wound up the proceedings with a roguish

"O No, John! No, John! No-o, John! No!"

The Bradfields laughed and clapped delightedly. Ma Brad, a little flushed from her exertion and from the gratifying response to her performance, modestly bowed herself off-stage center and became once more ringmaster.

"Dexter, how about friend Alice?"

Dexter, with a rather sheepish grin across the table at Maggie, rose docilely to his feet. Obviously he was good-naturedly repeating the motions of a long-since-established routine. He stood very straight and stiff, with his head thrown back. His hands were thrust into his back trousers pockets; it was clear he did not know where else to put them. He fixed his gaze intently on one corner of the molding, as though he expected the words to flash by the spot, like news reports around the belt of the New York Times Building. Without turning his head or moving a muscle of his face, he embarked on a deliberate recitation of "Gentle Alice Brown."

Maggie looked across at her husband with a rising sense of wonder. Why had Dexter never told her of this—she could not frame the word *accomplishment* to herself—this trick he had mastered? Heavens! she suddenly thought; if it is to be an evening of parlor tricks, they'll be calling on me any minute, as the only professional here, to give them something. She instinctively reached to adjust her hair. What should it be—a speech from *Cyrano*, or Noyes' "The Highwayman," mastered, with gestures, at the Arts Theater School? (Her hand hovered over her Adam's apple as a natural reflex to the mere thought of "the bunch of lace at his throat.") Dexter was winding up.

"He traced that gallant sorter to a still suburban square;
He watched his opportunity and seized him unaware;
He took a life preserver and he hit him on the head,
And MRS. BROWN dissected him before she went to bed."

Maggie found the performance excruciating. The word she used, disdainfully, to herself was *amateurish*. Only a year ago, fresh out of college, she herself had so passionately determined to become—magic word!—*professional*. When she had told her mother of her resolve to study for the theater, Mrs. Fraser had countered rather ineffectually, "I imagined you'd want to take courses, dear. There are such fascinating ones nowadays. Even in Boston," she added humbly. "But I never thought you'd want to be a professional actress."

"Heavens, Mother, whatever do you think I would take a course *in*?" Maggie's voice was withering, her unspoken challenge daring Mrs. Fraser to say, "The Garland School of Homemaking."

"Do you ever feel, dear," her mother ventured, "that perhaps it isn't quite fair to take a job from some girl who might really need it?"

"I certainly don't! It's just a question of who has the most talent."

Talent. There was the rub. Maggie had succeeded in almost expunging from her consciousness the gist of her interview with the head of the Arts Theater School at the beginning of her spring term. "You have *something*" had been the verdict. "We all feel it. You have a vivid, dynamic personality, and an enchanting voice. You're bound to make your mark some day, somehow. But as for talent for the theater . . ."

It was just there that Maggie rang down the curtain on the stage of her memory, leaving herself merely with the words ringing in her ears, *You're bound to make your mark some day . . .*

She turned her attention back to Dexter. "That's dandy, Brad," Sarge was saying to his brother.

"Thanks, Brad," Dexter answered Sarge.

Ma Brad was on her feet again. Her smile was as broad as ever, but this time it bore witness to the recent passage of two blueberry muffins and was dark blue.

"Now, girls, where are our Tessa and Gianetta?"

Kitten and Marcia had barely tripped through the duet from *The Gondoliers* before Ma Brad was calling on Aunt Katta for a story in Irish dialect. As the roar of mirth in response to this exhibition subsided, the mistress of ceremonies announced, "And now for our grand finale!"

There was a scraping of chairs. They were all on their feet, except Maggie and Roger. Ma Brad rapped with her fork on her drinking glass. Sweetly she sang

"On the first day of Christmas
My true love sent to me
A partridge in a pear tree."

Pa Brad sang

"The second day of Christmas
My true love sent to me .
Two turtle doves, and
A partridge in a pear tree."

Kitten sang

"The third day of Christmas
My true love sent to me
Three French hens,
Two turtle doves, and
A partridge in a pear tree."

They were off. Through all the days of Christmas they went, the pattern becoming more closely interwoven until they ended at the top of their voices, singing at once

"The twelfth day of Christmas
My true love sent to me
Twelve lords a-leaping,
Eleven ladies dancing,
Ten pipers piping,
Nine drummers drumming,
Eight maids a-milking,
Seven swans a-swimming,
Six geese a-laying,
Five gold rings,
Four colly birds,
Three French hens,
Two turtle doves, and
A partridge in a pear tree."

It was over at last, and they all sank back, puffing and laughing, into their seats. They had done ample justice to the blueberry muffins, but no one was conscious of his own appearance or that of his neighbor's. They applauded roundly, laughing, shaking hands with one another—delighted with themselves.

"Whee-ew!" gasped Aunt Katta. "Enough high jinks for one evening, Pa Brad!" She mopped her brow with a man's large folded handkerchief. "Bring on the pie."

"*I* think," said Kitten gently, "that as we now have in the family someone who has been on the stage in New York, it would be wonderful if she would do something for us. How about some *Cyrano*, Maggie?"

Maggie, from across the table, heard the words with a tingle of satisfaction. It was a tribute to the joint powers of imagination of the two friends that, between them, they had succeeded in transmuting

Maggie's few months of dramatic study into a brilliant, though brief career in the theater.

"*Parlez-vous* frogs legs?" her brother-in-law Sarge was calling to the company.

They stirred uneasily. Ma Brad spoke. "We all know how gifted Magpie is. But I think, dear, we don't wish to change the character of our Sunday evenings. We'll just stick to family talent, as we always have."

For a second Maggie felt as though hot ink had spurted through her veins. She was furiously angry—angry enough to shove her chair back and leave the table. But across it she caught the gently beseeching look from Kitten, flanked by both Dexter and Roger, looking somehow steadying and kindly.

"You're right, Ma Brad. It's much more fun this way." She smiled her warmest smile, complete with its two deep dimples, at her mother-in-law. It accomplished a general lessening of tension as the family turned back to the pie that is known in Boston as "Washington," and everywhere but in Boston as "Boston cream pie."

After dinner the family gathered in the "parlor," separated from the front hall by a screen of multicolored beads. Here, too, golden oak prevailed. Maggie, settling herself on an uncomfortable mahogany sofa, upholstered in black mohair, pulled a cigarette out of her bag. She felt a tap on her arm. Pa Brad was speaking to her in an undertone. "Not in here, Magpie," he said. "Ganny Bradfield never allowed smoking in Castle Adamant, and we've never changed the custom. Those who are slaves to the weed are always welcome to take a puff in my caboose."

Dexter had already shown Maggie the small shack, hardly bigger than an old-fashioned outhouse, that was Pa Brad's exclusive domain. Within its confines he practiced the hobby dearest to his heart: the mastery of knots. He had been at work for as long as his children could remember on a book filled with all he knew on the subject. He hoped it would be published posthumously.

"What'll you put in the old man's suit, Magpie?" Maggie realized that her sister-in-law Marsh, calling from across the room, was not merely addressing a question to her; she was leading a family scramble back into another wild orgy of laughter over their own wit and accomplishments. The game went on until they were out of breath with their efforts. It was Kitten who suggested, as a sort of mop-up operation, a round of "Up Jenkins." Only Sarge and Dexter abstained, preferring to retreat to a distant corner for their Sunday-night combat of Thumbies. The sound of the two struggling gladiators' heavy breathing was painfully audible to the rest of the family as, their right hands locked, each tried to flatten out the thumb of the other.

Just as the contest came to an end, with Dexter the victor, there was a scratching from the screen door of the front porch, accompanied by a frenzied yelping. Aunt Katta sprang to her feet, crying, "My animules!" and strode into the hall to open the door. Then came a clatter of claws and a rush of wool, and the three Shetland sheepdogs catapulted themselves upon their mistress. "Aw, Mummy's *babies*! Did oo det locked out?" The deep grooves in Aunt Katta's face softened; her eyes were transfused with tenderness. She opened her arms and clasped all three to her middy blouse. "Didums was! Didums *was*! Who's Mummy's bestest dirl? Who's de Moppsikom Floppsikom boy!"

Her face disappeared into their long coats as they chewed her ears, licked her nose, and clawed at her hair.

"Now we must show our Aunt Magpie what the Three Bears can do. She hasn't seen Mummy's own boys and dirls sit up in um's three chair-chairs and eat um's sup-sup."

At the word *sup-sup* the dogs obediently hopped onto three shabby chairs—already well covered by their own hair—and sat up on their haunches, their front paws crooked. Aunt Katta dove into her breast pocket, pulling out first a whistle and then a handful of small dog biscuits. She placed a small piece of biscuit on each quivering nose. There was a moment of hushed reverence, mercilessly ripped apart by a strident shriek from Aunt Katta as she threw back her head and then, in an all too accurate imitation of a squawking turkey, let loose in a descending scale with a wild "Gobble! Gobble! Gobble!" The dog biscuits vanished.

The clock on the mantelpiece struck nine. "Time for Bedfordshire," Ma Brad announced.

Maggie got up and went to her mother-in-law, smiling. In the warm tones that had a way of melting hearts she started to say, "Thank you so—"

A scream from Marsh interrupted her. "For heaven's sake, Magpie, what do you think this *is*? Don't start company manners on us. This isn't a *party*!"

Maggie turned around to look for Dexter. Before he could join her, however, her father-in-law was at her side. "Don't let anybody put you off, Magpie. You're being here has made it a party. You're a great addition to the family. We're all going to like you."

There was a murmur of assent from them all except Ma Brad. Aunt Katta proclaimed in a voice which roused the three sheepdogs once more to attention, "Like her? Why, she's one of us already!" And she clapped her new niece roundly across the shoulders.

4

THE NEXT morning at breakfast, on the porch of Titipu, Maggie announced to Dexter, "I've decided that at our party tonight there are going to be no games, and no singing."

"Then what shall we do?" Dexter asked almost woefully.

"We'll *talk*!" declared Maggie.

Her words had the desired effect. Dexter looked up from his coffee cup, thoroughly alerted. "The whole point of a family party is that you don't have to talk," he explained. "It would ruin it if you had to be thinking of things to say."

"But I don't have to 'think' of things to say. Tell me, *really*, darling," said Maggie, fixing him with her blue eyes, "don't you like people?"

Dexter swallowed a mouthful of buttered toast, wiped his mouth and stated simply his Yankee creed, "I don't mind them."

"*Mind* them? Well, I should hope not!"

"I just don't want to see them, that's all. I don't like having to make conversation with strangers."

"But aren't you curious about them?" Her own brow knitted with curiosity over the phenomenon across the table from her.

"No. Why should I be?"

"Because they're new! And then there's always the chance that a stranger may turn into a new friend."

"But I don't want any new friends. I'm all right the way I am." Dexter wound up the conversation to his own satisfaction.

Later that afternoon, meeting Dexter and Roger at the Dunster railroad station after their day in the city, Maggie managed to fall behind for a moment alone with brother. Moving fast and firmly to secure an ally, she said without preamble, "Don't you think I'm right, Roger? I've told Dexter that at our party tonight I want to have conversation instead of singing and games."

Roger appeared to take full measure of his ebullient older sister, as he had often taken it before. "Listen, Mag, don't start getting bossy around here. You'd be awfully smart if you didn't start out trying to make over your in-laws."

"I'd rather make them over before they take me over. Of course, if you plan to sacrifice all your own individuality—"

Roger interrupted her. "They're not trying to take over anybody. The thing to remember about the whole family is that they are just the nicest damned people that ever lived. But they're scared of their own shadows. They want to be kind and friendly, but they don't know how. We hoped you didn't feel miffed or anything at not being asked to recite last night, but I know Kitten is right: she says they're scared to death of you because you've lived in New York and been on the stage. She says they're all nuts about you but are scared pink you're going to high-hat them."

Maggie could feel her ruffled feathers subside. It was not the first time that Kitten's soft answer had turned away her own wrath.

In spite of her eagerness to make friends with her new family, Maggie found herself left to her own devices during the hours of the day that Dexter was in Boston. She was as much appalled as surprised to discover what solitary occupations her in-laws chose with which to fill their days. Gardening, canoeing in the inlet, carpentry, knot-making, bee raising, and dog breeding—each Bradfield went about his business as though he lived in a world uninhabited by other human beings. Maggie, used to the gregariousness of the swimming-club pool at Northeast Harbor, could not believe her eyes when she watched each member of her new family proceed singly and alone for a dip in the creek at the foot of the meadows. Pa Brad, with the elbow-length sleeves of his black bathing suit flapping loose about his scrawny white arms, would stop to record in his notebook both the start and finish of his hot trek from Castle Adamant across the fields of juniper bushes. Maggie longed to ask him the simple question *Why?* But somehow the very seriousness with which he made his entries appeared to offer its own excuse.

Aunt Katta alone seemed disposed to return Maggie's advances, or, indeed, to be aware that she was attempting to make any. Maggie perhaps went more than halfway as her heart opened in happy gratitude to the one member of her new family, aside from Dexter, who appeared to be aware that she and Roger were children of a great man. The first time that Maggie visited Tower Green with the rest of the family Aunt Katta said, "I still can't understand why I never knew Dr. Fraser until our chicks began marrying his chicks."

"Probably because he didn't go to Harvard," said Sarge morosely.

Pa Brad tried to brighten the gloom cast by such an epitaph. He spoke with tolerant kindness as he asked, "Where did your father go, Maggie? I'm afraid I've forgotten."

"He went to Leland Stanford. Then he came east to the University of Pennsylvania Medical School."

Sarge lifted his mallet to strike the chisel into the granite with a final *coup de grâce*. "Never heard of either of them," he said.

"Oh, Sarge, you're hopeless!" Kitten tried to keep a tone of sisterly endearment in her voice, but it had tears in it all the same. "My name's Fraser now, and I'll have you know Dr. Fraser has had an honorary degree from Harvard, which is more than any Bradfield has had."

"You've forgotten Uncle Frank."

"That was only an M.A. and because he gave them two million dollars. Dr. Fraser was made doctor of science not only of Harvard, Yale, Columbia, and heaven knows how many more, but also of Oxford and Cambridge as well. I'm so proud of having his name I don't know what to do!"

She slipped her hand in Roger's; at the same moment Maggie felt the pressure of Dexter's on her own shoulder.

After this, as Maggie walked past Tower Green, she was apt to come up to the door and call, "Yoo-hoo!" Her call almost always had the effect of materializing Aunt Katta, who would stride forward to say, "Come on in and chew the fat awhile, Magpie."

It was Aunt Katta's hand that could fill in for Maggie some background strokes needed to set her new in-laws in clearer perspective.

"I can't get *at* Marcia," Maggie said to her one day. "After all, she's Kitten's and Dexter's sister, and I'd love to be friends, but whenever I try she—well, she sort of sidles away from me."

"Poor Marsh," said Aunt Katta with sudden softening. "The child's afraid of her own shadow. Yet I'd be willing to bet that she'd give her eye teeth to be like you. She's the one of the Brad chicks that seems to have been—well, perhaps the kindest word is *extinguished* by the family. She worked for me once at Dover Street."

Maggie knew that the Dover Street Settlement House in the slums of Boston's South End was Aunt Katta's dearest "baby."

"When she was there she met a High Church Anglican priest—at least that's what he called himself. He was a charming, sensitive feller, and the two of them seemed to get on like a house afire. He had her going to Mass before breakfast and all sorts of shenanigans. I always thought something would have come of it, but the Brads did so much laughing about collars worn wrong side to, and the tomfoolery of any man in his right senses bobbing curtsies and wearing petticoats, that when he was transferred to a parish in New Jersey he didn't take Marsh with him. Ever since then she's shied away from human critters more than ever. Next winter her dearest dream is coming true. The family are going to let her live at Far Fields all the year round, with Sarge. She's going to raise Shetland sheepdogs—like my Three Bears—and she's happy as a clam at high tide at the prospect. Have you heard about her collection?" she asked abruptly.

"No. What's it a collection of?"

Aunt Katta hesitated before she said, "Well, when she really feels she knows you she'll show it to you herself some day." She seemed disposed to go no farther.

Maggie was enjoying herself. "And Sarge?" she asked. "What about him? Is he perfectly happy just to stay stuck at Far Fields with his sister?"

"Oh, I expect so" was the bluff rejoinder. "Sarge used to talk once upon a time about moving west, to run a ranch the family owns in Wyoming, but Ma Brad pointed out to him that someone in his generation has to look after the family finances, so he seemed to accept becoming a trustee like the good sport he is. I've never believed in having favorites among my nieces and nephews, but you Frasers have picked off the cream of the crop. Probably most New England families who've been around a goodly number of generations are much the same: the stock's a bit thin in spots, but in others it's still running with wim and wigor."

Maggie, looking at Aunt Katta, thought that she was certainly a walking advertisement for the vitality of the Bradfields. She was somehow not so much above male and female as beyond them. She was simply a good sort. It was too confusing to ask oneself, a sort of *what*? Maggie was grateful for her existence. She was a member of her new family with whom it was possible to communicate.

"It's not saying anything against your Dexter when I say that Kitten's the flower of the family," Aunt Katta went on. "She has some sixth sense that the rest of us haven't got—or anyone else I've ever known, so far as that goes."

Seeing her sister-in-law at Far Fields, Maggie felt as though her intimate college friend were disappearing beyond her reach. Here she was as absorbed in the pages of a Burpee catalogue as, a year before, she had been in the poetry of Emily Dickinson.

There was an evening, at dusk, when Maggie, leaving Dexter behind in his pursuit of hawk moths, wandered over to Barataria. Kitten was on her knees before her herbaceous border, intent on planting a row of heliotrope. In one hand was a muddy trowel, beside her a watering can. The scent of the heliotrope came to Maggie across the freshly cut grass; from across the fields she could hear the whistle of a whippoorwill. She stood still a moment, as neither Kitten nor Roger, who was standing beside her, had heard her approach, feeling as though she were seeing them for the first time together as a couple. Kitten's cheeks were flushed; her hair, dampened by the exertion of her exercise, curled in tight ringlets along her forehead. Her eyes were shining, and her mouth was half open in rapt absorption as she held each plant tenderly in her hands before slipping it into the little mud hole, filled with water, that received it with a welcoming gulp. Roger was watching Kitten with much the same look of concentrated tenderness that she was turning on her plants.

"Hello, you two!" Maggie called brightly. "Making mud pies, Kitten?"

"I'm putting out more heliotrope for my hummingbirds. They can't have enough of it."

"You Bradfields! I've left Dexter at home because he seemed more interested in his moths than me, and now here you are, more interested in hummingbirds—"

"Not than in you, Maggie!" Kitten exclaimed, getting to her feet. "Roger, take her inside and light the lights. I have only two to go, and I'll be right in. I'm *so* glad you came over, Maggie!"

Before Roger turned to do Kitten's bidding he stooped to kiss her. Kitten's face, lifted to return the kiss, shone with a light that caused Maggie to look away, embarrassed. She could not understand what could so illumine a moment that, so far as she could see, seemed to consist of nothing more than doing a grubby chore.

Kitten could not be pried loose from her house and garden even when Roger was not there. Sometimes, in the morning, Maggie would appear at the doorway and ask, "Wouldn't you like to come and do something?"

"Oh, I don't think so, Mag" popped out before she could stop it. Then, more politely: "I'm really quite happy the way I am. Thanks just the same. What did you have in mind?"

"How about a swim? I don't mean in the creek at this foul low tide. But how about coming down to the Little Beach?"

"I don't think I will, Mag, thanks. But why don't you go? You should!" Maggie accepted as a natural law that when anyone said *should* to her the exhortation involved her own pleasure.

It had not taken Maggie long to discover that all of Dunster, except the Bradfields, went every morning, as one woman, to a small private beach to watch over its young. She saw at once that to be one of these young matrons could not mean high adventure, but it would mean sociability—the next best thing. She soon formed the habit of being on hand. They appeared at the crest of the dunes, singly or in couples, dragging small children or carrying the still smaller ones. They plowed through ankle-deep hot sand, trailing after them knitting bags, water wings, back rests, and various large rubber seagoing toys. Their first stop was the primitive wooden bathhouse where there was always wet sand on the damp, splintering floor and the air smelled of wool bathing suits that had never dried. The still life behind each partition was much the same: an unclaimed bathing shoe, a torn bathing cap, a rusty safety pin, a bottle of citronella minus cork, a broken button, and, over all, a sprinkling of talcum powder. A steady stream of talk, in high-pitched voices, went on among the women across the tops of the partitions. It did not cease to flow as they proceeded onto the beach and settled themselves in a row facing the sea and their children. Knitting needles came out and clicked busily, stopping only for a shriek of "Ouch!" and a slap as an unscathed greenheaded or black fly sailed off for its next landing. Cigarettes, citronella, and various unguents and lotions were passed down the line intermittently. Those whose children were over a year old were pregnant. The atmosphere was one of buzzing fertility and so feminine that the mothers themselves would hardly have acknowledged any force aside from their own as being responsible for the fruit of their wombs. The talk touched on the little happenings of the day either among themselves or in the community—an infantile-paralysis scare, the news from somebody's mother-in-law who had had a stroke on Cape Cod, what the tennis pro at Manchester had said about playing at net, an itemized list of things to be given to the local Congregational Church rummage sale—buzz, buzz, buzz.

Only for a few days in late August that summer did the conversation turn to wider horizons when President Harding died and Calvin Coolidge became President. When Wig Newton, the wife of the distinguished gynecologist Newton, said, "It really makes you feel as though you were living right in the middle of history, doesn't it? I mean like Lincoln's assassination or something," she seemed to express the feeling of the group to their satisfaction.

The easy chatter of the young mothers on the Little Beach was generally interrupted later in the morning by the arrival of half a dozen of Dunster's older ladies. They, like their daughters, arrived chattering happily among themselves. Maggie, to whom it was natural to believe that any gathering was improved by an addition to it, was always first on her feet and halfway up the dunes to meet them. She had perfect good manners with her elders—enough respect to make them preen their feathers and enough familiarity to give them the illusion that the feathers were not molting but were still lustrous with youth.

One morning she had called gaily, "Here come the Culture Girls!" They had been delighted with the name, and thereafter they used it themselves to refer to their little weekly-morning gathering on one another's verandas. They assembled with knitting, darning, or embroidery bags, possibly a bowl of garden peas to be shelled, and an "interesting" book to be read aloud by one of their band in quiet, cultivated tones. (They had just started on Gamaliel Bradford's *Damaged Souls.*) They reminded Maggie nostalgically of her own mother; most of them actually had been young with Elsie Faneuil in the nineties. They looked out at the world about them as Mrs. Fraser looked, with sweet and inquiring eyes, appearing to expect it to be what it had been in the days of Miss Hersey's School, Papanti's dancing class, and their own particular sewing circle. Each one wore the distinguishing hallmark of her era—a small solitaire diamond, in her engagement ring, set high and lonely on a narrow band of gold—just as Maggie wore the badge of the twenties—a larger diamond embedded low in diamond-encrusted platinum filigree to match her narrow platinum wedding ring.

The ladies' bathing suits were all of durable black. Maggie shuddered to see that their dowdy folds did not quite conceal the wrinkled breasts, the swollen knees, the darkening veins, and the sagging stomachs, ravaged by the years which had not touched their minds and spirits. If they had been articulate enough to hit on a watchword, among them, to hand on to their daughters it would simply have been: "Be good, sweet maid, and let who can be clever." Whenever they were mentioned singly or as a group Maggie would exclaim, as she might over an unprotected kitten in the midst of traffic, their impending extinction implicit in her inflection, "Ah, they're *sweet*!" She did not fully realize that they were indeed the last stragglers in a species about to dip forever from the American horizon—gentle women.

Once or twice during the summer Maggie was included on what the Culture Girls called a "spree." This involved joining some half dozen of them on an "antiquing" expedition to one of several fashionable nearby summer resorts. For these outings they wore what amounted to a uniform. Their hair, marceled by Mademoisèlle Alary, was as freshly white as their flannel or homespun coats. Their tanned skin, like the dark velvet of a showcase, afforded a becoming setting for their modest strands of real pearls and their very good diamond, ruby, or sapphire rings and *diamanté* wrist watches. They carried large needlepoint bags, containing a 4711- or Yardley's English Lavender-scented "hankie," their knitting, their "specs," and plenty of fresh five- and ten-dollar bills. After wandering through half a dozen shops—eyeing here a spinning wheel, handling there a warming pan, and settling finally for a set of raffia containers for drinking glasses or a basket of pine cones treated to burn in a variety of colors—they would settle down to the real dissipation of the afternoon. With the greed and excitement of small children at a party they let go in a bacchanalia of cinnamon toast, devil's-food cake, ice cream, iced tea, iced coffee, or "horse's neck." The gusto, mingled with aplomb, with which these widows—because that is what they all were—tucked away the fare on their plates might have made an onlooker wonder if they had not perhaps also swallowed up their late husbands with the same relish. When the guzzling was over they wiped their mouths, gave a tug to their corsets, and placidly returned to the leather upholstery of their automobiles to expand in comfort.

When Maggie expostulated to Dexter that she wished that "somebody exciting" would turn up in Dunster, his rejoinder was "I don't know what you expect if all you want to see is summer people."

Maggie had yet to learn that the Bradfields' feeling for their year-round neighbors—those whom the "summer people" referred to as "natives"—was deeper than their feeling for any human beings on earth. Perhaps it was a sort of atavism, or reverting to type on their part. Dexter and Sarge never felt as much at home with their Harvard classmates and fellow club members as they did with these friends of their youth. And in return the Bradfields held a unique place in the affection and respect of these brothers under the skin.

Maggie could see with a sort of helpless despair that it satisfied Dexter in every fiber of his being to hang about Charlie Crowell's boatyard, up the Essex River, on Saturday afternoons. With his towhead bare in the hot sun and in khaki pants far shabbier than Charlie's, he seemed capable of spending an indefinite amount of time at his friend's side, watching him scrape barnacles off the bottom of an old catboat or replace a frayed peak halyard on one of the small sailing skiffs of Charlie's design that the children sailed up the tidal inlet. The men did no more than exchange a monosyllabic grunt of communication every quarter of an hour, but neither seemed to feel the need of a more intense or lively interchange. Maggie could see that the smell of the mud flats at low tide, the squawking of the sea gulls, the barely distinguishable whisper of fiddler crabs on the march through the eel grass, and the gentle splashing of water against the rotting planks of the old float at the end of the wharf, encrusted with sea-gull droppings, cast a mesmeric spell over her husband.

For her own part, standing beside him, first on one foot and then on the other, swatting at black flies, her ears droned to a hum of monotony as her blood quickened in panic born of a sharpening awareness that she was becalmed.

It was only in later years that Maggie learned that she had lived this chapter of her life through what the rest of the world came to call the "roaring twenties."

5

When I get back to Boston, everything's going to be different, Maggie said to herself often during that summer. If the words failed to carry immediate reassurance to her own ears, then she repeated them with the inflection of a challenge.

For one thing, she would have a house of her own as a base of operations, and at a safe remove from the Bradfield web.

When Dr. and Mrs. Fraser had offered her a house on lower Mt. Vernon Street as a wedding present, Dexter had expostulated, "I don't know what the family will say. I know they were counting on our living on the place in Milton." (Maggie was already beginning to know that, when Dexter spoke of the family, it meant simply his mother.)

"But, darling, Milton's *country*! Who wants to live in the country in winter?"

"What's wrong with the country, in winter or any time? It's the only place I've ever lived."

"But there's nothing *happening*—no concerts, no theaters, no parties, no people!"

It was obvious Dexter had never considered any of these adjuncts as having anything to do with his marriage. "I guess I never thought. I suppose all that is important to a woman."

"To me it is," answered Maggie.

When, then, her mother-in-law telephoned from Milton after their first night in the house to ask how Dexter had slept "through all that city traffic," Maggie could laugh her rich, good-natured laugh and say, "You must come and sample our guest room, Ma Brad. It's as quiet as the country."

Mrs. Bradfield did not answer. Instead, in a voice that closed the subject, she said, "We'll see you both on Sunday night."

Maggie's answer tumbled out. "I'm sorry, we can't come on Sunday. We're going to Mother's and Father's."

There was a pause. "Sunday night is a family institution. We were counting on you, Magpie, dear."

Maggie instinctively had already picked up the trick that a wife does well to learn in expressing a wish of her own to her husband's mother—that is, to present it as coming from her husband. "But it's because Dexter wants to talk over something about his work with Father," she said.

The answering voice sounded a little mollified. "Well, then, we'll expect you the Sunday after."

It was after this conversation that Maggie said to Dexter, "Summer's one thing, but winter's another." She seemed under no compunction to beguile her husband with fair promises. "We aren't going out to Milton every week for supper," she stated as a simple fact.

He had put up no opposition and seemed, indeed, on the next Sunday, to be as glad as she was herself to be back in her parents' house on Brimmer Street again. To cross once more the threshold of her father's library was to stir to life that part of Maggie which had lain fallow at Far Fields. No young Proust ever perceived more sharply the divergence of the Bradfields' "Way" from the Frasers' "Way"; Maggie felt that she had come home in a truer sense than any indicated by a mere street address.

The light of the setting sun, flooding into the room from across the Charles River, gave an added glow of warmth to its contents. Over and above the worth or value of individual pieces there was implicit in the total effect experience so richly lived, values so finely tested that *charm* was a thin word to describe it. Its furnishings were an unself-conscious potpourri of belongings gathered individually and jointly by her parents. There were Sheraton and Chippendale chairs and tables brought from Grandfather Fraser's rectory in San Francisco, objects so beloved that he, in turn, had brought them with him all the way from Scotland. A Gilbert Stuart portrait of an early Faneuil judge showed the same soft brown eyes and delicately chiseled mouth perpetuated in both Mrs. Fraser and Roger.

There were, as well, books, pictures and *objets d'art* given to Dr. Fraser in the course of his far-flung career—a pair of Georgian candlesticks from his colleagues on the staff of the Medical School of the University of Pennsylvania, a pair of Meissen vases from the Mayos in Rochester, a Taschereau edition of Molière from the Curies. There were signed photographs of Emmet, Osler, and Cushing.

Maggie, from her comfortable corner, watched and listened. Neither her father nor Dexter would have thought in 1923 of asking her to share the martinis they were enjoying. She said to herself how "typically Bostonian" was Dexter's baggy gray Brooks Brothers suit, his striped knit tie and heavy brown gum-soled shoes. The undercurrent of condemnation, however, petered out as she observed the attention and intention playing across her father's features as he talked to the younger man. Maggie watched the moisture that came and went in her father's eyes—eyes as light and bright a blue as her own—prompted by quick amusement or a spurt of tenderness, quickly hardening into a glitter of concentration or flashing with the fire of sudden temper. Maggie observed him now, as she had so often before, suddenly blow his nose, leaving the high-arched bridge flushed red—a weakness she could wish that she had not inherited. Then followed a thorough rubbing of his pince-nez, his long, delicate surgeon's fingers folding and unfolding his silk handkerchief with the finesse of a conjuror, before the glasses were replaced and jostled into position by a lifting and dropping of his bushy sandy eyebrows. His slender shoulders stooped in a dark-blue double-breasted suit, Savile Row tailor-made, whose lapel bore the small red insignia of the Legion of Honor. Both he and Dexter had forgotten Maggie's very existence as, with the same relish two artists might have shown in talking of a Turner sunset, they discussed female cancer. What they were saying floated across the surface of Maggie's consciousness; she galvanized into attention only when Dexter calmly said, "When it comes to dissecting test animals that have been radiated, give me rats any day. I forget every time I open a rabbit's belly how warm and nauseating the smell is."

"How disgusting!" she cried from her corner. "Can't you both talk about something else?"

"Such as Fatty Arbuckle? The theater has its disgusting aspects too, Maggie, if one is determined to be disgusted."

It amused Dr. Fraser, *en pantoufles*, to play the role of the world-weary cynic. The winds of scientific enlightenment had long since blown away any cobwebs of illusion from his perfectly ordered, richly stocked mind. It titillated that sensitive organ, when it was not concentrating on the practice and theory of surgery, to play at "getting a rise" out of his daughter. Her emotional responses to his hypodermic needling of wit and hyperbole were worshipful, violent, and instantaneous; her grasp of its intellectual content was almost nonexistent.

When, after dinner, at which her father had opened a bottle of champagne in her honor, she and her mother left the men to their coffee and liqueurs and went upstairs to her parents' bedroom, Maggie settled down into a comfortable old chintz-covered armchair and sighed. "It's nice to be back!" she said with warmth enough to make her mother look up sharply, her eyes intent with concern.

Maggie took in with one hungry, lingering look the whole, created out of so many parts—on her mother's dressing table the emerald-green velvet pincushion, growing like moss in an embossed silver slipper, and the little vase that held her mother's hatpins. There was the heavy mahogany four-post bed, in which she and Roger, as a special treat, were allowed to spend those days they were kept at home with any one of their successive childhood complaints, while Mother read aloud *The Would-Be-Goods* or *The Wind in the Willows*. The room was lined with photographs of herself and Roger back to and before the distant days Maggie could remember. There they were, on the

Champs-Elysées, balloons tied to the buttons of their coats, brandishing hoops. There were the countless snapshots of Northeast Harbor and, finally, in the place of honor on the mantelpiece, herself in a whirl of white satin and lace in all her Bachrach glory.

Instinctively, through their childhood, Maggie and Roger found their way to this room as soon as the front door downstairs closed out the world outside. The cry of "Mother!" was the first when they entered the house. Then, roller skates dumped or doll carriage abandoned, up the stairs the children rushed, with Mrs. Browning, their brown cocker spaniel, at their heels, to fling themselves, puffing and talking at once, into the welcoming nest. When, later, their father's key in the lock below was heard, a premonitory hush fell on them. They could tell by the very way his steps fell on the stairs what was his mood. Only Mrs. Browning refused to accommodate herself to it, but rushed to convoy him on his ascent. If Dr. Fraser's spirits were good he would kiss his wife, pinch each of the children by an ear, and sit down to entertain them with stories of patients or colleagues. On these occasions the atmosphere was electric for Maggie. She giggled more wildly than the humor of the stories warranted, and no sooner had her father stopped for breath than she would go at him with "Tell some more, Father!" But if he had had a harassing day, or was already preparing for a piece of writing to be done that evening, he strode in, without looking at any of them, and said, "Skat, kids." Maggie and Roger did not have to be asked twice, but shot from the room on the command.

Now, sipping their coffee together on either side of the familiar grate, Mrs. Fraser smiled across at her daughter with a happy welcoming smile, receiving her into the largest secret society in the world—two married women alone together. *How is it, darling?* was the unframed question that could not cross the lips sealed in Victorian reticence.

Maggie looked at her mother for the first time in her life as though, after all, she might have some secret, some wisdom, to impart which might be worth heeding. Not from her, as a general rule, came the exhortations, admonitions, charges, and challenges served up with the spice of wit and prejudice; by comparison with her father's pronunciamentos her mother's gentle truisms carried the flatness of a bland diet. Now suddenly, however, Maggie felt a longing to elicit from her some magic formula that she had never before suspected her of possessing. For the first time in her life she was confounded by the thunderclap of realization that her mother had once been young. If only she could communicate with her—*now*—as with a contemporary! For an instant it almost seemed as though their wings of longing brushed, each struggling with feet rooted, like a fly's on sticky paper, to her time and place, unable to do more than fan the air. Neither could advance toward the other. It was Mrs. Fraser who essayed feebly, "I can't believe that you're really *Mrs. Bradfield*, dear. I suppose you feel as though you belonged to a new family."

"Mother," Maggie brought out abruptly and almost harshly, "did you ever find your in-laws difficult?"

"If they were, they didn't have a chance to be difficult with me, living on the other side of the continent. It always seemed a little ironic that your Grandfather Fraser, who had gone all the way from Scotland to San Francisco to preach the Gospel, was so anxious for his son to retrace his own steps. It was he who insisted that your father come east to study medicine, and I really think he was delighted when he married a girl from Boston! It was certainly no personal compliment, as we met only once when we went out to the World's Fair, but he said Boston reminded him of Edinburgh, and that seemed to make everything all right!"

Maggie could see on her father's bureau a faded photograph in a small oval frame, taken in 1898, of Elsie Faneuil, her neck and throat bare and her soft round bust held tight in a fitted bodice of the period. Her hair was done as she wore it still—parted in the middle, rolling at either side toward the knot at the back. She was all freshness and sweetness as she looked out on the life that still lay before her to be lived. The very tilt of her head—a little deprecating but nevertheless gay—seemed to say that she was going to make no demands on life; she was sure to find it pleasing. The half-quizzical smile, turning up beyond the curve of her lips (even Dr. Fraser wearied of its being compared to that of the "Mona Lisa") seemed to hint at a secret that was sure to yield enjoyment—a secret, nonetheless, that she intended to withold. The living face, with the marks of years now etched into it, was still inviolate. Maggie knew her mother to be gentle, loving, and modest; now, more than ever, she knew her to be much more. As fragile, as invisible as gossamer, it was that much more which had held her brilliant, erratic husband's devotion chained to her. If she herself knew why, the undecipherable upturned smile did not betray the reason.

"But, even with Father, didn't you ever feel that you wanted to express *yourself*—quite independently of him, I mean?" Maggie spoke almost roughly in her desire to wring from her mother some admission that she too had been human, had been vulnerable, once.

"Perhaps it was very unimaginative of me, but from the day that your father first asked me to marry him—at Mt. Desert, when he was only an intern at the University Hospital in Philadelphia, meaning we should have to face a five-year engagement—I never wanted anything he didn't give me."

For no conscious reason Maggie suddenly felt that she was living again that terrifying moment so long ago when she had seen her father weep. She was only five years old at the time—it was in Philadelphia—and some men had come in a cart and put tanbark down the middle of Delancey Street outside their house because her mother was lying in a darkened room upstairs with typhoid fever. Maggie had stood in the downstairs hall and peered into the reception room where her father was in consultation with two doctor friends. They talked in hushed whispers, and then her father went abruptly to the window, putting his forehead against the pane, and she had watched, awe-struck, as his shoulders shook up and down. She knew that he was crying.

"Now, dear, I want you to look over some of the linen I've set aside," her mother was saying. "I know that young people nowadays don't want too many things to clutter up closets, and of course your trousseau sheets and pillow cases are lovely, but there's nothing like a little really *old* linen. . . . ."

With her father Maggie was able, as she said to him, "to take her back hair down."

He dropped in to see her in the new house the very day after she had dined in Brimmer Street.

Dr. Fraser had enjoyed the game of baiting his wife by telling her that perhaps their wedding present to Maggie had been a mistake.

"If you're trying to outbid the Bradfields for Maggie's affections," he said, "I'm sure it's not necessary. When we were young a house of our own was something to work for."

"Maggie is restless, Malcolm. I think it will be a sort of anchor for her. You should understand that."

"Meaning that she is all my child?"

"I wish she were—*all* of you. I'm afraid, for her sake, that she has only some of your qualities. Drive and curiosity aren't enough; she should have something stabilizing in her life."

"Well, so long as it's not stabilizing like a cage."

"Oh, no, dear. It couldn't be that. It will be something that she can feel is all her own—and Dexter's."

"Well, be sure you leave it that way. No clucking and brooding during the first months at least."

Mrs. Fraser made no comment of either reproof or irony when he told her on Monday morning that he thought he would take a peep, as a social observer, at the "lovebirds."

Looking about him with satisfaction at his daughter's living room, he asked her, without preamble, "How are you making out with your plain-living in-laws, Maggie?"

"All right, I guess." There was little conviction in her voice. "They certainly are awfully different from you and Mother."

"I don't count, with my crude California background."

"But Mother! She's Bostonian, and *she's* not like the Bradfields."

Dr. Fraser leaned back in his chair, and crossed his legs. He always enjoyed discoursing on the character of his adopted city. When he had arrived ten years before, via California, Philadelphia, and Paris, the reception he found awaiting him, in spite of his Bostonian wife, had been chilly. An international reputation at his back counted for nothing; he still had a local one to earn as well. Now he had done so. He was not only respected medically, but loved for his wit, urbanity, and charm. The constricted aborigines appeared to feel in his society as though they themselves were similarly endowed. With easy affability he explained for Maggie's benefit, "Don't forget that there are high-collared and low-collared Bostonians. Your mother comes from a line of judges, clergymen, and scholars, going back three hundred years, not to mention the Ambassador and the Senator. She belongs to the brand of Bostonian who knows what the amenities are. The Bradfields are what is known as good yeoman stock, shrewd enough in the eighteen hundreds to make their fortune in textile mills. But it never brought them any *savoir-vivre*." He stopped for the familiar ritual of rolling a cigarette. "I ran into your father-in-law at the Somerset Club last week looking like one of his own hired men. His cloth cap was stuck into his pocket. I'm sure his suit was ordered at Sears, Roebuck, and there was soil from Far Fields under his fingernails. It would be hard to convince an outsider that he is a very rich man." He paused to savor a few deep draughts of tobacco before asking abruptly, "How do you get on with your mother-in-law?"

Maggie felt a strong temptation to share some of her own reservations about Ma Brad with her discriminating father. But because she was as anxious to convince him, as she was herself, that her married state was entirely satisfactory, she tossed off with noncommittal good nature, "She seems very sweet."

"That's what I'd be afraid of. Look out for her, Mag."

"But how?"

"Henry Adams was never wiser than when he said the most important quality in a wife is *gentillesse*. I think that goes through the whole fabric of marriage. Just be *gentille*, Mag."

"You mean, just *nice?*"

"Dear me, did you learn French too young to know what it means? Be nice, with grace. *Gentillesse* is the cornerstone of all the other amenities. Don't forget."

There certainly was no effort needed by Maggie to be *gentille* during the first weeks in her new house as a married woman. She simply knew that she was happy. Dexter for his part seemed inclined to accept her happiness with the same placid assurance that he accepted his own. Had he been a Latin bridegroom he might have expressed his bubbling good spirits, on returning from work at the end of the day, with a nosegay of flowers, a bottle of wine, and, perhaps, a song. As it was, he walked home from the Massachusetts General Hospital along West Cedar Street, in his heavy gum-soled, unpolished brown shoes, with a give of the knees characteristic of a mountain climber on a long pull, munching a concoction of peanut butter stuffed between two salty yellow crackers, which he bought at the corner drugstore on his way. On his doorstep he stooped to pick up and bring in to Maggie the *Boston Evening Transcript*. He was blissfully content, and if it would have taken another Bradfield man to diagnose the symptoms of his state as differing from those of stolid indifference, that was only because Bradfields were not accustomed to wearing their hearts on their sleeves any more than they wore gloves on their hands or hats on their heads.

As he appeared on the threshold of the living room, Maggie was likely to let fly at him with a challenging question.

"How do you like them?"

"Like what?"

"Oh, Dexter! Use your eyes. The curtains!"

"They look fine to me."

"No, but really, do you think I chose the right material? I'm still afraid maybe the pattern is too large. Or too busy."

"Don't be silly. They look swell. Come here," he said, clearly bored with the conversation. "I want to kiss you."

The strength of Dexter's arms, as they enfolded her, was comforting to Maggie not only as an expression of the lover but as a reassuring adjunct of the handyman. Each evening on his return there was what he called a "change in the line-up" to execute. Perhaps it was a sofa to be carried on his bent shoulders up the small winding stairs to the living room where Maggie could get the "feel" of it; and then, twenty-four hours later, in response to a feel that it looked better in the front hall after all, it was carried down again. Perhaps there were crates of china to be unpacked, or mirrors and pictures to be hung. All these functions of the male in feathering his nest for his mate Dexter performed not only with docility but with conscious satisfaction and pleasure.

One evening, after about six weeks of this nightly ritual, Maggie, with her feet up, in pretty mules, on the Empire couch, looked out over the kingdom she had brought into being. Turning to her husband as she might to a trusted prime minister, she proclaimed, "Well, I must say I can't see another thing to do." There was the sound of a perceptible sigh. "I guess we can really call ourselves settled."

"Thank God," said Dexter, loosening his necktie.

"You're not *glad*, are you, Dexter? *I'm* not! From now on I shan't know what to do with myself." She suddenly brightened. "Except I do think we should have a housewarming." She looked out over the living room as a general might survey the scene of a victorious campaign and, sniffing the scent of gunpowder in the air, realizes that there are still fresh worlds to conquer. "If we moved the piano we ought to be able to get forty people into this room," she said.

"Speaking of housewarming, Fig Newton was asking me today if we wouldn't come out some Saturday evening to Belmont. He and Wig want to get some of the MGH crowd together who haven't met you. Naturally, there'll be a good many you'll know from Dunster. They want you to choose a date."

Maggie put down a copy of *A Lost Lady*. "Oh? You mean a party in my—in our honor?"

"Well, sure. Yes, I suppose it would be, though Fig didn't exactly use the word 'honor.' But Fig's not a very fancy feller."

"That sounds awfully nice. Get me my Phillips Brooks calendar, darling."

Dexter got up to remove from its nail by the telephone in the hall the indispensable field map for Boston's female strategists.

At one masterful survey Maggie had digested its contents. "Tell them we could come two weeks from Saturday," she said.

The curtain was going up—at last. She could hardly wait for the first act.

6

"MAGGIE! Hurry up or we'll be late!"

Dexter, from the downstairs hall, sounded the leitmotiv which was to ring through the years of their marriage, announcing that the Bradfields were going out to dinner.

Maggie yelled back from the bedroom, "Just two minutes. I'll be there!"

She stood before her dressing table strewn with opened jars and bottles, scattered jewelry, and a spilled box of powder. About her on the floor lay a mound of discarded underwear, a bath towel, a dressing gown, and several pairs of shoes, two of which had found their way onto the bed, along with her hat and coat. Now all she had to do was to transfer lipstick, comb, and compact from her daytime purse to her evening bag. Oh, dear, but the lipstick was the wrong color. Where *was* her new one? It was always the same; however early she planned to start dressing, there was always a scramble at the last moment. Vaguely she felt it was Dexter's fault. His punctuality made her nervous, and his tidiness irritated her as finicky. "After all, this isn't a laboratory," she had said to him more than once as she found him putting back glass stoppers and adjusting the tops of jars in her wake.

She twirled about in front of the mirror, delighted with her new evening dress. What fun it was to be one of the first to wear a new fashion! Maggie surveyed with satisfaction her hand-embroidered chiffon velvet, its top part of sky blue, a skirt beneath of royal blue, and a bottom skirt under that, reaching her ankles, of midnight blue. About her neck hung a long necklace of lapis-lazuli beads. She hoped it would knock Wig Newton's eye out.

Maggie, actually, had never been subject to twinges of female competitiveness. In her new life as a married woman she was less than ever in a position to be a prey to them. As the wife of a research physicist she felt herself to be at least apart from, if not actually above, what she called to herself the "run-of-the-mill" doctors' wives she had met through the hospital. She was so sure of the unique destiny awaiting Dexter—and herself as his wife—that she could afford to be entirely affable to her less privileged sisters. Indeed, she hoped at this moment that these very doctors' wives were putting on *their* best party dresses. Her credo was simple: a gay party dress was an ingredient of a gay party, and what in the world was more worth making an effort for than a gay party? Maggie had already been depressed by the Bradfields' aversion, not peculiar to the Bradfield family, to "getting all spiffed up." She had no intention of becoming a dowdy wife.

Arriving, the last guests by a generous margin, at the Newtons' threshold, she saw in a flash that there was something terribly wrong.

Wig greeted them at the front door. "Where've you been? Fig was just going to call up the city morgue!"

Maggie, looking at her hostess in a cotton gingham and sneakers, cried out as though she had been stabbed in the heart, "But we're *dressed*! I thought it was a party!"

"Whoever heard of dressing for Halloween?"

"But nobody told us." Maggie's voice broke; then she turned suddenly on Dexter. "Why didn't you tell me it was a Halloween party, Dexter?"

Wig was ushering them into the big hall and trying to make herself heard over the din at her back. "I told Fig to tell Dexter it was informal, but he probably forgot. You know husbands! They never listen to a word you say. What's the dif anyway? Come on in."

There were some twenty couples assembled. Maggie recognized most of them from Dunster. She had been on summer picnics with many of them—the men drinking MGH gin out of flasks behind a sand dune while their wives toasted marshmallows for the children, and all of them roaring out "Seeing Nellie Home" or "There's a Long, Long Trail a-Winding" into the face of the rising moon.

Maggie spied Sarge and Marsh, standing alone together in a corner. They, as brother and sister, looked even more alike than their parents looked, as first cousins. They differed in only two ways: Sarge wore steel-rimmed spectacles and Marsh's were tortoise-shell; Marsh's face was splashed with freckles, while Sarge's shone pink and white, as though he had shaved off more than a beard, getting down to a tender baby skin beneath. Neither of them had visible eyebrows or lashes.

Maggie, glad to see them as familiar landmarks in the strange scene about her, crossed the room to join them. "Hello, there," she said. "I didn't expect to find you two here."

"Hello, Magpie," they said in unison.

"Where did you drop from?"

"We drove up from Far Fields," they said.

"Won't you come back to spend the night with us?"

"Oh, no, thank you, we've got to get back, because—" they said.

Maggie could not hear the rest. The noise swelling around her sounded more like a barnyard than a gathering of civilized human beings. Maggie stopped to study those who were making it.

"What are they doing?" she asked above the din.

"Making mating cries. That's the way you find your partner. Here's your card."

Maggie took it and read *Orangutan*. She turned to Dexter for consultation and consolation only in time to hear him let out a high howl. Just before he became airborne in an attempt at a wheeling flight, he held out his card for her to read, which said, *Laughing loon*, and he was gone. Maggie saw Marsh, still in her corner, timidly meowing, while Sarge, with a sudden afflatus of self-confidence, curled his lip to emit a roar like a tiger. No one of the creatures about her seemed in the least inclined to offer her help or encouragement. Each was transfixed in an ecstasy of self-expression.

Maggie had no idea whether an orangutan walked on two legs or four, but an instinct to bury herself far out of sight made it not too difficult to drop on all fours along with many of the other guests. She advanced warily along the footboard of the room. Several men, involved in the same sort of progress, accosted her with grunts and growls. She was confident that an orangutan could never be guilty of either noise and, with as much self-respect as she could muster in the circumstances, pursued her way drearily and dejectedly. She saw, with a sideways glance and dour resentment, that Dexter had already found his lady laughing loon in the form of a hilarious pregnant blonde in a rather dirty white middy blouse and blue serge skirt. Suddenly Maggie's gaze was arrested by the antics of a large man advancing through the crowd in the middle of the room. His knees were bent, knock-kneed, and at every step he gave a bounding spring, his toes turned in toward each other. He carried his palms facing toward him and swung them in large loose sideways sweeps, stopping occasionally to go through the pantomime of scratching his chest or of seeming to remove a flea from his own head and eating it. He peered eagerly through the other moving figures, making a chattering noise with his teeth as he did so. Maggie, from her position on all fours in the corner of the room, wanted to hang her head as with a sudden fearful certainty it came over her that what she had been watching with revulsion was the preliminary courting skirmish of her mate.

He proved to be a pediatrician from Seattle who, finding himself in Rome, was conscientiously trying to do as the Romans did. When Maggie found that he too was in an agony of embarrassment she felt better and was not sorry to spend the rest of the evening in his company. Around them swished too many martinis and too much hard cider, in a kaleidoscope of shrieking, laughing and jostling.

After a chaotic buffet supper, guzzled for the most part off laps, as the guests sat cross-legged on the floor, there was *divertissement* of dumb crambo. Impersonations of scenes and personalities familiar to staff members of the Massachusetts General and the faculty of the Harvard Medical School, and nobody else, were enacted to the whoops of the initiated. The skits involved the humor of a mistaken diagnosis, the fantastic revelations of an X ray, the hypochondria of patients, and the lasciviousness of nurses. After they had all laughed themselves into what they diagnosed as "stitches," Wig marshaled her guests into two teams—Mammals and Reptiles—for more games. First came a relay race of string-chewing. Balloons were released up to the ceiling. The contestants then jostled and shouldered their way into position, each to stand openmouthed beneath one balloon. At a signal each contestant started chewing on the end of his balloon's string—the purpose of the game to be the first to swallow and all but digest the entire wet wad of string. Maggie's mortification was complete when Dexter, taller than any of the others, seriously went about the business (taking no time out for spluttering laughter), gobbled his piece of string down first, and, at the end of his sprint, brought the captured balloon to rest in triumph on his nose. He was banged on the back, his hair pulled, and cider brought him as a reward for his prowess.

Then someone called out, "Why doesn't Chas bang the box?"

Fig led Chas, the great heart surgeon whom Maggie remembered from Dunster, to the piano, saying, "Shoot, Luke." And Chas's fingers, with the same facility that guided them through the left auricle of the heart, sped knowledgeably into and out of the key of G. "Shame, Shame on Old Notre Dame" came first; then "Turkey in the Straw" and "The Old Gray Mare" as vaguely appropriate to Halloween.

Before Maggie had time to steel herself, there they were, all roaring, as they had roared on the sand dunes, "Seeing Nellie Home" and "There's a Long, Long Trail." "Nita, Juanita" in melting close harmony came next, with "Old Black Joe" close on its heels. And then, suddenly, there in sight was the musical haven where they would be. It was Fig Newton, hearty and wholesome, who lifted his voice first to proclaim the glimpse of the promised land, as Chas's fingers heralded the landfall. "With crimson in triumph flashing, Mid the strains of victoreee . . ." Sarge moved close alongside Dexter. Maggie, standing on the other side of the piano, watched the two brothers, their heads thrown back, hands in pockets, pouring out their very souls in abandon, declaring the only passion they were not ashamed to confess. What Rodolfo's lament to Mimi would have been to an Italian, what the martial notes of "Pomp and Circumstance" would have been to an Englishman, the words and music of "Harvardiana" were to the Bradfield brothers.

The next half hour was given over to Harvard football songs; and then, as suddenly as it had begun, the singing subsided, leaving Chas Harlow to his own devices. With no audience for his efforts he modulated his way surreptitiously into Rachmaninoff's Second Concerto and, out the other side, into the "Moonlight Sonata," which served as an unacknowledged background for Bobbing for Apples.

Mammals and Reptiles faced each other on all fours, in two lines. One representative of each team came forward at a time to a pan of apples floating in water. Screaming, spitting, and splashing were unleashed with a fresh abandon. Wig nearly drowned ignominiously in her own dishpan as, under the lash of uncontrollable amusement, she inhaled water through her nose and went into a choking fit. If there had not been so many doctors present, one of whom stepped forward masterfully and suspended her in the air by her feet while several others thumped her on the back, the game might have ended disastrously. As it was, it subsided like the deflating balloons underfoot. Most of the guests were dripping wet to the waist: rivulets streaming from hair joined rivulets running from noses to make one mighty stream splashing from the chin down onto shirt fronts and open dresses beneath. Turkish towels and blankets were passed around. Fig, with one heavy army blanket over his shoulders and two fingers held up at the back of his head to suggest feathers, with a jug of cider balanced on his shoulder by the other hand, flung himself into a wild whooping Indian war dance, on flat feet, toes pointed out, occasionally removing the hand which made the imaginary feathers to beat his own lips into an abandoned, bloodcurdling war whoop.

It was at the introduction of this further contribution to the bedlam that Maggie, taking Dexter by his dripping sleeve, firmly advanced on their hostess and said, "I'm sorry, but we have to go home."

"Oh, come on, *spoilsports*!" bellowed Wig. "It's only twelve-thirty. I hope we aren't shocking you, Maggie."

Having no answer for the bludgeon attack, Maggie murmured ineffectually, "Not at all, but—" she clutched wildly at the only lifeline that might prove strong enough to haul her out of the engulfing waves —"I don't feel very well."

"Oh, too bad. Not too much cider, I hope." Then, suddenly remembering that the Bradfields were newlyweds, Wig's leathery face crinkled into creases. "My dear, I understand perfectly." As she eyed Maggie's voluminous draperies her face was a jovial leer. "Go right along. You should take care of yourself."

To the almost inaudible background accompaniment of Chopin's "Funeral March" and the accompanying cacophony of further roughhousing, the Bradfields slipped away unnoticed. Maggie's closing of the front door was an unmistakable slam. The candle in the jack-o'-lantern in the front hall guttered behind her.

"Never again!" was the first detonation of the explosion which was to blast Dexter on the way home.

"Never again what? Don't you really feel well, Maggie?"

"I feel sick all right, but not the way Wig thinks I feel sick. If that's the kind of Boston party I'm going to be expected to go to—"

Dexter interrupted her. "Belmont, not Boston," he said.

"Don't be so *literal*, Dexter! It's the same thing."

He went on, implacable. "Well, you can't pretend you're a stranger, Maggie. Your mother's family is one of the oldest in Boston. You may have lived in New York one winter, but, after all, that doesn't make you—"

"Listen. It doesn't make me Bostonian. Don't forget, Father grew up in California, *his* father came from Edinburgh, and I lived in Philadelphia before the two winters we spent in Paris."

"But then you came to Boston." It was Plymouth Rock speaking.

"Yes, for a few years, at the Brimmer School, before I went away to Windover, and then to Vassar. Why, I even refused to come out in Boston!"

Maggie tossed her head proudly, almost believing now, after five years, that her decision had truly been one of repudiation. Actually it had been made because she instinctively felt that though she could never be anything so horrible as a "pill," she knew that she was not likely to sweep all before her at debutante parties on the ballroom floor of the Somerset Hotel. Even at the Kimball House Saturday-night dances at Northeast Harbor the highest title she had been able to earn was "loads of fun." Unfortunately, she was also loads of weight to maneuver about a dance floor—a gangling, too enthusiastic girl with the fine figure of a woman. Though she laughed and talked incessantly she was quite aware that the girls known to possess either "it" or "S.A." were the skinny, sultry John Held, Jr., vamps who rarely spoke and who danced sinuously cheek to cheek and spent a large part of the evening off the dance floor petting or necking—activities unknown to her. All the same she had felt stirring within her the conviction that a larger empire was awaiting her in a distant dazzling future. Pimply Harvard undergraduates were all very well, but they were not easily subjugated, and the time was bound to come when she would demand a larger public. The winter that Maggie might have been a debutante was the winter in which her father had been visiting professor of gynecology at McGill University in Montreal. When it became apparent that Maggie would really like to go to Vassar, it suddenly made everything much easier; Mrs. Fraser could spend the winter with her husband, knowing that she was in the place where the need was deepest. And Maggie, as she had always thus far succeeded in doing, got what she wanted.

Dexter was not going to let her off easily. "You're always talking about all those years on Brimmer Street," he said.

"Yes, and I was a child during them. And I went to lots of children's parties. But I certainly thought when I married I was going to get away from the level of pinning tails on donkeys or hunting the slipper."

I thought when I married. There she was again. *Married*—the magic state she had believed would touch, like a fairy wand, all the old familiar landmarks and turn them to sparkling gold.

Maggie turned squarely around to confront the phenomenon that was her husband. "Do you mean, Dexter, that you really didn't feel anything wrong?" Her father's words came back to strengthen her stand. "The Newtons have none of the amenities," she declared.

Dexter, quick to detect an alien vein in her tone, countered, "What the hell are they?"

"I don't know how to tell you if you don't feel it for yourself. Manners, charm," she fumbled, feeling futile. "They just don't know how to live, that's all. They behave as though they weren't civilized."

"Well, it was sort of—informal. But I told you that's the way Fig and Wig are."

"*Informal?* Is that all that you think was wrong with the evening?"

"Well, what kind of party do you want? I suppose you want everybody to be dressed up."

"Oh, you Bradfields! Why must you be so sneering if women want to wear pretty clothes and men aren't ashamed of looking as though they had at least brushed their hair and changed the shirt they've worn all day. There are worse things in the world than being dressed up, as you call it."

"Such as—? Go on. Say it."

This was the first time since her marriage that Maggie had heard temper in Dexter's voice. Its sound caused her to quail for a moment. Sheepishly she evaded his direct question, drawing a discreet red herring before him.

"Well, maybe it's just that our tastes are different. But I like people to be slightly—" she knew that the word she was going to bring out didn't convey the full height or depth of her meaning, but it would have to serve—"slightly more glamorous."

"Then you're right. We are different. I certainly am not interested in glamour." The word was spoken with an icy disgust.

"We might as well still be living in Dunster," Maggie pursued. "I certainly hope my life in winter is going to be different from my life in summer."

"Listen, Maggie, I can't see what you're working yourself into such a lather for. It's only one evening out of a lifetime. It doesn't really matter."

"But it does matter! Can't you see that it does?" She looked at him as though seeking out a chink in his imperturbability through which she could pierce, to stab him into an awareness of her own distress. "It matters because it's my life."

Dexter opened his mouth to say, *I hoped I was your life.* Instead he said, "I guess it's easier on a man who has a job. What happens in the evening doesn't seem very important one way or the other."

"It may not be important to you that I was wearing a beautiful and expensive new dress—and, if I do say so myself, a becoming one. Then to find myself in all that screaming and horseplay and spitting—it's revolting. Those deadly doctors and their deadly wives—"

Dexter broke in. "Have a heart, Maggie. Those fellows work hard. They have to relax sometimes."

Maggie was in full swing now and was not to be stopped. "The trouble with them is they're all constipated!"

The diagnostician stirred to life in Dexter. "How do you know?"

"Don't be so literal. They are the way *I* mean constipated."

The Bradfields did not speak to each other again before they reached home.

7

WIG'S DIAGNOSIS proved to be correct. Maggie soon found that she was pregnant. The horizon of her interest not only suddenly narrowed; it happily intensified. She found herself loving Dexter with a new and thrilling emotion. They were going to have a baby. God was in his heaven.

Maggie's own happiness of anticipation was doubled by the fact that Kitten was expecting her baby in the same month. Kitten expressed her deep emotion by secretly writing poetry; Maggie sent to Groton School for the necessary admission forms.

The news brought happiness not only to Maggie but to both sets of future grandparents. They showed a tendency to hover, if not to cluck —a state of affairs that Maggie, in her mellowed frame of mind, welcomed with entire good nature. Two years before, as the emancipated college graduate, she had patronized Mrs. Fraser with a withering "Oh, *Mother*! You just don't understand *anything*!" Now during her mother's daily calls she asked docilely, "Do you think I ought to do this?" or "Is it all right to feel like that?" or "Tell me what you think I'd better do about the other thing." The fact that Mrs. Fraser looked rather drawn and tired as a result of a succession of taxing visits from foreign doctors and their wives simply did not impinge on her daughter's line of vision. She was a fount of comfort and experience, to be milked; Maggie, as a dependent child, took suck.

Fridays came to have a special significance for Maggie, as they brought her a call from her father-in-law.

It was the habit of Ma and Pa Brad to drive the Franklin into Boston on that day for the symphony concert in the afternoon. For these excursions Pa Brad adhered to his boyhood custom of putting into the back of the car, as he had in the carry-all of his youth, a coil of heavy rope and an ax. He left his wife on arrival in the city so that he might deliver on foot his farm eggs to some dozen families up and down Beacon Hill, winding up his route by a call on Maggie. His first act on coming into the downstairs hallway was to whip out his little notebook in which he recorded the number of minutes it had taken him to walk down Mt. Vernon Street from the State House at the top of the hill. He was not trying to outstrip former records of his own; what he wrote down was merely a statement of fact. Statistics sustained Pa Brad. His hobby of making beautiful and intricate knots had developed a remarkable dexterity in his fingers so that when on these visits he brought booties, blankets, and bonnets for the unborn baby he took it much more for granted than did Maggie that they were the work of *his* hands, not of his wife's. As Maggie kissed her father-in-law's two rosy smooth cheeks, fresh from the stinging east wind, so bald and pink and innocent did he appear that Maggie felt that the pale-blue Shetland-wool bonnet were better popped over his own head. In these little visits, away from the overshadowing presence of his wife, Maggie came to know Pa Brad better and to grow increasingly fond of him.

One morning she said to him, "I am beginning to see where Kitten gets her sweetness and gentleness."

He blushed pinker than ever. "Oh, dear me, you're quite wrong. Kitten is an artist. I'm not. Far from it. I'm only a crackpot."

"You'd get on well with Spaff. She's always trying to save the world, too. I had a letter from her this morning, raving, as usual, about Bob La Follette. Would you ever vote for him for President, Pa Brad?"

"Oh, I never *vote*," he said serenely. "To me it's a choice between Tweedledum and Tweedledee. Neither party can do anything for this country without free trade. Free trade is my King Charles's head!" He laughed contentedly. "Mind you, my wife doesn't agree with me."

The mere mention of her name seemed to produce her in the room and bring him up short. "She sent some S.S.P. Chabiscos to Dexter. She's afraid that with a new diet he may lose out on some of his own favorites."

Maggie was fully aware of the little stinger intended for herself along with the bittersweet chocolate-covered hard crackers that Dexter loved so much to munch at odd times.

"Thank you ever so much!" she exclaimed, as *gentille* as could be. "It's a great help to be given ideas as to anything I can give Dexter in the way of a treat. You Spartan Bradfields are awfully hard to spoil!"

During the Friday mornings that Pa Brad was wearing out his shoe leather for a profit of a few cents (it was a matter of principle with him to sell his eggs for a little less than market price, disclaiming the role of middleman), Ma Brad was busy either clipping coupons in the vaults of the State Street Trust Company or conferring with Sarge over possible changes in investments, never spoken of beyond the confines of the shabby office overhanging the Old Granary Burying Ground where their conferences were held. The profits resulting from such changes were regularly plowed back into the family capital worth many millions of dollars. The transactions thus executed by Ma and Sarge were referred to by the rest of the family simply as "Ma's business," an activity in which they were all totally uninterested, apparently unaware that it had any bearing on their daily lives. Dexter himself would have been affronted if anyone had told him that his family possessed great means. Money was an unpleasant subject. Dr. Fraser had been amused when Dexter, as a potential son-in-law, presented himself without guile as a young man whose only "expectations" lay in the hope of an increase in the stipend from the research foundation that was backing his work. It was on this stipend, in addition to a modest allowance given Maggie by her parents, that the young Bradfields lived under the beneficent rule of Nellie, cook and maid-of-all-work.

Sarge came up sometimes from Far Fields, where he and Marsh had dug in for the winter, to spend Thursday nights with Maggie and

Dexter before these business transactions. Marsh, however, sent polite messages of regret when Maggie urged her to join her brother. Maggie was as far as she had ever been from knowing what Marsh's secret collection consisted of. Hints had got her nowhere, and there was something in the Bradfield reserve that made it impossible to ask a direct question whose answer was being so deliberately withheld.

Maggie enjoyed Sarge's visits, as there was absolutely no effort required to entertain him. He brought with him the very distilled essence of Dunster. Sometimes Maggie felt she even detected a faint aroma of clam shells about him. His presence came to be as welcome to his sister-in-law as that of Fetch and Carrie. In any case, he spurned the bed in her crisp little guest room, preferring to stretch himself out to sleep on the floor. When Maggie suggested that he might like to leave a toothbrush in the bathroom cabinet for such visits, he said simply, "No, thanks, I use this," and pulled out of his pocket a small rubber object that he placed on the end of his finger and, baring his teeth at her, proceeded to demonstrate.

On the rare occasions when Ma Brad came herself to see her daughter-in-law Maggie felt as though she were being inspected, as a gardener might a rosebush guaranteed to bloom by a given date.

"I'm certain it will be a boy," her mother-in-law stated, adding cryptically, "because of the name."

Maggie's expression spoke her lack of understanding.

"If there's not another male Bradfield, the family will die out," she added with a sternness that frightened Maggie.

Aunt Katta came too, like Balthazar or Melchior, to pay homage. "I must say you don't *look* very feak and weeble!" she would say with the hearty gusto of an embarrassed male. Her calls were paid on Saturday afternoons, after the Harvard football game in the Stadium. She attended these contests unescorted and unattended by the encumbrance of a male. Her brother Frank, a "ninety-niner," had died a bachelor. (The title affixed to any man Aunt Katta knew sprang from the date of his graduation from Harvard.) Aunt Katta suavely assumed the role of her brother's widow and in his name bought tickets to all Harvard sports events. There certainly was none stalwart enough on the bank of the Charles to say her nay. She wore her coasting costume (it was a matter of pride with Aunt Katta that she still careened down Blue Hill bellybumps)—red mittens, crocheted for her by Pa Brad, and a woolen cap, also the work of her brother's fingers. Her feet were encased in what she called *ahtics*; her broadcloth coat had belonged to the late Frank Bradfield and was lined with moth-eaten sable. She carried with her an old black buffalo sleigh robe, smelling faintly of stable straw and manure.

On one of her visits she arrived bearing a queer contraption padded with patchwork quilting whose skeleton appeared to be a wooden box once used for the delivery of groceries. She told Maggie with satisfaction that Pa Brad had measured a certain corner of the porch at Titipu and assured her that the box would fit it exactly.

Maggie had the disturbing sense that Aunt Katta expected her to be delivered of a puppy.

When July came Maggie was back at Far Fields, and Aunt Katta's crèche occupied by little red squirmy Priscilla. It was Kitten who had produced the boy—a Pyrrhic victory only, as his name was Roger Fraser, Jr. The name of Bradfield had yet to be perpetuated.

Maggie adored her little Priscilla. She wrenched her from kind Irish Delia's care (Delia was a present from Dr. and Mrs. Fraser) to bathe her every evening; she changed her dresses and bonnets several times a day. Other changes she left to Delia. She snuggled Priscilla, cooed over her when she brought up an obedient "bubble" after slapping on the back, and felt her heart turn over when the first toothless smile of recognition flickered across the tiny face. It pleased rather than piqued her to watch Dexter, home from the hospital, go at once to Priscilla's bassinet to poke at a bare toe or a tiny, waving, mottled orchid hand before turning to kiss Maggie herself.

Maggie laughed. "You know who's going to run this house from now on! You're very smart to pay homage to her first."

The habit stuck and through the first years of Priscilla's life Dexter, when he reached home each day, went directly to the bassinet, then to the bathtub, presently to the play pen, and finally to the dining-room table, where Priscilla was enthroned in her high chair brandishing an uncontrolled spoonful of apple sauce over her head.

Kitten during those years had borne another little boy and was pregnant again, while Priscilla remained Maggie's and Dexter's one and only. Maggie could fairly feel the implied reproof every time Ma Brad said, "Do bring her out to us in Milton on Sundays so the poor little thing can get some companionship with other children."

Ma Brad came regularly to see Priscilla on her visits to town.

Maggie complained, "She seems so slow about learning to talk. She just looks at us all with those huge wide-apart blue eyes. In some awful way she seems to have got my number!"

"Dexter was just the same," her mother-in-law told her. "It's the scientific approach, that's all. Priscilla is taking everything *in*."

"But, oh dear, I don't want her to be—" Maggie just didn't say "like Dexter," though her thought was implicit when she lamely came out with "I don't want her to be a scientist."

"Why not? Think of Madame Curie." Ma Brad seized the moment as a happy one to ask, "Just what *do* you want Priscilla to be, Magpie?"

"I want her to—" Maggie hesitated an instant, and then, almost without a thought, the wish of her own girlhood popped out—"to be a success!" Perhaps aware that she had proclaimed the words with more passion than their context warranted, she hastily amended, "Anyway, that's what I always wanted for myself. Maybe Priscilla'll make a name even if I haven't—" to her own surprise, one more word popped out— "yet."

Ma Brad's voice was disarmingly smooth as she asked, "I don't quite understand what you mean, Magpie. Surely as Dexter's wife you have a very important name."

"Oh, of course. Of course I have," Maggie responded too hastily. "I guess really all I mean is that I want Priscilla to—well, to *shine*! I want her to be both happy and attractive."

Ma Brad's eyes narrowed. "Attractive to whom?" she asked.

"If she's the way I want her to be, she'll be attractive to everybody! If she's pretty and gay and talented and has lovely manners, she'll be happy. And if she's happy she's bound to be attractive!" Maggie's flashing smile spelled Q.E.D.

"Perhaps you mean that if she's attractive she'll be happy. I can't say that I think either goal is—well, quite enough."

"It is for me," said Maggie, beaming. "I intend it to be for my daughter. I want her to have all that glitters!"

"*You* want? Have you thought, Magpie, that perhaps Priscilla herself may know some day what she wants?"

To her Grandmother Fraser little Priscilla was an object for demonstrative, overflowing love. In the face of all overtures, however, even from Maggie herself, the demure little girl remained alarmingly self-contained.

She was flaxen and straight-haired like all the Bradfields—a fact of nature Maggie did her best to refute by weekly attacks on the child with cotton rags and a stick. The unconvinced and unconvincing curls lasted only a few hours after such attempts, and presently the fine Bradfield hair would hang as limp and straight as ever. Maggie occasionally turned her maternal hopes onto Priscilla's blue eyes. "Isn't she just like a little china doll?" she would say, and then fling herself into some performance to waken response. She reverted instinctively to some of her own childhood favorites.

"Ainsi font, font, font les petites marionettes!" she would sing, jerking Priscilla's pudgy little hands from the pudgy little wrists as though she were manipulating a puppet:

> *"Ainsi font, font, font,*
> *Trois p'tits tours*
> *Et puis s'en vont."*

Priscilla merely stared at her mother with round appraising eyes, showing no flicker of amusement; rather they came nearer to expressing condemnation. Maggie sometimes would stamp and turn to her father as witness, saying, "I don't think the child has any normal reflexes."

Dr. Fraser was no comfort. "There's speculation in those orbs, Maggie."

"That's what's so creepy. Why doesn't she speak, then, or laugh?"

"Don't forget, she's a Bradfield."

"I *don't*!" Maggie's assent was nearly a groan.

Mrs. Fraser was apt to drop in on Delia's afternoon out, when Maggie rather featured "my afternoon with Priscilla." This involved putting Priscilla on her knee and carrying on a lively conversation on a plane assumed to be over her head, the assumption being that nothing could go through it. The conversation was apt to be carried on half in French and half in English, with perfect precision missing the very point for which it was designed.

"*Je commence vraiment à m'inquieter au sujet de cet enfant.* You know there *is* feeble-mindedness in the Bradfield family, and I wonder if Priscilla is going the same way."

"Please, Maggie, be careful. Little pitchers, dear . . ."

"*Elle ne comprend absolument rien. Elle n'écoute jamais un mot de ce que je lui dis. Et puis* the child never laughs. There's something very funny about her reflexes. She's just like Dexter."

The words served as signal for the familiar obbligato to many of Maggie's hyperboles—"Poor Dexter!"

"Poor Dexter," for his part, gave every indication of being entirely satisfied not only with the daughter the Lord had sent him but also with the wife whom he himself had chosen.

Maggie, as Priscilla grew older, found her days being inexorably filled in the same way that other young matrons filled theirs. She served on committees to benefit the North Bennet Street Industrial School, the Boston Dispensary, and the League of Women Voters. Her first allegiance, perforce, was given to Aunt Katta's "baby"—the Dover Street Settlement House for whose overworked staff she did volunteer work several hours a week, addressing envelopes and answering the telephone. Her father, quoting the title of a special department of the

Boston Evening Transcript, tortured her whenever he asked, "How are the Divers Good Causes, Maggie?"

Next, she was stalked by Wig Newton. Maggie had noticed that whereas the highest compliment she herself could pay another woman was to say, "She's so attractive!" Wig would narrow her eyes, cross her arms, nod her head and say, "She's doing a good job well, by heck." When she asked Maggie to serve on a committee of doctors' wives agitating for the repeal of the Massachusetts law prohibiting birth control, Maggie could think of no very good reason for saying no. After the first meeting she went home to Dexter to give an impersonation of kindly Miss Lena Cobb, one of Boston's grand old reformers, plucking her by the sleeve and asking, *sotto voce*, exactly what birth control *was*.

"Oh dear," Maggie said, "there's your we-are-not-amused expression. Now *don't* make me feel more unworthy than I already do!"

Dexter seemed not to have heard her words, but spoke rather as a result of a private impulse of his own.

"Maggie, you don't have to serve on that committee to please me, you know, if you'd be happier doing something else."

An unpleasant rumbling of an organ which might have been conscience goaded her to attack as the best defense. "You mean you think I'm doing more harm than good where I am?"

"I didn't say so." He looked at her a moment, his expression softening. "I love you the way you are. Don't let any doctors' wives make you feel that there's some obligation for you to get on their particular band wagon."

Her eyes smarted suddenly with tears. "You are a nice man, Dexter," she said.

"I'm not nice. I love you. Sometimes I wonder if you believe it—if you've ever really believed it." He floundered in the misery of the inarticulate. "Just having you around—gay and lively and lovely—and *happy*, Maggie, that's what I want. *I'm* not asking you to try to make yourself into anybody else's idea of what a physicist's wife should be. You—just the way you are naturally, the way you like to be—you are the wife I want."

Disarmed, almost dismayed, all Maggie could do was repeat lamely, "You *are* nice, Dexter. You're ever and ever so much nicer than I am. I'm so glad if you're happy with me. You hardly ever say so, you know!"

"That's because I depend on you so completely it doesn't need saying. Can't you feel what you are to me, Maggie? There's no other girl I've ever seen whom I could even imagine feeling about the way I do you. The social ones all seem like damned fools, and the other kind—the girls I used to see around Milton—they just seem sort of blah. But you—" he put his hand on her shoulder and turned her toward him almost harshly—"hell, must I say it every day? You are the one I love. Since you've given us Priscilla I love you more than I could have dreamed possible. You give me everything I could ever imagine wanting in the world."

If Maggie had been tempted into repartee in answer to the longest speech Dexter had ever made to her, or had felt the impulse to murmur that there were still things in the world *she* could imagine wanting, she could not have opened her mouth to say so, for the simple reason that Dexter closed it with a kiss.

8

"DEXTER, I've been thinking," said Maggie. Sitting after dinner in their Mt. Vernon Street living room, she was wrestling with the difficulty of knitting a sweater for Priscilla. The mothers of Priscilla's little friends at the Baby Beaver (the progressive school at the foot of Beacon Hill that educated most of the children on its slopes) seemed to have been born knowing how to knit. Maggie, protesting that she was "all thumbs," could progress at all only by turning over her work to her mother whenever she was confronted with a hurdle like a sleeve.

Dexter, deliberately at work in setting the wings, antennae, and legs of a big poplar hawk moth on a spreading board, made no response.

"Did you hear me, Dexter?" Maggie's voice sharpened.

"Sure." He gravely continued his occupation without looking up. "Am I supposed to ask what you've been thinking?"

"I refuse to talk while you're doing something else," Maggie declared over the clicking of her knitting needles.

Dexter's eyes lifted toward the work of her hands for an instant, but appeared to decide not to mention it. He put the spreading board aside.

"O.K. Let's hear what's on your mind."

"I don't want to go back to Dunster again this summer," Maggie said, loud and clear. "We've been there for five consecutive summers since our marriage, and I think it's time for a change."

The smile of amused indulgence vanished from Dexter's face. "For heaven's sake, Maggie," he said, "what's wrong with Dunster? It's where we live in summer, just the same as Boston is where we live in winter."

"How can you say anything so depressing and not want to cut your throat?" Maggie contemplated her husband with a wonder bordering on revulsion.

A frown darkened his brow. He clearly did not know what Maggie was talking about. "Why should I want to cut it?"

"Because in Dunster nothing ever *happens*!" She hurled the charge at him. "Every year the same old Brad Ballads in the barn—"

He cut her short. "What's wrong with the Brad Ballads? Everyone enjoys them."

"Every Bradfield does, you mean, because they do the performing. But have you ever stopped to think of the audience? You know as well as I do that your mother refused to go to Winthrop Ames's *Iolanthe* because she said, 'The Bradfields know Gilbert and Sullivan themselves. They don't have to hear other people sing it.' And when thinking that almost any change would be for the better I offered to put on a production of *Aucassin and Nicolette* with the kids, you know I didn't get to first base." Maggie, warming to her subject, drew breath and hurried on. "And last summer when I felt I just couldn't *bear* the monotony of it and sent out that postcard—well, I've been in the doghouse ever since."

The incident of the postcard had been a *cause célèbre*. Maggie had sent out some fifty printed cards to neighboring summer families announcing: "Mrs. Dexter Bradfield will do anything for fifty cents an hour." Dexter himself had been amused by Maggie's vagary, but his mother had appeared before them both more in anger than in sorrow. "If this is a form of practical joke, Magpie, it is in very bad taste. If you had stopped to consider how it reflects on Dexter's ability to support a wife you would never have composed it. The Bradfields never mention money. If they did, it certainly would be to suggest some way in which they might give, not ask for it."

The rehearsal of past grievances fanned the flame of Maggie's rebellion. "It isn't only that nothing ever happens at Far Fields," she went on. "The worst of it is that your family doesn't seem to want anything to happen."

"I just don't get what you're talking about. Everything that I want to happen has happened. What else do you want?"

"I tell you what I want!" Maggie put down her knitting and stood up. "I want to go to Northeast Harbor next summer! When you get there you'll see how flat Dunster is—and I don't mean just all those dunes and that eel grass either."

"But I can't go to Maine, Maggie. I can't be so far from the laboratory."

"You mean not even for your holiday?"

"No. Not for my holiday. I have to keep in touch."

"In touch!" she echoed derisively. "In touch with that dark, dreary little hole! Don't you realize, Dexter, that you're burying yourself alive? Nobody's going to know that you even exist if you don't let people see you and get to meet some new ones. You may not believe me, but I'm suggesting a change because I think it would be good for you—in your work. When we go out to dinner I can't tell you how often it happens that one of the women who have sat next to you at the table corners me afterward and asks, 'Just what does your husband do, Mrs. Bradfield?' All the other men seem to have something entertaining or interesting to tell about their work, and I could just die of embarrassment, because what can I *say*?"

"Do you mean, Maggie, that you think that the value of a man's work is to be measured by whether it's something to talk about?"

"If a man is a success he generally has something to say. I certainly hope you want to be a success. I'm only trying to help you." Maggie gave a gusty sigh in tribute to Dexter's two most irritating characteristics: she could not make him lose his temper, and she could not make him change his mind.

The Bradfields continued to spend their summers at Far Fields, and to make things "happen" Maggie had to work with the material at hand in Boston.

This material consisted almost exclusively of committee meetings and lunches or tea with friends. Often when Dexter came home late in the afternoon he would find three or four young women having tea with Maggie. The living room was heavy with cigarette smoke, and there were toast and cake crumbs on the carpet and in the upholstery. Maggie, settled back as queen of her court, would call out as he came up the stairs, "Yoo-hoo! Hello, darling!"

For a moment he would stand in the doorway while she surveyed him as an intruder in her feminine domain. His eyes looked tired, actually bloodshot, from peering into stone tanks, she assumed, or into a microscope. His strong shoulders hung as though some inner rod that generally kept them squared had been removed; his hair was rumpled, and even his shirt, everything about him spelling dead-beat. Wherever his attention had been all day, only a fraction of it had come down to earth, brought to bear on what was now before his eyes —his home, his wife, her friends. It did not occur to Maggie, looking at him in these moments, to change her own pace, to mute her own resonances.

"Tea, darling, or a drink?" she would ask brightly as she might of some casual stranger. "If you're not afraid of being the only man, come on in!"

Dexter was always afraid and never came in. He was, however, powerless to do anything about it when Maggie would press one of her friends to stay to dinner. Nor could she repress her natural reflex even when the guest got up to leave at ten o'clock, after a stay of five hours. "Oh, don't go *yet*!" she would exclaim.

The minute the door was closed Maggie might say, "Isn't it really pathetic what a one-track mind Martha has? All she seems to be able to think about in life is the Junior League."

"Then why did you ask her to dinner?" seemed a natural enough question for Dexter to ask.

"Why not?" was tossed out casually as an answer. "It seemed sort of unfriendly not to."

"You don't even have to like anyone very much to want them around, do you, Maggie?"

"No." She seemed interested in this discovery about her own nature. "I guess that's true. Even if they're not the brightest or most fascinating creatures in the world they're still somebody."

The next time the telephone rang Dexter would hear his wife answer "Hel*lo*" with the rising inflection that spelled delighted anticipation. The moment she had put down the receiver she might say, "What a dull girl! Why did I say I'd lunch with her?"

Dexter could only ask, dumfounded, "Why did you sound so enthusiastic when she asked you, then?"

"I can't be rude, can I?" she said and closed the subject, Dexter outside it.

It was not that Maggie did not enjoy hours of domestic happiness; the trouble was, she told herself, that there just were not enough of them. Like reading to Priscilla, before her bedtime, for instance. That was the rite Maggie enjoyed more than any other—doubtless because her own role was one of active participation. On those late winter afternoons when she didn't have to say to Priscilla, "Sorry, lamb, but Mummy has something she just *has* to do instead," even Dexter, coming in from the laboratory, would quietly tiptoe into the room and draw his chair, too, close to Maggie's knee, like Priscilla's, to listen to *Tom Kitten* or *The Tailor of Gloucester*.

There were the Sundays, too—spring and fall, and even an occasional beautiful wintry one—when they drove down to Far Fields for the day, taking a picnic lunch with them, Priscilla snuggled between her parents on the front seat. On these outings, more than on any other occasions, the little tongue was loosed, and the child chattered easily, generally about the animals Aunt Marsh was going to let her see—new pigs, new puppies, and a new colt. No sooner did the car come to a halt before Titipu than Priscilla shot from it, uttering a whoop—"Aunt Ma-a-rsh! Where are you?"—and was off to the kennels or the stable on the dead run. Dexter and Maggie, more often than not, did not see her the rest of the day and were free themselves either to fuss about the place—Maggie was dreaming dreams of a rose garden—or to take Fetch and Carrie on a long walk over the dunes. By the time they started for home again the ordinarily pale little face carried two sunburned splashes as a proud memento of her favorite spot in the world.

Birthday parties, too, were fun—for Maggie. She flung herself into their execution with abandon, staying up with Dexter late the night before, pinning up on the living-room wall the donkey who, in turn, was to have a series of tails pinned onto him, cutting out paper costumes, tying up grabs, writing names on favors. When the room was actually filled with a dozen or more children Maggie herself remained in the thick of the festivities to the bitter end, tweaking there a little girl's sash, offering here a hand to a little boy whose shifting feet and rolling eyes indicated the need of a personally conducted trip upstairs. The two grandmothers, smiling from the sidelines, were as much a part of the *décor* as the spun-sugar nest in which crouched the ice-cream bunny. Watching Priscilla bob a well-turned curtsy each time she shook hands, Ma Brad, standing particularly straight, as though there were no power on heaven or earth before whom *her* knee would bend, said, "It looks a little artificial to me, Magpie, like teaching a dog to walk on its hind legs."

"I don't see it that way at all" was Maggie's breezy rejoinder. "At her age it's part of good manners, and at any age a girl who hasn't got attractive manners is a plain, ordinary pill."

Mrs. Fraser poured her bit of oil over the troubled waters: "With her hair so beautifully curled—it must hurt the poor little thing with those rags on all night long—she looks like a little fairy!"

It was in the field of drama that Priscilla most disappointed her mother. In spite of secret coaching for her school Christmas play in the part of Tiny Tim she was allowed only to exclaim as a young Cratchit, "There never was such a goose!" And the next year, instead of thrilling Maggie as Jesus, Mary, or Joseph, her presence was manifested only through the twitching of the ears of an ass, inside whose large, hairy head her smaller one was concealed.

Maggie literally lay awake at night planning for Priscilla's future. She was already on the best "lists" in Boston, starting with the Friday-evening dancing classes. Maggie was making researches into the question of finishing schools in Paris, Lausanne, and New York. She used to say to friends, "I can't *wait* till she's old enough to be through all this boring progressive-school phase and be a real companion. I always knew I'd adore having a daughter, because there's so much one can *do* about daughters!"

But in the meantime the fact remained that, between school and nurse, there was precious little her mother could do for her, just as there was precious little the wife of a hard-working research physicist could do for him.

Maggie was a wife. Maggie was a mother. But still Maggie knew that there were energies within her straining to be unleashed.

She exploded to her mother one day in a sudden outburst, "I wish I could be like Kitten! She always seems so *contented*." The word carried the merest hint of disdain. "If only I could have babies the way she does probably I would be, too."

Mrs. Fraser confounded her when she answered, "I dare say you'll think I'm quite absurd, Maggie, but don't you think that if you slowed down your tempo a little you might be more likely to have another child? Remember that Kitten spends a great deal of time every day by herself, and spends evening after evening quietly at home. She says that even to write a few lines of verse there has to be a time of gestation. You're wound up so tight, like a beautiful bright top, my guess is there's no part of you, body or spirit, that's peaceful enough for creation."

"What do you mean, 'peaceful'? I certainly can't see that I'm leading a very *exciting* life."

"And yet you're never alone, dear. You know the photograph I have over my desk of my beloved Snowy Pine—that Japanese screen? That says better than I can what I mean. There's so much unfilled space on each panel it makes you appreciate all the more the little tip of pine that does show. That's the way I think we should feel about people: we must keep a sort of margin around each one if we're to get the deepest meaning out of him. Kitten has so much to give to Roger and the boys—so much, too, to give her writing because she is—well, what the saints calls 'recollected.' That's what I should like to see you, Maggie, dear."

"Honestly, Mother!" Maggie's tone was withering. "It's no good preaching at me. I'm a freethinker—like Father!"

It pleased Maggie to consider herself in every characteristic her father' s child; she had used this same argument to confound her mother on past occasions.

Her mother's usually gentle brown eyes flashed unexpected fire. "I wish you were entirely like your father, Maggie. He may be free in his thinking, but he's anything but free in his living. He knows what it is to serve something bigger than himself, as any scientist—as Dexter, too—does. He serves it through an iron discipline of himself."

"Oh, well, men are different!" Maggie airily dismissed the sex.

"But a woman can serve her husband," Mrs. Fraser went on implacably, "and sometimes the best way of doing that is to build up within herself a hidden reservoir of serenity and strength that will refresh and restore him when he needs it."

"Honestly, Mother!" The refrain was repeated. "You're simply mid-Victorian. Spaff would just die if she could hear you."

Even after five years of marriage Maggie still turned to the image of Spaff as representing emancipation incarnate. At least once a winter during those years Maggie pleaded an excuse for "playing hooky" by insisting that she would "die" unless she saw *They Knew What They Wanted, Charlot's Revue, Show Boat,* or Raquel Meller. Dexter could only affably save his wife's life by urging her to go visit Spaff, still living in the West Tenth Street apartment she and Maggie had shared on leaving Vassar. Spaff returned the compliment from time to time by appearing for a one-night stand in Boston, generally in the capacity of a spearhead in the crusade for pardoning Sacco and Vanzetti. She picketed Governor Alvan Fuller's house or the Massachusetts State House with equal zeal. After being graduated from Teachers' College, Spaff had become a member of the faculty of the Davenport School for Girls, the very archetype of all that was most progressive in modern education and most modern in progressive education. In her spare time, however, she flung herself into both civic and national projects for the commonweal that made Maggie, from her Boston backwater, point with pride. In fact, Maggie had come to look upon Spaff as a sort of *alter ego*, carrying into a public arena the torch of achievement that had fallen from her own hands. During the summer of '28 Maggie's own sense of being stuck in a quagmire at Far Fields was sharpened by letters from Spaff, who was actively campaigning for Al Smith. She wrote of her meeting Smith personally, as well as of shaking hands with John W. Davis, Newton D. Baker, and Governor Ritchie of Maryland. When Smith was defeated at the polls, Maggie decided that the time had come for her annual visit to New York, this time to be made a little in the spirit of condolence.

Landing in Grand Central Station on a snowy November evening, Maggie, her long legs twinkling under her knee-length leopard-fur coat, hurried up the ramp to find Spaff waiting for her on the other side of the barricade. The girls hugged each other heartily as Maggie exclaimed, "Oh, Spaff, it's good to see you! New York's in my blood, and always will be!"

That evening they went to see Zita Johann in *Machinal*. When they returned to the apartment, the girls stuffed a pile of cushions at their backs and sat on the floor before the fire in the grate to sip their nightcap, a concoction of Whitman's cocoa and condensed milk they and Kitten at Vassar had drunk so often and christened "miggles."

"Oh, dear," exclaimed Maggie, "how marvelous to have an evening like the one I've just had! If you knew how I missed New York, Spaff!"

"And if you knew how I still miss you," Spaff responded stoutly, " 'specially at Mrs. Bent's Sunday lunches," she added with a flashing smile of her large teeth.

"Don't tell me she still asks you!"

"Sure she does. Anyway, I never minded going as much as you did. But then she wasn't the friend of *my* family."

The one shadow that had darkened Maggie's first months in New York after college had been cast by the presence of her parents' great friend in the same city. Maggie, who had resolved to lead the dedicated life of a neophyte of the theater, had fled the majestic instancy with which Mrs. Bent pursued her with her "standing invitation" to Sunday dinner and to consider herself a "member of the family." The very tolerance with which Mrs. Bent would *not* show herself shocked at the idea of Maggie's becoming an actress infuriated her just as her affability toward Spaff irritated *her*. Mr. and Mrs. Bent serenely called her Caroline (obviously neither of them could be expected to frame the word *Spaff*) and received with indulgent good humor her championing the cause of Bob La Follette in his charges against Standard Oil. After all, wasn't Caroline the daughter of the president of the Spafford Chemical-Hydraulic Company? Such political vagaries amounted to no more than a rather endearing parlor eccentricity in a very young woman.

When the two Bent daughters, luminaries of New York's Junior League, would twirl their platinum-and-diamond engagement rings with what appeared to Maggie ostentatious nonchalance, and ask, "How's the acting coming, Maggie?" much as they might have asked a delinquent child about a new yo-yo stick, Maggie and Spaff would return to Tenth Street spluttering, "They're all so damned patronizing. We'll show them!"

Spaff could say to Maggie now, years later, "When Mrs. Bent asks me about you, it kills me to see how pleased she is that you are just a housewife in spite of the way we used to talk. Don't you have moments of wishing you hadn't married—I mean, until *after* you'd made a big success?"

"Of course I do. But then one can never have everything." Maggie sighed just a shade too melodramatically, as though, indeed, it was she who had turned her back on the New York theater, and not the other way round.

The next evening, after the friends had returned from a lecture at the New School for Social Research on "Why Stalin Ousted Trotsky," Maggie decided that attack was the best defense.

"Spaff, frankly, I'm worried about you" was her opening volley. "I wonder if you realize what's happening to you? I mean there you sat all evening with those repulsive, greasy pseudo-intellectuals." (It was fortunate that Spaff did not think to ask Maggie what test she applied to determine a true intellectual from a pseudo of the species. Anything that Maggie did not understand she feared; and anything she feared she derided.) "There wasn't one who looked as though he could possibly turn into a beau. If I were you, do you know what I'd do?"

The girls squared off, drawing away from each other a moment, as though to size up the most vulnerable spot to strike. Spaff's ordinarily good-natured smile froze on her face. Her voice was hurt and angry as she answered, "You always seem to know what you'd do if you were anybody but yourself, Maggie."

Maggie, fired by a vision which had just presented itself to her inner gaze, pounced. "Listen, Spaff," she said, "I'm only trying to help you. I want you to come up to Boston for a real visit and let Kitten and me introduce you to some decent men."

"If there's one thing I wish my married friends would not do," said Spaff with hauteur, "it is to try to marry off friends who aren't married. I'm all right the way I am, Maggie. As it happens I'm leading an extremely interesting life, and exactly the kind of life I always wanted, and that you did too, so far as that goes—once," she added with a deliberate thrust.

There was an uncomfortable pause. If Spaff would only accede to playing pawn in the exciting game Maggie envisaged, Boston itself could become not such a dull place to live in after all. "Listen, Spaff," she said, "please don't be huffy. I guess tact isn't my strongest suit. Please come on up after Christmas, when you have a real holiday, and we'll have fun—you and Kitten and I—just the way we used to." She could see that her prey was wavering. She drew closer and put her hand on Spaff's knee. "Please say you will, Spaff." And then, suddenly softening, she added, "You're right in lots of ways about me. I get awfully down in the dumps sometimes. Your coming to stay would do me good."

When Maggie returned to Boston the next day Spaff had accepted her invitation for the Christmas holidays. The friends parted as they had met—with a hug—each with an added glow of satisfaction induced by the knowledge that from the pedestal on which she stood she was in a position to reach down and give the other a boost up.

9

On her return from New York, Maggie's first instinct was to enlist the support of Kitten and Roger in her plans for Spaff.

Maggie's house had come to serve as the focus for all the social exploits of the Roger Frasers beyond the confines of Milton. Maggie insisted to them both that it was impossible for her to give a party without them as her first-to-be-invited guests. Entirely happy and self-sufficient, they would not, under their own momentum, have sought outside distractions, but when Maggie piped the tune it was different; they both obediently danced.

Adorable to look at, gentle and feminine in manner, Kitten had the faculty of making any man to whom she talked feel important. She charmed members of her own sex as well with her sympathetic attention to any recital of their grievances and the expression of admiration of their triumphs. (Her clothes, too, soothed them; their very lack of style stilled any spirit of competitiveness. Her one evening dress was of sky-blue lace, with moonstone necklace neither long enough nor short enough to count. By day she wore a "heather mixture" blue tweed suit exactly like the one she had worn at Vassar.) Both sexes, in short, talking happily about themselves to such a listener, fancied themselves as giving. The quality of interest they had aroused was devoid of anything either cloying or demanding because it sprang from an inner strength; therefore, all unconscious, they gratefully received the rarest of gifts found in society—sensitive, concentrated, unselfish understanding.

Roger, as a dinner guest, was the perfect foil to his wife. He left to her the business of drawing out new people, and gave himself up rather to impersonal but informed and intelligent conversation on subjects of general interest. In fact his appearance at Maggie's parties was a sort of reflex that he had obeyed since childhood. He allowed himself to be towed out, half reluctant, half pleased, onto the tumultuous seas of social intercourse in the wake of his dominating older sister.

Whenever Maggie found herself alone with her mother for ten minutes she was compelled to pick a fight, to proclaim some kind of declaration of independence; if she was alone with her father she continually overreached herself in an attempt to woo his attention by being funny or by dramatic exaggeration, generally ending up by being just plain noisy. It was only with her brother Roger that she was entirely herself—at her best.

Although she was two years older, Maggie could not remember the world without Roger in it. These two children of an unusually close-knit marriage had always been, in a sense, conspirators; Roger was Maggie's surest ally. Since childhood Maggie had been the commanding officer, Roger the docile foot soldier. "I tell you what let's do!" she would proclaim. "Let's play house. I'll be the mother, and you can be the baby." Or: "I know what let's do! Let's play theater. I'll be Stone. You be Montgomery." When Roger returned from his studies at the Beaux Arts in Paris, however, there had been a subtle reversal of the roles; in Maggie's eyes he had taken on a new stature. If he still appeared to find refreshment and stimulation at the fount of her abounding vitality, she herself came to depend more and more on his advice, approval, or admonition. She welcomed it because it came not from above but from her own level, as it were—from one who had abundantly, through the years, proved himself as being on her side.

Roger and his sister were as disparate on the outside of their beings as they were different within. A gentle nature was discernible in his sensitive mouth and deep-set, dark-brown eyes. There was nothing about him, however, that suggested softness—perhaps because his trim, wiry figure and the reputation that went before him proclaimed that he played a brilliant game of tennis. Where loose-jointed Maggie was "all over the place," Roger was co-ordinated and concentrated; where her handwriting was a "mess," his was as much the work of a polished artist as his precisely drawn architectural renderings. In the Northeast Harbor swimming pool Maggie churned up a surf all about her, splashing, kicking, and wheezing as she plowed through the water; Roger slipped beneath its surface, swift, sure, and noiseless.

Most observers would have said that after their respective marriages, to sister and brother, Maggie and Roger would have had more "in common" than ever, but actually the curtain that can divide twin souls of childhood into isolated adult entities fell inexorably between them. Maggie used to fume to herself, longing to tell and to ask so many things, but forced into the—to her—almost superhumanly difficult recourse of holding her tongue. She learned to talk of marriage or life in Boston or at Dunster in general terms, deriving what comfort she could from his equally general answers.

Exploding to him one day after a particularly dull committee meeting, she had said, "I just couldn't help feeling all those dreary women were trying to pull me down to their own dismal level. Is that what being married is—a sort of conspiracy on the part of other women to get you to be as stuffy as themselves?"

Roger looked at her, appraising, a moment before bringing out almost tentatively, "You shouldn't let yourself be *mangée par les autres*, Maggie. Why do you care what those women think of you? What if they do blandly assume you are one of them? You know you're not, and that's all that ought to count."

Maggie appeared interested in the diagnosis. "Maybe you're right. I never thought of it."

"I have an idea you're not sure yet who you are. With every new person you meet you hope you're going to find out. Your wanting to have people around you fools people into thinking you're kind of a cornucopia, overflowing with riches to shower on your hungry pensioners, whereas actually—" he hesitated, as though Maggie might not like what he was going to say— "I think it's you who are the hungry one."

Maggie, feeling that Roger was probing closer than usual to the bone, asked with a sudden intensity, her sharp bright eyes narrowing into an expression of worry, "Roger, do you think I am just hopelessly discontented?"

"Anything but." The mere tone of his voice carried balm. "You're hopefully believing, therefore capable of disappointment."

Whatever concern Roger may have felt about his sister's happiness he did not express, like his mother, in gentle counsel, or, like his father, in ironic teasing; rather, he made it his business to toss her way some entertaining activity or distraction. He and Kitten took her to see the Guitrys in *Mozart* on an evening Dexter had to attend a medical meeting, and it was Roger who suggested to Aunt Katta that Maggie might be more useful to the Dover Street Settlement House organizing a theater benefit than in doing humdrum office work.

Maggie herself felt a painful twinge when, according to the convention that proclaims the parasite more important than the flesh on which it feeds, she saw her own photograph rather than that of the stars in the *Boston Evening Transcript* over the heading: "Mrs. Dexter Bradfield in charge of benefit sponsoring Lunts' bow to Hub in *The Second Man*." It was not so much that she felt compunction for attracting limelight that should have been flooding other features than her own; rather, it was that she would so much have preferred to star as actress than as "socialite." In New York, the winter before, she had been to a party in honor of Eliot Cabot, who was appearing with Helen Hayes in *Coquette*, and felt again the tingle of mixed pride and envy for one handsome Bostonian from her own world who had shot across the larger heavens of theater renown, just as in her Vassar days she had admired Constance Binney as another who had made her mark in the world that Maggie herself longed so passionately to adorn.

Back in Boston it was easy to light the actual life she had lived after college in New York with the deceiving glow of imagination. She told herself today that in those precious days of independence she had been successful as a "career girl," and so stirred up in herself an uneasy mingling of desire and restlessness. Because Maggie constitutionally was unable to admit that she had made a mistake in her own life, she looked about her to suggest to friends how they might improve their lives.

One evening she cornered Roger and Kitten. "You've both got to help me," she exploded abruptly. "I'm going to get Spaff married!"

"Have you Spaff's blessing on your scheme?" asked Roger. "Do you happen to know if she wants to get married?"

"Oh, pooh! Who cares what she says? Everybody should be married!"

If Roger, eyeing the decisive toss of his sister's golden head, entertained thoughts of the fox with its tail cut off luring a fellow fox into the same trap, he kept them to himself. "Have you any particular candidate or candidates?" he asked.

"Well, I have several in mind," Maggie answered rather grandly, "though my first choice is Sarge. Now, Kitten, don't tell me Sarge isn't the marrying kind, because we're going to make him so!"

Before Kitten had a chance to speak, Roger interrupted. "Good God, Maggie, have a heart! Sarge is perfectly all right the way he is, minding his own business."

"That's just the trouble with him. He should be taken out of his rut. Spaff could make any man she married really important."

"Important to whom?"

"You sound just like Father! Don't be mean. Spaff would get him into some big work—philanthropic, educational, or political. I've always thought that Sarge might be—well, almost like Dexter, if only someone would just bring him out. The way he is now he's only sort of a rough draft of what he could be. I feel it in my bones that Spaff would make the perfect wife for a Bradfield man. The Bradfield men are so noble." Maggie did not observe Kitten wince under the edge of disgust in her voice.

With what she considered Machiavellian guile Maggie did not, within the hour of Spaff's arrival in Boston, produce an obviously eligible man. In fact, the first days of her visit were spent in the Triumvirate's giving itself up to the joys of reunion. "Have you heard anything from Frannie?" "You know Ellie's broken her engagement." "You'll never believe what Buzzie's been doing." "Will you ever forget the time? Will you ever forget the day? Will you ever forget . . . ?"

One evening Spaff went alone to have dinner in Milton with Kitten and Roger and their three boys. Coming in late, she said to Maggie, who was waiting up for her, "Don't they all seem happy? I should call that a really perfect marriage!"

Maggie was aware of the sensation of discomfort bordering on irritation that she had felt before now in the contemplation of Roger's and Kitten's marriage. It was not prompted by anything so crude as jealousy—Maggie's nature was not a small one—but it was the sense of baffled irritation that the extrovert must always feel in the presence of any power that defies definition, and does not *show*. Dearly as she treasured Kitten as her closest friend, she still could not truthfully understand how any man could have fallen in love with her as instantly and remained as unshaken ever since, as had Roger. Maggie supposed that it was because as a wife Kitten offered exactly what she offered as a friend—the unique quality of unquestioning and total acceptance. When Spaff spoke of a "perfect" marriage, though Maggie was tempted to explain that her own idea of such a state would have much more glamour, she could say heartily, "Oh, yes, they adore each other."

"Isn't it wonderful about her having a poem accepted by *Poetry* magazine? She's so modest she never told me a thing about it until Roger showed it to me."

"Yes, it's wonderful," Maggie said with warmth, adding with a cozy giggle, "Promise not to tell, but I really can't make head or tail of it. It *looks* so simple, and the title is easy—just 'Orion'—but I don't know what the poem means!"

Maggie had noticed, during the last summers, that Kitten was more and more apt to have a pad and pencil in her hand when she sat by the play pen of the current baby. Whenever Maggie asked her what she was writing she would say no more than "Oh, nothing. Just scribbling."

There had been an evening too when Maggie went over to Barataria to find that Kitten had gone to walk by herself on the dunes. Maggie attacked Roger, who had explained his wife's absence. "How can you let her, Roger? Aren't you afraid something might happen to her?"

"Not in the least afraid. But even if I were it wouldn't do any good."

"I suppose not. I'm glad to see that Dexter isn't the only Bradfield that likes to be alone."

"He certainly isn't." Roger had looked with sudden sharpness at Maggie. "Solitude has never been your cup of tea, has it, Maggie? Kitten says the only way she ever hopes to find out who she is is to be alone at night, out of doors."

"How *queer*! Imagine not knowing who you are." For a moment she had looked genuinely puzzled. "Well," she went on in an everyday voice, as though to reassure herself, "maybe there are some compensations in not being literary!"

But when Kitten's penchant for solitude and writing both had "paid off" in a poem actually published and accepted, even if in a magazine Maggie had never heard of, she was wholeheartedly excited and pleased.

Spaff's final comment was "All the same, Kitten's poems don't count for anything to her alongside those three boys. *They* are something to be proud of all right."

Maggie had already pointed out to Dexter, "Really, it's pathetic to see how much pent-up maternal feeling Spaff has." She had observed with amusement how Spaff, with all the assurance of the progressive educator, had launched a deliberate campaign of wooing and winning Priscilla's interest. Her large teeth bared, the craters of her dimples overflowing with merriment for some unshared joke, she advanced on Priscilla, who was gravely absorbed in a coloring book. Spaff proceeded to draw for her, with running commentary, in that treacle-sweet voice reserved for "disturbed" children, a picture of an old lady going out of her house for a walk, falling down and picking herself up, falling down and picking herself up, four times—the result being an awkwardly drawn picture of an improbable-looking animal. Priscilla studied the effort with sad adult eyes, as though Spaff were the problem child, and then, picking up her own book, sidled out of the room to resume her own activity unmolested. Maggie called after her, "Priscilla, that's not a *bit* a nice way to behave when Aunt Spaff is kind enough to show you a new game!"

On Sunday Dexter drove Maggie and Priscilla and Spaff down to Far Fields to spend the day, Roger, Kitten, and their brood going from Milton in their own car to join them.

Their arrival at Far Fields took place just as Maggie hoped it might. Sarge and Marsh were in the driveway to welcome the party; Marsh, blushing scarlet beneath her freckles at the sight of a stranger, retreated immediately to the barn, all the children at her heels. Sarge was left to do the honors.

Maggie, in preliminary soundings, had discovered that Spaff had no recollection of having met Sarge at her wedding. Looking at him now with the fresh eye she assumed Spaff would turn on him, Maggie was aware of certain features that had never struck her before. His Adam's apple, for one. Why had she never observed that it protruded into rather a sharp point and slipped up and down in its socket every time he spoke? She could have wished that he did not have to wear gold-rimmed glasses; in juxtaposition to a heavy plaid mackinaw and his very large red ears, they did not help to present exactly the figure of romance with which she had hoped to dazzle her friend.

But then there was no aura of romance shimmering about Spaff, either. At Vassar she had been called "outstanding." Off the campus, as on it, she still loomed as outsize. Her strong features, with the splendid dark eyes, and hair pulled straight back from her low brow, appeared worthy of perpetuation in a larger-than-life bronze, representing some impersonal benefaction to mankind, like Freedom of Assembly.

Maggie, watching Sarge take a step backward, said to him brightly, "While the sun is high, Sarge, won't you take Spaff through Castle Adamant? It is such a period piece I'd love her to have a guided tour."

"O.K.," answered Sarge, and, turning immediately to Roger, said, "You come too, Rah-Rah. An architect can explain it much better than I can."

Maggie shook her head and frowned at Roger, but he seemed not to absorb the drift of her pantomime as he walked off with Sarge, leaving Spaff to follow after.

Later in the morning they all took a walk along the dunes. A spanking ice-cold northwest wind was blowing, turning the sea a dark-reddish blue and whirling the powdery sand about their ankles so that it stung like needles. Roger, eyeing Kitten in her inevitable blue tweeds, Spaff in a brown leather jacket over a yellow skirt, and Maggie in a Peck and Peck crimson homespun, said, "You look like three bright, cheerful birds in this winter landscape."

"Oh, speaking of birds!" Maggie pounced on the topic tossed her. "Spaff teaches a nature class, among other things. I think, Sarge, she'd be fascinated to see some of your Dunster sandpipers!"

"They go south in winter" was Sarge's stolid reply as he turned on his heel to catch up with Dexter, who had gone on ahead. In no time the four long Bradfield legs had outstripped the rest of the party, who, faltering in the cold and wind, turned back to the seclusion of Titipu and an open fire.

When the brothers rejoined them they fell to on a picnic lunch, Maggie disgusted to see that Spaff seemed no more anxious to sit next to Sarge than he to her. It was apparent that she felt more at ease with the girls or their husbands than with the only single man.

Well, thought Maggie, *if they won't have a tête-à-tête, here goes for a little general conversation.* "Kitten," she said much louder to her sister-in-law than was necessary, "did Spaff tell you that she's had an article accepted by the *Junior League Magazine*? It's about her trip to Mexico and the causes of revolution. Sarge, you're such a swell amateur photographer you really ought to see the pictures she took."

"I'm sorry, I don't belong to the Junior League" was the repartee that reduced Marsh, in a remote corner, into a choking fit over her hard-boiled egg.

Spaff, never happier than in addressing a meeting, thawed suddenly, feeling the attention of what she would have called "the group" turned on her. "Those people have got something, do you know it?" Spaff challenged them. "It makes the rest of—" she just didn't say *you*— "us seem so damned spoiled and futile." Abruptly she wheeled on Dexter. "They've got plenty to give you medics to think about. There's a *job* to be done there on birth control. The Church has as much of a stranglehold as . . . as—" suddenly she brightened, remembering that she herself was in darkest Africa at the moment— "in Massachusetts!"

"Considering present company, isn't that a rather unfortunate topic of conversation?" Roger beamed happily at the perennially pregnant Kitten.

Spaff turned immediately back to Dexter. "I want to check some figures with you before I go back to New York. I've been doing some interesting field work on the problem. The place to attack it, of course, is on the community level."

Maggie, who always became instantly bored by conversation on a general topic, shrugged her shoulders and tapped her foot. Suddenly she announced to her brother in a voice just loud enough to disturb Spaff and Dexter, "Oh, by the way, Roger, I forgot to tell you I've been reading *Bella* by my friend Giraudoux. I just adore it!"

The desired effect was accomplished. Spaff stopped what she was saying to Dexter to ask Maggie, "Who knows Giraudoux? Madame, at Davenport, says he's one of the most brilliant writers in France today."

"He may not be a real friend, but I'm sure he'd remember Maggie all the same. Tell Spaff," urged Kitten, letter-perfect in every exploit of Maggie's past as well as present. Kitten often served as a better stooge than Roger.

"We-ell . . ." Maggie drew breath with the customary gasp and rapturous smile that preceded any anecdote concerning an adventure of her own. "During the war there were some French officers sent over to give military training at Harvard—probably ROTC or something. I studied their pictures in the paper and naturally chose the only one without a mustache as 'my' officer. So when Roger and I stood on the steps of Grandma Faneuil's house on Beacon Street to watch them on the day they arrived in Boston drive slowly by in an open car in a parade—didn't we, Roger?—when he was right in front of us I called out, very shrill and clear—I guess I was about sixteen and fresh as paint—'*Vive Giraudoux*!' He turned around with such a surprised look that anybody on dreary old Beacon Street could know his name, and waved his white-gloved hand, and smiled right at me. Naturally I nearly died of ecstasy, didn't I, Roger?"

"I remember I wanted to crown you."

"Yes, and not as queen!" Maggie giggled. "Poor Roger, I was always embarrassing him to death, dragging him backstage, trying to get the star's autograph—Pavlova, Yvette Guilbert. When we saw Hampden in *Hamlet* and Roger heard the lines 'Our one-time sister, now our queen,' for a whole month, whenever I asked him to do anything, the answer was 'Yes, Queen,' or 'No, Queen.' "

"I guess you were just born a lion hunter," Roger said good-naturedly.

"I'm *not* a lion hunter!" his sister retorted hotly. "I'm a lion feeder. It's quite different."

"Tell us the difference," put in Spaff, the professional moderator.

"Well, a lion hunter collects lions. She likes to have them around, like a new picture—something that will show and make people talk. I don't care whether anybody knows I know them or not. I just want to be allowed to—to worship!"

"Look at her eyes shine," said Sarge, all but recoiling before such an abandoned show of feeling. "Does she look at you like that, Brad?" he asked Dexter.

In parting, Maggie swallowed her sense of personal irritation and disappointment in her brother-in-law. With as much cordiality as she could muster she said, "When you come into town on Friday, Sarge, won't you spend the night with us? We want to take Spaff to a show or do something that would be fun." To Spaff she said, "Sarge is a character! On Thursday mornings he cuts wood in Dunster, and on Friday mornings he cuts coupons in Boston."

"Thanks, Magpie," said Sarge, "but I've got to get back to Far Fields. Flora's not entirely out of the woods yet."

"Honestly, Sarge, you and your sick cow!" Maggie tried hard to smile. "Well, don't forget I'm counting on you and Marsh for my New Year's Eve party."

Maggie tried to cheer herself on the drive home by the thought that perhaps the day had not been a total failure. Spaff had loved Far Fields and Dunster—an important entering wedge.

That evening Spaff got a long-distance call from New York. She came to Maggie with sparkling eyes. "I've had the most thrilling invitation! This friend of mine I met during the campaign has an extra seat for Roosevelt's inauguration at Albany on New Year's Day. She wants me to drive up with her. I must get back to New York tomorrow."

"Oh, Spaff, not tomorrow! I've asked *such* a nice man to dinner tomorrow night to meet you. He's Dexter's research assistant, and though he's not just my type I'm sure you'd get on too beautifully."

Spaff recoiled visibly. Maggie could see that she felt that she was being patronized. With quiet dignity Spaff said, "I'm sorry, but I certainly can't pass up a really important political event for a merely social evening that means nothing anyway."

When Spaff had returned to New York Maggie exploded to Dexter, "Aren't people the limit, the way they simply don't appreciate what you do for them!"

"Don't take it too hard, Maggie. Maybe you didn't succeed in marrying Spaff off in under a week, but I think she enjoyed herself."

"Do *you* think she's attractive, Dexter? Do *you* think I'm crazy to try to get some man to be interested in her?"

"She seems to me a very pleasant person."

In the face of such inadequacy of human perception, "*Honestly*, Dexter!" was all that Maggie could find to say.

10

Nature, abhorring a vacuum, would undoubtedly have sent Nini Deacon into Maggie's life eventually. As it was, the catalytic agent that served this force was, ironically enough, Mrs. Fraser's Wednesday Club.

Mrs. Fraser, distressed over Maggie's obvious disgruntlement after Spaff's return to New York, advanced on her daughter much as she might if she had been extending a bowl of calf's-foot jelly, saying, "I've been thinking, dear, that if Boston is likely to be rather monotonous this winter you might enjoy a little feeling of *belonging*. My Wednesday Club wants to invite a few young women this winter as guests, with the idea that one by one, as they prove themselves interested and interesting, they be invited to become permanent members."

Maggie asked challengingly, "Who belongs?"

Mrs. Fraser's evasive answer was "Well, they're all my friends, dear."

"You mean all members of your sewing circle?"

Mrs. Fraser attempted, by the airiness of her voice, to bleach all stain of the stigma. "Not all *mine*, although I think that most of us came out in the nineties. I suppose that seems antediluvian to you, but they're all interested in—"

"Worth-while things?"

"Yes!" Mrs. Fraser seemed grateful to have the word supplied foı her, oblivious of the sneer in Maggie's voice. "And interesting things too. We discuss a topic each time."

"How deadly!" Maggie's groan dissipated her mother's happy dream that she was winning a convert.

"But it's really not. We have a most entertaining time! We aren't trying to prove anything. We're all congenial, and enjoy being together. But we realize that we aren't getting any younger and must bring in some fresh blood if the club is not to die out. We thought half a dozen young women, as guests for this season, would be a great addition. Naturally it keeps it more in the family if we can bring daughters. Mrs. Calcott is asking her daughter-in-law."

"Dorothea? That Cambridge prig?"

Dorothea Calcott, with a substantial Boston name and an equally substantial Boston fortune, living in Cambridge as the wife of a Harvard professor, had long considered herself as leaven in the lump of academic society. The mere mention of her name was a thorn in the flesh of Maggie Bradfield. Dorothea, she heard, held a real salon. Dorothea had a remarkable knack for collecting "interesting" people about her (the Dexter Bradfields not among them). Maggie, from across the Charles, could only splutter, "Pseudo-intellectual," but she was disturbed by the unpleasant sense that Dorothea had succeeded in creating an entertaining life for herself where she, Maggie, had failed.

Mrs. Fraser spoke comfortingly. "Well, she may not come, dear. The meetings are always in Mrs. Calcott's house, because of her being such an invalid, so it did seem as though it would be appropriate to ask her daughter-in-law."

Before the era when it was decreed that all meetings were to be held in Mrs. Calcott's Chestnut Street house, one of Maggie's earliest childhood memories was the flurry in Brimmer Street on those days the club met there. The best lace tablecloth was on the dining-room table; there was tea served at one end, and hot chocolate with whipped cream at the other. Afterward she and Roger were allowed to nibble among the leftovers—paper-thin cress sandwiches and "favorites," a light cupcake crowned with hard bittersweet-chocolate frosting and edged with light white crunchy icing—a specialty of the Women's Educational and Industrial Union.

The almost wistfully good women in whose honor they had been ordered would never be guilty of a "let-them-eat-cake" approach to any of the problems of their day. They would simply eat the cake themselves, complacent in the knowledge that by so doing they were giving employment to the worthy women who made it, and work hard on the energy generated by its calories to see that their less fortunate sisters might have bread.

When Maggie arrived at Mrs. Calcott's on Wednesday afternoon she found the atmosphere electric. Mrs. Fraser was not the only one of the ladies to have put on her "best" dress—a rare occurrence. Each of them possessed a "rainy day" costume and an "everyday" costume, the latter covering almost all exigencies, even a trip to New York. (What was the point of "sitting out" a nice dress in traveling, which, if left to hang in the closet, would remain perfectly good for years to come?) Mrs. Fraser had already told Maggie the subject of the afternoon's discussion: "What hero of fiction would you choose for a husband, and why?" Maggie was reminded, before the discussion opened, of the twittery atmosphere in the girls' dressing room before a dance. These kindly matrons whispered behind their hands to one another, "I'm not going to tell who my husband is going to be!" "You'll never believe whom I've chosen!" "Oh, my dear, that's not fair. He's mine!"

She settled into a back corner to watch the proceedings, which began to get under way only after Mrs. Calcott was helped by her daughter-in-law into a comfortable chair in the front row. Even the rather dampening influence of her formidable presence did not completely still the flutter until, sipping first from a glass of water to give her courage, the president rather meekly asked for order. Maggie was interested to see Jane Deacon for herself. The ladies of the Wednesday Club, by electing her president for this season, though she was still only in her early thirties, had crowned her with the highest honor it was in their power to bestow. Although a public tribute, it was also something in the nature of a martyr's crown. She was their Joan of

Arc, immolated in that ever most popular of all popular lost causes—the outraged wife. Maggie had heard her mother's friends inveighing against the "Chicago adventuress" who had bludgeoned Dick Deacon into abandoning Jane and her five children and, adding insult to injury, had herself moved into Boston to reap what she anticipated would be the rich harvest of her deed. The Wednesday Club was dedicated to the proposition that she must reap, instead, a whirlwind. This was the first appearance of Jane Deacon, at once discarded and elevated, in her new role. She was out to do a good job well, by heck.

With admirable, if ever so slightly strained, gaiety she led the discussion, which turned out to be less of a debate than a guessing game.

"My husband would have to be a man who has spent seven years at sea. He must be a naval officer and he must be serious and deep in his feelings, although he has charming manners in the world." Hands shot up with blood pressures, the ladies growing "warm" as they advanced upon the quarry. The final tally proved that, after Jane Austen's heroes and a few contemporary ones—Mark Sabre of *If Winter Comes* and Young Jolyon of *The Forsyte Saga*—it was in the Elysian fields of Victorian fiction that these paragons burgeoned. Maggie also observed with pleasure that almost invariably each lady chose as her dream husband the very opposite of the one she possessed in real life. Ralph Touchett was chosen by the wife of a boorish bullying amateur yachtsman; there were several Darcys chosen by the spouses of dim cotton brokers or investment trustees. There were three Captain Wentworths; one Eugen Courvoisier, from *The First Violin*; one Hamilton, from *The Initials*, one Henry Sumner from Robert Grant's *The Chippendales;* and a Mr. Baer. *The Gentleman from Indiana* brought forth even louder cries of protest than did Heathcliff. And the one vote cast for Hamlet was thrown out entirely, as it was maintained that drama was not the same as fiction, though Mrs. Bastion went down fighting, asserting that the right kind of wife could have "put some gimp" into an otherwise charming man.

Maggie, who, in summer as an outsider looking in, could coo affectionately over the Culture Girls, now, watching some of the same women or their equivalents, was aware of a shudder of panic: it was a conspiracy, closing in on her, to make her one of themselves. As she walked home afterward with her mother she struck out violently. "Mother! *Really!* It's too silly—all those old women sitting around having wish fulfillments about their dream man, like manicurists reading *True Romance*."

When, therefore, several months later Maggie was asked to come "in on the ground floor" of a new young club, founded as a deliberate protest against the Wednesday Club, she accepted with alacrity, even though the instigator of the palace revolution was the distrusted Dorothea Calcott herself.

Maggie thus became one of the charter members of the Hub Club, dedicated to the proposition that all its members must be "interesting" or "amusing." Adhering to the classic pattern of revolutions, however, it presently found that compromise with the world of harsh facts had to be made: the admissions committee was forced to lower its sights from the interesting and amusing and settle for the interested and amused. (It was also understood, although not put into words, that the income, social standing, and lack of professional occupation of its members bear the imprint of *The Social Register*.) The meetings, held in a sort of studio-loft on the back of Beacon Hill, consisted of lunch, followed by "skits." The older women, perhaps as a reaction from their serious committees and discussion clubs, fell upon this outlet with the excitement of small children. Maggie watched otherwise respected and respectable matrons blacken their teeth with cork to parade about in their husbands' union suits, superfluously adding cushions fore and aft; they reddened their noses, to their own hilarious shrieks of amusement and to Maggie's—she could not have said why—excruciating embarrassment. With the addition of Nini Deacon, freshly arrived from Chicago and hailed as a "patron of the arts who knows everybody in the music world," Maggie was fired with the hope that shock troops had landed. The fact that Nini was the "adventuress" who had snagged Jane Deacon's husband only added to her luster in Maggie's eyes. Unimaginative as she was unsuspicious,

Maggie Bradfield could not guess that Nini Deacon might use her to serve her own ends.

Even Nini's enemies—and their number was not negligible—were forced to admit, "You've got to hand it to Nini." Taking life by assault and battery, she had built her own personality like a pioneer woman building a stockade. She was small and dark. Her own idea of her face was that it was piquant. The idea was founded on the fact that she had a pointed little nose and a pointed little chin. Her very expression was pointed. Her tiny clawlike hands busied themselves unceasingly with the small area of her face like a gardener tilling a plot of soil. The eyebrows had been plucked long since, and in their place there ran a thin penciled black line. Over the sharp thin twig which was her mouth she painted on, two or three times a day, a heavy sticky rosebud where, if left in a state of nature, a thorn would more likely have sprouted. If hats were small, Nini's were the smallest; if skirts short, hers the shortest; if shoulders wide, hers the widest. One trade-mark she made her own; she never wore any other color than black, and she was never *décolleté*. If, in the evening, she did not wear sleeves to the wrist, then she wore long black gloves. She thought of herself as *petite*; perhaps a black-widow spider does the same.

A little black widow, in point of fact, was just what she had been for several years before she met the Deacons on the *Ile de France* on the way to Europe. After her husband's death it was glibly said among her wide Chicago acquaintance, "My dear, she killed him." Not that she was so much accused of outright murder with stiletto or poison as of devouring him whole, as her insect sister might have done. Like a Victorian heroine he had simply gone into a decline, and then, obligingly, died, leaving her what she referred to, with just the right attitude of dismay, deprecation, and delight, as his "pork-packing millions." With those millions in her husband's lifetime she had been guarantor of the Chicago Opera Association as well as a trustee of the Chicago Symphony Orchestra and had cut a swath on the Gold Coast as hostess to visiting celebrities. If the European musician, appearing as guest artist with either the opera or orchestra, suspected her of wanting either to seduce or endow him, he was wrong. She found ample reward for her lavish hospitality in simply being allowed to call him by his first name in public. Leaning comfortably back on a node that she maintained had formed years ago on her vocal cords, she let it be known, with the sublime assurance peculiar to a woman of means, that it was mere chance that her own name was not in lights today on the marquees of the opera houses of Europe and America.

When she met the Deacons on shipboard, on her way to Salzburg, she flattered Dick by the assumption that he had the soul of an artist because he was a trustee of the Boston Symphony Orchestra. As both he and Jane had heretofore thought of the position as one of the many purely civic responsibilities he dutifully shouldered in the community, he enjoyed being seen in this becoming and interesting new light. Eyeing the couple from Boston with a calculating eye, Nini decided that Jane Deacon must, if not actually be thrown into the cold Atlantic, be tossed overboard. The maneuver was executed with such slickness that Dick Deacon was the last person to realize that the grand passion which seized him did not spring from his own loins but rather from Nini's head. Repeating by rote, he assured his wife that it was more "honest," for her own sake, as well as for that of his five children, to grant him a divorce. Jane forthwith went docilely to Reno.

Nini, who had plotted every detail of the swath she was going to cut in Boston with Dick's old Boston name and her new Chicago money, was offered Boston's chilliest cold shoulder. She was at first incredulous, presently disappointed, and, in short order, defiant. She glared across the invisible barrier and spluttered imprecations on the stuffy, absurd, provincial, hypocritical has-beens who passed for society, while those on the other side glared back and pronounced the intruder as an "adventuress," hard, scheming, and—behind their hands—"ordinary."

Nini's defiance, however, aroused a tingle of sympathy among some of the daughters of her repudiators. In their hearts there was not one of these young women who found any quality to like in Nini, but they espoused her cause not for what it stood for but for what it stood against. It was in this spirit, even more than because she knew talented people, that they railroaded her election into the Hub Club, giving the ladies of Boston a *cause célèbre* over which to lick their chops. A few of Jane Deacon's friends were vociferous, lobbying with the slogan, "Who next?" Surely Dick Deacon's behavior should not be condoned to the extent of welcoming his second wife among them. The curiosity of Jane Deacon's friends, however, overruled their loyalty. They were not only anxious to see for themselves what this foreign import might be like; they looked forward to reporting to Jane on her lack of charms. Both factions could vindicate Nini's election by saying, "After all, it's not like the Chilton Club or the Wednesday Club, which *stand* for something. The Hub Club is only for fun."

There were times during the ensuing winter that the words thus lightly spoken were well on their way to being eaten, along with the chicken patties and peas of the club luncheons. Nini promptly assumed the role of renovator, pointing out to its members how the club could be better run along the lines of Chicago's Sock and Buskin Club. (The fact that the members of the Sock and Buskin were at that moment sighing gusty sighs of relief and saying, "Thank God she's bossing the Bostonians now," would have worried Nini no more than the letters many Chicagoans had sent via the underground to Eastern seaboard friends, asking, "Do tell us about the poor man she's married. Does he know what he's getting in for?") She assailed the amateurishness of the productions, saying, "They're no better than charades. Why don't we give something *good*? In Chicago I put on Molière's *Le Bourgeois Gentilhomme*. We gave it for a charity benefit and it was a huge success. There's no reason we shouldn't do it here." No one of the members daring to say, "Except that we don't want to," they found themselves in short order brushing up rusty French, learning lines, attending rehearsals at inconvenient times, and working on costumes and sets far harder than their cleaning women worked for them.

Dorothea Calcott, although metaphorically holding her upturned nose not because Nini Deacon was bad but because she was rich, played the part of the heroine Dorimène. Maggie, with her father's recording of the Comédie Française performance of the *leçon de danse* as model, was assigned the part of the *Maître à danser*.

Nini called Maggie one day, soon after rehearsals had begun, to ask, "Couldn't we get together for half an hour just by ourselves? I'd love to work up the scene of the minuet with you into something that will stop the show. Your accent is so perfect it will be a relief to get away from the boarding-school French of some of our other members, and besides, just anyway, I'd love to see you."

Maggie tingled to the agreeable sensation of having her back scratched in just the right place, and asked Nini, just as Nini had intended her to do, to drop in for a cocktail before the next luncheon meeting.

She arrived, chic and competent, wearing a small black grosgrain hat, low and tight, that covered the top of her face, and a huge silver-fox fur that covered the bottom of it, so that little was visible except two bright eyes and a sharp little nose.

She opened her coat, looked about Maggie's living room and said, "How sweet!" with an inflection which conveyed some of the things the room was not. Maggie quickly proffered a martini, which was accepted in the offhand way that told Maggie it was as natural to Nini before lunch as coffee at breakfast.

At this moment Priscilla, at home from school with a cold, chose to come into the room to look for a missing box of water-color paints. She wore a plaid skirt and a rumpled tan sweater. Her hair needed brushing, and the fingers in which she held a peanut-butter sandwich were covered with paint.

She came forward obediently, bobbed her curtsy, and said, "How do you do," and gave a loud sniff, proclaiming her need of a handkerchief.

Nini asked in a brittle social tone, "Do you play the piano, Priscilla?"

"No," said Priscilla and sniffed again.

"Do you act, like your mother?"

The child withdrew into a painful silence of confusion, clearly not understanding the question that had been put to her.

Maggie interpreted. "Mrs. Deacon wants to know if you act in *plays*, Priscilla. Not if you behave like me!"

"I was part of the ass in the Christmas play," she stated soberly.

"How nice! Then you're going to be talented, like your mother."

Priscilla shifted from one foot to another as though the chains of her thralldom were cutting down to the quick.

"Run along, dear," Maggie said, lightly setting her free. "And *do* tell Delia to wash your hands!"

Priscilla bolted from the room, and just as Maggie opened her mouth to explain away some of the obvious reasons why her child had not put her best foot forward, Nini made it clear that the interruption had been entirely irrelevant to the matter in hand, lifted her glass toward Maggie, saying, "Here's looking at one of the few women I've met in Boston who is both decorative and gay!"

Maggie's responsive blush was instantaneous; her dimples deepened as she flashed a delighted smile in return.

"Heavens, I'm afraid I'm not either. But I love to be allowed to enjoy life!"

"A pretty hard thing to do in this bourgeois provincial city."

Maggie started to speak, to express concern for the stranger within such grim gates, but Nini, with her nose to the ground, was on Maggie's trail and was not going to let even interest in herself distract her.

"What I want to know is what you're doing here at all. Have you always lived in Boston?"

Again the pleasant little tingle. "Well, I lived in Paris when I was a child, and after college I studied for the stage in New York—" she let the images thus presented linger in all their attractiveness a moment before she added, with the merest hint of a rueful sigh— "and then I married."

"I'm sure if you had gone on with your career you would have had a huge success." Maggie opened her mouth, but closed it as Nini lifted a hand in protest. "No, don't say anything modest, and don't tell me it's also possible to be a success as wife and mother. We both know that's not what we're talking about. After all, there's no success like—*success*!"

The responsive gleam in Maggie's eye flashed the answer that she knew just what her new friend was talking about.

"Well, I do hope we're going to get to know each other much better. It's such heaven to find someone who is—cosmopolitan!" Nini smiled brightly, pinning the decoration on Maggie.

"Isn't Dorothea Calcott that? She speaks beautiful French." Maggie just didn't add *too*.

"Perhaps, my dear, but isn't she a little pallid? You have such *élan*!"

Nini, who had been diligent in her homework, had already discovered that Dorothea presented a bit of a threat to her own ambitions. She had literary and intellectual pretensions, as well as social ones, and surely Boston and its environs did not afford enough artistic lions to feed those bent on their blood. Nini had already decided just which followers of Dorothea's she might herself capture in a skillful, well-planned raid.

In Maggie Bradfield she scented a potential ally of the first magnitude. She was Social, with a capital S, as well as sociable, bored, and hungry for something and someone new. Through both her husband and her parents she touched many strands of Boston life; if properly flattered and cajoled, she could be induced to place these strands in Nini's own clutching little talons.

"I know so well what it is to make sacrifices for one's marriage." Nini sighed gently. "Dick and I are so tremendously in love, and yet, when one's husband is a businessman . . ." She let the sentence hang suspended and asked abruptly, "What is your husband? I ought to know, but I don't."

"He's a research physicist."

Nini looked blank.

"He works in a field where he says physics and chemistry meet with biology," Maggie explained. "They hope, among other things, to find a cure for cancer."

"Oh, how fortunate you are!" Maggie's new friend exclaimed with sympathy. "He must be a fascinating talker, and you must share in the excitement and the importance of his work. But the paper business—there just isn't much to be said about paper at the end of the day! And naturally, for a woman who has been surrounded with artists, writers, musicians—I did have a really heavenly apartment on the lake—it is just a little lonely sometimes. I do so hope we can cut out all the silly conventional bowings and scrapings and simply behave as though we'd known each other always—which is the way I feel! I hope you'll let me come and take my back hair down with you from time to time and report on my progress among the Pilgrims."

It was at least progress to the third martini. Thoroughly in stride now, she went on, "You must let me meet your distinguished husband soon. I'm so anxious to see the man for whom you gave up—well, all the things you might have done."

"Oh—" Maggie felt her face burn hot—"oh, you'll meet him all right. He . . . he—" how could these parallel lines, Nini and Dexter, ever be brought to meet?— "he's terribly busy," she said lamely.

"But not too busy to come and have dinner with us in the slums!" said Nini as she eyed Maggie brightly over the rim of her cocktail glass.

11

"Maggie! We'll be late if you don't hurry!" Dexter sounded the familiar refrain—into deaf ears, as usual.

When the Bradfields finally crossed her threshold Nini showed no irritation over their late arrival; she had tried for this evening for a long time. She kissed Maggie as she might her closest friend and greeted Dexter with easy familiarity.

"Hello, there. I'm going to call you Dexter right away. I feel as though I've known you forever."

Close at his wife's heels, like a well-trained dog, came Dick Deacon. The spirit of his smile would have been better conveyed by a wagging tail; one felt he was about to extend a paw.

"Hello, Dexter feller. Great stuff you could come over and see us in the slums."

As the Deacons' address was on an old square in the south end of Boston, Dick Deacon had just the foundation in fact he needed for the fantasy that he had moved if not to Montparnasse at least to the Rive Gauche. Actually, his wife's large drawing room, with tall French windows and two fireplaces, filled with museum pieces of French furniture, had more true elegance than any he had ever been exposed to in his stodgy, overstuffed segment of Boston.

"Now—" he rubbed his hands together enthustiastically—"I'm not going to offer you a cocktail because I've got some bully wines for you with dinner. How about a small Montilla?"

"A what?" said Dexter, remembering that Dick at the Tennis and Racquet Club had never been one to discriminate between a Budweiser and a Pabst.

"Sherry. A bully, light little unfortified sherry. Nini discovered it in the village of Montilla south of Córdoba in Spain."

Some faint music, of which Dexter had been only dimly conscious, came to a sudden stop. Dick moved quickly to a cabinet, which he opened, uncovering a concealed victrola in the bottom shelf of the bookcase, glowing with the bright jackets of the newest books. He put on a record. "Nini and I are sold on this Bartók feller. Can't get enough of him. I'm afraid, Dexter, that Nini and I must seem crazy to you, but the truth is, feller, these moderns have got me."

He let Dexter have the flash of his full smile—full, that is, as to teeth. Dick gave the impression of possessing more than the average mouth could hold. Perhaps it was only that they were as large as they were shiny. In fact, his lips were cracked literally to the breaking point as they were forced to stretch into an incessant smile. Since his second marriage this smile was induced by an excess of being interested. Dick was interested in music, he was interested in writing, he was interested in painting, he was interested in politics; he was particularly interested in sex. His marriage to Nini had represented for him a sort of spiritual change of life. He smiled more than ever. He had developed a habit of shaking his head, like a dog with an earache, and at the same time making his blue eyes, behind their steel-rimmed bifocals, twinkle in unison with the shake. But in his pursuit of the *vie de Bohème* and his dedication to the modern, he could be serious with the best of them. When he wanted to add weight to his words—one would have said already heavy enough—he had developed a habit of closing his eyes and turning his veiled lids on his interlocutor. The listener was so afraid that the eyes might open suddenly to find that one's attention had wandered that it had the effect of holding him, no matter how inwardly restive, as though spellbound. Closing his eyes tight, he would say, "To me, there is no question that Wagner was the greatest genius that ever lived." This opinion was arrived at by dint of Nini's private coaching. The sport of spotting leitmotivs made Wagner his favorite composer. He would murmur "Fafner," "Power of the Ring," "Golden Apples" as though he were calling out scores from the sidelines of the Longwood tennis courts. It was a question whether the *Liebestod* might not pop out as Love Set.

Now he was showing Dexter the ingeniously concealed loudspeakers in each corner of the room. Dexter, always respectful of a good job of carpentry, gravely congratulated him. "That's a damn good job, Dick."

"Glad you think so, Dexter. Nini and I have a bully time in the evenings. We turn down the lights and flop on the floor on a couple of cushions—none of your Beacon Hill straight-backed stuff, feller—and then we listen to something that's *damned good*." He shut his eyes tight and turned the closed lids intensely toward Dexter. "And I don't mean just music either. Poetry! Yes, sir, I'm quite a devotee of some of this modern poetry. Nini has shown me that the only way to come to know modern poetry is to listen to the poet himself, or herself, as the case may be." Here he opened his eyes to take a quick peek to assure himself that Dexter had not escaped. Seeing that he had him tight on the end of the line, he closed them again. "This Sitwell gal. Damned interesting stuff she's turning out. And Eliot. That *Waste Land* of his is *bully*."

Nini came to join him. "Did you tell Maggie we've got some of the Harvard people coming in?" She referred to the expected captives as though they were Outer Mongolians and her own skill in bagging them correspondingly remarkable.

"You know it's the damnedest thing," Dick went on to Maggie, his battery of enthusiasm recharged, "how all these highbrows just naturally gravitate to Nini. I've lived in Boston all my life, and I can't remember ever spending an evening with a Harvard prof, but, by golly, they turn out in force for my lady wife. We have old 'Puffer' coming—they say he's really something of a character—and a young poet feller—writes his own, and reads them, too." He rubbed his hands over the arena of his living room with all the anticipatory gusto he would once have shown for a scheduled scrimmage between the Boston Bruins and the Toronto Maple Leafs.

He had hardly finished speaking before Professor Wiggam came into the room, followed by Harry Kent. The older man wore a single eyeglass and a velveteen smoking jacket, a pipe rather ostentatiously apparent out of one pocket. He was dressed in character, identifiable at once as what he was—the beloved "Puffer," authority on English literature of the nineteenth century, who had sublimated fairly well his suppressed desire to be an actor by the establishment of his reputation as a raconteur. Harry Kent, delegate at large from Harvard's English Department to preach the gospel of modern poetry (some of it his own) to the Philistines, was as studied in the protective coloring he presented to the world as "Puffer" was flamboyant. Harry operated socially on the lines of the "modern" clergy who, through backslapping, collars worn facing front, and rough tweeds, give the lie to those enemies of the Church who believe it to be served only by sobersided killjoys. Harry Kent was slick, handsome, well dressed; he did not suggest a man used to handling the intricacies of iambic pentameter so much as one skilled in assembling the ingredients of a good cocktail.

They came into Nini's drawing room, if not on tiptoe, finger to lip, at least sharing a common sense of guilt: they had not confessed to Dorothea Calcott their acceptance of Nini's invitation. Refugees from her salon, they considered themselves spies dropped behind enemy lines. If the evening was to prove amusing, then Dorothea herself must be included in the next expeditionary force. If, on the other hand, they were to be bored, then their guilty secret would die with them.

Formalities were passed between guests and hosts along with the canapés, and abruptly dropped when Nini sprang to the threshold. "Joseph [she called it "Yoseph"] *darling*!"

Maggie's first thought, on being introduced to the Hungarian rhapsodist toward whom she had yearned over the footlights in Symphony Hall, was *But he's simply tiny!* Without waiting, her voice vibrant with the emotion that thrilled her, she exploded, "You're the most wonderful pianist I have ever heard in all my life!"

Joseph Szaknary looked into her face, his own gleaming with pleasure and perspiration. "Denk you, denk you, Madame."

The rest of the evening was a series of kaleidoscopic impressions for Maggie. At one moment across the dining-room refectory table she witnessed Dexter's struggle with a huge Russian woman with side-burns, said by Nini to sing gypsy songs. Dexter, making ineffectual jabs of conversation in her direction, got no more response from her than he might from a hippopotamus in the zoo at feeding time. She was not to be distracted from shoving her garlic bread about the edges of her plate, mopping up the last of the *scaloppine*-of-veal gravy, and allowing her glass to be refilled by her zealous host. "Da, da" was the only repartee Dexter could woo from her. After dinner, when the ladies were powdering their noses upstairs, Maggie did not fare much better. She asked, "What do you find to do with yourself, Madame, in Boston when you are not singing?"

The answer came stolid and placid. "I vas kookink."

There were, as well, several actors from the Copley Theater and several members of the Boston Symphony Orchestra. Only a Chicago friend of Nini's, well grounded in her powers of long-range planning, could have explained to Maggie the underlying purpose of the evening. Tucked away under all the window dressing was an unostentatious French woman whom Nini, in her excitement at having charmed across her threshold at all, introduced, forgetting to mention her name, with the title which explained her importance—"an intimate friend of the Koussevitzskys." Pianists, singers, violinists in Nini's jungle were panthers, bears, and antelopes (poets no more than parrots) compared to that king of beasts, a conductor. Nini, newly arrived in this alien jungle, was on the prowl for the big kill.

When the men rejoined the ladies, Nini moved firmly to shake up the contents of her drawing room. She herself advanced on "Yoseph darling." Seeming to have her prey pinioned with his back to the wall, however, she shifted her bright little shoe-button eyes back and forth, seeking whom next she might devour. She was uncomfortably aware that the Harvard professors were restive; they were far less sure of themselves than the star performer. He, conditioned to the acclaim of multitudes, demanded only less of the same from his individual admirers. The words "you are wonderful" established at once the assurance that he and Maggie were going to have everything in common. Highly paid and widely recognized, he could afford to be socially genial. But the professors, underpaid and known only to the *cognoscenti,* were prickly to cope with. Demanding subtlety in the flattery they inhaled, they looked for knowledgable discourse on their own particular field of endeavor. Maggie, knowing herself unable to give it, instinctively drew away from them as they showed every inclination of drawing away from her. Breezy and enthusiastic in company, she naturally opened her mouth and talked, without suffering the discomfiture of knowing that the words she spoke might be weighed. The prophets of Cambridge did just this: fearing that it might be they themselves who would be found wanting, they judged against Maggie.

Nini flung herself into the breach, and presently the professional performers, glad of an evening off, drew up in a polite circle around Harry Kent. After a few nervous sips of water and a rattling of papers, he began to read.

" 'Portrait of a Sad Tea Party,' " he announced. "A fragment of my work in progress, *Massachusetts There She Stands.*"

A sigh of mingled admiration and expectation filled the room as the reading began.

"The tea table is set with faultless care,
Tippit is sitting backwards in a chair
And murmurs in a husky voice, 'Can't we be friends?'
The daylight, dismal as a mashed potato, ends."

Maggie was making a concentrated effort to understand the drift of what was being read, but it seemed to become harder as Harry went on, and on.

She peeped surreptitiously at Dick. His head was lifted toward the reader, his eyes squeezed tight closed, as though he were receiving the fine needles of a shower full in the face.

"*. . . Am I so dreary?*
Still twisting the scone—dreary!
The very word is like a bell
To make me know I've got to get the hell
Out of this dump. Like as the waves make toward the pebbled shore
I sidle slowly toward the open door.
Mi ritrovai per una selva oscura
How much less boring to be dead
Than simply to be going home to bed.
Video meliora proboque deterior sequor.
Here, creep, wretch, under a comfort serves in a whirlwind
Philomel with lullaby
Sing in your sweet lullaby
Lulla, lulla, lullaby
Now it's time to say good-by.
Blah blah black sheep
Good night ladies good night ladies goodnight sweetheart
I'm going to leave you now
It's about time
Blah, blah
Blah
Blah."

There was a respectful hush. "Of course, it does help to know one's Bhagavad-Gita," said Harry Kent.

"Naturally." "Of course." "But that's obvious" was said in unison.

Professor Wiggam merely pulled audibly on his pipe. To ears attuned to this special Morse code, his message conveyed, "Don't forget me. I, too, have a parlor trick up my velvet sleeve. How about a Browning monologue?"

Appearing to sense the risk of just such a disaster, with the intuitive powers given to a man in desperate straits, Dexter loomed suddenly before Maggie, saying, "I told you I had to cut it short this evening. It's time to go home."

The minute they were outside, the roles they had played on leaving the Newtons' Halloween party were reversed. It was Dexter who exploded, "You can go there by yourself after this! What a bunch of phonies!"

"Do I gather you consider Nini a phony?" There was a splinter of ice in her voice.

"I don't like the cut of her jib."

"Because she doesn't look as though she came from Milton, I suppose?"

"That's not fair, Maggie. I like plenty of people who don't come from Milton."

"You don't like Nini, I suppose, because she's cosmopolitan." Maggie, pursuing the advantage she believed she had gained, pressed further. "Did you by any chance resent seeing other people perform in public? Is it only Bradfields who are allowed to display their talents?"

"You know that's absurd, Maggie. What makes me sore is to see you fall for someone like that woman. She's trying to get something out of you. That's why she butters you up."

"Nini! Get something out of me! That's a joke! Why, she has everything—" She just stopped herself from adding, "that I haven't." Instead she said, "Maybe she just wants a little fun, a little life. And in a bourgeois provincial city like Boston it isn't easy to find."

Dexter looked at her quizzically, as though the unacknowledged quotation marks had sprouted from her head like two horns. He lowered his eyes abruptly; whatever it was he had seen, it looked menacing.

12

DURING THE next two years, in spite of any objections from Dexter—and he learned in time to keep those he felt to himself—Maggie's intimacy with Nini Deacon became her chief preoccupation. Under the leadership of her new friend Maggie was to awaken to the dictates not of style but of fashion. When Nini founded a small chamber-music club—the players drawn from the Boston Symphony Orchestra, the concerts given by candlelight in her high-ceilinged drawing room—Maggie learned to catch forty winks—after all, were not her host's eyes closed?—and still snap open her lids in time to exclaim with the last note, "Isn't Hindemith *un*believable!" It was her idea to start in her own kitchen—on Nellie's night out, which in due course also became Dexter's—an intimate wine-and-food supper club. She could smack her lips knowledgably over a "nice little Chilean Rhine wine" and prided herself on her *moules marinières*. Relegating Fetch and Carrie to the care of Marsh at Far Fields—"they really are country dogs"—she presented Priscilla not only with a goldfish bowl of guppies but also a French poodle whom she christened Silhouette and whom Priscilla called Silly.

It was in the late fall of 1930 that Nini, seated one day in Maggie's living room, said, "I've been thinking what I might do when the Chicago Opera is here in January. I adore Mary Garden so, I thought it might be fun to give a party for all the principals after one of the *Pelléas* performances. For me, Mary simply *is* Melisande, and Melisande, Mary."

"That's exactly what Father says," said Maggie. "It's his favorite opera."

"How perfect!" Nini's rosebud broke into sparse bloom. "Then perhaps *this* is the opportunity to get your mother and father across my threshold! Isn't it fantastic that in two years it hasn't happened yet? It's months ahead, so they really can't have another engagement. But Boston has got me so cowed I couldn't bear that they might think me even the tiniest bit pushing, so won't you, Maggie darling, ask your mother for me which of the *Pelléas* performances would fall on the best date for them? Once they choose, then I'll plan my party around them!"

Maggie's heart sank. She had not forgotten the one meeting face to face between her mother and her new friend when Mrs. Fraser had somehow managed not to shake hands either on being introduced or on saying good-by. Maggie, taxing her with her coldness afterward, had been treated to the first flash suggesting dislike that she remembered ever to have seen from her mother when she said, "That Mrs. Deacon is simply somebody I'd prefer not to know."

It was then with a foregone assurance of failure that Maggie passed on the invitation. The refusal was already pronounced while Maggie was still foundering among the alternative available dates.

"Oh, Mother," Maggie expostulated, "I knew you'd say that! What *shall* I tell Nini?"

"If she is so thick-skinned as to extend such an invitation, then she lays herself open to being snubbed. I am afraid you will have to tell her the truth—that your father and I are devoted to Jane Deacon and don't care to know her successor."

"But how smug! You of all people! How can anyone on the outside know why a marriage breaks up? Taking a stand like that makes you seem so . . . holier than thou."

"If Nini has a right to choose a husband, Maggie, then I have a right to choose my friends. From what I know of her, she's not one I care to have."

Aggressively, Maggie asked, "I suppose that's another way of saying you disapprove of my having her for a friend?"

"You know very well, dear, I've never 'disapproved' of your leading your own life and making your own friends. I'm merely speaking for myself."

For an instant she hesitated, glancing half wistfully, half apprais-ingly at her daughter. Then, with the humble docility of the parent whose child has sent her on an instructive attendance at *The Silver Cord*, she ventured only, "I'm not talking about morals, dear. I'm only talking about *taste*."

"Well, I think it's revolting!" Revolt was in the very way Maggie stood, in her mother's bedroom, with her arms akimbo, her hands on her hips. She hurled her defiance. "I can only say that Nini's coming to live in Boston has made life over for me!"

Mrs. Fraser's expression grew suddenly graver. "Maggie, dear, it worries me that life can be made or unmade for you by any friend. Dexter and Priscilla are your life."

Though the last words were spoken as a declarative sentence, there was just the hint of interrogation in her voice that seemed to ask, *Aren't they?*

When Maggie brought herself to tell Nini the gist of what her mother had said, with her own softening embroidery added, Nini said almost kindly, "Never mind, darling. It isn't your fault. I don't hold you responsible for Boston!"

To Maggie's surprise the episode closed with a sense of closer sympa-thy between herself and Nini—a sympathy bordering on collusion. Nini's course, at least, was clear. If, after two years of valiant struggle, Maggie had failed as an entering wedge to open certain of Boston's closed doors she could at least urge Maggie to come out from behind those same bulwarks.

When Nini asked Maggie one evening to meet Raymond Masters, even she could not have dared to hope that Providence had placed in her hands the ideal weapon for her purpose.

Maggie was feeling particularly lighthearted as she set out for her friend's house. For one thing, Dexter was satisfactorily accounted for at home. When he had told her that he must work on his progress report on Radiation Scatter for the National Research Council she had enthusiastically agreed that his work should come before everything. If anything could spoil her pleasure in one of Nini's parties, the brooding, unco-operative presence of her husband was enough to do so. But this was to be a very special evening. Nini was producing the literary catch of the season, the author of the best-selling new novel *The Joneses*, as the only other guest, protesting that he was one of their "most intimate friends." Maggie wanted free rein.

She came breathless, after hurrying upstairs, into the drawing room to find the guest of honor alone.

"Oh!" She faltered at the threshold. "Oh, dear, I'm afraid I'm early."

"How do you do?" A tall, slender man was standing with his back to the fire. "Nini and Dick haven't come down yet. I'm Raymond Masters."

"I know you are!" Maggie smiled radiantly at him. "Why else do you suppose I'm so prompt? Of course you couldn't be expected to know that I'm generally late wherever I go."

"I'd like to know more than that about you. For instance, your name."

Ray Masters came forward to draw up a chair in front of the fire. Maggie stood for an instant facing him before seating herself in it. Firelight and candlelight played over her. She was dressed in an emerald-green taffeta dress, with long rhinestone earrings that swayed and sparkled. The dress was low-cut, showing the line of her rounded ample breasts. Her response to the flattering look of appraisal that she could not miss was a spontaneous deepening of her already heightened color. A sudden expectant smile turned the switch on her two dimples.

"Maggie Bradfield," she declared.

The fire gave a pop as she spoke, as though giving vent to the animation of a highly charged moment. An electric shock of mutually recognized attraction crackled in the room. The brown eyes, with their heavy lashes that looked almost boldly into Maggie's, conveyed assurance of pleasures to come. "Delighted to meet you. Won't you sit down?"

Maggie could feel her physical heart skip a beat as she took the proffered seat. *Very attractive*, she said to herself as she watched Raymond Masters seat himself opposite her across the hearth. Her first impression was one of casual ease. The thought of Dexter's masculine solidity appeared rigid alongside of this almost lazy grace. He spoke slowly, the West in his speech softened by a hint of the South. She knew Raymond Masters to be clever, if not actually brilliant, and his quizzical, humorous face only reaffirmed his gifts. But there was, as well, an oddly detached ironical manner, as though he found himself not only in the position of best-selling author but even as existing in the twentieth century at all by some queer mischance to which his debonair spirit was not entirely reconciled. Maggie decided on the spot that whatever else Raymond Masters did not have, he had charm.

Nini hurried into the room, with Dick at her heels.

"Oh, you two have already met?" she asked briskly, all but rubbing her hands. "Ray, did Maggie tell you that she is not only our dearest friend, but is Mrs. Dexter Bradfield? And if you know your Boston ABC's, you'll know that's very good."

"I learned my ABC's away from Boston," Ray answered with a smile, "but I still know what's very good when I see it."

To Dick's query as to whether he could interest anyone in a martini Maggie exclaimed, "You certainly can interest me! I need it," adding, with a disarming smile, "to cover up my nervousness."

"What's the matter? Don't you feel among friends?" asked Ray Masters.

"I *feel* as though I were!" Maggie turned full on him, all confiding, and her words spilled out in accompaniment to the cocktails Dick was pouring for the others. "Oh, Mr. Masters, I may sound a fool, and I'm sure you're bored to death with people gushing all over you about *The Joneses*, and I swore I wasn't even going to mention it, or treat you like a celebrity, and all that, but I have to get it off my chest—right now, at the beginning of the evening. I just think it's the very best book I have ever read in my entire life—*ever*! I feel as though nobody in the world but me could know how excruciatingly good it is. I can't help feeling that I know you very, very well! I'm a complete stranger to you, and naturally you don't care what I think. But I can't help it. I do think all the same that you're a *great writer*!"

Ray Masters grinned a broad grin and said, without affectation and with obvious pleasure, "That's nice of you to say so. I'm delighted that you like the book."

Nini followed up Maggie's attack as though it had been of her own planning all along. "It's true, Ray. Maggie really doesn't flatter just any mangy old lion."

"I am not a lion hunter." Maggie beamed at him over her Steuben cocktail glass as she produced her self-stamped passport. "I am a lion *feeder*! I absolutely worship people who are smart enough to be successful. But then clever, creative people must have an audience, mustn't you?"

"Thanks for the 'you.' "

"And—may I go on?" Maggie was beside herself with excitement and delight.

"Please do." Ray turned to his host and hostess to share with them his pleasure in this new-found dynamo.

"If I were you, do you know what I'd do?"

"No. What?"

"You better listen to her, Ray," put in Nini. "Maggie's terribly smart about people."

"Well, you'll probably think I'm a terrible buttinsky, but I'd write a play of *The Joneses*!"

Ray's attention was focused. "I've thought of it, of course. But my theater friends tell me it would be a tough assignment. There's not enough 'story line,' they say. If it carries at all as satire, or holds up as a book, they say it's due to the accumulation of small details."

"But details can be as fascinating in performance as a good plot! If you get the right director, the right actors. Oh, I know I'm right! *Please* try it!"

He seemed to enjoy the contemplation of Maggie's flushed and eager face, responsive to the conviction that she was talking to an unusual man.

"Well, who knows, maybe you'll give me courage." He lifted his glass. "If it comes to Broadway, you're invited to the opening night, Mrs. Bradfield."

"Oh, call her Maggie," Nini interposed. "You'll be doing it by the end of the evening anyway, so we may as well cut a few corners."

After dinner Maggie repeated, "Oh, how I worship talent!" This was after Nini had closed her bony little hand over Ray's and drawn him to the piano.

"Here, what is this?" he protested. "Nobody told me I was to sing for my supper."

"Dick, put a brandy here beside him" was her only answer. "And now, please."

Ray sat down, shoving himself away from, rather than closer to, the keyboard. Maggie remembered how, in Symphony Hall, Szaknary had stooped to hang over it as though imbibing the elixir of life. By contrast, Ray's attitude, his head thrown back, his arms held almost straight, nonchalantly proclaimed the casual amateur who pretended to offer nothing more important than "background music." His fingers wandered lightly through a variety of modulations and rhythms until they led him into "Tea for Two," "Smiles," and "Yes, We Have No Bananas," ending up with a brilliant rendering of "Kitten on the Keys." As casually as he had begun his performance he closed the piano, in spite of vociferous applause, and shrieks of "*Bis!*" from Maggie and Nini, and twirled around on his piano stool, saying, "And that's that."

Looking at the gifted performer in awe, Maggie wondered how it was that he suggested rather more a hero of musical comedy than the serious writer of a best-selling social satire. With his pin-striped dark-blue suit, bow tie, and wing-tipped shoes, she thought him as engaging, as jaunty as Fred Astaire.

Later, when Nini's party was over, Maggie found herself sitting beside Ray Masters on a banquette in the small bar of the Ritz. The stop-off, as he was taking her in a taxi to Mt. Vernon Street, had occurred as the most natural thing in the world.

"I really ought to be at home with my husband right this minute!" Her eyes danced. It was fun to feel she was playing hooky.

"He can wait. He must be an awful dope if he lets a beautiful gal like you far out of his sight. What *is* your husband, Maggie?"

"He's a research physicist."

"God, how depressing!"

"*He* isn't depressed. Why should you be?"

"Maybe it's better to be than see one." He shot a quick, canny look at her. "I bet he's the strong, silent type. Come on, is he?"

She laughed evasively. "Nini's been talking, I bet."

"Nini. There's a smooth little operator. Did you get all that 'darling' stuff she was handing me this evening?"

"But I thought you were old friends."

"I've been a friend of Dick's for twenty years. When he married Nini she practically held her nose when she had to see me. What could be duller than a poor dope of an adman who has to buy Deacon paper for sales campaigns! But I write a book. The damned thing sells. Suddenly I find I'm 'darling.' Actually, I'm anything but darling, but once you get to know me I shan't have to tell you that."

"I hope I am going to get to know you." Maggie filled her lungs with a deep breath. Like springing a diving board up and down under her feet, in anticipation of the final leap of commitment, she stopped for a moment to take what preliminary soundings she might, merely by what she could see on the surface. The prevailing winds were favorable, the barometer was rising, the visibility was good; in her own vocabulary this translated into a repetition of ***very attractive***. There was no more delicious moment, she had told herself often, than that in which one stood poised, on tiptoe, just before the swooping dive into a brand-new personality.

Maggie looked again at Ray Masters. His hair was very dark, cut short, *en brosse* at the forehead, and receding at the temples. Across his low forehead ran a row of deep horizontal furrows. He appeared constantly to be attempting to eradicate these lines through applied pressure of thumb and fingers just above his nose. His eyebrows were dark and bushy, intermittently shooting up into an *accent circonflexe* of wry amusement or ironic query. His lashes were heavy and dark. His swarthy complexion had as foundation a naturally olive skin. Maggie wondered whether a tendency toward purple ruddiness was due to the rays of a sun lamp, or whether he was simply flying the club colors of the alcoholic with overtones of a heart condition. The curve of his mouth was sensitive; it conveyed both humor and discontent. At each corner of the lips ran a narrow vertical channel into which a smile could be funneled upward, or a pout downward. Indeed, the very pliability of expression, the intensity of coloring, bespoke an explosiveness of nature, whether in violent amusement or uncontrolled temper. Maggie found it a sensuous, funny, unhappy, clever face. Yes, *very attractive.*

He was lifting his glass toward her. "You're not going to be able to help yourself." His voice was sympathetic.

"I hope you won't be disappointed in me," Maggie brought out in sudden panic.

"A fine way to start a beautiful friendship. I'm too old. I refuse to be disappointed ever any more."

"Have you been disappointed so often, then?"

He seemed to shy away from the brink of autobiography. "There are those who make a pretty good case for my having disappointed them," he said.

" 'Them'? Have there been so many?"

"I am using the chivalrous plural. Do you ever use it about your husband?"

Maggie laughed a fresh good-natured laugh. "Heavens, I'm certainly not chivalrous to Dexter!"

"No, it would be the other way, of course."

"Would be is right." The freshness had gone, though the good temper remained.

"Are you, too, unappreciated, Maggie?" The expression of his face lightly mocked the words he had spoken.

"It depends on who by," she answered.

"Well, I hope your husband knows what he's got."

"Oh, he knows all right!" Now she skipped backward a few steps in the Virginia reel in which they seemed to be engaged. "Yankees, though, don't bother very many times in the day to *tell* their wives what sirens they are." She waited a moment as though toying between a choice of routes to lead her back to him. "You're not a Yankee, because you live in New York, but what are you? I know nobody's a New Yorker!"

"Uh—uh," he said, conveying the negative. "I was born and raised in St. Louis. Came east to Princeton, wrote the book of a Triangle Club show, made the *Nassau Lit*, fancied myself as the heir apparent to Scott Fitzgerald—and actually wrote some fifty sonnets, believe it or not. Left in my sophomore year to join the Navy, came back to graduate with my class in twenty, and marry the girl next door."

"But you didn't stay next door?"

"No, we came back to New York, where I was always just on the point of writing a novel. To keep the pot boiling I got me a job at D.D.D. and T.—supposed to be one of the top advertising agencies in New York. Then the kids began arriving, we moved to the suburbs, and that's where I've been stuck ever since."

"And don't forget you couldn't have written *The Joneses* anywhere else."

"Pollyanna, eh?" There was neither kindness nor humor in his voice. Then suddenly softening, he moved his glass closer to hers on the table before them, as though to make an outward and visible sign of a forward move toward intimacy. "Both my wife and my boss tell me I'm an 'idea man.' By which both imply I never follow through with anything. Go on, say it," he urged. "You think I'm pretty mixed up."

Maggie, the doer, was roused. This shadowland of introspection was not her line of country. "I don't at all," she pronounced firmly. "And what's more, I certainly shouldn't call anyone who had written *The Joneses* only an idea man. I'd call him an *accomplishing* man!"

The flattery and the alcohol softened his expression. "And yet," he said, "Alice would like to forget I ever wrote the book."

"Why?"

He ducked under Maggie's glare, aware that its target was several hundred miles away. "Oh . . . Alice." A cloud came over his face. He spoke the single word of his wife's name as that of a vast, mysterious continent. He might as well have said, "Oh, Asia," seeming to plead that explanation of the currency, dialects, and tribal customs was too vast for exploration. "Alice is somehow embarrassed by the book," he went on. "She thinks there's implicit in it an unkind comment on her—on our marriage, even though the details aren't the same. The point about Alice is that she actually likes the 'nice' part of our life."

"Such as?"

"The Cedarside Women's Club, the Cedarside Heights Golf Club, even the Cedarside PTA. She turns up her nose at my advertising friends—anyway, at their wives—doesn't want our kids to make friends with their kids, and seems to be happy doing her shopping in Garden City. She never wants to come in to New York." He checked the list of grievances in midstream. "Here, I don't want to crab about my wretched little existence. Tell me about yours, Maggie. Maybe you like the same sort of things my wife likes. Maybe all women—'nice' women—crave the sense of security."

"I don't! I'm terrified of security, of getting in a rut. My father used to tease me when I got dressed to go to a party and say, 'Rings on her fingers and bells on her toes, and she shall have music wherever she goes.' There's no music in women's clubs—I don't care if they're in Cedarside or if it's the Chilton Club in Boston—and there's no music in a PTA, *any*where! If I lived near New York I'd be hurling myself into the night lights every night!" Her dimples appeared like two twinkling beacon signals of promise.

A film dimmed the look of admiration Ray had turned on her. He spoke with a certain wariness, with a hint of suspicion in his voice. "You're not a party gal, are you, Maggie?"

Instinctively she felt the implied condemnation. "Oh, heavens, no! I loathe a conventional, stuffy, formal party. I like an evening like the one we've just had. A few drinks, talking about interesting and exciting things—*not* our children's education! I love people who do things! You do things," she said abruptly, "and I think it's wonderful." Maggie was suddenly embarrassed to hear a catch in her own voice. She hastened on, brisk and diagnostic. "But what else do you do? Have you a hobby?"

"Not so's you notice it, unless you count Long Island Railroad bridge, which I play, going and coming from work, for stakes Alice considers wickedly high. And, let's see, what else? I like to sit around and bat the breeze with something long and cool in my hand, and I suppose I don't mind playing the cap and bells at an occasional party, the way I did tonight."

"But when do you write?" Maggie asked earnestly.

"Write what?"

"Have you forgotten you've written a best seller—*and* illustrated it?"

"That was a fluke. Will probably never happen again. It was sheer blind boredom on a business trip to California that drove me to it. I don't expect ever to have four days to myself again in this world."

"But you *draw*!"

"Sure, my own layouts, and not bad at that."

"Well, I call you bursting with talent!" Maggie returned happily to the citation it pleased her most to accord him.

"And I should call myself Jack of all trades, master of none—or perhaps the archetypical adman."

Maggie confronted him boldly, not ashamed of the envy in her voice. "You must know all sorts of brilliant people in New York."

He looked suddenly serious, twirling his glass in his hand. "Maybe I'm what the psychological boys call ambivalent. I'll tell you one thing: I don't get any kick out of arty show-offs."

"You suddenly sound like Dexter."

Though there was only amusement in Maggie's voice, Ray shied away from her words as though they had been a rebuke.

"Have I written my own death warrant?"

"No. But I'm always warning him he mustn't become a Philistine."

"Christ, I hope I'm not that." Thumb and fingers traveled across his forehead, but the deep lines remained. "It's true I do get fed up with Alice's kind of woman." Quickly he added guiltily, "I mean the kind she has made her friends. Their ambitions seem so damned cheesy, so trivial."

"You probably prefer women who are artists."

"Could be. I know one thing, though. Give me a hard-bitten career babe, and I want out." He looked unfeignedly sheepish. "Maybe I'm no good with any woman. God help me, I still like a lady—if that word isn't too blush-making. Literally a *gentle* woman—shades of feeling and understanding. Like a good wine, I guess, the bouquet can't be built overnight." His eyebrows shot up in a question. He did not need to ask her in words if she thought him a fool. "God knows I've been had on the lady deal. A man thinks he's found something feminine and sweet, but brother, is there an iron hand in that smooth, soft, velvet glove!"

Maggie was aware of the rising within her of the familiar sensation of wanting to better or at least to rearrange somebody else's circumstances. "But it's absurd! If I were you, do you know what I would do?"

"How could I? Tell me."

"I'd get out! I mean, of course, after you've written your play! You oughtn't to stay on in an advertising agency."

The muted note of nostalgia and regret grated into a scratch resembling simple crossness, unrecognizable as such to Maggie, who had never heard it in her own husband's voice. "Alice is probably right. She says I just naturally like to gripe, and that I wouldn't have the guts to throw over the life I'm in, even for one year, to write. She says my book was only a form of immaturity, like a little boy scrawling words on the barn door, that it's the only form of rebellion I have guts for, and that it's much less trouble and much more comfortable to practice my self-indulgence in Cedarside than in Peterborough or Yaddo."

Ray had come to the end of the highball and peered, blinking through the festoons of smoke hanging around them, in search of a waiter.

"How about another drink?"

"I mustn't, really. My husband will begin to be worried about me."

Ray acquiesced, accepting the fact that the evening was over. On her doorstep on Mt. Vernon Street they shook hands. Maggie stood on the step above him. As he looked up at her, she loomed, thus placed, a head taller than he, a sort of triumphant *Winged Victory*. There was almost supplication in the look he turned toward her, as though to some all-powerful goddess sent to sunder the bonds of the fettered.

She shook hands cordially, saying, "Don't forget, I'm counting on you to write that play! And I hope I see you again sometime!"

"You will, Oscar, you will," Ray said, more to himself than to her, as he turned and left her.

13

THE NEXT steps on the path to the inevitable fell smoothly into place, one after another.

First came a series of lighthearted postcards to Maggie from Raymond Masters, reporting progress on the play he had undertaken. In the spring, on his way through Boston to inspect potential New England boarding schools for his son, he stopped over to spend a night with the Deacons. Maggie, once again, was summoned to entertain him. They met with the pleasure of reunion known to old friends—he called her his "lucky mascot"—and repeated the ritual of a nightcap at the Ritz Bar. When, in the fall, the pre-Broadway tryout of *The Joneses* opened in Boston, it was obvious that Ray, with the help of an expert play doctor, had turned out a hit. The audience of the play enjoyed, as much as the readers of the book, the sense of identification with the middle-class couple whose lives were dominated by keeping up with the Joneses, the couple next door who never appeared on stage. Not only did Maggie meet Ray again at the Deacons'; he himself came to Mt. Vernon Street.

On his second visit he brought Priscilla a pair of guppies and confounded Maggie by a half-hour conversation with Dexter, excluding her entirely, on the subject of the second battle of Bull Run. "Why didn't you tell me you had a Civil War addict in the family?" he asked genially. After he left, Dexter pronounced him "a decent enough sort of guy." Impossible for her to recognize any other facet of a human personality than that which turned its face toward her, Maggie found it hard to believe that there could be any meeting ground, in outer space, beyond the confines of the separate compartments in which she kept them in her own mind, where the two men might converge.

Next came the heavily disguised blessing of Nini's removal from Boston to New York.

Nini had begun to groan with mounting despair to Maggie over Dick's proclivity to talk about nothing but the Depression. Maggie, daughter and wife of a professional man, was half ashamed of her own sense of insulation from the world of business. Even Ma Brad and Sarge, after their clandestine consultations about family investments, must have hit on the policy "Mum's the word." To discuss the fear, or even the actuality of losing money, was as ill-bred as to admit that one had a great deal. (Their very placidity in maintaining this stand bespoke louder than words the substantial backlog on which the family could rest in times of stress.) Now, in view of worsening business conditions, Dick Deacon appeared reconciled to getting out of the family business and leaving it in the hands of his brother, who had always wanted to run it anyway. By way of a consolation prize Dick was accepting an offer from New York to head the fine-paper division of a wholesale house of paper jobbers. Actually Ray, representing D.D.D. and T., an important client of the company, had acted as liaison in the transaction. Nini was delighted. When Dick would murmur an occasional and rueful, "I'd always expected to end my days in New England," "How dreary!" Nini flashed back in answer. "Don't brood about where you're going to end them. The point is, where are you going to *live* them!" Both knew that her own fortune would help to ease their lot, wherever it was cast.

Before Maggie had begun to realize how much she was going to miss Nini in Boston she was visiting her in a luxurious apartment on the East River, in honor of the New York opening of *The Joneses.* During her stay Ray took Maggie to lunch and came to dine with the Deacons, on Nini's invitation, without his wife.

Back in Boston, if any further stimulant were needed to rouse

Maggie's responses to the thought of Ray and his success, it was supplied by the arrival of *Time*, with his picture on the cover. Indicated faintly in the background behind a colored picture of Ray was a lawn mower, a suburban villa, and a station wagon. The words under the picture were: "Could the commuter transmute . . . ?" The review of *The Joneses* as a play, inside the magazine, told of ambivalent Adman Masters' attempt to pull himself up by his own bootstraps. "Strangled by his white collar," could a commuter, *Time* queried, become a transmuter of the minutiae of daily living into the whole of a work of art? The reviewer asserted that Adman Masters had wrought the transmutation first as novelist, now as playwright. He had lifted the particular to the universal. His voice was that of the American Everyman—henpecked and hagridden at home, hearty and hail fellow well met with his fellows. The review closed by saying that the playgoer, just as the reader at the end of the book, knows what is going to happen to the hero stepping off the club car behind Mr. Jones at Cedarside; but the reviewer added, "With the appearance of a really important new American talent, we wish we could be sure which road Adman Masters himself is likely to follow."

When, later that winter, Maggie received in Boston a cable from Nini in the Bahamas, urging that she come for a visit, she could show Dexter the invitation in all naïveté because it was in naïveté that she read it herself. She could say to Dexter, "I might never have such a wonderful chance again. Don't you think I should go?" and he could reply with the instinctive generosity of his nature, "Sure you should."

When Maggie found Ray as a fellow guest under the roof of the same cottage on the island of Eleuthera, she simply accepted his presence as one of those delightful surprises that fall out of the heavens into one's lap. It did not occur to her that Nini Deacon, in inviting her, knew exactly what she was doing, nor that she was hitting back, with malice aforethought, at the Boston that had snubbed her. Sizing up the only remaining factor necessary to create the situation she desired between Maggie and Ray, she resolved to provide it in its most seductive guise—propinquity.

As background for the drama she chose to bring into being there was pink sand, soft as tooth powder, water so green that Maggie had never seen anything like it outside a swimming pool, and palmetta trees bowing before the tropical wind that never stopped blowing. If the denizens of this Garden of Eden were tempted by no tangible apple, they had only to open their mouths to admit the seductive infiltration of rum in a seemingly unending stream: daiquiris, rum Collinses, and planter's punches, and more planter's punches.

The very day after her arrival Ray confronted Maggie with *Time*'s implied query about his future, *What next?* They lay side by side on the beach in their bathing suits. The deep mahogany of Ray's smooth skin was broken only by his abbreviated salmon-colored trunks. Maggie smiled to herself, thinking of Pa Brad's black-cotton outfit.

Ray, flat on his stomach, arms and legs taut, asked his question without preamble. "Maggie, tell me—what do I do now?"

"You mean right this minute?"

"No. I mean my future in general."

"Your writing, or your life?"

He was clearly thawing under the nicety of her focus. "I didn't want to talk about it in front of Nini—" the light in Maggie's eyes melted into a new softness— "you know the way she is. She knows everybody's business better than they know it themselves. But the truth is I've had a damned exciting Hollywood offer. My agent thinks I should have my head examined if I don't accept it."

"Tell me about it."

"In the first place, it's a possible sale of *The Joneses*. Anton Chelek—I suppose he's acknowledged as one of the most brilliant producers in Hollywood—got his studio to offer me a deal. They want me as writer of the screenplay as well as technical adviser. So that makes a three-way profit for me—author of the play, Hollywood writer, and a finger in the production. The idea is that in return they want a three-year option on me as writer."

"And what's worrying you? Don't you want to accept?"

"It's pretty grim. If I accept, Alice says she won't come with me."

"Why?"

"Well, she talks about the kids—their schools, their friends. She's got it all figured that the PTA wouldn't approve of Hollywood as the place in which to bring up young adolescents. She's been calling my mother long distance in St. Louis every day, trying to get her to influence me."

"Oh! Have you a mother?" There was only the faintest accent on the *you.*

"Shouldn't I? Most people do, you know."

"Never mind. You were talking about your children. I should think Hollywood would be an absolutely marvelous experience for them. Wouldn't the children themselves adore it?"

"You're darn right they would. Skipper would die happy if he could meet Tom Mix and Trigger face to face, and since Sister's got it all planned *anyway* that she's to be a movie star when she grows up—no, what Alice is afraid of is that they'll like it too much. Just as she's afraid that I'd never come back—that I'd be bound to stay more than three years. She flings in my teeth the years I spent in the advertising business instead of—" he fumbled for an instant— "instead of getting out long ago."

"What would you have got out *for*?"

"Well, I always claimed I wanted to write, that I was using the job at D.D.D. and T. simply as a means to an end, so that I could afford to knock off for a year or two and give myself a chance. But you get going round in the squirrel's cage, and set up a sort of framework for existence in the suburbs, and the moment to break out of it never seems to come."

"I suppose Alice herself has become pretty attached to that framework." There was now a little tingle of animosity in Maggie's voice as she used the first name of a woman she had never met.

She did not notice the evasion as Ray said, "It's a cinch she wanted no part of my life in New York."

"Ah, it's a shame!" The sympathy on Maggie's features would have brought tears of self-pity to a far sterner man than Ray; but at the thrilling note of deep concern in her voice his defenses crumbled utterly.

Maggie, seeing the effect she had made, followed up her advantage. "But would it be so awful to go alone? You'd probably have a wonderful time," she said. The ravishing smile that accompanied the words "wonderful time" proclaimed the highest reward earth has to offer.

"I'm not so sure." He seemed inclined to back away from, rather than advance toward, the apocalypse. "I don't much like the prospect of my own society, alone in a hotel, and I don't see myself as a gay bachelor setting up housekeeping."

Maggie cut him short, the brisk social-service investigator not to be distracted from her questionnaire. "Do you want terribly to go?"

He squirmed under the stepped-up intensity of the probe. "I'm only afraid it might be more or less kissing good-by to the hope of doing my own quote serious unquote writing."

"But if you make all that money couldn't you *then* be in a position, after three years, to write a good book?"

Ray shoved his toe deeper into the sand and gave a snort. "Famous last words! No one can explain to me *why*, but the road to Hollywood seems always to be a one-way street. First-rate writers go out there and make a success in pictures. But whoever knew the man who made a success in pictures and left the place to become a first-rate writer?"

"That's not to say it couldn't be done."

He turned over on his back, his arms crossed under his head. "It's obvious Alice doesn't think I'm the boy to do it." He kicked the sand with his heel as though settling a debt with Alice herself.

"O-o-oh!" Maggie's exclamation was on a descending scale, carrying one theme of condemnation and another of allegiance.

"You think she's wrong?"

"Utterly!" Her eyes flashed courage and challenge to his rather dimmed ones.

"So, what do I do?"

"Why, it's easy." She stopped just short of saying "Get out." Sitting up, she ran her long fingers through her hair, shaking its length out behind and pulling her natural pompadour back from her high rounded brow. In full face Maggie's forehead was narrow, and her eyes were close-set; only in profile was her character fully emphasized. With her hair blowing out behind her in the wind she might have been the figurehead on a ship. She was no more strictly beautiful than an archaic carving, but Ray, lolling on one elbow looking up at her, appeared to respond to an arresting thrust, a forward motion which, like a magnet, drew him up to sit close beside her as she exclaimed, "Why, you just *go*, that's all!"

She turned now to face him squarely; the robin's-egg blue of her bathing suit intensified the color of her eyes. "When do you have to give them your answer?" she asked.

"I told them I'd think it over down here, and if I don't wire I'll tell them as soon as I get back to New York."

"What are you waiting for, Ray?" There was a taunt as well as a challenge in her inflection.

"Moral courage, I guess. What I've been waiting for all my life."

The days rolled over one another in a delicious iridescent haze, like the warm waves themselves. Hardly aware that it was happening, Maggie and Ray, in a matter of a few weeks, arrived at a plane of intimacy that it would have taken months, or even years, to establish in other surroundings, in other circumstances. For Maggie, the image of Dexter, showing fainter and more flickering behind the haze, diminished until it virtually disappeared from sight. She did not tell herself anything so blunt as that she was falling in love with another man because she had fallen out of love with her husband. But, using as a yardstick a man who was strongly attracted to her temperamentally as well as physically, and was easily articulate on both counts, she could measure, with mounting dismay, the limitations of her marriage. For Dexter, lovemaking was a simple direct assertion of the bond between husband and wife—that he accepted as the bedrock of existence. It was an assertion that demanded no light and shade of variety, no finesse, and certainly no words.

Now Maggie found herself being wooed both more boldly and more subtly and, at all times, articulately. With a lift of his eyebrows Ray would ask, if he saw her looking pensive, "Why so *piano*? Something worrying you?" If she laughed, he joined in, and then said, "That laugh could raise a man from the dead, Maggie. It's delicious, but it has such lustiness behind it." He was unabashed about noticing her clothes. A white sharkskin bathing suit drew forth the simple comment, "Nice." His eyes said so much more that she could feel her color rise and her pulses quicken as she turned her own eyes away to avoid the look in his.

It seemed no more than an unfolding of the natural order of things when one moonlight night Maggie found herself in his arms. They had been sitting side by side on the steps of the veranda watching the riding lights of a newly arrived yacht flicker across the still velvet of the harbor. Ray held her close for one quivering instant before they exchanged a long and passionate embrace.

As they separated and Ray lighted a cigarette, Maggie could see with her first conscious thrill of power that his hand trembled. His voice was husky as he spoke. "I've wanted to do that for a long time," he said.

Maggie's voice, faint and unrecognizable to her own ears, quavered, "I've wanted you to."

His hand reached out to catch hers. They sat, with fingers interlocked, breathless in the first delicious moment of mutual discovery.

"I don't make passes at women, you know." The little catch in his voice, supposed to represent a laugh, was nearer a sob.

The practical sex spoke. "What do we do now?" asked Maggie.

"What do you think?" He threw his cigarette away and drew her down beside him.

This time the intent of his lovemaking was clear and nearly irresistible to them both. Maggie freed herself abruptly. "No, Ray!"

Ray's powers of adjustment were not so precipitate. Presently, however, he deliberately lighted another cigarette. "You're right," he said.

"This sure is one hell of a mess to be in, Maggie. We'd better go inside."

The next morning, when the men were playing tennis, Nini, with her eyes almost crossing in concentration as she applied Fatal Apple nail polish to her big toenail, said casually, "You and Ray have fallen in love, haven't you?"

Maggie would rather not have confided her emotion to anyone just yet, but her need was acute. With a grateful sigh of relief she dumped it at Nini's scarlet-tipped feet. "I'm afraid so. Isn't it awful?"

"*Awful?* Are you crazy? It's divine! It's exactly what I hoped would happen."

"Nini!" A light slowly broke. "Why . . . I believe . . . is that why you asked us to Eleuthera together?"

"What do you think, silly?"

"But, Nini, how can you say it's divine? We're both miserable!"

"It's always darkest before dawn. Dick and I were miserable, too—just for a little. And of course I must say Reno *is* a bore, and breaking up a household is never any fun, but . . . well, look at us now!"

"Reno!" Maggie echoed the word. There was panic in her voice, but an unmistakabe catch of excitement as well. She hadn't even thought of such a thing (so she told herself). And yet, hearing the word spoken aloud, almost casually, suddenly crystallized for her much of the unnamed restlessness and desire that was increasingly disturbing her. Could she really divorce one husband to marry another? Because the very thought of becoming Ray's wife made her heart turn over, Maggie protested with even more vehemence. "For heaven's sake, Nini, please! Nobody's even thinking of Reno!"

Nini, appraising the protest for just what it was worth, attacked. "Maggie Bradfield, don't tell me that you are a coward and couldn't stand the gaff of being ostracized in Boston."

"I wouldn't give a damn about being ostracized!" The words popped out of Maggie with gusto. "It's just . . . it's just . . ." Her face clouded now into deep seriousness. "I couldn't hurt Dexter."

"Listen, Maggie, I'm not saying that Dexter doesn't love you. Of course he does. Who wouldn't? But he loves you only to the extent of his capacities, and I'm sure you couldn't mind my saying—*now*—that his capacities just aren't up to yours. Do you have *fun* with him?" She did not need to wait for an answer before firing shot after shot, *ping*, into the bull's-eye. "Do you enjoy things together? The arts—*any* of them? Is he interested in other people as you are? Does he ever tell you he loves you? Or does he, like so many Anglo-Saxon husbands, take you utterly for granted? It's awful of me to say so, darling, but ever since I met you I've been shocked at what a mismated couple you are!"

"I don't know why we're even talking like this." Maggie writhed on the cleverly baited hook. "But even if I were to consider such a thing, what makes you think Ray would leave *his* family?"

"We'll come to Ray. You know as well as I do that his life could be simply made over by the right woman. But *you*, Maggie! You mustn't show the white feather now!"

"But *Priscilla*, Nini!" Now there was passion in her voice. "Nothing, nothing would induce me to leave Priscilla."

"Who's asking you to leave her?" was the practical retort. "Take her!"

The expression on Maggie's face changed as radically as though the two words, like hard shot, had fractured the target at which they were aimed. Unconscious, suggestible, malleable, she lay wide open to the battery of the intriguer. Never suspicious, rarely perceptive, Maggie was vulnerable as the stupid and selfish are always vulnerable in the hands of the clever, conscious mischief-maker. Guileless and guileful confronted each other. For an instant Maggie was aware of a sharp thrust of something approaching fear. *Really*—although she would rather die than admit it to a human soul, she told herself—*Nini was pretty hard-boiled. Maybe a good many of the things her mother and the rest of Boston said about her were true. . . .* Maggie blinked. Then, quickly snapping off the switch that had flooded the picture before her with the clear light of revelation, she reinstated the image of a wise confidante guiding her in the ways of worldly wisdom. Her mouth a little open, her eyes widened into a stare.

Wondering rather than fearful, she murmured tentatively, "But it would be so mean to Dexter."

"Look. Let's stop talking about what would be mean to Dexter. Besides, you could be generous to him, silly! There's such a thing as right of visitation. Let him have Priscilla for as many holidays as he wants. It's about all he sees of her anyway. She'll be going to boarding school or college before you know it, and the next thing she'll be married. Just for the little time she and Dexter might have together—weigh it in the balance, Maggie, against *your whole life*! And you'd have life with Ray—the sort of life you deserve. Think of it—Hollywood! There's no question Hollywood is the coming place in this country. New York has had its day, but Hollywood has room for all the talents. Ray is bound to make a huge success out there."

Success! Like the sudden cessation of a toothache Maggie could almost feel a slackening of inner tension. She saw that if Ray were her husband she could make over to him her own restless longing, and perhaps be free of it forever. She would be married to a successful man. In her sign he could conquer—for them both.

The more the prospect attracted Maggie, the more she felt it would be unseemly to show anything but reluctance. "But *Ray*, Nini! What makes you think for one moment that he would consider leaving his wife and children?" she asked.

"Listen, Maggie, you haven't seen Alice Masters. I have. Of all the dim, dull suburban matrons it would be a pleasure to leave, she's it. Read his book! Only a miserable, frustrated man could have written it. He needs strength, courage, *hope*! Maggie Bradfield, if you're half the girl I think you are, you're the one to give them to him. And make no mistake about it, if you don't some other woman will. I know my unhappily married men. Ray is just ripe for the picking."

All the same Maggie's hand faltered. She said to herself, and she said to Ray with the frequency born of panic, "I must go home."

She believed she was saying it for the last time when one afternoon they crossed to the beach side of the island. They had gone at Nini's behest, to buy a grouper caught by a native fisherman and sold from the small boat in which he would row ashore. When they arrived they found themselves alone on the beach. Side by side they sat down on the sand.

Ray suddenly kissed her; there was more of harshness than tenderness in his embrace. Maggie felt his unhappiness clutch drowningly at her own and knew that their physical desire would only intensify it for both.

"I must go home!" The pain in her voice frightened Ray as well as herself.

"You can't. You mustn't," he said gruffly.

"I . . . I must." Her voice was low.

"Why must you?" His eyes blazed.

She lowered her own. "You know very well why."

"Are you unhappy, Maggie?"

"What do you think?" She turned away.

"I'm dead in love with you, Maggie." He covered her hand with his own. "Head over heels in love," he added almost angrily.

Their fingers tightened. For a few moments more they sat without speaking. Abruptly he brought out, "It's one hell of a mess, isn't it?"

"That's why I tell you I'm going home."

"You can't." He released her hand. For a moment he covered his face with his own hands, rubbing his eyes violently, as though he might clear his own vision. Then, looking off and up into the cloudless sky, he gently released his trial balloon. "I suppose we've been crazy to think this could go on. I know I have no right to ask you to go through any mill for me."

A second before, when he had been pressing her not to leave him, Maggie's feminine instinct of encouraging pursuit prompted her to turn to flight. Now, for a moment, the man at her side all but visibly teetered, apparently reconciling himself to life without her. The pursuing female sprang to aggression, although her voice was silken and her moves were stealthy.

"Why are you so sure I wouldn't go through—" she hesitated before the ugly word each shrank from naming— "a lot for you?" Her blue eyes fixed his, meekness and fealty touchingly mingled.

"Do you believe, Maggie, do you really believe we might have a chance at happiness together?"

His thought appeared to falter a moment but suddenly lifted to a higher, firmer atmosphere as Maggie ringingly proclaimed, "Yes! I know it!"

"You mean even if we went through all the mess of a divorce?"

It was he who had said it first, not she.

Now Maggie brought forward the reinforcement of her own resolve. Lady Macbeth could have spoken no more unflinchingly. "Yes, even after a divorce," she said.

14

THE WORD *divorce*, once spoken between Maggie and Ray, took on a weight for Maggie that it had failed to carry on Nini's lips. It was a tremendous step to envisage taking, but its sheer magnitude called out in her dormant potentialities of character. She had courage never before tested; she had passion never before fully roused. Because she had also the supreme arrogance of the spoiled woman who has never been denied anything she wanted, she found herself learning to live in the contemplation of such drastic action with an easier and easier familiarity. Not only did she adapt herself to this new climate that was freshened by the prospect of daring revolt; she found herself impatient of any ruses or delays suggested by Ray in advancing on her goal.

She arrived back in Boston well briefed on the procedure that she was to follow. The sum of it was "Do nothing, say nothing."

"There's no point having the sky fall about your ears," Ray had said. "I've got to get out of D.D.D. and T. first. Then once I'm settled in Hollywood I can let Alice know, after a merciful interval, that she may as well head for Reno, that I don't plan to come back."

Maggie had demurred on the spot. "But that doesn't seem *honest*, Ray! Why can't you just tell her right out, when you get home, that since she's been given every chance to go to Hollywood with you you've found someone else who will go with you, who believes in you and loves you. You're not ashamed that we love each other?"

"No, no," Ray had answered. "It's only—well, hell hath no fury.

One thing at a time, darling, makes much more sense for us both in the long run."

Her very first evening at home Maggie promptly disobeyed Ray's injunctions. Her motives, never clearly faced in any action, were mixed. One part of her was genuinely outraged at being called on to practice deceit. Even if she could have convinced herself that such dissembling was decent, she was constitutionally incapable of carrying it out; guile was no part of Maggie's make-up. There was at work, moreover, a subtle instinct for making sure what was so close within her grasp. If she was to burn her own bridges, put herself in such a position that Dexter could do no other than open the door to let her go, then surely any potential retreat for Ray was forestalled. If she made no move, said no word, how could she be sure that on getting back to Cedarside he might not find that the strands of habit which had bound him so fast through the years might not prove their strength? Or what, simply, if Alice talked him round?

By whatever processes of reasoning or lack of them, by whatever promptings of love or simple aggression, Maggie and Dexter were no sooner alone together, with Priscilla tucked into bed upstairs, than she steadied herself an instant, took aim, and fired.

"Dexter, I wish you'd sit down," Maggie said abruptly.

Dexter, standing feet apart before the open fire, moved obediently to a chair on the other side of the fireplace. He gave a self-conscious tweak to the bow of the brightly colored plaid tie Maggie had brought him as a present.

"I want to talk to you," she said in a voice she wished had not been quite so loud.

"What about?" was the casual, faintly disinterested answer. When Maggie took on a slightly imperious manner, he knew he would more than likely be told of some forthcoming social engagement in which he must participate for "his own good."

"Us. Our marriage."

The words, seeming to stand there before him on the hearthrug, unheralded, stark, and unclothed, caused him to look up sharply.

"I hope you don't think there's anything wrong with it?" He looked suddenly bleak when no answer came. Feeling perhaps that any words, even if only his own, might help matters, he tossed out for their joint comfort, "My only complaint is that we've been away from each other for too many weeks."

"Oh, Dexter! Please! Please try to understand that I'm trying to say something very difficult." Maggie contemplated the broad façade of his incomprehension. "Have you no idea?" she asked, almost querulous, then abruptly, but with undisguised emotion, "Can't you guess at all what it is I have to say?"

He stubbornly refused to take it from her in any outlines but the harshest. It was to be castor oil, without orange juice, and the jaws wrested open to receive it, at that. "No, I can't" he said, and snapped his shut.

"I . . . I just don't know how to tell you. I thought my letters might have given you some inkling, but I can't stay under the roof with you one night even, without your knowing the truth—I mean I wouldn't feel *honest*, Dexter—"

He was looking at her now with such a fiery concentration that the words ceased to tumble out of her mouth, but huddled, afraid, at its threshold.

"Say it, Maggie," he commanded her. "What's wrong?"

"Ray Masters and I have fallen in love with each other."

She got up and walked quickly to the window, turning her back on him. It seemed indecent to witness the actual splintering impact of the truth she had hurled at him. By turning away she ceased to be involved with it; it became solely his, to meet with what resources his manhood might muster.

There was dead silence, except for the spitting of the fire. She fumbled with the folds of the curtain at the window and turned at last to see him, standing now, to confront her. The color, she noticed, that had been in his face a moment before had gone. He looked quite gray. *He's going to faint,* she said to herself. *Standing up, he's going to faint.*

"I suppose I ought to have thought it might happen. I just never did. I thought you *liked* him, and I knew you admired him professionally—the way you always go for people who are talented and who can do things. And—" he hesitated, suddenly aware that the climax was inadequate—"I knew he was married." His mouth was too dry to achieve the swallow he attempted.

"He is. But that doesn't prevent people falling in love," Maggie explained tolerantly.

"I suppose not. I don't see how they do it, all the same."

He turned on his heel and went to the farthest table in the room for a cigarette. After he had lighted it, he asked, not looking at her, "Well, you've told me. Now that I know 'the truth,' as you call it, what do you want me to do about it?"

"I want a divorce, Dexter."

"You're not serious!" There was fire now in his eyes and in his voice.

"I'm afraid I am—I'm afraid we are."

"So Ray is going to divorce his wife—for you?"

"Well, I suppose actually he'll ask *her* to divorce *him*."

"I see."

"I know. I know, Dexter. It—it must seem incredible, just coming at you like this, if you've had no suspicion. But we just *know* it's the only thing for us both. Ray has been miserable for years." She clutched wildly now at the offstage figure to serve as distraction. "He was married when he was much too young. His wife simply doesn't understand him at all. Talent is just beyond her. She only wants him to be a successful businessman who belongs to the best clubs."

Dexter ignored the distraction. "And what about you? Have you been miserable for years, Maggie?"

The direct question was so painful that it seemed easier to ignore it. "I . . . I've fallen in love, Dexter. You *remember* when you asked me to marry you that I didn't think we were especially suited to each other. It—well, it's *fate*. I mean if only I'd met Ray then I would have married him. He's the kind of man I should have married in the first place. I don't mean anything against you. It was a mistake for you too, Dexter." She hurtled on feverishly. "I'm sure it was. I'm sure I haven't been the right wife for *you*."

"I'm the best judge of that," he answered without expression. Then, suddenly turning from defense to offense, he moved forward his own heavy guns. "Maggie, listen. You know you do things impulsively." He hesitated a moment, wondering if she would reject his evidence as irrelevant. "Why, even the way you accepted me, walking down the aisle at Kitten's wedding—maybe you're doing the same thing again. Give yourself time to think it over. It's a terrible thing you're talking about."

"I know it is. I know. That's why I feel so badly."

"I mean terrible for you. You don't know anything about this man, Maggie. Nothing that he doesn't tell you himself, that is. You don't know his background, his family, his friends . . ." Suddenly an inspiration swooped upon him. "What does your friend Nini say to this? Or doesn't she know?"

"She's the only person who does know." Unconsciously Maggie aimed and wounded him afresh. "It would have been pretty hard to miss, seeing us together every day."

"I'm sure she's delighted." The color mounted into the temples beside his angry eyes.

Remembering her own flash of insight into Nini's duplicity of character, Maggie, cut off from the possibility of lashing at herself for collaboration with such a shabby schemer, could only lash out at Dexter instead. "That's not fair! Nini appreciates talent, and it so happens that she has a lot of courage. She's not afraid to lead the kind of life that interests her instead of just staying stuck in a poky rut where people are afraid of their own shadows."

"You mean the way *we* live? Has Nini got it all figured out that you and I aren't living courageously?"

"Let's leave Nini out of this. It's got nothing to do with her."

"I wish I could believe you." He interrupted the words she was about to speak. "I'm sure you believe that yourself. That's what makes me sick." He too, however, seemed disposed to drop the unappetizing subject, returning instead to a fresh area of pain. "I suppose you've thought about Priscilla. What would you plan to do about her?"

"I thought, Dexter, you'd agree—I mean I think *everyone* believes that a child really is better off with its mother." Her words wavered as she looked at his face. "I mean as a permanent thing. Naturally so far as holidays, or summer visits I'd be just as generous—"

"Thanks."

"Don't be sarcastic, Dexter. That won't help anyone. I'm only trying to work things out so they'll be as satisfactory as possible for everybody."

"Losing both my wife and daughter is hardly what I'd call satisfactory."

"But, Dexter, your *work*! You know that's more important to you than anything in the world! I can't help feeling—and I do have hunches that are right, you know I do—I can't help feeling that maybe, in the end, in the really long run—I don't say right at first, but in the long run—you may come to see this is the best thing all round."

"I'm certainly a long way from there now, I can tell you."

"But you wouldn't *hold* me, Dexter? You wouldn't hold me, against my will?"

The cloak of bruised womanhood did not fit her. It seemed to shrivel under Dexter's blazing look of accusation. Feeling stripped to the bone, she dropped her own look, unable to meet his.

"This is getting us strictly nowhere" was Dexter's only answer. "We'll have to talk about it some more. And now, if you don't mind, I have some work to do." He turned, and left the room.

15

In a matter of weeks Dexter was marching forward with the tight-lipped courage of the Light Brigade, convinced that he was executing a stupid order, but unflinchingly loyal to his commanding officer.

If Maggie deserved punishment for her contemplated action, she was to receive it in full measure during the next year simply by having to continue life under the same roof with Dexter. To pretend at the same time to family and friends that there was nothing wrong was an affront to her nature, particularly when there was hardly an acquaintance who did not say, in one form or another, "Don't let Dexter work too hard, Maggie. Hasn't he lost a lot of weight? These research fiends need watching." In the next breath they would add, "Incidentally, I've never seen *you* looking better! What have you been doing to yourself?"

Maggie's loss of weight—she was delighted to find that she was sensitive enough to lose it—brought the emergence of a new beauty. From the heart of the unshaped marble, form became apparent; for the first time there was softness in her eyes, gentleness on her lips. She looked yearningly into the mirror, telling herself that suffering was responsible for the obvious change; but the telltale truth was apparent: the sheen and gleam upon her could have been caused only by her having been dipped, or positively drenched, in the elixir of awakened love.

Dexter, for his part, joined Maggie in putting the mechanics of the coming dissolution of their marriage into the hands of Mr. Parker, a

State Street lawyer, agreeing to let Maggie have the custody of Priscilla. The particular travesty of the truth that could be made to serve Maggie's ends bore the label "mental cruelty."

As the year drew to an end and Alice had docilely and all unsuspectingly gone to and returned from Reno, and the time came for taking the wraps off her secret, Maggie decided that her first and best move should be to enlist the support of her lifetime ally, Roger.

When she asked him to take her to lunch, telling him she had something personal she wanted to talk over with him, Roger suggested the Parker House. Between swallows of her Cotuit oysters, without preamble, she confronted him with the stark outlines of her situation.

"It may be a shock, Roger, but Dexter and I went over it all a year ago, so it's no good trying to talk me round now. We're going to be divorced, and I'm going to marry Ray Masters."

Maggie had not been prepared to see the color go out of her brother's face almost as it had gone out of Dexter's a year ago. "You're crazy, Maggie," he said, and he pushed his plate away, his appetite lost before he had begun the meal. "For Christ's sake, *why* are you going to be divorced?"

Maggie, rhythmically popping an oyster into her mouth between sentences, explained how the attraction between herself and Ray had grown since their first meeting. She told of his unhappy marriage, of Dexter's agreement to let Priscilla go west with her, repeating by way of peroration, "It's no good to ask me to change my mind, Roger. But I do need your help in how to tell Mother and Father."

"I should say you needed help in plenty more ways than that."

"What do you mean?"

"I mean you're out of your mind, that's all. I still don't see what you're being divorced *for*."

"Because I'm in love! I've told you." The fact that the waiter, with the menu, was witness to her proud declaration did not disturb Maggie. She paused merely to let Roger order her a mixed grill.

Roger, however, intervened before she could describe further the interesting condition of her heart. "It's damned foolishness to talk about love. Married people don't fall in love with other people's husbands and wives unless they want to. You're looking for a way out of something you don't like. I've known for some time that you were too restless for your own good. I'm sure Mother and Father have known it too, though we haven't talked about it. Maybe we've all made the mistake of being too New England—in not talking to each other or to you. But who would suppose you would need a keeper to explain the facts of life to you after—how many years of marriage is it?"

"Ten." The answer came with surprising meekness. "What facts of life do you mean?" Maggie asked in a small voice.

"For one, the caliber of man that Dexter is. I assume you've faced just what you're doing to Priscilla in letting her be brought up with a divided allegiance. But Dexter—I thought you appreciated him. Hell, I thought you loved him." The very gruffness of Roger's voice spoke clearly how much he himself loved his brother-in-law.

"But I *do* appreciate him! And I do love him—in a way."

"A damned queer way. Don't you mind hurting him then, if you love him?"

"Of course I mind! I . . . I just hate it!" Maggie's voice grew teary. "You may not believe it, but it's been hell this last year. He's been so noble and so gloomy it's nearly killed me. Sometimes we lie there in the middle of the night in our twin beds, and I can just feel he's awake, and I try not to let him know I'm crying. I can't bear it then to think that I'm really leaving him." It was Maggie's turn now to show distaste for her food. She shoved her plate away.

"Then, Maggie, why in heaven's name are you doing it?"

"I can't help it. Roger, can't you understand that?" Her eyes looked at him with sudden pleading. *"I can't help it!"*

Her brother looked at Maggie with a sudden intensification of interest. He never remembered to have seen her look so wretched, so nearly lost. His voice was kind for the first time; he spoke with the gentle reasonableness he might have used to a hysterical child. "O.K. Let's leave love out of this for the moment, because I think even you would admit that falling in love with Masters is the occasion and not the cause of your marriage breaking up. There's something inside you, Maggie, driving you, eating you. Can't you tell me what it is?"

She returned his searching look bleakly, blankly. Her brow was furrowed. He could see that she was making an effort to understand what it was that he had asked her. He saw also that his words had failed to convey any meaning to her. How could he expect her to describe to him the force that devoured her if she did not recognize even its existence?

"Well," she brought out at last, "I've always known that I hated to get stuck in a rut. There's so much of the rest of life I'm dying to know!"

He cut her short. "That's absurd. It's nothing outside you that you want. If it were you know perfectly well Dexter would give you your head and let you travel if you wanted to. It's something inside you that hasn't been satisfied. It doesn't seem, either, to have much to do with *you.* I mean the nice you."

"Do you think I'm sort of a monster? A sort of Dr. Jekyll and Mr. Hyde?"

"Could be. There's certainly some kind of chained beast in you that you don't know yourself that seems to goad you into doing strange things."

"Maybe it's ambition. Nobody ever made a success without ambition." There was a flash of her old perkiness; she seemed to feel on firmer ground.

"What kind of success are you talking about, Maggie? I should say you had everything right now that the average woman could want."

"*Exactly*!" she pounced. "And whoever said I wanted to be an average woman? I want to *live*! Can't you understand that? The way I am now I might as well be dead."

Roger did not seem disposed to pick up the gauntlet she had flung down. He sidestepped, saying merely, "Unless you hold that demon of yours in check, Maggie, he can destroy you utterly."

"Don't you think I'd be happy with Ray?" All that Roger had been trying to convey to her seemed to boil down to this.

Roger looked across the table. Was it possible that Maggie had not understood a word of the warning he was trying to spell out for her? It was not that she would not face his words; it was simply that she could not. Her eyes were bright with straining toward the far horizon of a world as flat as a cooky. She was as handicapped as an albino; she was incapable of seeing in the dark, most of all the dark within herself. She could not see because she was afraid to look, and because she was afraid to look she settled for the broad light of day in a two-dimensional world. Roger realized suddenly that Maggie was still waiting for his answer to her question, *Don't you think I'd be happy with Ray?*

"It's not a question of what you'd be getting in Ray—" his voice was more tired than kind; it was also very sad—"so much as it's a question of what you'd be giving up. I think you'd miss it all much more than you realize. Not just Dexter and your life together. Not, even, just Mother and Father and Kitten and—"

"You, Roger. I'll miss *you*," she said warmly, her eyes filling with sudden tears.

"I wasn't fishing. I'm trying to tell you it's a question of getting away from your own center, your own roots. I'm only afraid that if you kick over everything, everybody you've ever known, in the long run you'll be the one to pay."

Maggie's attention was alerted. "But I don't see how that could happen to me with Ray," she said argumentatively. "He's everything I admire. He's talented, he's—"

Roger interrupted again. "Are you sure that you're not identifying the name he's made for himself with the desire you yourself have always felt to make a splash in the world? I'm only afraid that secondhand fame may not make up to you for—well, all the values you've known firsthand."

"That's for me to decide," Maggie said with sudden decision. "In fact I have decided. I *know* I'll be happy."

"Fine. All I've been asking is that you face up to all the implications of what you're doing."

"Of course I've faced them. Why else would I make all this fuss? You don't think I *like* being divorced, do you?"

Because the way Roger had received her news disturbed Maggie more than she cared to admit to herself, she took with her mother a top-lofty attitude; she would not again risk being put in a position where her firm stand might be shaken.

After blurting out the bare facts she presented her challenge. "From now on, Mother, you'll never be able to say anything against Nini again. People who live in glass houses—"

"What do you mean?" Mrs. Fraser's face flushed suddenly as the full implication of Maggie's words engulfed her. "You mustn't think of yourself just as—just as—" She refused to bring her wandering thought to the destination toward which it seemed determined to hurl itself.

"Yes. Just as bad! Face it, Mother. I'm leaving my husband to marry another woman's husband. I don't think you'll ever be in a position again to stand in judgment on other people's divorces."

The next instant Maggie regretted her words as she watched her mother, inadequate but dauntless, floundering in heavy seas.

"It's not possible to lay down hard-and-fast laws, dear. I'm sure that the second Mrs. Deacon is a hard and scheming woman. And you—you're restless and high-spirited and warmhearted. Quite a different thing. I will not have you lump yourself with a person of that sort."

"The world will lump me with her sort, so you may as well get used to it."

"I'll never think of you as anything but a loving, generous child." Her mother's eyes filled with tears, and Maggie saw that the wings of her sheltering, forgiving love would remain forever spread over her; she could all but hear their whirr, feel the tickle of their feathers. Brush them away she never could.

Her father, on the other hand, whose urbane worldly wisdom Maggie was sure could gloss over any human predicament, did not attempt to disguise his distaste for the step she was about to take. He said to her bluntly, "I don't like what you're doing, Maggie. What's wrong with the husband you have?"

Maggie, ducking, as she would a bullet, from the one question she could not answer, instinctively reached for the only defense—her enemy's discomfiture.

"But, Father," she said as her voice broke and her eyes filled, "I never thought that *you* would be conventional. I thought . . . I thought you were more broad-minded," she said lamely.

"Have an affair with this man by all means, but why leave Dexter?" he countered. Mrs. Fraser opened her mouth to interpose. "No, Elsie, don't you support Maggie in this," he said. "The best that can be said for her is that she is a victim of a stupid system of Anglo-Saxon morality superimposed on an explosion of a half-baked discovery of 'the new freedom.' The French have always known how to handle these things. Upsetting two families, each with children, because of a sudden infatuation is immoral. A love affair, conducted with discretion and human consideration, is preferable. The bland assumption that there's nothing so important as one's own libido—or whatever we please to call our lack of principle and lack of grace—is puerile."

Maggie was trembling with hurt and temper, and surprise.

"You ought to be the very one to understand, Father," she asserted. "You're ambitious, and—well, *you've* never got stuck in a rut. You've always wanted everything that life has to give."

"It's true, Malcolm," Mrs. Fraser put in. "It's hard for a high-spirited girl to find an outlet. Maybe if she'd been born in the days of the covered wagons she'd have done better. The young girls nowadays are given everything. No wonder that when they feel they'd like to move on, all they can do is move—out."

Her mother's support irritated Maggie. She was grateful that her father could make their joint repudiation articulate. "Bosh!" said Dr. Fraser. "The covered-wagon women were laying down the foundation just so that girls today could enjoy some of the advantages of indulging their femininity—of being whole women, and not merely hewers of wood and drawers of water."

"But you seem to forget, both of you, I've fallen in love!"

"And I tell you, you're in the throes of an infatuation. I dare say you've fallen in love with the world's image of a successful man. But I tell you, Maggie, if it's importance you're after, Dexter Bradfield will be head and shoulders above this other feller some day."

"I'm not worrying about my husband's place in history, whatever you seem to think. I'm thinking of the kind of life we can have together. Ray is a gifted writer. You always claim to respect artists, Father."

The nostrils of the long thin noses of father and daughter, so much alike, quivered in the charged air of temper that pulsated between them.

When Maggie, that same evening, asked Dexter how he had made out with his parents he would say no more than "I promised Ma I wouldn't even talk about it, Maggie, until after the family powwow. She's called one in two weeks."

"But I don't understand. What can a powwow do? Everything's all decided!"

"I told you, Maggie, I've promised not to talk about it."

Suddenly Maggie felt a spurt of blind hatred for her mother-in-law. "Thank God my parents are at least civilized! I certainly hope your mother will be too."

Maggie had at last named her. There was no question who was going to prove to be her most formidable enemy.

16

When Dexter came into the room, after returning from the family powwow in Milton, Maggie thought to herself, *He looks beaten. Something's happened.*

"What is it?" she fired at him without preamble.

"It's tough, Maggie. It's—it's going to upset you terribly. You've just got to believe that it wasn't my idea."

"What are you talking about? What has happened?" Her voice rose with the heavy pounding of her heart. Frightened, she still did not know what she was frightened of.

"It's Priscilla. You're not going to be able to take Priscilla with you." Dexter did not lift his eyes to meet Maggie's.

"What do you *mean* I'm not?" The question was very nearly a shriek. "Who's going to stop me? Answer me that, Dexter! Who's going to try and stop me?"

"Ma is. Ma has," he answered, abject.

"But how? She can't! It's all fixed! You've agreed to her coming with me! You're not serious!"

"I am, Maggie. It's all pretty unpleasant. Most people don't realize that Ma's a real fighter. She's tough." The unconscious tingle of admiration in his voice caused Maggie's look of incredulity to blaze into one of revulsion. Dexter did not see it as he plowed stolidly forward. "It seems she's had the wind up for some time. She got Mr. Parker to admit that a divorce was in the works, and on her own she went ahead and employed a private detective who is able to produce witnesses to prove that Ray has been seen more than once at his country club—well, if not drunk, at least having had an awful lot of cocktails. That weakness, coupled with his move to Hollywood, could make a practically unbeatable case to prove that he would not make the right stepfather or provide the right background for Priscilla. Apparently, if there's the slightest indication of what they call alcoholism, the courts bend over backward to protect the child."

"But, it's—it's—I simply can't believe it! It's not true. It's *revolting*! And I shall fight it!"

"It wouldn't do any good. There'd not be one in a hundred chances of your winning out. In any case the publicity would be terrible for Ray. Ma pulled no punches. She seemed determined, if it came to a showdown, to call in every newspaper in the country."

"She? Look here, Dexter, what has *she* got to do with all this, anyway? You're Priscilla's father, and you've agreed to let me have the custody of her. All you have to do is to stand up to your mother, for once in your life, and tell her that this is none of her damned business!"

"I—I can't do that, Maggie," he answered, diminishing before her very eyes.

"What do the rest of your family say?"

"Well, you know Ma. She rules the roost. Pa always agrees with her, and naturally Sarge and Marsh go along too. Aunt Katta and Kitten stood up for you, Maggie. They made the point that any child, not just Priscilla, is better off with her mother. But Ma won out."

"But if she doesn't win out with you, she can't hurt me. You're not going to—you can't—side with your mother against *me*?"

"I have no choice, Maggie." Guileless, he gave her the truth and the completeness of his involvement. "Remember, I've got all the rest of my life to live with Ma."

"But *why* have you? Kick your family in the teeth! They deserve it! And what's more, if you had the guts to do it they'd probably come crawling to you and have more respect for you in the end."

"You don't know Ma, then."

"I wish to God I never had known her, I can tell you that!"

The minute the words of open, flaunting rebellion were spoken Maggie could see that she had made a mistake.

"This isn't getting us anywhere," Dexter said, stiffening into unassailable dignity.

"You—you—" Maggie spluttered. "I thought you were so strong! I thought you were so unselfish—that in spite of this thing I'm doing you understood *why,* that I didn't *mean* to do anything cruel, and all the time you're nothing but a great big, cowardly mother's baby!"

She stormed from the room. Even from behind her bedroom door upstairs Dexter could hear the paroxysm of sobs and tears that all but shook the little house.

Sobs and tears, too, were presently being transmitted across the continent, via the Bell telephone system. Letters, as well, bore screeds of invective and despair. Ray agreed that the old witch hunter, as he called her, had all the cards on her side; any attempt to buck her was patently futile. Summoning all his reasserted manhood, he was able stoutly to say that in spite of the fact that his own marriage had been dissolved in the hope of a brighter, happier one with Maggie, still he could not possibly ask to hold her in the present circumstances. She must, of course, consider herself free.

"*Free*!" she had cried across three thousand miles. "But I'm not free! How can I be? It's too late now to be free!" Her physical desire, the thrust of her ambition and restlessness, her passionate insistence that her own will be done, were but a few of the chains that held her. Sweepingly she dubbed her enslavement with a title as high as her distress was deep. "I'm in *love*, Ray!"

"So am I in love, Maggie." His chains rattled antiphonally.

In letters she wrote, "How can we just pretend that it hasn't happened between you and me? It isn't possible to turn back now."

And he replied, "I know darling. It's hell. Don't think I don't want and need you terribly. It's no fun leading this wacky life out here without an ally, without my love, but I can't be the one to ask you to leave Priscilla. . . ."

And there they were, once more, biting the bitter core of their sweet fruit. Or, to soften the metaphor, Maggie, having eaten her cake, was confronted with the incontrovertible fact that she was not going to have it too. Gay, golden, gregarious, all her life she had been headstrong and spoiled; she had never known the whip of discipline or been put in a position where unselfishness might be demanded. Suddenly before her, stern and inexorable, loomed two possible choices that demanded of her ironclad strength—either way. As she set her feet on the path that it was inevitable that she, being she, must take, there ran through her a toughening of fiber. Where a short while before she had been self-willed, today she must be no less than ruthless.

Maggie was unable to achieve a meeting with her mother-in-law face to face. She had high hopes of her own powers of persuasion (heard herself pointing out the disadvantages to a sensitive child of parents avowedly incompatible), but Dexter, acting as ambassador, had always the same message to transmit: diplomatic relations were broken off; Ma Brad had no intention of talking to Maggie (he did not need to add *ever again*); her mind was made up once and for all. As for Dexter, Maggie had learned in one stricken moment, when it was too late, that setting herself in direct opposition to his mother had been fatal. He was set to stand fast to the end.

Once the news was general Maggie spluttered to Roger at the stand Ma Brad was taking. His only answer was "I don't know why you're so surprised, Maggie, at the way everyone's taking this. For a bright girl you seem to have figured out everybody wrong. I could have told you Ma Brad was something to be reckoned with."

"I don't know why everybody can't be like Kitten," Maggie countered. "After all, Dexter's her own brother, and she doesn't try to make me feel like some kind of monster."

"You know as well as I do that nobody can be like Kitten, and I certainly hope you aren't naïve enough to think that just because she doesn't call you names she likes what you're doing. She assumes that you must have reasons that are nobody else's business."

Maggie did not like the turn the conversation was taking. Actually, the first time she had been alone with Kitten after she knew the state of affairs, Kitten, looking rather strained, had said gently, "I'd really rather not talk about it, Maggie. You know I'll do everything I can for Priscilla, just as though she were one of my own." At the time Maggie had put down the one rather bleak little statement to Bradfield inarticulateness rather than to an excess of feeling.

Roger did not intend to let her off easily. "Have you happened to notice how Kitten has been looking lately?"

Maggie was loath to admit that she had, in point of fact, thought that Kitten was looking ill, with circles under her eyes, as though she had been crying or had been losing sleep; she was also much paler than was usual with her.

"Then why hasn't she *told* me if she doesn't approve?" Maggie asked not without petulance.

"Kitten never sets herself up as approving or disapproving of anyone else. You know that. In hurting Dexter it's as though you're hurting her. And because she never yips when she's hurt herself, she's not going to start now—even to me. In a funny way maybe your own family—Mother, Father, and I—are tougher on you for hurting a decent guy like Dexter than his own sister. Kitten's never judged anybody in her life, and she's not going to start now." And Maggie was forced to the unpleasant admission that in her brother's presence from now on she would never entirely escape the icy breath of judgment.

This terminal interchange with Roger took place on the day that Maggie and Dexter had put their signatures to the final settlement. In it Maggie waived all rights to Priscilla until she was twenty-one years old. At that time the child herself would be at liberty to choose whichever parent, if either, she wanted to live with; in the meantime it was understood she was never to become part of Raymond Masters' household.

Maggie still had to face, with a sinking heart, the prospect of telling the little girl herself how her future had been signed away.

She picked an evening when they were alone in the house—Delia's and Nellie's night out. She had tucked Priscilla into bed, and after the usual goodnight kiss she sat down on the edge of the bed and took the bony little hand in both of hers.

Stroking it gently, she began lamely, "Darling, Mummy has something to tell you."

"What is it?"

"I'm going away, dear. Mummy's going all the way out to California."

"When are you coming back?" The clear small syllables struck straight to their target.

"We-ell, I don't know. I—I'm going out there to live, dear." This was awful, dropping these words, so heavily weighted with adult perfidy, into the fresh, unpolluted waters. Incapable of hatred for herself, Maggie could feel her mouth go dry, the taste of venom toward her mother-in-law on her tongue. "I—I'm leaving you and Daddy behind," she went on.

"Why, Mummy, why?" There was a slight sharpening discernible in the thin little voice, pointing upward, toward panic.

"Because, darling—it's hard to explain. But sometimes when a man and woman marry, the way Daddy and I did before you were born, it turns out to be a mistake. Daddy likes to lead one kind of a life, and I like to lead another. And out there in California I—I—" How *could* she say it? She swallowed hard and hurried on. "I'm going to be married to a man who likes the same kind of life I do. You know him, Priscilla!" Her voice brightened cozily. "It's Mr. Masters who gave you the guppies. Remember?"

"But how can you marry him if you're married to Daddy?"

"Well, I won't be married to Daddy then. I—we—we'll be divorced first."

"Like Jenny's mother and father?" There was not only interest but there were excitement and pleasure now. A sudden unexpected weapon to help her to gain dominance over an envied friend was too good to be true. "Will I have two fathers then?"

"In a way, yes."

"Will I have two mothers? Jenny has."

"Well, not right away!" Maggie chuckled indulgently. "Maybe *some* day Daddy will marry again too."

This all was suddenly going much better than she could have dared to dream. "And, darling, I'm going to be married at Northeast, at Grandma's. Won't that be fun—a real wedding? And I want *you* for my flower girl! You've never been in a wedding, dear, and we must choose a dress for you specially. I shan't have any other attendants, so it can be just the way we decide is the prettiest for *you*."

"How long will you be in California?" The voice was tense.

"Well, I don't know exactly. Mr. Masters—I think you must call him Ray, the way I do—Ray is going to work out there, but I'll come back, darling. On holidays we'll see each other at Grandma's and—"

"Aren't you ever coming home any more?"

"My home will be in California, Priscilla."

"Where will my home be?"

"Here. Where it has always been! With Daddy." She felt herself now hurrying faster and faster, as though merely by brushing them aside in conversation the very years themselves would accelerate their passage. "And you know, darling, it won't be long before you'll be going off to boarding school, and then, maybe, to college, and *then* some day, when you're all grown up, you can choose, and can come and live with me all the time if you'd like to."

"Oh."

Maggie had come to the end of her resources. It was all she could venture, as a starter. Quickly she began whisking about with opening the window, arranging an extra blanket, talking about the dress to be laid out for tomorrow morning. She stooped to brush Priscilla's forehead with her lips, not trusting herself even to say good night, then, quick as a wink, she had closed the door behind her and stood on its other side with a racing heart.

She felt she could better have borne the sound of sobs, curses, or recriminations hurled after her. There was only silence on the other side of the closed door.

—II—

Margot

17

"ANY COMPLAINTS, Maggie?" The eyes of the new bridegroom squinted into the late-afternoon sunshine as he surveyed his bride.

"When you call me that, smile. The name is *Margot*."

"You win. All right then. Margot. Darling."

Maggie flashed a rapturous smile at her bridegroom and all that he had already brought her. They were sitting on the terrace of their Hollywood house, with its tubs of camellias and gardenias and bright outdoor furniture. Her nostrils quivered expectantly; the minute the sun set the air would be sweet with the perfume of night-blooming jasmine.

So far, it was proving a little difficult for Ray to remember the new name that Maggie had insisted on.

"I'm really superstitious about it!" she declared. "I want to forget that Maggie Bradfield ever even existed. Can't you just feel it in your bones that Margot Masters is bound to have a dazzling future? I can! She just can't miss. I know it!"

"You make me a little uneasy. Am I going to be held accountable for producing this future for you?"

"I'm not worried. So why should you be?" had been her assured answer.

As Ray lifted his cocktail glass toward his Margot, she certainly presented the appearance of a young woman who had already won her victory. She might have modeled for a travel advertisement of Happy

Hawaiian Honeymoon; her smooth skin, tanned by the tropic sun, seemed to glow with her body's consummation of a strong physical love. Only as the sun struck her directly did it reveal a few lines ringing her brown throat; like telltale markings around a tree trunk, they silently announced that this springtime blooming was not the first.

"I toast you, darling," said Ray. *"Aloha nui loa paoli!"*

"With all the love there is!" Maggie echoed the words they had both painstakingly learned from friends on the Island of Maui. "I *feel* as though it were all mine. That's why I'm happy! I'm happy! I'm happy!" Each proclamation exploded from her center into widening ripples.

"The best of it is you don't have to say it." Ray's voice was full of deep feeling. "I think anyone accidentally touching your little finger would get an electric shock. Darling, if you knew how good it makes me feel to know that it's all mine!" Tenderness had replaced jauntiness in his smile.

"Of course it's all yours. You made it!"

"Then keep it for me—always. I could inhale it forever."

"Do you know what *I* think is nice about a second marriage?" asked Maggie abruptly. "It's the fact that one is—I won't say old enough, but experienced enough to appreciate it." She put her hand in Ray's. They sat for a few moments without words, the warm current running back and forth between them.

Maggie still could not believe in the total transformation of her surroundings. The Masters' house, perched several hundred feet in the air on one of the pueblolike cliffs above Sunset Boulevard, was also only five minutes from Schwab's Drugstore and from the supermart where Maggie had gone to shop the day of her arrival, to be served by a starlet-in-waiting whose costume was a pair of shorts, a bra, and roller skates. Now, however, that Maggie was officially "settled," Mrs. Maitland had taken over the shopping. Mrs. Maitland, who drove to work in a lime-green Packard, was the Masters' "housekeeper." (Maggie had learned already that the word *cook* was as taboo in southern California as the word *undertaker*.)

"Tell me what happened at the studio today, darling." Even as Maggie said the words she felt a tingle of delight. How different, how different it was to have a husband who had work that it was fun to *talk* about! Her life would be his life. To that end she had already bought a little notebook and written in bold letters on the cover: *The J's.* She told him that she was jotting down, as they came to her, ideas that might be helpful to him in his work on the screenplay of his novel. Ray's year in Hollywood, before Maggie's arrival, had netted him simply a postponement of the assignment for which he had been engaged. Now, however, with Chelek back from loan-out, things were bound to hum at the studio. It was fun, Maggie thought, to toss off the enchanted words "the studio" as though she were part of its all-embracing life. Sovereign to its subject, mother sow to its sucklings, deity to the faithful, to Maggie it was a new and thrilling allegiance. Ray had told her that the studio could get a man tickets to the Rose Bowl or reservations on the Super Chief, keep his name out of the paper when in trouble, put it in when he wanted it provocatively "linked," mend his shoes, buy him a typewriter, design his Christmas cards, or sue his wife for divorce. Her husband's god would become her god as well.

"We-ell—" Ray did not seem in a hurry to give Maggie's question a direct answer—"there were a hell of a lot of conferences, but the way it looks now—"

"I hope you're going to start on *The Joneses* tomorrow!" Maggie finished the sentence for him.

"Not so fast, not so fast." Ray patted his wife's hand as it lay on his knee. "The mills of the gods grind slow, darling. No, it seems that Fremont is bringing a lot of pressure to bear to get the studio to finish up the one more picture he's committed to do this year, so he can get off to Mexico."

"But wouldn't *The Joneses* be a perfect vehicle for him?"

"Apparently not. He says the part isn't sympathetic enough. Don't laugh, but Chelek's trying to sell him the idea of *The Bostonians.*" Quickly and kindly he added, "By Henry James. I haven't read it since college, and don't remember much except that it's about two women. Apparently the man's part can be built up. They're talking about my doing the treatment and, if they like it, the screenplay as well."

Within a week Maggie had received from her mother the Boston Athenaeum's copy of *The Bostonians* and had started a new notebook, labeled: *The B's.*

Ray told her that Chelek was going to produce the picture as a covert study in Lesbianism; he was quite sure that he could easily rig it to get by the Hays Office. He was to use an all-British cast with the exception of the Basil Ransom role, which would be played by Alexander Fremont.

Surprisingly, it was to Nini Deacon that Maggie owed her introduction to this great motion-picture star at just the moment she most wanted to meet him.

The gist of a letter from Nini was to say, "I've written Alexander and Dotty Fremont all about you both, and I'm sure they'll be calling you. We were very close last winter in Jamaica when I took them everywhere in my car. Not only is he still the biggest name in Hollywood, but he is such a *gentleman*, and Dotty is just precious. They'll do anything for me, and after they've met both of you they'll adore you for yourselves. Obviously! I'm jealous already to think what fun the four of you are going to have together."

When, therefore, the Masters received a telegram from the Fremonts —"Celebrating our twentieth wedding anniversary with a few friends. We want you both so much to be there"—Maggie accepted forthwith.

Driving up, on the appointed evening, to the Beverly Wilshire Hotel, in a rented Tanner limousine, Maggie gave her husband's arm a squeeze. "Darling, pinch me to make me believe that I'm really here!" Her dimples deepened with the sheer delight of realization that she had achieved the impossible. Maggie Fraser, Maggie Bradfield were forgotten wraiths. Here rode, along with the nation's movie stars, as one of their colony, Margot Masters—new name, new husband, new *world*!

Just as they drove up to the hotel one of the swarm of teen-age fans that lined the sidewalk, sensing in the air all the excitement generally attendant on a "premeer," broke loose from the crowd to jump on the running board of the Masters' car. Cupping his hands like blinders about his eyes, the better to blink at the glamour of the occupants, he announced in a disgusted yell to his companions, after one look at Maggie, "Aw, she ain't nobody!"

Maggie essayed a feeble laugh, for Ray's benefit; but she was put out. These were not the words that she had torn up her life by the roots and traveled three thousand miles to hear.

Inside the hotel, Maggie took the crowd of guests jostling their way toward the Florentine Room to be intimate friends of the Fremonts. She and Ray fought their way through the photographers, with their *ack-ack* of flashlight bulbs, to reach the receiving line at last. She was yet to learn that flashlights popping about her head, if never at it, were as customary at the most "informal" Hollywood party as black flies on the beach at Dunster. The native inhabitants simply came to accept their presence as part of the local fauna. For her own part, Maggie, in spite of her instinct to duck, slap, or scratch this new brand of marauder, learned in time to move about among them, serenely immunized by the citronella of anonymity.

The Masters fell into the receiving line. It consisted of the celebrating couple and their three boys, each squirming beneath the pinch of a stiff collar and the scratch of a blue serge suit. Maggie, making the one all-embracing gesture that includes hair, shoulder straps, and girdle, and plastering her best party smile on her face, advanced on Mrs. Fremont.

"We're Nini Deacon's friends—the Masters," she said.

Dotty Fremont was dressed in white bridal tulle, her low *décolletage* bordered with fresh gardenias. Diamonds flashed from among the gardenias as from other strategic outposts. Her smile was radiant, incessant, and unfocused. It shone on like the sun itself; it was up to each guest to jockey himself into its rays. Her eyes traveled, unseeing, over the person with whom she was shaking hands as she sought a sight of the next in line. Before Maggie knew it, without having caught her hostess's eye, she found that her hand had been passed firmly and diagonally across Dotty Fremont's bosom and placed in her host's hand. Along with it were tossed the words, "The Martins, darling. Friends of—darling, *hello*!" and Dotty was kissing the woman who followed Ray. Alexander Fremont shook hands warmly with them both, and his million-dollar vocal cords gave a tremolo of delicious warmth as he said, "It's wonderful of you both to come."

Maggie hastily resolved to try another line of attack with the great man himself. "We're the Masters," she said, smiling inclusively at Ray over her shoulder, "the Raymond Masters," she repeated, to make assurance double sure. "You and Ray will be seeing a lot of each other for the next few months."

"Tell them they're damn slow about serving the champagne," Alexander Fremont said over Maggie's shoulder.

"My husband is writing the screenplay for *The Bostonians*," Maggie said loud enough to command the attention of their host.

"Is that so?" he said. "Chelek takes care of the production details for me." Grasping Ray by the hand, he almost lifted him off his feet as he eased him decisively out of the way to make room for the next in line.

A man in tails, who, for one happy instant, Maggie mistook for Lewis Stone, stopped them first to ask their names and then to tell them the number of their table. "Drinks are served at the buffet at the farther end of the room, sir," he said to Ray.

There, in a hornets' nest at the bar, Ray's arrival seemed to stir up a buzz of recognition. Maggie realized with gratitude that they had reached the asylum offered by colleagues from the studio.

Ray started off the introductions by taking Maggie up to Chelek. He was wearing a Windsor tie; a black ribbon hung from the pince-nez on his nose. His only response was repeated by each of the half-dozen other men with whom she shook hands. "I want you to meet my wife." Maggie found herself abruptly shunted off onto a siding with the women as a superfluous load to haul.

She heard herself being talked to by Mrs. Gull, a short, stout little woman dressed in pale-orchid satin; hairdo and dye were both harsh. Several smooth, comfortable double chins and several smooth, comfortable rolls of flesh on her upper arm flapped in unison as she rattled on to Maggie. "Isn't this the most ex*quis*ite affair? The Fremonts are the loveliest couple in Hollywood! Everything they do is in perfect taste."

"I'm afraid I don't know them at all. I've only just come here to live."

"Is that so? Well, dear, you'll *love* it. In spite of all the bad publicity Hollywood gets, it's just a city of homes. Cy and I have lived here twenty-five years. What does your hubby do at the studio, dear? Mine is studio manager."

"He's Raymond Masters, the author." Maggie spoke with unconcealed pride.

"What has he done in pictures?"

Maggie, ignoring the question, moved to tuck her arm into Ray's as he talked to Chelek. Cheerfully interrupting their conversation with all the assurance of a woman used to charm, she said, "Mr. Chelek, I'm terribly thrilled that Ray is to do *The Bostonians*! I don't know whether he's had a chance to tell you, but it happens that I come from Boston, so don't hesitate to feel perfectly free to call upon—"

"Maggie—" Ray nodded toward a new arrival—"this is Leonard Blatz, another colleague of mine at the studio."

Leonard Blatz shook hands and immediately called over his shoulder, "Beverly, come here, honey."

A fantastically beautiful girl, dressed in skin-tight bronze-metal cloth, slouched over to join them with the gait of a fashion model.

"This is Mrs. Masters, dear."

"Pleasure," said Beverly Blatz, holding out her hand in its long white glacé-kid glove with three diamond bracelets, and immediately dove into her evening bag to pull out a compact and mirror and began working at repairs on the Cupid's-bow mouth she must have created only a very short time before. First she puckered her lips into a mean little kiss, and then suddenly shoved them far apart into what failed to pass for a smile. Wielding her lipstick ferociously, she followed the perimeter of her lips, swabbing deep inside the lining of her mouth.

Ray and Leonard turned their backs immediately on the two women they had united. Beverly was too involved with the project under execution to initiate any topic of conversation, so Maggie ventured, "I'm so interested to be here. This is my first Hollywood party."

"Pardon?" said Beverly as unintelligibly as though her mouth were full of dentist's fingers.

"I said that I'm thrilled to see a real Hollywood party." Maggie spoke a little too loud, as she might in speaking to a foreigner.

Beverly pursed up her lips again, crinkled up her eyes tight and, peering into a hand compact, blew a gust of powder across the surface of Maggie's cocktail. "This party is in perfect taste," said Beverly as she turned her back on Maggie and walked away.

Mrs. Gull fluttered close again. Maggie this time grabbed at her as a welcome spar to cling to. "Ought I to know who she is?" she asked, nodding in the direction of Beverly's undulating rear view.

"Oh, that's lovely Beverly Blatz. She was a mail girl at the studio. That's where Lennie met her. He divorced his wife and married Beverly. They say she can do *any*thing with him."

There was no further opportunity to expatiate on this theme; a roll of drums from the orchestra announced dinner. Ray came to take Maggie off to find their seats at one of the tables alongside the dance floor where they had been told they would find their place cards. Maggie was as surprised as Alice at the mad tea party to find that next to Mrs. Ray Masters' place card was Mr. Ray Masters' place card. She pointed and whispered to Ray, "Probably a mistake, but don't tell anybody." It took them only a few minutes, however, to discover that the other five husbands at the table were also sitting next to their wives. It took her only a few more Hollywood parties to learn that such a seating arrangement was a prevalent practice. Like other folk customs in other lands various explanations were offered: some said that, like an institution founded at the time of King Arthur and his Knights of the Round Table, it had sprung out of the mists of antiquity in the reign of Doug and Mary. Some said that husbands and wives wished to make the most of their moments together before being parted by divorce. Others said that neither would trust the other out of sight for half an hour. There were the kindly few, like Mrs. Gull, who continued to state that Hollywood was a city of homes.

The floor show of the evening started with the soup. To a roll on the snare drum and the opening measure of "Here Comes the Bride" from the piano and violin, Dotty Fremont skittered forward, with the little steps of a ballerina, arms spread wide, into the circle of baby-pink spotlight waiting for her in the center of the room. As a matron of an older time might have waved a languid ostrich fan, Dotty Fremont closed her jeweled fingers about the chic accessory of the day—a microphone. Through it she cooed a welcome to her guests. "Hello there!" (Wild cheering.) "Zan and I want you all to feel warm deep down inside just the way we're feeling ourselves this evening. We want every couple in the room to feel that they're lovers again, just for tonight. And now to start the ball rolling!" she turned to the orchestra leader—"Guy, play something just for the newlyweds here tonight. We want those couples on the dance floor who have been married within the year!" (More wild cheering.)

At the few chords of announcement Maggie's pulses quickened. She pushed back her chair and, catching Ray's hand, they stepped forward, through the shadows in which the tables were placed, down into the light waiting at the center of the dance floor. *I suppose it will be practically an exhibition dance, and I do hope Ray won't mind. Maybe there'll be one or two other couples so we won't be too conspicuous,* she thought to herself. All the same she was smiling with anticipatory pleasure as the luscious notes of "The Way You Look Tonight" swelled louder. *It really will be fun,* she thought, *Ray and I whirling around while all the stars sit by and watch. This does give me something to write home about!* As she walked forward, in a delicious trance, she was suddenly jostled from behind. Instinctively she turned to Ray for support, in time to hear him saying "I beg your pardon" to someone he had jostled from the other side. The floodlight was playing on them now and in its enclosure she could see first with confusion, then with incredulity, that the dance floor was not dotted with one or two couples, as she had imagined; rather, it was filled to capacity with so many newlyweds clasped to one another's hearts that there was only a handful of couples left to serve as audience to such mass witness of the power of romantic love.

With the next course Dotty asked the couples who had been married ten years to dance. This time the orchestra wailed "Thou Swell" as a far more modest assemblage stepped forward. Maggie recognized Beverly and Leonard Blatz in the middle of the room among them.

Her companion on her right, who had introduced himself with a laugh as "Rod Branch, an attorney who knows enough to put everyone in this room behind bars," explained for her benefit, "These are the boys who've got hooked, but good. That last batch were most of them on their third or fourth time around. Once a man can get out of a second marriage he's good for an indefinite number more, but these second-marriage gals are tough. The ones a man has left his first wife for who've got their teeth into something good—wisdom teeth, big-girl teeth—they are the gals who aren't going to let go and don't intend to—models, receptionists, showgirls, has-beens in pictures. Look, there's Larry LeClerq waving to Arlene Tremaine on the sidelines. That's a good one! Everyone in Hollywood knows Larry's been keeping her for years, but Francine—she's an old Mack Sennett girl—is willing to grin and bear it. Larry'll never get out of that one!"

Catcalls and wolf whistles from the sidelines assailed many more couples than the LeClerqs. Maggie had the sense of missing some family joke, just as long ago at Fig Newton's she had missed some of the purely Massachusetts General Hospital humor. Now she studied, not with complete detachment, what common denominator seemed to exist between these women who had held their husbands ten years and who, if Rod Branch was to be believed, were each one, like herself, a second choice. Each had been pretty, that much was clear, but now, ten years later, all were struggling to preserve the figures and faces that had once been their fortunes. A few, having given up the struggle, had obviously sought refuge in dissipation, revealed in telltale pouches under eyes and lines about mouth and chin, duplicated on the faces of their mates.

With the dessert Dotty tripped forward once more. "And this dance is for those lovers, like Zan and me, who have never stopped loving for twenty years, and plan to go on loving for twenty more!"

The orchestra retched up the portamento strains of "Let Me Call You Sweetheart" as the switchboard of lights went into convulsions to produce a shimmering spectrum of color. Six couples advanced to the center of the room: the Gulls, the Branches, the Fremonts themselves, an unidentified couple from out of town, and a team of writers whose marriage was said to be the most stable in Hollywood, held together by the bonds of a mutual-security pact pledging heterosexual loyalty—only.

By skillful stage management the few extraneous couples were presently liquidated so that the anniversary pair were left alone to do an exhibition dance, cheek to cheek. Rod Branch, back beside Maggie, mopping his forehead, explained to her that the couple had been hoofers together as kids on a vaudeville circuit long ago. "I have firsthand knowledge," he said, "that it was her personal savings that kept Zan's name out of the papers in at least one unsavory scandal."

Now Dotty followed her husband's intricate footwork on the dance floor with as much adaptability as she had shown in life. Under the hypnotic aphrodisiac of the orchestra the eyes of both were closed in a positive orgasm of infatuation with the same object. That object was Alexander Fremont. His eyelids fluttered apart for a quick adoring glimpse into the mirror, past which he led their steps.

When the suspirating music breathed its last, hosannas and applause resounded as the Fremonts, hand in hand, bowed first to the audience and then to each other. Dotty, taking her husband's hand, drew him to the microphone.

"And now, before the party goes on—for the rest of the night, we hope," she gasped—"I should like, at this time, to make the presentation of an Oscar. It's an Oscar for the outstanding performance not just of one year but of twenty years. It's an Oscar for the greatest star in the whole firmament of husbands—Alexander Fremont!"

She reached into her bag and brought out a leaf-thin gold cigarette case, which she handed to her husband.

With boyish charm Alexander Fremont wonderfully managed a blush to accompany his modest smile as he took it from her.

"Why, what do you know?" he drawled. "And something written on the durn thing, too, in Dotty's writing. She must have got it processed down at Grauman's." (Laughter and applause.) Then he read aloud, "For my darling of twenty years—and always." There was an instant when the coating of vanity in which he was sheathed appeared to have been pierced. He knitted his brows over the object in his hand, as though indeed he were holding the tangible shape of the love she had given him. The moment passed, and suavely he slipped the cigarette case into his inside pocket and patted it with the proprietary satisfaction suitable to drawing-room comedy, before turning to his wife, with the easy reflex of the accustomed driver putting his foot on the accelerator, and, enfolding her in his arms, pressing upon her lips a lingering Hollywood kiss.

Maggie and Ray stayed until four in the morning. Waiting for their car under the marquee, they could hear pronouncements on the evening's entertainment tossed out into the night.

"Don't be crazy. The studio pays for the whole thing, tax-deductible."

"Why all this talk about marriage? I've been living in sin for seven years. Nobody asked me to get up and dance."

"Excuse us, please"—and two men pushed past, carrying the inanimate form of a prominent New York playwright. Nobody looked twice. The last words Maggie heard before the door closed behind her were "Perfect taste."

She did not see the Fremonts again in Hollywood.

18

It took Maggie nearly six months to admit to herself that she was not likely to become a collaborator in Ray's work; the struggle to admit that she was not his professional confidante came even harder.

"On Eleuthera, darling," she said, "you told me you wanted a wife who was interested in your writing and believed in it. Now you never tell me anything."

"I know. It's only that I'll get the hang of the work better if I don't keep pulling it up by the roots every night to see how it's going. I'm making a hell of a lot of dough, so why worry?"

"What I worry about is your making a name. I was talking to a woman last night after dinner who told me *her* husband was doing the continuity on *The Bostonians*. I thought it was all your picture. That sort of thing makes me feel so—so insecure, somehow." Maggie had trouble in finding a word for which there had never been any use in her vocabulary. "I'm afraid maybe you don't stand up for yourself enough at the studio," she said.

"I tell you one thing. I'll get as much visibility out of this picture as Henry James will, so relax. What does it matter anyway, so long as I have you?" And he took her in his arms as a means, not for the first time, toward inducing his wife to step down off her soapbox.

Being made love to by her husband had gradually become the only excitement in Maggie's life; it had not yet occurred to either of them that it might not be enough to last her forever. Actually she would have been only too glad to allow her physical love its natural flowering in bearing Ray a child. He, however, was adamant. "Alimony for Alice and support of my kids is enough. No one knows how long this Hollywood gravy train will hold out. Why stick our necks out? Besides, we've got enough emotional complications as it is—your kid, and my kids, without throwing in *our* kids."

For all the expansive happiness that came of being married to a husband with whom she was passionately in love, Maggie was increasingly aware of an insistent malaise that she, who had never known an hour's homesickness in her life, was at a loss to define. She expostulated to her mother, in letters, saying with her old insensitiveness to any feelings on the part of the person addressed, "Why doesn't *anybody* write me but you and Kitten?"

She hardly counted Spaff's communications as letters, bristling as they were with unintelligible arrangements of the alphabet. "What thrilling things are going on in Washington!" Spaff wrote. "I have good friends in the FCC, the NEC, the FHA, and the FDIC, though of course my first love is the CCC, which is giving work to so many of the unemployed youngsters I've worked with in our neighborhood boys' club." There was very little that Maggie could write in reply that did not sound too frivolous to put on paper.

Her sharpest pang lay in the difficulty she found in reaching through to Kitten, chiefly because Kitten seemed to find it difficult to reach through to her. Although her sister-in-law wrote faithfully and fully, it was clear that she considered that Maggie was as far removed as though she had settled in outer space. She wrote:

> I remind myself of what member of the Forbes family was it who deplored Cousin Cam's going to the Philippines as Governor because she was afraid he would get quite "out of touch with Milton Hill." As I'm sure, what's more, that you're delighted to be out of touch it's impossible to follow you in your thrilling new life, even in imagination! All I can do is tell you of our tame little happenings here.

Priscilla is growing into a very interesting child, Maggie, and *so pretty*! I try to get her to Milton almost every week end. It's such a civilizing influence on our boys to have a little girl to consider! Though I'd bet on Priscilla anywhere to be able to take care of herself. She seems as pleased with our new house as we are ourselves. I think it's Roger's masterpiece to date, and expect he has started a trend for modern houses in Milton, as inquiries are pouring in on him. We're all thrilled with the beautiful bird-feeding platform that's built off the sunroom. So far our family consists of an occasional downy and hairy woodpecker, juncos, evening grosbeaks, brown creepers, nuthatches, and my beloved fat cheerful little chickadees.

Kitten herself did not tell Maggie, what Mrs. Fraser did, that *The Atlantic Monthly* had accepted two of her sonnets on the very subject of her winter visitors.

Roger did not write at all.

Aware as she was of the barrier that divided her from the adult members of her family, Maggie poured out an unending stream of volubility on Priscilla's small head.

"Don't forget your Mummy, my precious, who thinks of you often and always," she would write.

Once a week would come a sedate little answer: "Dear Mummy. How are you? I hope you are well. I am well. I saw a baby seal and his mother at Franklin Park Zoo. She was liking him on the nose and he was eating a fish. I hope you are having a nice time. I got your letter. Love from Priscilla."

She would toss such communications to Ray for diagnosis.

"She sounds happy, and that's the important thing, isn't it?" was the verdict.

Maggie did not dare to answer, *Not as important as that she should miss me.*

Where Ray's children were concerned Maggie paid dutiful lip service to her new role as stepmother and would ask solicitously about

Sister and Skipper when their father opened their letters. He, however, refused to be drawn into any discussion concerning them; when Maggie made affable inquiries she felt as though a door were closed in her face. Sometimes when she was alone she would study their pictures on Ray's bureau: Sister, dark and lovely, was unmistakably her father's child; but Skipper, with the wide-apart eyes and upturned nose and obviously blond coloring, must be what friends were fond of saying, "All Alice." And yet, perversely enough, Ray seemed to love him nonetheless for this distinguishing mark. In fact, he was always picking up what he called gimcracks that the boy might like. Both children were part of a life he did not care to share with Maggie but, clearly, a part he was far from forgetting.

With Mrs. Maitland to take care of the house and no friends stopping in during the day to disarrange it, Maggie had, for the first time in her life, hours of solitude on her hands. Ray, in their first months in Hollywood, seemed aware that she was called upon to adjust herself to a way of life that was hard for one of her temperament and background to accept. One day he said to her, "You're in a tough spot for a sociably inclined gal. Don't forget, Margot, that I had a year in this town to observe its *mores* before I had a wife of my own, and so far as I can make out, in Hollywood unless a woman rates in pictures she might as well be dead—that is, unless either her fame or her fortune are such that even this town can't afford to ignore them."

"Oh, well, I'm not worried. You know me! I adore talent, and one of them will probably come along who'll be glad of the good old lion feeder."

"You're in about the only town in the world where that doesn't go down socially. A lion feeder, however thin you slice her, is still just one more fan. And over the dinner table stars don't crave fans. What they want, pure and simple, is to talk shop—with experts. It's a one-industry town, darling."

"Don't think I *mind*, dear." Maggie was quick with her reassurance. "It amuses me to death to watch! But I was thinking about Hollywood wives in general. Can't the men at a party talk rationally to a woman who's married to somebody else?"

"Men in Hollywood don't think of women in connection with talking, my sweet, whether rationally or otherwise. A woman is either a babe, a name in pictures, or your own wife."

"Then what about the women among each other? Can't they at least be friends?"

"Uh-uh," came the debonair negative. "They're afraid of their own shadows. They can't move out of their husband's salary echelon without losing face or of being accused of sucking up to a higher-up. It's dog eat dog all the way."

For the first time in her life, because she had so many long daylight hours of solitude to fill, Maggie fell into the habit of lying down after lunch. She found something enervating in the climate that made it easy for her to fall into a heavy drugged stupor, half waking, half dreaming. The noise of their Japanese gardener's rake on the gravel path outside her window could magically be transformed into the scraping of a snow shovel on a Brimmer Street sidewalk. The clicketty-clack of her next door neighbor's children's roller skates on the asphalt under the palm trees became the clicketty-clack of her own and Roger's roller skates on the esplanade along the Charles River in Boston. How she used to tear along, her hat held on by an elastic under the chin, her eyes swimming under the lash of an icy east wind, when she spurred Mrs. Browning, tugging at the leash, to race faster and faster, barking at Roger's receding wheeled heels!

This sensation of being pulled on roller skates became the frequent prelude to a recurring nightmare which came often to disturb Maggie's nights. The fierce, desperate creature that dragged her was no longer a gentle cocker spaniel. Whatever it was, it tore her, streaking through space, against her will, farther and farther away from something, somebody very precious that she was abandoning behind her. She could hear over her shoulder first a whimper, and then the sound of sobbing, more and more violent. She longed, she strained, to let go, to go back to the rescue of whoever it was who needed her so, who was sobbing so deeply . . . until she woke to find her pillow wet with tears and Ray patting her shoulder, asking, "What's the trouble, honey? What's wrong, Margot?"

"Oh, I don't know. I dreamed I couldn't go back to—"

"To whom?" he asked kindly.

Her thoughts became confused, confronted with a direct question. "I don't know. Someone that belonged to me. I mean, somebody left me behind. I was lost and she wouldn't stop for me."

"Who wouldn't stop for you? You really aren't talking sense, darling."

"Oh, I don't know. It was just—sad." She didn't want to be questioned, or to question any further. She curled close to Ray, who held her in his arms. But the sadness remained, even through the following day.

Maggie found herself longing for just one friend. So when Ray told her that Enid Forrest had showed up at the studio, fresh from England, to play Verena Tarrant in *The Bostonians* she welcomed with delight his prophecy, "Here's a gal that ought to be just what you're looking for. Very un-Hollywood and civilized, I should say. I suggested that she and her husband drop in for dinner just with ourselves."

As Enid Forrest stood in the doorway a few nights later Maggie thought, with a lifting of the heart, *At last! This is what I have been waiting for. Here is quality.* The pale, intense, heart-shaped little face was innocent of make-up, framed in a whirl of blond hair which hung to her shoulders, like a child's.

"I'd know you anywhere!" said Maggie, going forward to shake hands enthusiastically. "You look just the way you did in *Ballade for Dead Ladies* and *Echo*—my two favorite pictures of all time."

Before acknowledging the greeting, Enid simply stood a moment, framed in the doorway, drew in a deep breath, and, clapping her hands pattycake fashion, exclaimed, "Grumpin, darling! Look! *Books*!" Her husband, a large red-faced tweedy sort of country squire joined her as they both came forward. As she shook hands with Maggie, Enid said,

"I fancy you must think me frightfully rude. But I'd really not expected books in Hollywood. How lahvly! You have our Trollope."

Maggie was only too happy to explain, all smiles, "You mustn't think of our house as 'Hollywood.' We aren't, you know. We've only been here a very short time."

"You're English, surely?"

"No. Boston."

The silky hair was flung back, the little pointed chin thrown in the air, and a gay ripple of laughter which would pass for silver spilled out. "Ah, now I see why Ray's doing *The Bostonians*! I shall come to you for advice on my characterization. May I?"

Here was response to fill Maggie's hunger. "Please! I adore being used as a guinea pig. And Ray will tell you I'm one with even a glimmering of intelligence!"

They all laughed with the ease of old friends.

Cocktails and dinner were cozy as cozy. After dinner Maggie lighted a fire and put a cushion at Enid's back. "Here, now, pretend that you're really at home," she said.

Enid picked up the cushion, plopped it on the floor, and herself on top of it, with her knees clasped in her arms. "What heaven, Maggie" (they had got onto first names with the lobster bisque) "—books and an open fah, and I'm sure you'll let my Grumpin have his pipe. Grumpin, darling, come and sit beside me on the carpet, and—like who was it in Dickens?—let's look at pictures in the fah."

Grumpin, rather like an obedient retriever who has been told to charge, gave a grunt and, lumbering to her side, lowered himself to the floor. Lacking a choke collar to tighten about his neck, Enid buried her sharp little chin into the padded shoulder of his Harris tweed and held it there.

"Oh, darling, I see us all so happy in California in our Seven Dwarfs Cottage—you, and The Dumpling, and Nanny, and I." Now she buried her nose in the tweed, and then, first ruffling it up the back of his head with her hand, she buried it in his—Maggie could not help observing—rather oily hair.

She turned to Maggie. "I hope you don't mind our going on a bit. Grumpin and I have been married seven years, and every day we wake up and say to each other, 'Perhaps *this* is going to be the last day of our honeymoon,' and do you know it's too *extrawdnry*, it hasn't ended yet!"

Maggie laughed good-naturedly. "Don't mind us," she said. "We haven't been married a year ourselves."

"Darlings! What heaven! What fun we'll have—just the four of us! Oh, I do see a picture in the fah of just the four of us having frightful fun together and letting the rest of Hollywood go hang."

"Do you like your little house?" asked Maggie.

"Darling, I couldn't like it more. The moment I saw it I said, 'It's simply *us*,' didn't I, Grumpin?"

"Rath*er*."

"It *is*, actually, rather like our little house in the Cotswolds which we call The Smidgin, as it *is*, actually nothing more than a smidgin of a house. It was dear funny Nanny who was quite heartbroken at our not having a swimming bath, as she'd quite set her heart, poor lamb, on writing home about how very grand she was in Hollywood. Hahver, perhaps one day when we're all veddy grand, we may have one. It's only my poor Grumpin who does so depend on his game of tennis. I had rather hoped for him, as I'm away so much at the studio, that there might be a tennis court. Yes, I do see one picture in the fah which is a house with a swimming bath, and a tennis court, *and* a garden where we might have real English tennis parties on Sunday afternoons, with tea and hot scones. Do I see that picture in Pacific Palisades?" The little white face turned to Ray. "Isn't that where the really big stars do live—*ecc*tually?"

Ray agreed that many of them did.

"My dear good old Grumpin will never ask for a thing for himself, and of course I think it's too absurd to bother where one lives, but, Ray, since without you there'd be no picture, perhaps you could just say to them at the studio that I'm rather uncertain about my performance if I have to worry about my poor old Grumpin at home, with no garden and no court."

"And no pool?" put in Maggie.

"Well, a swim is fun after tennis, isn't it? I know they simply grow like gooseberries here, so perhaps let's just say a court, a garden, and a pool. I'm sure there'd be no trouble about getting someone else to take on the Seven Dwarfs cottage, because it is too *sweet*. And since moving is such a bore, and so distracting when one's working, don't you think it might be better all round—I mean for the sake of the picture—that the studio moves us straight away?"

The picture Ray saw in the fire made him clear his throat, get up and say, "Well, we'll have to see about that. How about another drink?"

When the glasses were filled all around Enid again turned to her husband and said, "Grumpin, darling, you tell what pictures you see in the fah."

"I don't know that I see much of anything, you know."

"Oh, Grumpin, *darling*. But you do! Don't you see a picture of that billing you were talking about? *Tell* Ray, my sweet."

"Oh, yes, quite. Why . . . er . . . as a matter of fact it's the question of billing for the picture. Enid feels rather strongly—"

"Grumpin, it was *your* idea." The chin sank deeper into the tweed.

"Quite, quite. Well, as we were saying, it's the question of billing. Enid . . . er . . . I don't feel that Enid and Natalie Davidge should have just the same billing, don't you know?"

"Darling old Nat," purred Enid. "Over here you probably don't quite realize what a national institution she is. She's been in simply film after film but has become what we call in England a hack. It's natural for her, poor pet, to feel that her name is a big one. And, quite frankly, darling, she doesn't seem to understand how much bigger my name is than hers." The pictures in the fire now were making Enid's eyes dance ever so prettily. "My draw in Europe is quite extrawdnry—quite as large as Michele Morgan's—and in the States—well, you know yourself, darling, I've been on the cover of *Life*, and when has old Nat been anywhere near that?"

"I'm sorry you feel that way," Ray murmured uncomfortably, "but after all that sort of thing is arranged by the agents, and I'm sure

Natalie Davidge's agent must have got the thing set before she left England."

"I know, but that's what's so unfair, because you can't realize over here how—well, darling, I don't mean to sound unkind, but old Nat is a bit of a joke with us. And it *is* possible that I'll have to tell Chelek I simply can't give the sort of performance he will expect from me unless something is done to change that billing. I mean to say, either one is the star of a film or one's not, and it's impossible to have two stars. You do see my point, don't you?"

Ray saw the point of her chin as it lifted toward him like a sharp little lance, to do battle.

"Come on," he said without conviction. "I've been telling Maggie here that she was going to have one Hollywood evening that wasn't business. The picture I see in the fire is her giving me hell once we're alone together."

When Enid and Grumpin had left, by midnight, Ray came to Maggie.

"Ah, Mag, I apologize, darling. There goes a girl friend glimmering." He took her in his arms, and they laughed together.

The next day Maggie received a sheaf of lilies with a card enclosed reading, "I can't tell you, darling, what a difference it makes to have found *you* in Hollywood!" The message was signed, "Fondly, E."

Maggie did not see Enid again, but perhaps that was because soon afterward she moved to Pacific Palisades. Presently Maggie heard through Ray that Grumpin had returned to England. It was not until Maggie was no longer living in Hollywood that she read of Enid Forrest's marriage to Anton Chelek.

Maggie's growing sense of isolation increased, rather than decreased, with time. If only there were just one person in Hollywood who knew, as she told herself, who she *was*. Uncertain for the first time in her life as to her own identity, Maggie resorted to a direct attack on Ray's way of life. Something must be responsible for her own *malaise*, something outside herself.

Almost insensibly the Masters formed the habit, after leaving an evening party, of indulging in an altercation, generally precipitated by Maggie. The course of these exchanges ran true to pattern.

"What a dreadful evening!" was Maggie's opening volley.

"Aw, honey, come on. I didn't see anything wrong with it." Ray, washed into a lambent frame of mind by the intake of plenty of alcohol, would give a sudden and rather aimless guffaw. "It undoubtedly wasn't much like Boston's upper crust, if that's what you're missing."

"You know very well I'm missing no such thing. But I will say, in Boston they can ask a stranger some other question than 'What do you do in pictures?' "

"O.K. Here they ask, 'What do you do?' There they ask, 'Who are you?' Obviously you prefer the latter."

"I *don't*! It's just that the yardstick here seems—well, so crude."

"Wait a minute. Wait a minute. If some of my studio colleagues here came to Boston, would your father take them to lunch at the Somerset Club?" He could read the answer on her face. "The inner circle here just happens to be interested in something besides family."

Without thinking, out would pop Maggie's answer. "They're certainly interested in something besides me!"

"Don't tell me you're miffed, darling, because you weren't the center of attention?"

"I don't know how you can have any idea of whether I was the center of attention or not. You seemed to be in conference all evening and certainly couldn't notice what was happening to anybody else."

"It's not fair, Margot, to blame a bunch of craftsmen—artists, whatever you want to call them—for talking shop when they get together. I thought you were interested in pictures."

"I am. But I'm interested in a few other things too." Maggie could think of nothing further to say—until the next time.

About the end of their second November in Hollywood, Ray came home one afternoon earlier than usual. Without waiting to give Maggie her evening kiss or attempting to soften the blow, he simply announced, with bravado, in a voice that told her he'd been drinking, "Chelek is out on his ear."

"What do you mean? How can they *do* such a thing!" There was no answer. "Did you have no idea of it?" Maggie moved vaguely toward Ray, as he showed no sign of coming farther into the room.

"There's been a lot of gossip at the writers' table for some time. I didn't want to tell you till I knew for sure."

"What does it mean?"

"It means that I go too. I'm known as his man."

Maggie sauntered with deliberate casualness to the sofa, where she sat down and lighted a cigarette. She addressed her next remark to the center of the ring of smoke which floated from her lips, her tone of voice pleasantly detached and affable.

"You know the funny thing is, Ray, that this may be a blessing in disguise. You may find something you like much better—something—" she paused serenely to let another ring sail away—"not in Hollywood, something back in New York." It was hard to keep the excitement out of her voice.

Ray's eyebrows shot up as he came forward to slump into a chair beside her. He appeared, in the quick look he turned on her, to measure the weight of the opposition she was capable of offering.

"So," he said at last. "You're trying to get me out of Hollywood."

"I'm not trying to do anything except to see that you don't let yourself be ruined as a creative artist."

"By what right can you make such a snide crack? I haven't completed my first picture, and here you are telling me I'm through."

"I'm not! I'm just telling you to watch where you're going."

"It looks like maybe I don't have to. Maybe you're doing the watching for two."

"I don't intend to sit by and watch you go downhill."

"Look here. Let's get this straight. Are you talking about my work or my social life?"

"It's impossible to discuss anything with you rationally if you're going to be sarcastic. You know I'm not worried about your 'social life.' I'm worried about . . . about . . . well, call them your associations. They're cheap, that's all."

"Maybe it's yours that are worrying you. I'm not crabbing."

"Nobody's crabbing. I'm just trying to think of your own good."

"Huh. Where have I heard that before? I'm quite capable of looking after my own good, thank you."

"Oh—" her voice was faint with temper— "so you mean that I remind you of Alice?"

Ray spoke in a suspiciously conciliatory tone. "I've been tactless, Margot, and I'm sorry. It was a rough trick, just blurting out a piece of news like that to you, without any preparation first. Actually, there's no need for either of us to go off the deep end. It makes me superstitious to talk about possibilities before they jell. But there really is the chance of something damn good coming my way, and fairly soon, too. Believe me, as soon as I know anything definite we'll talk it over."

"May I ask if it's in Hollywood or New York?"

"How could it be in New York?" The same savage unpleasantness was back in his voice. "Who's talking about New York anyway? I've made my break, and there's nothing that could take me back."

It was that evening that Maggie wrote:

Dear Nini:

You're the only friend I can turn to. I've got to produce an alternative, quick, in New York to Ray's most unsatisfactory set-up here; but naturally it mustn't look as though it came from me. I know that Dick has so many of the big advertising men as clients—even some of Ray's old D.D.D & T. colleagues—don't you think one of them might come up with something? Naturally, I don't mean in the same office, because wild horses wouldn't get Ray back into that harness again, but surely they know of things that are going on in other fields where Ray's gifts might be used. Here he is utterly wasted, and though I know he'd *kill* me if he knew I were writing like this, still I can't bear just sitting by without *doing* something which will really be for his own good. . . .

19

"Margot! Hurry up or we'll be late!"

Ray stood at the front door as Maggie, still in the bedroom, hovered for one last moment before her dressing table, spraying perfume first behind one ear, then behind the other. She was determined not to be bullied out of a festive mood. Chelek was giving a big party, she adored her new dress, and, besides, Christmas Eve was her favorite evening of all the year. She simply refused to acknowledge the mess that lay about her on the bedroom floor. Along with the familiar stage properties of opened cold-cream jars, wads of greasy tissue, silk stockings, and far-flung lingerie, there was a generous contribution supplied by Ray—odd socks, shoes, discarded shirts, soiled handkerchiefs, and inadequate neckties. With Alice and Dexter three thousand miles away there was no one to pick up the debris.

The first Christmas of their marriage Ray had borne Maggie off to the desert. In the somnambulistic trance of a honeymoon whose end she could not bear to admit, it would have made little difference if he had taken her to an igloo instead of the Desert Inn at Palm Springs. This Christmas, however, they were to be together in their own house. Maggie told herself what fun it was going to be. All the same her spirits would have been considerably lighter if her letter to Nini had yielded fruit. She had received merely a short note in reply, saying she would do what she could, but of course with these Brain Trusters in Washington she wouldn't be in the least surprised if they all ended up in the poorhouse; jobs weren't easy to find.

Ray had not mentioned his last days at the studio, which were to expire with the year, nor had he referred again to the mysterious and exciting possibility that was in the works. To evade any danger of a repetition of their painful disagreement he and Maggie had assiduously avoided any talk of business. With Christmas in the air it had not actually been too difficult.

As they drove to the Chelek party through Beverly Hills, although one lobe of Maggie's brain was all attention for the scene before her, another was sharply contrasting that scene with all the Christmas Eves she had known before. Ray was obliged to put his Cadillac into low gear to accommodate his pace to that of the crawling traffic with its loads of sight-seers. These peered reverently at a group of white reindeer, keeping watch under a cluster of chartreuse and "aqua" Christmas trees at the door of Abraham Lincoln's old Kentucky log cabin, across the street from Diane de Poitier's château, down one of whose chimneys, lighted by floodlights on the sidewalk below, a larger-than-life-size papier-mâché Santa Claus had already flung one leg. Out of the pipe in his mouth at regular intervals there floated iridescent soap bubbles onto the awe-struck upturned faces of the onlookers beneath. Dressed in "chubbies," wedgies, babushkas, and slacks, their jaws rotated rhythmically over their gum, as the sheep in the fields of Bethlehem must have chewed their cud in full view of the heavenly vision.

How different from Christmas Eve on Beacon Hill! How could she conceivably be anywhere else in the world on this magical night?

She and Roger, as children, had been allowed to stay up and accompany their parents, each holding a hand of each, as they wandered up and down the streets of Beacon Hill in the first darkness of evening, which on that one date of all the year was so cruelly coquettish about putting in an appearance. Every house had its shades up and was lighted from within by the light of candles in the windows—all real candles in those days, showing interiors that did not so much call for (they were too hushed for that) as invite a contemporary Holbein to come and record them before it was too late. The soft flickering light, edged with encroaching shadows, brought into relief good books, fine furniture, handsome paintings, sparkling glass, and gleaming china. These inanimate objects seemed to exist not so much for any utilitarian purpose as to offer a suitable frame for the regulated lives of which they themselves were a part taken sublimely for granted.

In those faraway days, weeks of work preceded the singing on Christmas Eve. Which of her father's friends was it—the distinguished medieval architect, Ralph Adams Cram, or Dr. Richard Cabot—who had had the inspiration in the first place? She could still remember Dr. Cabot standing on the front steps of a Mt. Vernon Street brick house, with a flickering lantern held aloft with which to beat time, his head with its characteristic tilt to one side, blowing on his tuning fork to give the pitch to his faithful band. There was no sound anywhere on the street, among the small and attentive groups of listeners, until, clear and sweet, the voices sounded, "Silent Night, Holy Night." When the repertoire was completed, the owner of the house, and close friend or relative of the singers, would open the door and come out onto the top step and call, "Thank you! Merry Christmas!" before the carollers quickly trudged off to another rendezvous. By some miraculous law of nature it seemed to Maggie, looking back, that it almost always began to snow on Christmas Eve just as the singers set out. She could remember the hush and thrill in watching the first quiet snowflakes float down in the cold night to be blown about by the festoons of icy breath garlanded about the singers. Tomorrow would be Christmas!

What were they all doing on Beacon Hill right now, right this minute? she wondered. Priscilla was probably trailing around after the Bradfields as she and Roger had once trailed after their parents. Of late years the whole Christmas Eve ritual on Beacon Hill had become so publicized and debased that many of the old families had come to dread the evening, with its hordes of suburban sight-seers and teen-age rowdies stamping through the streets, roaring out any carols that happened to come into their heads. Louisburg Square was always the storm center of these untamed forces. While "Good King Wenceslas" was being yelled in full voice on one side of the square, "The First Noel" was being bellowed forth from the other. In this disorganized bedlam the Bradfield family had come to be known as an institution. Dexter joined the clan as its members came up from Dunster or in from Milton. There were Sarge, Marsh, Kitten, Aunt Katta, Ma, and Pa, all wearing red mittens, red mufflers, and galoshes, the family symbol of good cheer and good health. They made no concession to "popular" taste in the program they offered, drawn from a selection of medieval French and early English Christmas music. The program had been rehearsed with such loving care over the whole year that its delivery caused a hush of awe even among the noisiest street revelers, and the family found itself like a sort of amalgamated Pied Piper, trailed from corner to corner through their evening itinerary, the end of each selection drawing forth spontaneous hand clapping from their followers. Maggie, as Dexter's wife, had shown no compunction in making fun of the seriousness with which the family took themselves, utterly lacking self-consciousness as they closed their eyes and knocked their stocking-capped heads together in that ecstasy of concentration known only to amateur choral singers. It amused her, as well, to witness the spectacle of such a stalwart Unitarian, if not downright agnostic, tribe flinging itself with such proprietary abandon into the proclamation, in its most orthodox idiom, of the Incarnation. . . .

"Well, are you impressed?" The car door slammed. They had reached their destination. Ray was handing over his car keys to the boy in charge of parking, and was speaking to her. Maggie did not hear. Roger's words echoed in her ears—*You'd miss it all more than you realize.*

"How late do we have to stay, Ray?" Maggie asked in a small voice, and abruptly reached for her husband's hand.

"That's *one* question I've never heard you ask! Is something wrong, darling? Are you sick?" Ray drew her toward him solicitously.

"No. Yes. I don't know. I just feel sort of funny" was as close to a self-diagnosis of homesickness as Maggie was capable of achieving.

The sight of her host was no restorative. In white dinner jacket and cummerbund he was receiving his guests by the brink of his swimming pool. The pool was lighted by floodlights and reflected not only the brilliant jewels and mink of the women but the façade of the temple of the Ptolemies that Chelek called home. Somewhere from back of the five-car garage floated the strains of Schubert's "Ave Maria." A white-coated bartender in the foreground was gyrating a cocktail shaker over his head in rhythm to its strains.

Chelek greeted the Masters, saying to Maggie, "You'll know everybody. It's a strictly studio affair. Just because it's my swan song is no reason for not making merry."

Maggie, eyeing the columns of the huge mansion, so different from the houses she had tenderly peered into in her recent vision of home, asked politely, "What are your columns made of, Mr. Chelek? Are they marble, plaster, or wood?"

Chelek flicked one beside him with a manicured thumbnail. "Thinsetic," he said.

It was almost noon when Maggie opened her eyes on Christmas morning. She had drunk too much champagne the night before. It was the champagne that must have been responsible for bringing on another spat with Ray. Echoes of it still buzzed in her heavy head.

Maggie couldn't remember much of what they had said to each other following the usual unpleasant interchange. Maggie vs. Hollywood—the cause of the scrimmage was the same. She did know, however, that when they reached home, both thoroughly angry, the sight of the familiar room, with its frosting of Christmas joy, confronted her as a rebuke. Unconsciously, she had placed herself under a spray of mistletoe in the doorway. Ray, seeing her framed as she was, without words advanced on her and almost roughly took her in his arms and kissed her with passion.

"Come to bed, sweetheart," he murmured urgently, his breath warm against her open lips. "There's nothing wrong with either of us that being in bed together won't fix."

Maggie stretched. Heigh-ho. After all, today was another day, and not just any old day at that. It was Christmas! Now, Ray waking too, they exchanged a rather rueful yuletide kiss and presently toasted each other in Alka-Seltzer.

With cups of black coffee to reinforce them, dressed in their wrappers, they opened the stockings that Maggie had hung on the mantelpiece the last thing before turning out the light the night before. After skimming the cream of useless knickknacks, jokes, and fripperies, Maggie, with a sense of the recurring thrill of past Christmases, turned to the business of unwrapping some of the more impressive-looking packages.

Presently, over the ruins of paper, boxes, and curling ribbons her new radio-phonograph floated the strains of the "*Valse des Fleurs*" from *The Nutcracker Suite*. Abandoning herself to the rhythm set by Stokowski and the Philadelphia Orchestra, Maggie, flinging her arms wide, swirled about the room in a new pale-yellow satin negligee.

"I'm feeling better by the minute! I suppose I should be thinking of dressing."

"Wait a minute." Ray spoke with a flicker of belligerence. "You're not going to drag me anywhere today, I hope?"

"Drag you? Why should I? And where?"

"I don't know. Christmas is always rush, rush, rush. Alice is forever—"

Maggie cut him short. "Never fear. Nobody expects us anywhere today. We expect nobody. We're in Hollywood. Remember? And we have no families."

"Nirvana. It suits me fine. Look, how's about cocktails on the patio?"

"Already?"

"The sooner the quicker I can get a little of the tail of that dog."

Maggie had let Mrs. Maitland go for the day, leaving behind her a stuffed turkey to be put in the oven for dinner. The lack of routine or obligation suddenly appeared delicious.

"We'll have champagne cocktails," she announced, "and caviar and *pâté de foie gras*—all courtesy of the studio!"

A little later they were rocking back and forth on the hammock outdoors in the sunshine. The warmth had brought out the scent of the gardenia blossoms; a hummingbird buzzed among them. Ray was wearing a bright aloha shirt, open at the neck, and sandals on his feet. Maggie's Christmas present—a heavy gold-link bracelet and watch which told the month and day as well as the hour—showed to advantage on his brown wrist. He lifted his glass toward Maggie, who was dressed in a pair of navy-blue slacks and a pale-blue hand-tailored shirt.

"To Christmas cheer, southern California style, free of fuss, friends and family!"

They ate off trays on their laps from an array spread on a glass-topped table before them—fruit, salad, cheese, plum pudding, and *marrons glacés*. The warmth of the sun, the tingle of the champagne, their closeness to each other worked on the flesh and spirits of both: a delicious amorous sleepiness claimed them. When the last *marron* had been washed down by champagne they returned inside to the darkened bedroom and the still unmade bed.

When they returned to the living room nobody had picked up the mess, nor had anyone washed the dishes. Maggie, turning in disgust from the wreckage, went back to the bedroom to complete the long-distance telephone call she had placed earlier in the day. Presently the magic carpet of imagination had done its work. Rocky Mountains, prairies, and rivers were spanned, and she was in the pantry of her parents' house on Brimmer Street.

"Mother?" she quavered into space. In spite of herself her voice gave a telltale break.

"Maggie, *darling*! Merry Christmas!"

Then came the pearls of dialogue, valued at more than a dollar a minute. For all the feeling behind them, as they popped into place, the completed strand did not differ, either in originality or inspiration, from other strands being strung that night from coast to coast.

Mother and daughter called back and forth to each other in unnecessarily high-pitched voices.

"How *are* you, dear?" called Mrs. Fraser.

"I'm fine! How are you?"

"We're fine! It's wonderful to hear you! What's the weather like out there?"

"We had our lunch outdoors."

"I can't believe it! It began snowing here last evening, and it's been snowing all day."

"Really? I wish I could see it."

"Isn't it wonderful to be talking! You sound just as though you were in the next room!"

"What? I can't hear you!"

"I said you sound just as though you were in the next room!"

"Oh."

"We certainly wish we could see all that wonderful sunshine! Darling, your father and I are thrilled with our presents! You were much too generous!"

"Don't be silly."

"She's right here, dear. She's dying to talk to you. I'll put her on, shall I?"

There seemed to be some sort of shuffling at the other end. Then, unexpectedly there was her father's deep voice.

"Hello, Mag. I just wanted to put in a word. No matter what money Ray is making he'll be broke after this call, so I'll leave the talking to you women. I just wanted to say Merry Christmas."

"Oh, Father, it's wonderful to hear you. Merry Christmas to you, too."

Then came the sound of further shuffling. After a little pause she heard a third voice, as tiny as that of the third bear.

"Hello," it said flatly into the unhearing ether.

"Baby!" The word Maggie had not used for years bubbled up spontaneously. Then, unconsciously echoing her own mother's words to her, Maggie asked, "How *are* you, dear?"

"Fine." Another pause. "Thank you for all those presents. I loved them."

"*Did* you, Priscilla?" Remembering how her child had always loathed *baby*, Maggie reinstated her promptly in her proper rank. "I'm glad, darling. I should have loved to have sent you a whole lot more."

The wire carried a thin little laugh. "I guess there weren't any left after you bought all those."

"The picture of you and Silly is perfect. Did you really make the calendar yourself?"

"Well, Daddy took the picture, but I pasted it on and did the lettering."

"Well, I just love it. I have it on my bureau."

Maggie felt the longing to probe a little beneath the surface on which she and her child were cutting such conventionally acceptable figures. She wanted to know where Dexter was this very minute, and what he had been feeling all day.

All she dared venture in the way of exploration was "Did you have a nice day, dear? What have you been doing?"

"I went out to Milton for lunch—" the hesitation was fractional—"with Daddy."

"I'm glad. How is—how is everybody?"

"Oh, fine."

"Well, darling, it's wonderful to talk to you, but I guess I'd better say good night to Grandma before I hang up. Put her back on the telephone, will you? I'll write you, dear, and you write me, won't you? I love to get your letters."

"O.K. Here's Grandma."

There was her mother's voice again. "It's been lovely to talk to you, Maggie dear. I suppose we must hang up now."

Neither seemed to want to be the first to snap the thread that held them. "We miss you, dear child."

The words, a little tremulous, were not completed before the answer was gulped out, "And I miss you!"

Maggie hung up the receiver and buried her face in her hands.

From the living room she could hear Ray calling her. His voice was warm and loving. "Come in here, honey. I have something to tell you. Something nice."

Maggie wiped her eyes guiltily and put an ineffective dab of powder on her nose before she joined him.

"Come sit beside me," said Ray, holding out a hand and moving over to make room beside him. "I have a nice surprise for you."

"Really? What is it?"

Her husband smiled as the sun burst out from behind the clouds. "I told you I was superstitious, and I suppose I shouldn't tell you till it's finally in the bag, legal papers signed and all the rest of it, but the hell with superstition."

"I can't bear the suspense, Ray! What is it?"

"It's a dream come true, Margot, for any creative writer in this place. I'm one of three who are forming our own independent producing unit. Chelek's to be the producer, and Ralph Gerber, the smartest director in Hollywood, is leaving Global to come in with us; he has been able to get the necessary financing. I'm in charge of the whole writing end, on a guaranteed salary basis—*with* percentage, mind you—to do at least three original screenplays a year, with a very good likelihood of more if I want them."

"That's wonderful, darling! That's really wonderful," she repeated with only a little less enthusiasm.

Ray reached into his pocket and produced a letter. "It certainly makes this easy to answer," he said, handing it to her.

Maggie opened the enevelope. The letter, written on Stembler and Reed stationery, with a Park Avenue address, read:

Dear Mr. Masters:

We understand from our good friends the Golden Oil Company that you may be returning to New York in the near future. They have expressed an interest in your producing their Stage Classics radio program. The program is to be considerably widened in scope and expanded to a running time of an hour and a half weekly. It therefore is a spot for which they want the top talent—executive as well as literary.

As we handle the G.O.C. account we should ourselves like to talk the matter over with you personally.

May we hear from you as to the chances of your being in New York in the near future?

Very truly yours,

Maggie did not stop to read the signature before she exploded, "But, Ray, *darling*, you won't turn them down without knowing what the job is?"

"Sure I will. Besides, I have a damn good idea just what it is. I'm not interested, period. Why should I want to get myself ulcers adapting Shakespeare, Ibsen and Shaw for radio when I have a chance here to do my own writing for pictures?"

"Yes, but, Ray, out here it's not really *writing*."

"What do you mean, it's not writing?"

"Well, I mean it isn't a book, or even a play that anybody *sees*."

"So nobody sees pictures—is that your idea?"

"Don't be so literal, Ray. You know what I mean. You owe it to yourself to go on to New York and simply listen to what they have to say to you. All you have to do is listen."

"I tell you, honey, the contracts are in the works. They'll be ready to sign before the end of the week. It's a waste of time, of money, and of energy. I know what I want—this is it. Once, long ago, I thought I might be a poet, or at least a serious writer. Now my sights are lower, but can't you understand, Margot, I'm still interested in expressing the little spark of creation that I hope still burns in me? It seems I have a sort of natural flair for situation, dialogue, character. This is my chance to prove whether I can create something original out of the gifts I have. How *could* I want to go back to a job of hack editing? What gets me is where Stembler and Reed ever got the idea that I was planning to come back to New York. Everyone who knows me knows it's the last thing I plan to do. It all sounds pretty damned phony to me."

Maggie spoke with the sweet reasonableness born of determination. "But, darling, if you're so sure this setup is right for you, then you're in a very strong position! It means the New York people would have to offer you something terrific to make you even consider it. Surely you would dare just to listen to them."

"Don't be crazy! Of course I dare. I'm merely talking sense, that's all. Dollars and sense, if you want. Why spend all that money for a trip east?"

"Because I want to go with you, darling. *Please!* Let's just swoop down out of the skies and surprise our families and friends!" Maggie became moved to a new pitch of intensity by her own eloquence. "It would be *fun*—to see some plays and have a change. We'd only have to stay a couple of days, darling. Tell Chelek you have a highly nervous wife who has set her heart on a trip east. You'll sign their agreement when you come back. It's important, Ray. I know it is. *Please.*"

"Important to whom?"

"Well, then, to *me.*" All that was feminine and appealing was written in her eyes and her features. Her husband looked at Maggie *imperatrix* become suddenly suppliant. Her very body seemed to soften with her eyes, in whose depths he could read the promise of undreamed-of gentleness and gratitude. She did not command or exhort. In a voice Ray had never heard before from her, Maggie softly beseeched. Reaching for his hand, she pressed it to her beating heart, murmuring, "Just one more Christmas present. Please, darling. Say yes."

20

A WEEK later Maggie ran up the steps of her parents' Brimmer Street house, turned her own key in the front lock, and swept into the front hall, dropping her pocketbook, throwing open her coat, and calling out, "Yoo-hoo! Mother! Father! Here I am!" with all the breathless triumph of a channel swimmer. She had just parted from Ray at the North Station, on his way to spend Sunday with Skipper at boarding school in New Hampshire. The very name Masters was forgotten. She was Maggie Fraser again.

Her mother hurried down the stairs, arms outstretched to welcome her in an embrace as tender as it was complete. Dr. Fraser stood on the landing at the head of the stairs and let his daughter come to him. "How's the Hollywood glamour girl?" he asked.

"Oh, Father, don't be silly!"

Maggie turned suddenly from him so that he might not see the tears in her eyes. Something was wrong about this home-coming. She had looked forward to it as a child to her own birthday party, but somehow the candles hadn't taken light. In one look she saw, to her surprise, that both her parents had aged. Her father was a little paler and a little balder at the temples. Her mother seemed to have dwindled in size, even as the front hall itself had dwindled. The illusion lasted only for a minute, and presently they were having tea together in the library, questions and answers popping simultaneously.

"Let's look at you!" both parents said almost in unison.

Maggie, wearing her first mink coat, thrown back from her shoulders to show a bright coral dress, with two large gold clips at the neckline and two heavy gold-link bracelets at her wrist, looked for one thing simply—richer. She had put on weight: Hollywood's good food, Hollywood's basking in the sunshine, Hollywood's early hours for going to bed (Maggie, exempt from the discipline which forced actresses onto the set, made up and ready for work at nine o'clock, had been privileged to lie in bed late in the mornings as well)—all had done their share. Very likely without any of them sheer sexual satisfaction alone would have accounted for a certain florid look.

Both Dr. and Mrs. Fraser exclaimed on her appearance, how happy, how handsome she was looking, until her mother hurried on to say, "Priscilla will be here presently, dear. She's spending the night with us. She was going home from school to pick up her bag. I'm so anxious to know if you think she's changed enormously."

"Two years—oh, I expect she has." The suspense was making her nervous. Maggie could feel that both her parents, too, rather dreaded the impending meeting. It was a relief when the doorbell rang. This time it was Maggie herself, as mother, who ran down the stairs to open the door. There, on the step, self-contained, with a small valise in her red woolen-gloved fingers, stood Priscilla. She wore a dark-blue reefer with brass buttons, white socks and brown shoes; her arms and legs looked longer and skinnier than Maggie had been prepared for. Maggie opened her arms wide, clasped the scrawny little figure tight, feeling the brass buttons bite into her own flesh, and smothered her with kisses.

"Oh, baby! My precious baby! Priscilla, darling, I can't believe it! Come in, come in out of the cold, dear."

She closed the outside door behind them and flew at her for another kiss, then held her off at arm's length.

"But, darling, how you've grown! Look! You're up to my shoulder. Aren't you much taller than the other girls in your class?"

"Not much. Some, I guess."

Maggie called up to her mother, who was standing at the head of the stairs, "She looks so like a Bradfield I can't get over it!"

Her mother smiled down on them both. "That's what everyone says."

"I don't feel as though I'd had a thing to do with you, darling. I hope you believe I *am* your mother!" The little fledgling of humor didn't quite get off the ground.

The next hour between mother and daughter, alone up on the third floor, passed happily on both sides. Maggie pulled out a dress and two sweaters from Magnin's for Priscilla and helped her try them on. There were two telltale spots of color on the little girl's usually pale cheeks. Here was her mother at last, close by, to touch and to listen to. On the bureau she picked up a bottle of her perfume, took out the cork, and sniffed deeply. "I haven't smelled that since you went away, Mummy. I just love that smell."

"So do I! I'm glad you remember it, dear."

"I remember a lot of things. Have you still got that flannel cover to your hot-water bottle with a kitten's face on top?"

"Oh, dear, I'm afraid not!"

Priscilla stood alongside the still half-full valise and looked ruminatively at its untidy contents. "Those must be new bed slippers, with that pink fluffy stuff on them. I don't remember those."

"Well, in two years, I should hope I would have a new pair!"

As she unpacked and took off her dress to change for dinner Maggie questioned Priscilla about school, her friends, and her riding lessons.

"Oh, I like my riding better than anything else I do. Nancy goes with me now every Saturday."

"Who's Nancy?"

"She's my best friend."

"Do I know her?"

"Oh, I guess you don't. She was new at school last winter."

"And do you still like that nice mathematics teacher as much as ever?"

"Oh, yes. I hope you won't mind, Mummy, but I'll have to do my homework after supper."

"Of course you will, darling. I don't want you to make any change in your ordinary schedule because I'm here."

Dinner was fairly gay. Her father opened a bottle of champagne in Maggie's honor. Maggie had written her parents to say nothing in Priscilla's presence about the possibility of her returning east to live, so the conversation was deliberately focused on Priscilla's activities and interests. There were jokes and references between her and her grandparents that Maggie did not follow, but she was so determined not to feel a stranger that she joined in, asking questions and expressing an almost too eager interest in everything they touched on. Dinner over, Priscilla retired upstairs to do her homework.

Maggie, turning back to her parents, said, "Now I must call Kitten and Roger to fix up a time for seeing them. I can't wait to see the new house. A modern house on Milton Hill really should be worth the price of admission!"

In a minute the former sisters-in-law were exclaiming rapturously over their delight in hearing each other's voice.

Maggie bubbled, "Kitten, darling, I can't wait to see you all, *and* the house! When is it going to be convenient for me to come out?"

There was a split second of hesitation before Kitten answered, "We'll talk about it tomorrow. I have to come in to town with two of the children—Kim and Braddy—for dentist's appointments. Roger'll drop in after work to your mother's house, and I'll come along and join you both there."

"How would it be if I drove out with you, and maybe spent the night, and then we could all have the evening together?"

"We're going out to dinner, I'm afraid. We'll talk about it, Mag. Look, could I speak to your mother a minute? I want to tell her something about some shoes I tried to exchange for Priscilla."

Maggie, feeling she had been all but brushed out of the telephone, could hear them pick up a subject they obviously had been over many times before. "Didn't they have them in double-A?" she could hear her mother ask. Maggie began to talk to her father in an unnaturally loud tone of voice to drown out the sound of the two women discussing details of the burden of fitting out her child with shoes.

Kitten arrived the next afternoon, a little bedraggled from shopping downtown and coping with two squirming, now both thoroughly irascible, boys at the dentist's, her hat on the back of her head, revealing her golden hair fading out to drab. There followed after the first warmth of meeting the inevitable comparison of children's heights, past and present, hailed with cries of incredulity and congratulation, between escorted trips to the bathroom and to the pantry for milk and cookies. Afterward Kitten fished down from its special shelf in the library the box of toys kept by Grandma for just such incursions. Then she and Maggie crossed the hall into the living room to be by themselves.

"Now, let me look at you," said Kitten, sinking down into a chair and reaching for a cigarette. "Oh, Mag, it's good to see you." And then, as though the barrier of Maggie's remarriage had never existed, she said simply, "You'll never know how I've missed you."

"With four children? Darling, don't tell me you have time to think of yourself, let alone anyone else!"

"You'd be surprised what I have time to think about. Tell me—" she went at once into the subject which was clearly paramount with her—"how does Priscilla seem to you? I love her like one of my own, and then she's our only girl in the family."

"I gather, poor darling, you're doing all sorts of dismal errands for her. Soon she should learn to do some of them herself. Mother says you've been simply angelic coping with her."

"It's nothing, and both her grandmothers are a little old to bother too much over fussy little things." Maggie did not know whether to bless or writhe at the forbearance that did not add, *Somebody has to.* Kitten went on. "Tell me how she seemed to you."

"She seems fine. At first I was afraid she was going to be shy with me, but I could tell, by the light of her eyes and the spots of color in her cheeks—oh, I could tell she was glad to see me." There were lights in Maggie's eyes, and her own cheeks flushed as she spoke.

"She talks about you, Mag. I know she thinks about you all the time. She always shows off the things you send her. She keeps your letters in a special little leather box on her desk, and Dexter says she herself is the one who says, regularly every Sunday, 'Now I'm going to write to Mummy.' She's a faithful little soul."

"Look, Kitten," Maggie brought out abruptly, "our plans are uncertain, but probably Mother has told you there's a good chance of our coming back to New York to live. I'm sure Ray is going to see that it's the sensible thing to do. If we do, may I count on you for one thing?" Before Kitten had time for assent or dissent she hurried on. "Use your influence to see that Priscilla is allowed to come to New York for at least one school holiday each winter—*not* to stay with me, but at a hotel, with either Mother or Father. If one of them brings her it's certainly none of your mother's—" Maggie intercepted the words *damned business* on the end of her tongue—"concern. Surely she'd trust her with Mother or Father."

"I—I should imagine she would, Maggie," Kitten faltered.

"And I'm sure Dexter could have no objection either," she said a little too aggressively.

"I—I don't see how he could."

"You may tell your mother I'm willing to guarantee that Priscilla won't sully her feet by crossing my threshold, or corrupt her morals by so much as seeing Ray. But I should consider that I had the right to see her, as long as she was under her grandparents' supervision. Wouldn't you think that fair?"

"Yes," Kitten was forced to admit. "Yes, I should think so."

"We *must* come back to New York to live!" Maggie announced suddenly and decisively to herself and not to Kitten. "We've simply got to!"

The explosion seemed to clear the air to her own satisfaction. She got up and kicked the log that was burning in the fireplace. She did not look at Kitten as she asked in a gentler voice than she had used at all, "How is Dexter?" The second's stillness widened, so that she flung herself quickly to close it. She could feel her cheeks burn as she hurried on. "I mean, how is he *really*? Has he—er—got over the . . . shock, do you think?"

Kitten looked unhappy. Maggie appeared to have forgotten her plea at the time of the divorce that they should not mention Dexter. Kitten spoke reluctantly. "Dexter is a faithful soul too, Maggie. I don't think he will ever 'get over' you, if that's what you want to know. But he has never worn his heart on his sleeve. I've never heard him say a bitter word about you. Actually, he doesn't seem to want to refer to you any more than is absolutely necessary."

"But—" Maggie felt now that she could turn her face to Kitten's to ask her question—"he's all right, isn't he?"

Constitutionally unable not to speak the full truth, if she was going to speak at all, Kitten could only say, "It depends on what you mean by 'all right.' He's working harder than ever—almost every evening, I gather, and often over week ends too."

"That's what he cares about more than anything in the world," Maggie pronounced decisively. "It's what he always did care about more than anything. Human beings will always come second to his work."

"I think the very few human beings who are close to him come before anything. I'm sure he'll never forget you, Mag. But he's not going to let anybody ruin his life."

"That's what I mean!" Maggie said with complacency, as though she had won a legal case. That her action had not been the means of destroying Dexter seemed to carry its own built-in excuse for leaving him.

Tacitly the decision was made to change the subject. "Been writing any more poetry lately, Kitten?" Maggie asked as brightly as though she were questioning Roger about his tennis game.

"Nothing to speak of. I don't believe I'll ever be able to call my soul my own until the boys are all grown up and I'm an old lady."

"Pooh! You'll never be old." Maggie almost frowned as she looked at the serene, unruffled expression on Kitten's features. It was true that the gold was no longer as bright in her hair as it had once been, but what *was* there in her expression that looked so innocent and so happy? Maggie, used to scrutinizing her own face in a magnifying mirror, was forced to the admission that it told a different story.

Her line of thought was interrupted by Roger's arrival from the office. As the brother and sister kissed each other Kitten got up. "I'll go and keep the children from getting too much in your mother's hair while you two catch up a little." Maggie mildly wondered why she seemed nearly to bolt from the room.

"I don't know why we're being shut up like this." Maggie laughed with a nervousness inexplicable to herself. "Don't you want a drink?"

"Not just now, thanks." Roger lit a cigarette.

"You're looking very well, Roger." Maggie had taken in already the pleasing appearance her brother presented. Men in Hollywood, she thought, with their play suits, slacks, aloha shirts and sandals, didn't look—well, as *convincing* as Roger with his gray flannel trousers and shabby tweed coat with the leather patches at the elbows. His gentle, serious face with its quick smile was such a relief. The face was a little thinner; otherwise he looked just the same. "I'm frightfully impressed with Kim and Braddy," Maggie told him. "I honestly don't believe I'd have known Braddy, he's changed so."

Like Kitten, Roger seemed more interested in Maggie's child than in his own. He used his wife's very words as he asked, "How does Priscilla seem to you?"

"Kitten and I were just talking about her. I'm very pleased with her. She certainly looks awfully well, and she seems as happy as—well, as she ever was. I never have been able to understand those buttoned-up Bradfield natures, you know—with the exception of Kitten, who isn't buttoned up. But when am I going to see the rest of your brood? *And* the house? That's what I'm waiting for!"

Roger blew a short puff on his freshly lighted cigarette and then crushed it out almost roughly in a nearby ash tray. Maggie began to see that his walking up and down had been simply a preliminary—to what she could not guess. He sat down, planted both feet before him, rested his elbows on his knees, and, holding his temples firmly in a tight grasp, presented the appearance of preparing to be sick on the carpet.

"Look, Maggie," he said, but did not look himself, continuing rather to stare at the spot between his feet. "I seem to be the one that's hooked with the unpleasant job of breaking the news to you. Kitten's such a gentlehearted creature it about kills her. The truth is, I'm afraid it's not going to be possible to ask you out to our place in Milton."

It was Maggie who suddenly felt as though she were the one who was going to be sick.

"What's the matter? Why not?" she asked, but already knew the answer.

"Because Ma and Pa Brad have asked us not to."

"But I shouldn't see *them*! I shouldn't even want to! I'm not going to their house. I'm coming to yours! If it would make it any less painful, couldn't you smuggle me in after dark?" Her irony teetered painfully over the precipice of temper.

"I'm afraid that wouldn't help." Roger tossed her the lifeline of a wan smile of amusement. "You see, after all, though I built the house, it was they who gave it to us and it is on their land. I suppose we are morally bound to respect their feelings—and they're pretty strong, as you may imagine."

"So they've forbidden me so much as to set foot on their property," Maggie announced angrily into the middle of the room, as though the decree were her own.

"Well, yes. It amounts to that."

Roger looked up now to meet her eyes. They confronted each other in a long unblinking look.

Roger did not need to say aloud, *I told you so.*

When he spoke his words were simple, to the point, and as free of malice or reproof as they were of pardon.

"I don't see how you can blame them much after what you've done," he said.

"O-o-h!" Maggie gave vent to an inarticulate sound on a descending scale, as though she had been suddenly physically hurt. "How can people be so sure? So sure they have all the right on their side? People just don't behave that way nowadays about divorce! That sort of Puritanical holier-than-thou attitude is what makes New England and Boston ridiculous!"

"Maggie, aren't you trying yourself to have all the right on your side?"

"Certainly not! I merely—"

"Just a minute. Listen to what I was going to say. You decided, with your eyes open, to leave Dexter and marry again. It seems to me you've got to have the guts to stand up to the consequences of what you did. I don't think it's so damned extraordinary that the Bradfields shouldn't want you back on the place after what's happened."

"But they ought to understand! If they were human beings they would. I can tell you one thing. They're not going to stop my seeing Priscilla. I've just been talking with Kitten. If we come back to New York to live, and if Priscilla comes to New York with Mother or Father to stay in a hotel, no power on earth is going to prevent my seeing her."

"That sounds reasonable enough," Roger acceded, "but that's quite different from your turning up on their home base. It's the way they are, Mag. They can't help themselves. If you do a rather . . . well, violent thing in leaving a husband whom a lot of people admire and who's idolized by his family, it's asking a good deal to expect that very family to give you three cheers of rousing support. You can't really count on having everybody admire and like you, Maggie."

"So that's what you think I'm out for? Just to be admired and liked?"

"Not purposely. Certainly not. Only on the whole, most people do seem to fall for your well-known charm. I suppose you're spoiled. You expect too much, that's all."

The memory of their last intimate talk was too green in the minds of both for either of them to wish to pursue the subject further. For a moment Maggie sat without speaking, soaking in her sense of what Roger had always meant to her. There was not a memory of childhood which she did not share with him. She knew that either would have gone to the stake for the other, without thought or, indeed, reason. All the same today she shivered in his presence. Being alone with her brother was like being alone with herself, and, for the first time in her life, after a long separation, instead of feeling cozy with him she felt uncomfortable. The fact that his presence brought her more pain than pleasure showed how far she had traveled. *Oh, well, he'll probably snap out of it,* she said to herself.

As though he had been reading Maggie's thoughts, Roger jumped out of his chair, saying in a voice tinged with unmistakable relief, "Come on, let's go find the others. I guess we'd both feel better for a drink."

21

WHENEVER RAY capitulated to his wife's wishes—and, as time went by, he found himself doing so more and more often—he rather ruefully explained to any interested bystander, "My Margot is a force of nature." To himself he murmured, "Peace at any price," as he licked old scars inflicted by Alice in past campaigns. When, therefore, he recognized the full impact behind Maggie's single purposiveness to move east, he simply bowed his head and accepted the inevitable. The Masters became New Yorkers.

One morning, after they had been living in the city two years, as Maggie was reading her mail she uttered such a shriek that it brought Ray tearing in from the next room.

"Spaff is going to be married!" she proclaimed. "I've just had a letter from her."

"Wonderful! He's a lucky man."

"You may not think it so wonderful when I tell you *who* she's going to marry."

"Who? Has he two heads?"

"She is going to marry *Dexter*!" Ray blinked under the impact as she shot her bolt full in his face. "*Dexter*!" she almost shrieked.

"I'll be damned!"

"Damned? *Damned*? But it's the most fantastic, ridiculous, hypocritical, deceitful—"

"I don't get you, Maggie. I don't see why it's hypocritical or deceitful."

"All this great talk of a career! She's pretended to be so interested in teaching, when all the time she was plotting to set her cap at . . ." She choked on her own temper.

"It might be quite nice, actually," Ray said mildly.

"Poor Dexter, is all I can say! He must be out of his mind. Spaff must simply have made a dead set at him and grabbed him. Why, Dexter would never *look* at a woman if she wasn't at least attractive."

"I've always told you, in her own way Spaff is attractive, and she's intelligent and has a lot of character. Margot, I'll tell you one thing—you ought to be awfully glad for Priscilla."

"*Priscilla*! It's *awful* for Priscilla! Spaff won't understand her at all! She'll try some revolting progressive-education theories on her and treat her like something in a test tube. Oh, you wait! I'm going to hit back at those precious Bradfields now. If it isn't safe to expose Priscilla to *you*, I'm going to begin to protest and say that I don't care to have my child brought up by *Spaff*!"

"Listen, Margot. Keep your shirt on. I thought Spaff was one of your very best friends. I always understood you thought her good enough for Dexter's brother."

"This is something quite different. She's always pretended to be my friend, but now she goes and marries my husband!"

"But, Margot, *I'm* your husband. Remember?" Ray spoke mildly.

"Dexter was my first husband, and Spaff knows it! She must know this would upset me and make me . . . well, upset."

"I don't think you're being any too sharp, Margot, if you honestly believe Spaff set her cap at Dexter—or any other man, for that matter. I'm sure the reason she and I have got on so well together was because I am married to you. For all her bluster my guess is that poor Spaff is as shy as a schoolgirl with men."

Maggie had been surprised, on her return to New York, to find how much Ray liked Spaff. He accompanied Maggie with good nature to an occasional Sunday-morning brunch on Tenth Street and was always glad when Spaff came uptown to dine with them. When Spaff told the Masters that she was accepting the position of headmistress in a new progressive school in Milton that Kitten had helped to organize they exclaimed in unison, "Spaff, we're going to miss you!"

And here was Ray, obliging Maggie with a kindly objective character analysis of one of her best friends. It made her furious; he spoke with as much smug assurance as though he understood her better than Maggie herself. "She's probably felt the same way with Dexter as she has felt about me. Just because he had been your husband she felt she could relax with him and be as nice as she really is."

"Oh. So you mean that it was Dexter who chased Spaff?"

"I mean no such thing. From what you tell me, at the best of times Dexter's a bit on the quiet side. The poor guy has probably been lonely as hell with you gone. Along comes Spaff—intelligent, friendly, and kind. Why, it's a natural—on both sides. They should be very happy together. You must have known, Margot, that Dexter would marry again sometime. In fact you must really have wanted it for his sake. It's a grim life for a man living alone, 'specially with a kid to bring up."

"If Spaff had let him alone, I bet he never would have remarried."

Ray opened his mouth to speak, closed it again, and then said merely, "I'm sure when you think it over, Margot, you'll really be glad. Since Dexter was bound to marry some day it's much nicer to have it . . . well, sort of in the family. Spaff will be wonderful with Priscilla, I'm sure, and she's so close to Kitten and Roger it ought to make it much easier for you than if you had to deal with some perfectly strange dame."

When, in due course, a year later came the news that Dexter, Jr., had been born, Maggie again seized Priscilla as the excuse for protestations.

"Any woman who has a baby late in life is bound to make a fool of herself over it. You watch. He'll either turn into an insufferable prig or a roaring pansy. But either way she certainly isn't going to bother about a half-grown stepdaughter."

"What do you *call* her, Priscilla?" Maggie asked, shameless of her own inquisitiveness, when Priscilla came to New York for a holiday.

"Aunt Spaff, just the way I always have."

"She really is great fun, isn't she? And so kind," Maggie said with a smile that felt to herself like a leer.

"Yes," said Priscilla.

"Do Daddy and Aunt Spaff—" she faltered, not knowing how to ask all the questions that were burning on her tongue— "do they seem to have a lot of fun together?"

"I don't know. I guess so. Mummy, do I have to wait till I'm twenty-one, now, to come to live with you?"

Maggie's heart leaped as she answered sweetly and seriously, "I'm afraid you do, dear, but maybe something can be worked out."

The something was the decision to send Priscilla to boarding school. The Bradfields pulled in the direction of Putney. Anything experimental, and involving two sexes, Maggie was sure would appeal to Spaff. Therefore, Maggie pulled enthusiastically in the direction of Farmington, where, she said, she was sure that a telltale Boston surface could be removed and a nice cosmopolitan coating put in its place. Again a compromise was reached. The rather sulky little pawn was sent to a new boarding school for girls in Maryland—Pemberton Woods.

But the little pawn's sulkiness began slowly to boil over into spouts of active protest. Maggie received more letters from Priscilla in her first six weeks of boarding school than she had during the last two years. The gist of them was the same: "I hate this place"; "I know I'll never learn to like boarding school"; "My roommate is horrible"; "I wish you wouldn't make me stay at such a terrible school." And then one night, after midnight, Maggie was awakened by a long-distance call from the headmistress of Pemberton Woods, telling her that there was no trace of Priscilla anywhere in the school buildings or about the grounds. No one had any idea where she was.

Maggie was to remember the next days for the rest of her life—one impression superimposed on another, time stretching out to an unbearable infinity and then suddenly telescoping shut into oblivion. She seemed to be talking on the telephone to Dexter at one moment, to Spaff at another—and yet the sound of both those voices, which twenty-four hours before would have set emotional reverberations ringing within her, did not touch her, in themselves. All that counted was the purport of what they were saying, and what they were saying was merely the echo of her own agonized cry, *Where is Priscilla?* She talked to her father and mother, to Roger and Kitten, to the police, to several teachers, to the school doctor, and to Priscilla's roommate. Neither she nor Ray slept for two nights. Ray was transformed into the master, Maggie the child, clinging with abject gratefulness to his firmness and hope as well as his kindness. "She'll turn up, Margot. Here, drink this. If you can't sleep you still must keep your strength up." And with a shaking hand she would attempt a few sips of Ovaltine or Bovril.

And then as suddenly as the cloud had fallen on them it lifted.

Marcia Bradfield called from Far Fields. "She's here, Maggie. Don't worry. She's all right."

Within a matter of hours Maggie herself was at Far Fields, forgetting, in her passion of relief and concern, that she was defying a family injunction.

She all but collapsed around Priscilla's neck, sobbing and laughing at once.

Priscilla wriggled free. She was not in the least hysterical and only a little shamefaced.

"I don't see why everyone's so upset. I don't know what you all thought I'd done."

"But we didn't *know*, darling! That's just the point! How could we know?"

"I took the bus because I didn't have enough money for train fare, and I just missed one, so I had to wait about seven hours in a bus station."

"What did you *eat*?"

"Nabs."

"What?"

"They're a kind of cracker and you can get them at the bus station."

"But *why* did you run away, Priscilla? Why? Why?"

That was the gist of an hour's colloquy between mother and daughter. Priscilla, although self-contained and not garrulous, showed herself a rather astute diagnostician of her own plight.

"I kept writing that I hated boarding school, but nobody seemed to believe me."

"Darling! But so many girls hate boarding school at first and come to love it later."

"Well, I won't come to love it later. I just know I won't. And then I knew I couldn't come to you in New York, and I didn't want to go back to Daddy . . ." She faltered, but her mother held out an encouraging hand, urging her on.

"I can imagine," she said, "it must be hard, with the new baby."

"Well, Dexy's darling, but I don't know. There just doesn't seem really much point in my living with them too. And so I remembered that Aunt Marsh had often asked me to come and live with her and help with the dogs."

"But school, Priscilla! You have to go to school somewhere!"

"What's wrong with Dunster High School?" she asked blandly.

What's wrong with Dunster High? was the subject for the discussion arranged by Marsh to take place between Maggie and Dexter under the roof of Titipu. When Maggie came into the little sitting room, so poignantly familiar in every detail, to find Dexter standing before her on the hearth, she felt far less in possession of herself than if she had been Priscilla's age. They shook hands with embarrassment on both sides, though it was Dexter who mastered himself first, appearing not to notice the quaver in Maggie's voice as she said, "It's too bad you had to come all the way down here, Dexter."

With firm masculine aggressiveness he said, "That's all right. It's important."

Maggie reached for a cigarette and sat down on a sofa against the wall. "I suppose you know. Marsh has told you? Priscilla wants to live here and go to high school."

"How do you feel about it, Maggie?" Dexter sat down in an armchair before the fire.

"I might as well tell you right off—I don't like the idea at all. But then—" her voice quavered— "there's not much I do like about Priscilla's setup."

"What, in particular?" Dexter looked at her as he might have looked at a partridge that had stirred in the woods; he was alerted.

"I think it's pretty hard for her, trying to adapt herself to a new baby in the family. I suppose she must feel rather left out."

"That's ridiculous! She knows she was there first and will always—"

"I'm only saying what I think she *feels*, Dexter. I didn't say she was right. A second marriage is never easy for a child," she added primly.

"Don't forget whose second marriage came first." Dexter's eyes sharpened. He might have been on the point of cocking his gun to take aim.

"Priscilla was getting on *perfectly all right* until you and Spaff decided to get married." Maggie spoke with spirit. "It's only since then that she seems to feel rejected. I'd take her to live with me, with us, in New York like a shot and fight your family in the courts, too, if necessary—" her eyes were flashing fire now—"except that I really don't think she'd be happy at school in New York. She prefers the country."

"She had that at Pemberton Woods."

"Yes, but she hates the regimentation. It's no good blaming her. It's just the way she is—a complete individualist."

"Do I gather that you'd object very strongly to her living here with Marsh?"

"You don't 'gather' anything. I haven't said one way or the other, though I admit it's not the way I'd choose to bring up any girl."

"Probably she'd get all she'll need in the way of education," said Dexter calmly. "She's never shown any signs of turning into a great intellectual light anyway."

They talked for another half hour. The sparks of recrimination which had popped back and forth, probably an instinctive safety valve for releasing pent-up sadness and sentiment on both sides, had spent themselves. They now talked quietly—simply as parents of the same child. Agreement was reached. It was not a perfect solution; both admitted they would have liked something different, and neither would say outright that this complicated, darkened childhood for Priscilla need not have been if Maggie had not left home. Under not ideal conditions they agreed that spending her winters with her aunt at Far Fields seemed to offer a workable makeshift.

Dexter saw that the time had come to go; he got to his feet and stood for a moment shifting uneasily from one foot to the other. Looking at him, standing there before her—familiar, irritating and substantial—Maggie could have cried aloud, *You're my husband! Why must you go? We have so much more to say to each other!* Instead, she stood up too and, because she was moved and did not want to show it, spoke crisply, as though she were winding up a business interview. "Well, I think that's everything, then. After all, Marsh can reach either of us if any problems come up."

"Sure," said Dexter. He looked now full in Maggie's face so that she could feel her color mount in response. He held out his hand. "Good-by, Maggie," he said.

"Good-by," she said, and then almost meekly, "Thank you for coming."

He had gone. Maggie looked wistfully after the sturdy back of the husband she had never been able to dominate. She sighed.

From that day, under Margot Masters' surface agitations on behalf of her husband's career, ran a deepening undercurrent of determination. Priscilla must become hers, and hers alone. She yearned as a mother both to claim and to cherish her only daughter. But there was, as well, another satisfaction to look forward to: that of shaking her fist at Ma Brad and Spaff, separately and jointly, and saying, *Come and get her if you dare! She's all mine now!*

In the meantime Maggie squeezed every moment's satisfaction she could from the holidays Priscilla spent in a New York hotel with one or both of her grandparents, as well as a visit every summer, shared with Maggie, to Northeast Harbor. Priscilla began, to Maggie's delight, to take an interest in clothes, relying unswervingly on her mother's taste. She was too much of a Bradfield to covet anything that looked "dressed up," but as she became fifteen, sixteen, seventeen, her tweeds became better and better tailored, and her sweaters, scarves, and coats had a good country style of their own. As Maggie trailed about with her, supervising fittings, picking up samples on counters, she was pleased to hear everywhere agreeable murmurs. "Doesn't she look lovely in that!" Or: "My, isn't that perfect with her coloring! You don't often see a real peaches-and-cream skin." Priscilla was a beautiful, attractive and affectionate daughter. What plans for her future was Maggie busy hatching!

If Ray, because of Maggie's written agreement with the Bradfields, was denied any right to know his stepdaughter, Maggie's disposition toward Sister and Skipper Masters was all affability. Irritated by Ray's secretiveness where they were concerned, she would say to him from time to time, "You might as well be having an illicit affair with another woman. Why don't you ever *talk* about your children? You go off to visit them at school or get letters from them and won't tell me about them. I'd love to hear, you know!"

Free from any sense of either guilt or sin in the course she herself had taken, Maggie was blandly unaware that Ray was prey to the pangs of both. Having kept his feelings for and dealings with his son and daughter inviolate, he found it difficult to consent to so much as a lunch with them at the Princeton Club in Maggie's company. During a Christmas holiday, however, he capitulated.

It was Sister who floored Maggie first. Used to a daughter who served merely as a foil to her own brilliance of appearance as well as of personality, she was disturbed by the mere dazzling physical beauty of Sister Masters. Her nails and lips were scarlet and her beautiful figure was clearly already, at fifteen, a weapon whose deadly potential was appraised to the full by its owner. She was dark, sultry and totally enveloped in the suffocating folds of the boredom which can envelop, without a chink for the air of mercy, an adolescent in the presence of her seniors. She languidly accepted the obvious fact that there was nothing in the world she could possibly have to say to Maggie.

Maggie, hating herself, heard her own voice exclaim as she looked about the far-from-exciting dining room, "Isn't this an attractive place to have lunch!"

Sister's stare told her that her remark was too fatuous to be acknowledged. The child turned toward her father as though no one had spoken and asked, "Can you get Cokes in this place?"

Her wrists clanked with bracelets, heavy with small charms. Maggie hurled herself upon them conversationally.

"Oh, what pretty charms! I've been trying to think what to get for a birthday present for my Priscilla. I think it would be fun to start her with a bracelet with just one or two little charms, and then add to it. Do you mind my asking where you got that little poodle, Sister?"

Sister's pouting lower lip stuck out as she looked down disdainfully at the trinket. Addressing herself to the prancing gold poodle at her wrist, she said, "I don't know. Mummy gave it to me."

No one could think of anything to say for a few minutes. Then Maggie decided to tackle St. Paul's intrepid quarterback. "Skipper, your father tells me you're going to be a writer, too."

She wished she hadn't sounded so condescending. Clearly Skipper wished it also. She had been thinking that he looked a little less formidable than his sister. There was something of his father in the wry twist at the corners of the full, sensitive mouth, offering her at least the hope, if not the promise, of humor and responsiveness. She assumed his complexion would clear up in time.

"I'd like to be," he said in a sudden high falsetto that plummeted abruptly to a cracky bass, "but I'll probably never make the grade."

Ray threw out a merciful lifeline. "How does the football team look for next year?"

"Gee, it's hard to tell. Two guys graduating this spring are the best ends they've had in the line in years, but some of the kids in the squad—"

They were off. Maggie and Sister were left to shove their chicken patties and peas around their plates undisturbed.

After the children had left them Ray, aware of more awkwardness in the occasion than he cared to admit, tried to gloss it over.

"I'm afraid it was a little tough for you, Margot. Naturally it's a bit confusing for kids. If I know Alice, she'll give them the third degree when they get home, wanting a blow-by-blow description of everything. They probably felt awkward—a bit like two rather inexpert spies in enemy territory."

"Sister's a real beauty" was all Maggie could find to say.

"Yes, she is. I imagine she's going through the phase of resenting any female interest in my life," he explained with thinly disguised self-satisfaction. "She's filthy to her mother, and I'm afraid she wasn't all plain sailing for you."

"Don't forget I'm used to a prickly daughter!" Maggie answered valiantly. "Next time, you wait and see, I'll do better."

"Listen, Margot, there isn't going to be a next time," Ray said in a voice that appeared to startle himself.

"Whatever do you mean?"

"I mean that, by your leave, there's going to be just one area of my life that I intend to keep to myself. My kids live with their mother. I don't want them confused by having to absorb you, too, as part of their universe. There would be nothing to be gained from anybody's point of view."

"But what about mine? I don't like to have a failure. I don't like to feel that—well, that—"

"That there are two human beings, even if only adolescent, whom you're not going to get a chance to charm?"

"Ray! That's unfair! And you know it. I would only like everything to be friendly and easy and natural."

"Well, I'm telling you that there's nothing either friendly or easy or natural about divorce, so don't be so insensitive as to try to pretend that there is. It's enough of a strain on me knowing that I have two wives in the world at the same time, and I'll be damned if I'm going to put the burden on my children of having to recognize two mothers. It's proper that they should see you once, to prove to themselves that you exist in fact. But once is enough."

"All right. Suit yourself." The first and only stand that Ray had taken in direct opposition to Maggie since their marriage caused her to speak almost meekly.

Surprisingly subdued, she did not try again to inject herself into Ray's relations with Skipper and Sister. But the effect of finding one outlet for her energies blocked was to turn them with redoubled zeal elsewhere. If Maggie could not share with Ray the fruit of his first marriage, she could determine to make his present marriage burgeon. She would show him what fruits *she* could supply, fruits that would be sweeter than either of them had ever tasted—yet.

22

"HERE'S LOOKING at you, and many happy returns!" Ray lifted an ice-cold Gibson in Maggie's direction. They were sitting at a table in the middle of the dining room at "21." "No more feeling blue," he said. "You may be forty, but you've not begun to fight! You're still a terrific gal."

Margot Masters accepted without wincing the title accorded her. She knew that at forty she must stop thinking of herself as an attractive girl. Certainly, her ambition had never centered about maturing into a wise, witty, or otherwise wonderful woman. The very word *maturity* suggested old age, and old age for herself was unthinkable. The only recourse open to her was to assume the role of one untouched by the years, to be played with more bravura than is possible to youth. She had become a *gal*, and, since she was still the same vital, hard-driving Maggie, a terrific one at that.

The unformed, colt-legged Maggie Fraser was not discernible in, under, or behind the patina that glinted from Margot Masters. She was pounds thinner than she had been twenty years before, her figure trim and shaped for the wearing of clothes. She flashed a brighter lipstick and a redder nail polish than of old; there was a new high light of gold in her hair. Miss Jean, who had urged her giving up a blond rinse in favor of the Golden Blond, said, "It's only your own natural color, dear, that has gone out of the hair that we're putting back in again." So far as she went, Miss Jean was right. Where Miss Jean did not go, however, was into a certain relationship between the youthful sheen of the hair and the skin and the eyes, no longer youthful, in proximity to it. The once fresh, ruddy skin of youth was now merely ruddy, with a tendency to blotchiness after a second cocktail.

Margot Masters did not look dissipated, but the very fiber of what once had been Maggie Bradfield had toughened. The bright colors of her youth had been abandoned for the New York matron's customary suit of solemn black—tonight of faille—accented by the inevitable pearls ringing the horizontal lines around her throat. The brilliance of her smile and the sparkle of her eyes were as vivid as ever. There was rather more glint than glow to both.

"Now, darling, put your mind on the menu," said Ray.

Maggie looked up to the captain as to her best friend. "Philip, what have you tonight that's absolutely delish?" she asked, wrinkling her nose.

"What about sweetbreads à la Dreux?" volunteered Ray.

"No, darling. I don't feel like sweetbreads." Maggie turned to include Philip as she might a trusted family lawyer who had been asked to sit in on a knotty personal problem. "It's the queerest thing, Philip, because *you* know how I generally love sweetbreads, but tonight I don't know why—if you gave them to me I simply shouldn't take them!"

Philip appeared pleased that the complexity of his client's whim offered him only further means of demonstrating that he existed but to please her.

"What about shad roe, Mr. Masters?" he asked, stooping solicitously over Ray, in whose hand, after all, were the true keys to the kingdom, to indicate to him the spot on the menu where the delicacy might be found "in season." Both men knotted their brows in tribute to the seriousness of the business before them. "What about it, Maggie? *Belle meunière*? What do you say?" asked Ray as spokesman for their joint efforts.

"I say, wonderful! I feel just in the mood for something special. Philip, you always save the day! Oh, Ray, *look*." Maggie interrupted herself abruptly. "There's Wendell Willkie! How exciting! *Look* at him, Ray."

"The highest compliment of respect I can pay him is ***not*** to look at him" was the answer that would have irritated Maggie except for her high resolve to enjoy herself to the full this evening.

Maggie surveyed her surroundings with satisfaction. Where but at "21," where but in New York, in the winter of 1941, could life be as exciting as it was? There was even an added filip to the taste of luxury and pleasure in the knowledge that they might be short-lived: the hot breath of Europe's conflagration was making itself felt as it approached nearer and nearer. For the moment, however, it was possible to be in love with Panama Hattie *and* Mrs. Miniver.

As the waiter disappeared to do his bidding, Ray said, ignoring his wife's interruption, "I think I saw him serving the shad roe to Nini." With a jerk of his head he indicated the direction of a table across the room where the Deacons were dining.

Maggie and Ray had already spoken to their friends, sitting at a table against the wall. If Maggie had not been in a determinedly gay frame of mind she would have allowed herself to be put out at the sight of the Deacons in what appeared to her a more favored position than her own. Since Ray had lost his job as producer of "Stage Classics" she was on the lookout for a public snub, intended or otherwise. If you weren't around a lot, showing your face in public, it was so easy to be forgotten. Because the Deacons were dining early Maggie assumed that they must be going to the opera. That winter Flagstad and Melchior could not have sung without Dick Deacon to keep score from his wife's box; with every performance he was able to chalk up a higher number of recognizable leitmotivs. The Masters had stopped only long enough for Maggie and Nini to exchange a *Hello-darling-how-divine-you-look*.

Over Ray's shoulder Maggie warily observed the Deacons—looking as much of a fixture in the room as the Sheffield silver and the dark wainscoting behind them. Maggie smiled to watch Nini scan her fellow diners at other tables through her lorgnette. Grown so nearsighted is to be almost blind, she was far too vain to wear glasses. She merely carried over into her café life the same *sang-froid* she had developed on Monday evenings in the Diamond Horseshoe. There, Maggie had watched her scrutinizing her fellow subscribers through her opera glasses with all the deliberation of a bird-watcher. Nini could even frighten herself as she brought into focus the features of a female of the species whose sharp beak or pair of huge glittering eyes in the center of her lens was returning the compliment of appraisal from only a few yards away. Now Maggie watched her wave across the dining room as she cried, "Darling! Your Don yesterday was the best yet!"

Dick Deacon, like a slightly rusty mechanical toy beginning to run down, could be heard, under the clatter of dishes, to rumble out a faithful "Bully. Bully for you, feller." All color and life seemed to have been drained from him. As he looked many years older than his true age, this anomaly happily served to make his wife look younger. Even at "21" Nini would point with pride to the milk toast to which he was sentenced. "Dick has ulcers. All the big men do, you know."

Dick's lips were as cracked as ever, but his teeth seemed more prominent in his skull-like face. He looked as though he were being gnawed away from the center; though he still periodically closed his eyes as of old, the expression conveyed more pain than interest. Maggie had laughed to Ray about the fact that whenever she and Dick met he drew her aside, as he might a fellow White Russian in exile, asking for news of the motherland. "What do you hear from Boston, Maggie? I hear they're going to tear up the Embankment."

Pursuing the "poor Dick" motif, Ray said, "For heaven's sake, you're not beating that dead horse again, are you, Mag? We poor saps who pulled our necks out of one noose only to stick them into another don't deserve sympathy. All we need is to have our heads examined."

"Ray, you make me sick! I will *not* have you putting yourself in the same class with Dick Deacon!"

"I can't see any difference." Ray's smile was all good nature.

"You *look* different, for one thing," Maggie told him with emphasis.

Maggie looked at her husband with pride of proprietorship. He still wore a bowtie. If he did not look quite as casually attractive as he had the day she first met him (the day she fell in love with him at first sight, she told herself) he looked indefinably more important. His hair had not grayed but receded slightly at the temples. Though the lines in his face were more deeply etched, they only added to the pliancy of his mask. As in a tragic or a comic muse, the same lines could effect a total transformation. A look of set and brooding unhappiness could brighten suddenly into an expression of such intense amusement that it beguiled the beholder to laugh too. He had proclaimed to Maggie that for this evening's celebration he intended to suffer "strictly no pain." His spirits, like his face, were capable of showing the reverse side of his moods of depression and irritability, and could expand into a wise-cracking, faintly aggressive bonhomie. "My wife pulls me around by the nose quite as much as Dick's pulls his. Come on, admit it."

"Then *you've* got to admit that I've never . . . well, hardly ever—" Maggie flashed her own disarming smile— "pulled you round, as you call it, if it wasn't for your own good. Certainly you see now that I was right to put my weight on the side your coming back east," she was not afraid to ask at a removal of six years.

"Shall we call it throwing rather than pulling?" Ray held aloft the huge pepper grinder to strafe liberally his slabs of smoked salmon.

Tonight was no occasion for recrimination. In a tone of rather ample, easygoing detachment he asked, "Have you stopped to think, Margot, that there is a grim irony in the fact that after eight years of marriage this is where we came in?"

Maggie, devoid of any sense of irony, was never amused by the result of her own actions. Performed with a high hand, they were their own justification.

"Such as?"

"For one thing, here I'm back in the advertising business, which I always said I'd rather drop dead than have anything to do with again."

And yet, thought Maggie, as she looked for words to refute the charge, she was so sure at the time that each step Ray had taken at her instigation must bring him nearer her goal for him.

With such high hopes she had thrown herself into his weekly radio program, "Stage Classics." For a while she had thought it contained all the ingredients of the perfect job. Ray, with his power to hire and fire talent, was a magnet toward whom gravitated stage and motion-picture stars, playwrights, columnists, agents, producers, and sponsors. It was Maggie's happy, self-appointed function to screen these candidates for her busy husband's attention. It was during those two years that "21" had been her throne room. There were evenings when she would look along the banquette on which they sat against the wall and exclaim, *"Everybody* is here tonight! Hello, Aleck!" First names went table-hopping, like their owners. "Hello, *darling*!" Darling, darling, darling—they were all darlings to Maggie. Clowns, comics, wits, and showoffs—she offered to them all the heady wine of unstinted praise and uninhibited laughter. Peal on peal, till her sides ached, she had offered it to them, so that she felt tonight that its echoes must still linger in the room.

It was not only in public that Maggie and Ray were dedicated to the proposition that gags make for gaiety, and gin for geniality, for it was during their first years in New York that the Masters drifted from the first ecstasies of what they had believed to be a love match into the easy camaraderie of what Maggie proudly labeled "fun." Fun was the order of those days. After an evening with some of "the crowd" Maggie would exclaim, "Come on back to our place!" There, their friends would howl with delight over some recent acquisition to Ray's collection of Victorian trade cards or other Victoriana. It seemed to reinforce for the Masters their occasionally flagging conviction that the twentieth century was the pinnacle of sophistication and maturity to laugh down from its heights at their jejune predecessors of the nineteenth century. Framed religious mottoes and devotional poems were plastered over the walls of their apartment. Above the bed, on Maggie's side, hung the legend "I Need Thee Every Hour"; on Ray's side:

"God Give Me Strength." In contradistinction, the four contemporary pieces of furniture were a bar, a mini-piano, a low king-size double bed, and a typewriter. At the first, on coming home at night, Ray would reinforce the stimulus he had been applying all evening to his sagging spirits; at the second he would release these spirits in song (this winter his favorites were "The Last Time I Saw Paris" and "A Nightingale Sang in Berkeley Square"), and into the third he would fling himself beside Maggie in the early hours of the morning, still hoping to recapture there some glimmer of a vision that was receding farther every day. It was not surprising that the fourth, in the morning, would rebuke him mutely for neglect.

Their apartment house was situated in the East Fifties, appropriately enough almost next door to the Gay Nineties. "You can walk from it *everywhere*!" they boasted. Home, for them both, was no green oasis in a weary land, for peace and mutual rediscovery; rather, it was a functional GHQ, stripped to serve as resilient springboard to catapult them into the torrent that roared about them, which they told themselves was life.

It was then that Margot Masters became accustomed to seeing her name shine in its own right in the Broadway gossip columns. In the society christened *café* she was a "personality." It was common Broadway knowledge that to get on the right side of Ray Masters—in fact to get on any side of him at all—one had first to ingratiate oneself with Margot. "Ask my Margot. She knows my commitments better than I know them myself," Ray would say. Or, "My Margot really knows what's what. I'd forgotten until she reminded me what a damned good piece of work Anatole France did in *Penguin Island*." (Maggie had not felt it necessary to confess that it was her father who had reminded her of the existence of both book and author.)

One columnist quipped, "Ray Masters' Margot is some Girl Friday. There's real public relations for him in that gal. How about the private relations, Ray?"

Oh, she had enjoyed it all hugely, sitting in on Ray's rehearsals, always eager to "come up" with suggestions. And for a while she had believed that Ray himself had seemed happy: even if they were not his own original plays or novels he was presenting, he was still reaching millions of people. If only the final debacle hadn't come over a program decided on through her insistence! But how was Maggie to be expected to know that the sponsor's wife was a bad sailor, and that listening to *Moby Dick* for an hour on the radio made her feel squeamish, and that she was sure she was a representative American woman and if *she* couldn't wait for the program to come to an end, just smelling brass polish and dead fish, she was sure that thousands of other American women were feeling the same way? Surely this man Masters didn't have sound judgment. Suddenly it appeared that a good many other people close to the sponsor had wondered themselves whether . . . etc., etc.

And so Ray, in his own words, had been "kicked upstairs." They called him literary consultant instead of executive producer. The net result of the shift was that he laid down the pencil in favor of the scissors; he was no more than a hack editor. And he'd be damned if he was going to spend his life doomed to that ignominy.

Maggie was quick to take up the cudgels in defense of her own image of the husband she had married. "But, darling, you may be back in the advertising business, but your setup isn't at all what it used to be."

"That's right." He pulled an ear and smiled. "I'm working for an outfit a good many cuts beneath D.D.D. & T."

"But the novel, Ray."

"Sure. The novel. An immortal work, if I can only get it off the ground. Listen, darling, if I get cross sometimes and make like I'm blaming you when things don't pan out, pay me no mind."

It was very confusing to Maggie that Ray, who had complained so much about Alice's lack of interest in his writing, didn't seem to want Maggie to express her own interest—or at least in the way she did. When in their apartment he did actually close behind him the door of the room they called the "study" to confront his neglected typewriter, the door never stayed closed more than a half hour. With a creaking of floor boards, Maggie would tiptoe in, whispering, "I thought perhaps you might like a glass of milk," or, "Don't mind me. I just want to see if I can find my old checkbook in the bottom drawer. Go right ahead and write." Then, with a loud pop of her knee joint, she would be rattling around on all fours, between his feet on the floor, before she tiptoed out again, to whisper from the door, "How's it coming?" as though she expected Ray might open his coat and say "See!" showing a Blake-like emanation issuing from his diaphragm.

Now, sitting across the table from her at "21," Ray felt a twinge of compunction that was becoming more frequent with him: perhaps Margot was bored. As instinctively as he would have reached for a cigarette he pulled out a funny story. A few minutes later Maggie's laugh was ringing out as it had rung so often in the same surroundings. It was interrupted by Nini's voice. Maggie looked up to find her standing beside their table.

"Can you share the joke?" she asked.

"Oh, it was nothing. Just another shaggy-dog story Ray picked up at the Dutch Treat Club." Maggie felt like a child discovered red-handed by an adult with her hand in the cooky jar. Nini's manner was severe, perhaps simply because the sight of another couple sharing a joke sharpened her own awareness that she and Dick never laughed together over anything.

"We're celebrating a very important birthday," Ray explained ingratiatingly.

"Don't tell her which!" cried Maggie. "It's too depressing!"

Nini lifted her lorgnette to scrutinize her friend with the bird-watcher's bright eye, belying the cordiality of her manner as she said, "Whatever it is, you don't look it, darling. Come on, Dick. We must run or we'll miss the curtain."

"Opera as usual, I suppose?" asked Maggie.

"No, no, not tonight. It's the opening of Tony Capehart's play. He did the dramatization of the novel himself, you know. I've been sitting in on the rehearsals, and Dick's one of the backers. We're both sure it can't miss." She gave a high, brittle laugh. "I certainly hope not, as I have some people coming in afterward to celebrate."

After she had left there was a moment's pause before Maggie said, with no attempt at softening the bitterness of her tone, "Not the most tactful way of letting us know that she's giving a huge party to which we're not invited."

"How can you be so sure it's huge?"

"She gave a huge party for *you* after *your* opening night, didn't she?"

The two pictures, the counterfeit presentment of two novelists, each of whom had adapted his own best seller for the theater, confronted them. In Nini's eyes Maggie's husband was a has-been; in her own eyes—Maggie could only turn her head away. Like the Bad Fairy at the christening Nini had spoiled the birthday party.

Ray, reading her mind all too easily, broke into her reverie. "I'm sorry, Margot. Just being the wife of a mediocre adman isn't enough for you. Admit it," he challenged her not unkindly.

"Does that make me some kind of monster? I think most wives would feel the same."

"I'm not sure. I know you love me. Natch. And want me to be happy, fulfilled, all the nice, kind things any little woman wants her man to have. All the same, I think you mind my being a washout more than I mind it myself. There's something almost frighteningly important to *you* in my being a success. It's like throwing on another wing to the house of your personality. It's as though you craved more stature for yourself. Am I crazy?"

"I don't know." Maggie looked troubled. "Roger used to tell me that most people think I like to have them around because they believe I have a lot to give, when I really am hungry for something from them."

"I agree with him. Another pair of eyes, not so much to admire you, another tongue, not so much to sing your praises as to tell you who you are. Maybe it's a case of mistaken or rather not yet located identity. You crave a sort of confirmation of yourself, or selves, and in each new friend, maybe in each new husband even—" his eyebrows shot up and then down—"you even believed that your own new name, Margot, would land you on the top of the heap." Feeling, perhaps, that he was probing deeper than Maggie's depth of understanding, he stopped. "You know what I think?" He spoke with sudden cheer. "I think it's time for you to become a success in your own right." Maggie's interest sharpened. Ray was continuing, resigned and affable. "Maybe my function is already fulfilled. I've run interference for you through the jungle of New York. You know your way around now. A lot of people know you. Why don't you take the ball and carry it from here on out?"

Maggie often charged Ray with being difficult to "figure out." She told him she could not tell when he was fooling. This was one of those moments. It was, as well, though she did not know it, one of those decisive moments that occur in every marriage. They take place not so much in words spoken or action taken as in a change of atmosphere as imperceptible as a shift in wind or a drop in temperature. The balance of power between them teetered.

Then Maggie spoke. "Are you just joking, Ray? Do you really think I could, on my own, make a name for myself?"

"You could be spectacular. I feel it in my bones."

"Then tell me how to begin! What am I going to be spectacular *at*?" Ray was to remember afterward the way his Margot looked—eyes flashing and nostrils wide—at the prospect of a rosy future all her own.

"Maybe Mrs. Bent will tell you—on Sunday."

"Oh, Ray, *honestly*!" There he was, fooling again, just when she most wanted to be serious.

Mrs. Bent had called a few days before, asking Maggie to come with Ray to lunch, saying, "I want to talk over a big job that I think you could swing, Maggie." Maggie had entertained herself since then by imagining the dreariest possible duties the older woman might be plotting to stick her with.

Ray filled his wife's glass, and then his own, his sad eyes beseeching her not to lose her temper, not to spoil the party he had planned for her more than it had been spoiled already. "I'm not joking," he said. "You're one terrific gal, Margot. You've not yet begun to fight. Down the hatch!"

Putting his head back, he gulped his own drink down in one swallow.

23

Maggie and Ray arrived in time for Sunday lunch at the comfortable double stone house in the East Seventies. Mrs. Bent, dressed in a plum-colored wool dress with the sort of pale-pink satin piping around the neck that bespoke a French maid to keep it fresh, shook hands cordially with Ray and kissed Maggie.

"Dear child, how nice. Am I not in luck to have caught you both? It's like the old days when I had my own young people at home. Now with all of them insisting on country week ends, Rhinelander and I rattle about like two peas in a pod, don't we, Rhinelander?"

"It's good to see you, Maggie. How are you, Masters?" Mr. Bent shook hands roundly with them both. He was a tall, handsome man, with eyes of a blue to match his wife's, ruddy complexion, and thin gray hair. If he had been dressed in overalls he would have been instantly identifiable as one of "nature's gentlemen." As it was, standing on the white bear rug in front of the fire in the high stone fireplace, his hands tucked under the tails of his morning coat complete with carnation in the buttonhole, he came up to the standard applied in terms of linear measurement: every inch the gentleman. Above the fireplace was a Simon Elwes portrait of Mr. Bent at his desk. The skill of a master's hand was apparent in the elevation of the particular to the general. It was not only one American banker; it was all extroverted American manhood, caught in a moment not so much of relaxation as of suspended tension before locking horns with the chosen form of action which, for him, spelled life.

Maggie looked about her at the room, with its gold brocade Louis XV furniture, thinking, as she had thought before, how buttressed it seemed against the city beyond its walls. Two heavy cloisonné vases, overflowing with sprays of pink dogwood and forsythia coming into forced bloom, were reflected in the Chinese Chippendale mirror. The flowers and vases on the heavy mahogany table served merely as a background for ranks of large silver-and-brocaded framed photographs. There were Albert, King of the Belgians, Queen Marie of Rumania, the Abbé Dimnet, General Pershing, the Prince of Wales, John Galsworthy, Nicholas Murray Butler, John Buchan, and Anne Morgan.

The next guests arrived all together.

Mr. and Mrs. Task came into the room first, followed by Mr. R. Basset-Basset.

Mrs. Task floated not only herself but the other arrivals into the room on a river of her own conversation, which showed no signs of stopping for any obstacles. She leaned on an ivory-handled cane. Flopping against it was a capacious black velvet pouch topped by an ornate wrought-silver clasp. Her pale-orchid pink powder must have been chosen to match the pale-pink tulle through whose flattering meshes the sagging folds of her soft chin were barely discernible under the grip of a fine lilac bead dog collar. Her suède pumps, with pointed toes and inset Cuban heels, had large silver buckles; her stockings were of heavy iron-gray lisle cotton.

"Oh, how cheerful and pretty!" she exclaimed without looking about her. "I love spring flowers and an open fire. Somehow I have the pleasant feeling that I am cheating nature, and it's such a struggle to cheat nature, isn't it? What did you say your name was, young man?"

"Masters, Raymond Masters."

Mrs. Bent intervened. "Mr. Masters is a novelist."

"Oh, dear, really? Then that must mean you're clever, and I'm sure you're going to put me in a book. I'm scared to death of clever men, though give me a clever man rather than a clever woman any day.

A woman is clever only if she's unattractive. You'd better talk to R. here. R. Basset-Basset reads everything."

Mr. Basset-Basset at the moment was giving his undivided attention to the silver tray that was extended to him by the footman. He was hanging fire over a choice of daiquiris, martinis, sherry, and tomato juice. Giving a little sigh to bear witness to a lost battle, he took a martini.

"R., come here and tell this young man about all the books you've read," Mrs. Task prompted.

Wiping away with a small napkin the effects of a hot cheese *canapé* from his clipped gray mustache, he joined them. Mr. Basset-Basset eyed Ray tentatively. He had not heard of him as a writer. That was a good sign. If a writer was famous in present-day America, it was axiomatic that he was a bounder; if he was unknown it was just possible that he was a gentleman. Mr. Basset-Basset told himself that he would find out in short order.

"I flatter myself that I've read everything worth reading up to the year 1900."

"May I ask, sir, why you stopped there?" asked Ray.

"Because I'm afraid I'm just an old-fashioned has-been who insists on reading the fellers who can polish up the handle of a good English sentence. Then too—and I hope I'm not stepping on any toes—" he bowed low and achieved a gulp of his martini on his downward sweep —"I must say I like to read about ladies and gentlemen."

"But there are so few left to write about, Mr. Basset-Basset," said Ray with a friendly smile, looking about in vain for a second martini.

Mr. Basset-Basset turned sharply to look at him, but Ray's expression seemed to emanate good nature. The sunshine, firelight, good food and drink, all helped to create an amalgamating atmosphere of luxury in which it was impossible to feel truculent. Mr. Basset-Basset found it pleasanter to assume that he was not in the presence of an enemy. "You're quite right. There are damned few of them left. And look at those there are—like Franklin Roosevelt, who fouls his own nest. When a man begins to prattle about a New Deal it's a pretty fair sign that he's betrayed his own class because his class repudiated him, and I'm not merely speaking of 1904, Rhinelander."

Mrs. Bent patted him placatingly on the arm. "Poor R. You've been born into the wrong century."

"I certainly have. I'm afraid, what's more, I'm in my usual Sunday-morning bad humor."

He was, like his host, dressed in his Sunday occupational uniform—gray spats, pin-stripe trousers, and morning coat, also with white carnation.

"That new young whippersnapper we have in the pulpit got sounding off about tolerance. If we go about *tolerating* a lot of wild-eyed radicals and long-haired New Dealers—"

"If you're going to have a heart attack, R.," said Mrs. Bent kindly, "do wait until after lunch. I want your opinion on a scheme I'm going to broach to my young friend here," she said, putting her arm around Maggie's waist and drawing her to the threshold in answer to the announcement of lunch. "Shall we go down?"

Seated at the table in the dining room, Mrs. Bent placed herself at its head with the authority natural to a woman accustomed to preside at committee meetings. She interrupted the instinctive move each guest was making to engage his neighbor in conversation, and addressed Maggie in a voice that needed no gavel for accompaniment. The heads of her guests swung obediently toward the head of the table.

"And now, my dear," she said, "I wish to lay my little project before you. Rhinelander and I feel that there's nothing too much we in this country can do for Britain. After all, she is fighting our battle for us."

"Hear, hear! Hear, hear!" rumbled and rippled down both sides of the table.

"I absolutely agree!" declared Maggie's voice above the others. Ever since word had reached her, via the Boston underground, that Spaff was an isolationist, Maggie resolved to Fight for Freedom.

"Rhinelander and I have had an idea that the visiting British naval officers in New York must often feel very lonely. Of course a great deal is being done for them, but not enough. And we thought of opening the ballroom—it has its own entrance—as a small recreation center. A good many tables and chairs could be squeezed in, so that the men could come and play cards, have beer and pretzels, perhaps even dancing and music and, if possible, some entertainment."

"Delightful!"

"An inspiration!"

"Splendid!"

"But I want some attractive young thing in charge to act as hostess and sort of general mistress of ceremonies. Naturally, Rhinelander and I would *hover*, but we should wish to keep in the background. The last thing we should want is to be *thanked*."

"Quite. Quite."

"Entirely understandable."

"The most modest people in the world."

"It's quite shocking—and Rhinelander and I are really ashamed of ourselves—but we simply don't *know* all the gay, attractive, talented Broadway set. We do know, though, how generous many of them are, and how they would consider it a privilege to entertain these men who are so far away from home, and *that's* how I happened to think of Maggie. Because I know, my dear, that you touch so many lives and are such a charmer yourself that not one of them would think of saying *no* to you. What do you say, my dear?"

As Maggie hesitated, uncertain just what to answer, Ray spoke up. "It's a natural, Mrs. Bent. Margot would do it superbly. It's a swell idea, and I'm sure the Britishers will eat it up. But it's also a swell idea for Margot. She could swing it to the Queen's taste."

"What Ray really means," said Maggie with a good-natured laugh, "is that it's wonderful for him, as it will get me out of his hair, so he can have peaceful evenings by himself for writing!"

They all laughed.

"Splendid! I'm delighted," said Mrs. Bent. "After lunch you and I will go over the ballroom and see what we shall see."

Apparently feeling that the dictates of good manners had been stretched to the limit, she dropped the business of the day as emphatically as she had taken it up and turned to Mr. Task, speaking in her off-the-record tone of voice.

"Tell us, Chesborough," she said, "what did you get in the way of a sermon this morning?"

Mr. Task looked across the table, a little fearful, at his wife. Although he was senior partner in Grimes, Task, Hollingsby, Strucke, and Grinnell, removed from Wall Street he was not apt to open his mouth without benefit of Mrs. Task as counsel.

It was she, therefore, who serenely answered the question, allowing Chesborough to pursue unmolested a slice of hard-boiled egg in his black-bean soup.

"The subject was 'What Is Your Rod and Staff?' Of course, the rector was bound to tell the congregation that it was the one in the Twenty-third Psalm. After all, we pay him to tell us that. But he asked each one of us to answer truthfully for ourselves what is our own rod and staff."

"That's an interesting question." Mrs. Bent nodded official approval. "Have you decided what is yours, Muriel?"

"Certainly. I decided on the spot. Money."

There was a moment's pause. "*Prenez garde, il y a des oreilles qui écoutent tout,*" said Mrs. Bent suavely.

The features of the two footmen removing the soup plates were imperturbable.

"Don't be absurd! Your two men know the value of money quite as well as the rest of us. Don't you?" Mrs. Task beamed up at Ovens as he placed a Crown Derby plate in front of her.

Ovens knew his place sufficiently to make no other answer than a remote and ghostly smile which flickered out as promptly as it had appeared.

"Muriel! You are refreshing! You're like nobody else I know!"

Mrs. Bent promptly decided that the way to slide over the awkward moment was to make a joke of it; she prayed that the servants would see the humor too.

"On the contrary, I'm like everyone else you know. Only I happen to be frank. I could have none of the things I most depend on without money. Patrick, for instance. I never thought I'd find a chauffeur to replace poor Noonan after he went to pieces, but I have. Patrick can park anywhere at any time—the opera, Altman's, the Colony Club. There seems to be no problem at all. It may be our money, but it's his nature that makes him cut out to be the policeman's friend. Now, Chesborough, please don't start one of your coughing attacks. I'm not going to be indiscreet. And last summer Patrick was simply a tower of strength on the yacht. *Chesborough!* There you go again. I suppose he doesn't like my using the word *yacht*. Very well, then, our elongated motor boat."

A violent spasm of coughing appeared to be Mr. Task's established method of dealing with his wife's inanities, as, perhaps, the inanities in turn constituted her revenge for his infidelities. His face became purple, the veins on his temples protruding from the effort, conscious or unconscious, of getting attention.

Today the Task yacht was sunk without a trace in the cyclone that nearly swept away even the table linen and sent the salt flying. When the waters had closed and calmed, Mrs. Bent, as the experienced chairman not to be deflected from the business of the meeting, turned for further polling to Mr. Basset-Basset. "R., I long to know what is *your* rod and staff."

"Easy! The Metropolitan Opera."

"How delightful!" In spite of a high-minded attempt at impartiality, an audible sigh of relief escaped the Chair.

"Mind, I didn't say anything as broad as music. I mean everything that goes with the Met—the Opera Club, the Saturday-afternoon broadcasts, opening night and, of course, Monday evenings. I enjoy the singing, but quite as much as the music I enjoy hearing it in the company of ladies and gentlemen. I always used to go over to Philadelphia for their Tuesday nights and stay with Fanny Cadwalader. I've always preferred the single-l Cadwaladers. Dear Fanny!"

Looking at Mrs. Bent facing Mr. Bent the length of the dining-room table, and their friends lined up between them, Maggie was aware afresh of the sense of something approaching incredulity in the presence of her parents' friends. They simply didn't seem to be real human beings. Could Mrs. Bent ever really and truly have been young? Had she ever been a bride on a wedding night? What had been the succeeding nights of her marriage? As Maggie watched her host and hostess facing each other across the roast beef and Yorkshire pudding, with the trophies of their life in common around them, she felt that they must have sprung into being, full-panoplied, as Mr. and Mrs. Rhinelander Bent—one a trustee of the Metropolitan Museum of Art, the other a trustee of St. Luke's Hospital, one on the board of the English-Speaking Union, the other quondam president of the Harvard Alumni Association. To fill their box on Monday night at the opera, to buy a Rembrandt for the Metropolitan Museum was simply as much of a civic obligation as to endow a hospital bed or found a scholarship. Neither came under the head of pleasure, nor, indeed, did its pursuit figure at all in the pattern of Mrs. Bent's days. Her four years in London as a girl, when her father was Ambassador to the Court of St. James's, had given Mrs. Bent the firmest belief she held: that a strong tie between the United States and Great Britain was the salvation of her world. If she had been asked, point-blank, whether the possession of a great deal of money was a necessary passport to this world she would have cringed at hearing the unmentionable word spoken.

Contemplating them now, Maggie remembered that when her mother had urged her to accept at least one invitation from them she had said, "Perhaps you won't find their house in New York very exciting, dear, particularly after Hollywood. But there's no question that Rhinelander and Lulie Bent *stand* for something."

Walking away from the house, at four o'clock, Maggie exploded to

Ray as soon as the Task's limousine rolled off out of sight. "I knew it would be just like that! Aren't they incredible?"

"Don't take it so hard, Margot. I've known worse." Ray's face broke into a good-natured smile. "My only peeve with the ice-water rich is that they don't give you anything to drink except one lousy warm martini, nine-tenths vermouth, which you feel they coach their servants to make bad on purpose. No wine at table, no liqueurs, no brandy. Otherwise I don't see what was wrong."

"How can they bear those other old Peter Arno fossils?"

"They have the one necessary credential, after family. Money."

"But the Bents have so much themselves! What do they care whether anybody else has it?"

"It's because they're touchy about having it themselves. It's the skeleton in their closet. They don't refer to it, even to each other."

"Ray Masters! You're just romancing!"

"No, I'm not. I tell you the Bents don't think of money as a means to pleasure but as a heavy responsibility they're conscious of bearing every minute."

"But I still don't see why it should make them have such boring friends."

"Because they feel *safe* with them." Ray spoke in the argumentative voice he might have used to a child. "Their friends all have just as much money, they're all old New York too, and not parvenus like—"

"Us?"

"Yes, and Nini, and a lot of other out-of-town big shots whom they vaguely fear—and rightly so—knowing they're out to dethrone the old guard not only downtown but uptown as well. When they huddle together, no matter how bored they may be, at least they feel protected against alien pressures and the violence of the modern world. It helps them to believe in their own existence."

Ray stopped to light a cigarette. Slowly he exhaled its smoke as he walked along. He was enjoying himself. "So far as I can see," he pursued, "Manhattan is not so different from most other American communities. It's a matriarchy. You've done pretty well to have made the grade with at least two of its crowned heads."

"How do you mean? Who are they?" It was fun to get her writer husband "going." She welcomed the contrast to Dexter, whose most searching comment on his fellow man was covered either by the word *pleasant* or the word *blah*.

"Nini, and Mrs. Bent, of course" was Ray's pronouncement. "Mrs. Bent is obvious. She is custodian of the past. Her segment of the city consists of all that is left of them—left of the Four Hundred. It may not get around much, but, brother, it still counts. The fly-by-nights blowing in from other parts of the country—no credentials asked or given, other than the power, the kingdom, and the glory they have carved out for themselves here—attach themselves to some already established institution, the way Nini has to the opera, to add to their own prestige. It's the Mrs. Bents who, by allowing their names to appear on the masthead of a museum or a hospital or a university, lend the institution *their* luster."

Maggie was enjoying the game. "But Nini? Surely she's not important."

"Isn't she just? Operating from '21,' she has her finger on almost everyone who is either very rich or very famous right *now*, today. Her realm is the present."

Maggie could not breathe the thin air of generalities for long.

"What do you really think of this recreation-center idea of Mrs. Bent's?"

"I tell you it's a natural, Margot. 'Scorn not the nobly born.' You've run a long way to escape from the Mrs. Bents of this world, but you'll find even in this Babylon she may give you something you want."

"But it makes me *mad* that she can live in this day and age and seem to be so out of touch with it! In all the years we've been going there I've never heard her once mention your radio show, when you had it. What is she *thinking* of?"

"Not Hooper ratings, that's a cinch!"

Maggie's dimples suddenly deepened, and she began to giggle. "I can tell you one thing she's got on her mind. When we were skidding around the ballroom after lunch she tucked her arm in mine and asked me whether I could tell her if there was any truth in a distressing rumor she'd just heard. Somebody has told her there's not a single virgin in the freshman class of Vassar."

"What did you say?"

"I told her I was afraid I didn't know. And *then*—imagine, after knowing me the way she does, how she could think for a moment I'd even consider such a thing!—she asked if I wouldn't like to sit in as a guest this winter on some grisly discussion club. Just the kind Mother belongs to in Boston, all old crones who think they want a little new blood. And *then* she asked if you and I would like to join the Present-Day Club!"

"What in Christ's name is that?"

"Well, the members, I gathered, are all at least seventy-five and have belonged since they played in Washington Square in diapers, and they meet a few times a winter, in a few of the half-dozen houses left in New York, and listen to things like a Columbia professor or a conjuror. Anyway, I told her that clubs just weren't my dish or yours either. What I can't get over is that it's all so exactly like Boston!" Maggie exploded.

"*And* St. Louis" was the dour answer.

"St. Louis?" Maggie turned on him, incredulous. "But St. Louis is the West! Westerners aren't puritans!"

"Look, Margot, this Boston bee in your bonnet has got you all wacky. You think you're reacting against the puritans. But your youth was no different from mine. The shadow that hung over us both—and still envelops the good souls we've just left—is Queen Victoria. The true puritan is fierce and passionate and hard. It's the Victorian who is sentimental, which is another way of saying he's dishonest. The relics we've just left are simply smothered in Victorian gentility—as were we," he added almost shamefacedly.

"Well, at least we've got over it!" said Maggie rather grandly.

"Speak for yourself, John" was Ray's only answer.

24

THE MASTERS, along with the rest of an uprooted world, were not exempt from the impact of history. Events fell so fast on their heads that Maggie, looking back, could hardly remember in what order they had fallen.

The attack on Pearl Harbor occurred on the day Ray arrived back in New York after a hurried visit to St. Louis, where he had been called because of his mother's having suffered a stroke. In a matter of weeks Skipper had left Princeton to enlist in the Navy (in spite of the protests of his father, who had done the same thing in 1917). Then came Sister's wedding—to be followed by her removal with her bridegroom to Fort Riley, Kansas. Ray's storm of protests at having to fish his cutaway out of mothballs and at having to sit in the front pew of the Cedarside Episcopal Church beside Alice had hardly died down when he was back in the same pew in quite other circumstances. Alice had telephoned him after midnight one night to choke out through sobs that reached even Maggie across the wires that she had received word from the Navy Department that Skipper had been killed in "operational maneuvers" off Pensacola.

When Ray returned from Cedarside after the memorial services he brushed aside Maggie's barrage of questions—her instinctive gesture toward consolation.

"Listen, Maggie," he said, "there's nothing to say, so there's no good asking. The church was full. It's all over. Now, let's talk about something else."

"But did you just leave Alice all alone, Ray? With Sister not able to come on it seems awfully grim for her. I wouldn't have minded at all if you'd wanted to spend the evening."

"Thanks. But I didn't." His mouth snapped shut as his eyes darkened with the pain he was determined not to share.

During the weeks and months that followed, Maggie had still to find the subject of conversation that would rouse Ray from the black depression that enveloped him. One Saturday he went out to lunch with Alice in Cedarside. She wanted to discuss with him alternative plans for design and the wording of a marble tablet that both parents were giving jointly to the chapel at Skipper's school in his memory. After this expedition Maggie felt more futile than ever in her attempts to interest him in anything beyond the confines of his own grief.

Who, in his presence, could ever again dare frame the word *fun*? When he closed the door of his study behind him in the evening, Maggie was aware of the disturbing sense that on the other side of it, instead of writing (his ostensible excuse for being there at all), he was more than likely sitting as he had sat when he put down the receiver after Alice's call, his head bowed on his arms before him. One day she found on his desk a package of Skipper's letters, beside it another package on which he had scrawled, "They all did more for him than I." Maggie knew that they were letters from schoolmates and teachers, friends from college, and, more recently, Navy friends, his commanding officer and others. Ray had let her look at one or two, no more; he seemed determined to exclude her from sharing his remorse as well as his grief.

Maggie could only stand by, frustrated, during the next months as she watched him dwindle before her eyes into a figure that receded farther and farther from her grasp. When he was accepted for Reserve Officers' training in the Navy in June 1942 she was aware that the step was merely the outward and visible sign of an inward isolation that was almost complete.

Protesting that he was unable to do any work since Skipper's death, he made no claim to heroism. "I suppose I'm a sentimental fathead," he said to Maggie, "but I'd rather be a flat tire in uniform than out of it."

Maggie showed what passed with Ray for surprising tact by saying nothing. He, in turn, expressed awareness of her restraint by treating her with a gentle consideration she did not recognize. She wondered whether perhaps he felt these might be the last days they would have together, and he was trying to put into them a little more of what he now wished he had shown her sooner and oftener. She was ashamed to admit to herself a rising sense of exhilaration at the approaching prospect of unimpeded independence and activity.

Within five months Ray was on proceed orders, via San Francisco, to ComAirPac, Pearl Harbor—taking a four-day "delay" in St. Louis with his mother. From there he wrote to Maggie, "Perhaps it's her recent stroke that has softened her up, or Skipper's death. But whatever it is, Mother seems prepared to come off her Queen Mary high horse and receive you as one of the family. After the war, darling, I want very much to bring you out here to see her. She's as much of a *maitresse femme* in her way as you are in yours; there's no reason you shouldn't establish some sort of grand alliance with her."

By the time AirPac had assigned Ray a berth on a carrier Maggie not only had moved herself from the Fifty-fourth Street apartment into the Hotel Wrentham, but was talking about moving the headquarters of the A.O.E.O. from Mrs. Bent's ballroom along with her.

With America's entry into the war, the full-grown Allied Officers' Entertainment Organization had hatched from Maggie's fledgling enterprise, incubated under Mrs. Bent's wing. It was barely off the ground before Chez Francette, exiled from the more immediate contribution her sisters in the *maquis* were making, had donated the design for a uniform to be worn by Maggie and her staff of Junior League assistants. It was a smart apple-green, with A.O.E.O. picked out on the lapels in the same shade of emerald-green velvet that was repeated from the becoming beret.

Maggie, seeing the ensemble for the first time, exclaimed, "Wonderful! Now we'll be Green Ladies!"

The name stuck, and presently a talented debutante had done a crayon sketch of the beret which became a little emblem, to be reproduced on posters, paper napkins, and matchboxes. Margot Masters' Green Lady had become New York's most chic officers' recreation center.

During the next months there whirled and flashed about Maggie sparkling streamers of excitement; as combined impresario, mistress of ceremonies, and hostess she stood as the pivotal figure of an operation that had spelled spectacular and instantaneous success. Broadway performers whom she had known in the days of Ray's radio program, claiming her as an old friend, were as happy and flattered to be invited to cross the threshold of the mansion that belonged to Mr. and Mrs. Rhinelander Bent as they, for their part, were thrilled to receive under their roof "real Broadway stars." Each world made much of Maggie as the possessor of the magic key that could unlock the door into the other. If Maggie did not consciously revert in memory to that moment in Boston when Nini, deploring her state, had exclaimed, "There's no success like success!" it was only because she was daily refreshed with draughts of the precious elixir for which she had thirsted so long.

Nini, witnessing the present triumph of her friend, was only too happy to expunge the recent past which had skirted perilously close to the precipice of failure. Practiced as she was in the fine art of distinguishing "right" from "wrong" in the strictly social sense, she perceived that any organization whose angel was Mrs. Rhinelander Bent was not only right but tops. In due order she threw over a previous commitment to the Stage Door Canteen to march behind Maggie's banner. Mrs. Bent's favor had been, so far, the one uncrackable nut on Nini's New York bill of fare, and, therefore, the most toothsome and desirable. It did not take her long, in her trim little uniform, to sell both Maggie and Mrs. Bent herself the desirability of staging a big benefit for A.O.E.O. She pointed out that with an increase of funds a move such as that envisaged by Maggie could be achieved—the Wrentham would give them a favorable rate on a suite, which would include an office for Maggie where she could have a secretary on eight-hour duty, a checkroom, and a small ballroom with a stage and proper lighting. Mr. Bent, inspirited at the thought of being restored to the privacy of his own ballroom, volunteered to match whatever such a benefit might net. The rest, Nini assured Maggie, they could manage between them. She was sure they could enlist the talent to put the evening over with a bang.

Maggie, waiting backstage in the ballroom of the Waldorf on the night of the Bal de Tête to make her "few remarks" to the huge audience that roared on the other side of the curtain, pulled the well-fitted jacket of her uniform down over her hips for a last time and, peering in a mirror, poked at her hair under the rim of her beret and applied a final dab of powder and application of lipstick. She looked smart and attractive; more, she looked important, and knew it. She heard her name spoken; a wave of applause floated her on stage. It had taken her years to get there, but at last Maggie Fraser, greeted by the applause of a huge audience, stood behind the footlights.

She took her place by the side of the master of ceremonies, whose scalp, so to speak, was dangling for the evening from Nini's belt. It had been Nini's powers of persuasiveness that had produced as master of ceremonies Alexander Fremont, no longer living in Hollywood as a motion-picture actor. His marriage of twenty years to Dotty the hoofer had been superseded by his marriage to the twice-divorced daughter of the owner of a large chain of hotels. Alexander Fremont's role in his father-in-law's hierarchy was covered by the vague title "public relations." His duties consisted of being set down, or set up, in a series of executive suites in the most expensive resorts across the nation to serve as bait to a flashy and, if possible, international clientele.

His smile was full and heart-warming as he stooped to take Maggie's hand in both of his, and then lifted it to his lips. Then, facing the audience, he said, "And now, ladies and gentlemen, this is one of those moments that make being in show business a pretty swell thing. It's the fun of sharing a personal friendship with all you wonderful people here tonight. 'Way out in Hollywood, before she became known as the personality she has since become, I'm happy to say that I was one of those who recognized that the world was going to hear from Margot Masters. I loved her then as I love her now—as all of you love this big-hearted gal who's doing one whale of a job for the best damned fighting men in the world today. Here she is—the one, the only—Margot Masters!"

It was certain that the platitudes that fell from Maggie's lips could not have charmed a large audience in themselves. But speaking in a voice of God-given timbre that could electrify without conscious effort, she achieved an instantaneous triumph. She smiled, she spoke—and she was loved. What she said involved simply the A.O.E.O.'s need for its own headquarters, and the overflowing of gratitude to all the wonderful people present for their generosity in having filled this need. Mutual delight fairly sizzled back and forth across the footlights. When Maggie had finished she retired, gasping from the excitement of her success, into the wings. From that strategic point of vantage she could peer out at the professionals, who, for the next hour, gave the sort of performance that Maggie, as their amateur entrepreneur, could lie back on, feeling that their triumph and their talent, by some magic alchemy, had become hers. When it was all over she mopped her brow as though it had been thanks to her personal efforts that the huge audience had been so royally entertained. She returned to the ballroom floor to join Nini's table for supper and to watch the fashion show, in which the "mesdames" who had baited the invitations as patronnesses were to act as models.

Looking vaguely about her, aware that she knew nobody in the party, Maggie heard a voice asking, "Won't you sit beside me? My name is Paul Prentiss."

Still breathless with the sense of her own accomplishment and unaware where she was, she took the proffered place without thinking.

"You were terrific, did you know it?"

The words, like a powerful magnet, turned her in her chair toward her supper partner. "Heavens, *I* wasn't anything! But wasn't the show marvelous?"

"Have you heard of *Fun* magazine?" her new friend asked abruptly.

"Should I?"

"Not necessarily. We're brand new, and hope to achieve something halfway between the old *Town Topics* and *The New Yorker*. We are definitely a class publication. I'm its editor. Known to the trade as Mr. P. or Sweet Pea. As you've only known me two minutes I assure you the 'sweet' is ironic."

Maggie, looking more closely at her interlocutor, remembered Chelek's Hollywood adjective *thinsetic*. Put positively, Paul Prentiss was nearly a gentleman and nearly a man; put negatively, there was a suggestion of the bounder about him and a whiff of the effeminate. He must have been, Maggie assumed, somewhere on the shady side of fifty; she was sure that the shock of evenly dark-brown hair was dyed. Although his mouth was loose and he spoke with a lisp, his hazel eyes had a steely glitter.

She found herself, however, absorbed in what he was saying to her. "I was watching you very carefully as you spoke up there on the stage. You've got a very attractive, natural, *breathless* quality about you. Have you ever thought of putting it on paper?"

"Do you mean can I *write*?" Maggie asked in a voice full of consternation.

Mr. Prentiss shrugged a shoulder in the direction of Nini. "Little pitchers," he said. "What I'm saying to you is confidential, for the moment. I have an idea that you might be useful to our outfit. I keep hearing about you as one of these fabulous women whom everybody knows, and I'm sure you know who's who in the world we're interested in."

"But I don't!" Maggie burst out. "I only know who's fun!"

"There's the name of your column."

"My *column*!"

The tête-à-tête was suddenly interrupted by Nini, calling down the table. Her shoe-button eyes were fixed sharply, and not kindly, on her two guests, as though glittering from the strain of ineffective lip reading. "Just because your own act is over, Maggie," she said, "don't forget to give the other performers a break. Aren't you going to look at the fashion show?"

"Yes, yes, of course!" Maggie, feeling as though she had been rapped over the knuckles, turned her attention obediently to the spectacle before her.

Slowly the undulating trail of society beauties got under way, weaving and swaying across the dance floor, each carrying her head with its elaborate jeweled headdress as though she had recognized its existence for the first time. The beholder was half afraid that it might come loose, fall off, and break on the floor. Even the weariest river of amateur exhibitionism winds at last to sea, and the climax was finally achieved in the form of the new Mrs. Alexander Fremont, whose headgear proclaimed her Columbia. She was dressed in a skin-tight sheath of midnight-blue sequins; her cap glittered with rubies, diamonds, and sapphires. Maggie's thoughts darted back—and wondered if Alexander Fremont's did too—to Dotty, in the Florentine Room of the Beverly-Wilshire, in her bouffant white tulle. What chance could she possibly have in the league where this dark, disagreeable but wholly assured beauty operated? Like the professionals backstage she, in her own way, was big-time too.

Maggie heard the same persuasive voice close to her ear, "Call my office tomorrow for an appointment if you're interested."

Maggie put a warning finger to her lips. She was in no mood to receive another public reprimand from Nini.

At that moment a burst of applause swept the ballroom. Maggie extended her own hands far out over the table, so that Nini might witness her enthusiastic response to the spectacle. Raising her voice over the hubbub, she cried to Mr. Prentiss, "Don't worry, I'm interested, all right!"

She turned her happy smile and sparkling eyes boldly on Nini as she redoubled her applause.

25

"Do YOU realize that you are having dinner with a *professional*?" Maggie asked her father across the first corner table in the dining room of "21."

"A professional what?"

"Stop it, Father! I refuse to be teased. I'm in much too good a humor!" The words Maggie spoke were unnecessary to proclaim the happiness that fairly bubbled from her.

"Since I take it that you consider your status an elevation, I rejoice with you."

"Of course I do! My first check is already hanging in my office—framed. And my second is to be spent this evening—on you."

"Also framed?"

"Yes!" Maggie laughed her most infectious laugh. "You're framed to order everything in the world you like most."

Her friends at "21," from Red, who opened the door of their taxi, to Jimmy at the entrance, were conspiring to give what she had asked for—the red-carpet treatment for her father. Proud of herself in her becoming apple-green uniform, Maggie was ten times prouder of her father in his colonel's uniform of the Army Medical Corps. People would turn to look at him anywhere, she thought. *Distinguished*—that is what he was, and that is what he looked. It was wonderful, for a man, she thought, taking him in with her admiring eyes, to be in his sixties and as spare as he had been at fifty. His shoulders were a little stooped, the blue of his eyes a little less intense than it had once been. and there were reddish-purple veins on his cheeks—but all the same the total effect was one of verve and keenness.

On the way from his hotel they had talked of the most important piece of family news—a serious operation that Kitten had recently undergone.

With Roger in North Africa, a major in the Army Air Corps, it was natural perhaps that Maggie's first concern should be for him. "What have you told him, Father? How much does he know?" she asked.

"He's known ever since Button was born that Kitten hasn't been well, so I rather think he must have been a bit prepared, but naturally it wouldn't be fair to tell him anything but the truth. I shall hope to see him soon face to face. The MGH unit is at Casablanca, and if luck is with us we should be meeting."

Maggie, flinching before the stark word *truth*, sprang forward to soften its outline for her own comfort. "But you're not worried yourself, Father? Kitten will be all right, won't she?"

"I'm very hopeful that she will be. A hysterectomy is one of the cleanest operations there is, when it comes to malignancy. The biopsy has shown no other adjacent tissue affected, so the prognosis is extremely encouraging. The X-ray treatments were simply an extra precaution. She's tolerated them amazingly well and is going ahead with her life as though the whole business is a closed chapter. There's every reason to believe it is—with fingers crossed."

"I still wish she'd told me first," Maggie said. "It seemed so awful for me not to be there with her."

"You know Kitten as well as I do. She wanted to make the least possible fuss, and actually until she was under the anesthetic we didn't know how much the operation was going to amount to. By the time it was over, and she felt like seeing people, I suppose she felt there were just too damn many Bradfields around her bed to make your being there also exactly relaxing."

"I bet Ma Brad probably stood guard on purpose just to keep me away!" Maggie burst out angrily.

"You weren't the only one she's had to keep away. It's amazing how people spring out of the ground who feel they have some demand on Kitten. Even when she's sick it's they who need her and not the other way around."

"Is she worried about herself, Father?"

"Certainly not. That girl has some magic key to life. Skeptic though I am, I'm bound to admit that there exists the genus *mystic* and Kitten belongs to it. She's at home in the universe. Perhaps it's simply because she's at home with herself. I agree with Roger that she has the true *feu sacré* as far as her poetry goes. I'm sure it's the real thing. And yet there she is, stuck on Milton Hill with no help, no gas, no husband, and a household of boys to act as chief cook and bottle washer for, and she's neither angry nor resentful."

"I don't know how she stands it!" Maggie burst out. "I know I never would."

"You certainly wouldn't. Neither would I." Dr. Fraser smiled at his daughter. "But then the likes of us will never inherit the earth."

Now, over their jellied green turtle soup, he recalled that Maggie had a husband. "You haven't told me what's the news of Ray," he said. "Your mother and I are so interested in all that you're up to in New York I hope you don't think we're callous not to ask more often about him."

"Oh, my no!" Maggie, feeling no compunction that she never mentioned Ray herself either in letters or in telephone talks with her parents, pulled out a letter from her handbag as though she had been reminded of an agreeable mutual friend. She skimmed through the first page. "Of course he can't really tell anything important. He's still on the *Essex*, and I figure he must be in the Solomon Sea. He talks about the 'spectacular precision of the launching and recovering of aircraft,' and writes, 'Wish I could tell you in detail of the day-to-day carrier operation.' Oh, yes, here's the part about a gas-attack drill. 'The Old Man appears to have a wry sense of humor all his own. Unbeknown to us squadron people, he had someone release ammonia fumes from back of the scuttlebutt outside the ready room. We were all in

Condition Able, which means General Quarters, but were horsing around not taking life very seriously when the gong signal for gas attack sounded. In a casual kind of way one of the pilots opened the door of the ready room to see what was going on and was met with a great wave of whitish fumes. He slammed the door and there was bedlam—a scuffle for gas masks, which were stowed in the locker under each pilot's adjustable seat. I wish you could have seen Hose-nose Johnson—he's the big joker from Texas I've told you about who's forever playing "McNamara's Band" on his harmonica—trying to mash his face into his gas mask, forgetting to remove the metal frame that keeps it properly stretched.' Well, you get the idea," said Maggie. "He seems to be enjoying himself, like a boy at boarding school."

"It's in the nature of the beast, Maggie. Man has always, on the whole, enjoyed himself in wars or he wouldn't arrange to have them so often. Perhaps woman, too, is enjoying herself in this one. Looking at you in that very becoming outfit, I should say offhand I'd never seen you looking better—fresh and on your toes."

"I guess that's because I'm so thrilled about the job on *Fun*. Not that the Green Lady hasn't been simply fascinating, because it has. But the staff can practically run it themselves. They've all been wonderful about understanding that now that I've got a professional job I'll have less time to give to a volunteer one, though actually the two really tie in. My column, 'Who's Fun,' is supposed to be bristling with the names of celebrities, and as they all come to the Green Lady, one hand sort of feeds the other," she said with satisfaction. "Maybe you'd like to see the way *Fun* introduces me."

She handed him a page of proof, which she brought out of her military satchel. Dr. Fraser read, "We welcome Margot Masters to the pages of *Fun, because* her 'baby,' the Allied Officers Entertainment Organization, is now grown to full stature and is rapidly expanding into a nation-wide influence for maintaining officer morale, *because* she has dared to laugh at being a lady, and in so doing has become a terrific woman, more interested in sampling the mixed flavors of her fellow humans than in picking at the Upper Crust of the Back Bay into which she was born, and finally *because* she has that one enviable possession which makes any other unnecessary to the woman who has it—personality."

"Splendid! I'm proud to know you. And what do you tell your public about the good and great who come to the Green Lady?"

"Oh, anything! Sweet Pea—he's the editor, really, but that's what we call him—says not even to think about grammar but just to rattle on as I talk. *Breathless* was the word he used. He said that's what people like."

"Maggie," her father said, shoving his plate away from him and crossing his arms, "are you happy?"

"Yes! Terrifically!" she answered without hesitation.

"You've got the success you always wanted?"

"I'm getting it."

"So far as I can make out you're happy because you know a lot of people who are known in a certain world, and you, in turn, are known to them. Is it that that makes you happy?"

"Why, I suppose so. Yes. Is that bad?"

"No, no. *Bad*, certainly not. *Intelligent* is something else. If you'll excuse a bit of Poloniuslike advice, I hope that since you've set your sights on success, you'll occasionally stop and ask yourself what you wish to be a success *at*. I submit that it makes a difference."

Maggie blinked, uncomprehending and a little hurt, at her father. She wanted this evening to be gay, lighthearted, and wanted so dreadfully for him to be as proud of being seen in public with her as she was proud of being seen with him. She could not understand the twist the conversation was taking.

"Don't you like what I'm doing, Father?" she asked.

"I haven't said that I didn't, my dear child," he answered gently. "I don't know. I simply have an unpleasant sensation of something very close to self-reproach. I feel perhaps that I've rather shamefully neglected your upbringing. Perhaps as a father I've been frivolous."

"I don't even know what you're talking about," Maggie could say with the ring of wholehearted conviction.

"In fact, I'm being kind to myself when I say frivolous. Selfish is probably more nearly like it. I'm afraid I thought of my only daughter as created for the express purpose of my relaxation, entertainment, and delectation. And you have, Maggie, always delighted and refreshed me." Father and daughter exchanged a happy look of mutual pride and love. "But the business of 'bringing up,'" Dr. Fraser went on, "I considered what my father used to call 'squaw's work'—I left that to your mother, and she, poor dear, in those days was so busy catering to my vagaries that she had little time to give to it. I now have the nasty feeling that perhaps you've been shoved off into the jungle of the twentieth century without the proper weapons in your hands."

"What kind of weapons, Father?"

"Discipline, for one thing. We've been too easy on you. I was reacting so violently against the Calvinistic repressions of my own childhood that I was determined that freedom should be the order of the day for my own children."

"But I would have grabbed it if you hadn't given it to me!" Maggie looked him brazenly in the eyes.

"And yet I don't think you've had the real thing. Perhaps if one's economic, social and even religious—" he hesitated for the word—"pattern is fixed, it's easier for the mind and spirit to soar off on their own. By hitting against the bars of my cage—my father's standards—in a sense I knew not only where I was but who I was, and knew what I didn't like about either. With you, we simply opened the door of your cage and said, 'Fly!' leaving both goal and direction to you." Dr. Fraser went on, more for his own edification than Maggie's. "Perhaps the standards of anyone in a profession are a little tepid. I think you always craved, Maggie, a little more dash and color than doctoring, teaching, or architecture could yield. Or maybe you're just plain spoiled." He smiled disarmingly, as though he had just paid her a rather charming compliment.

"That's what Roger says!" Maggie exclaimed with a spurt of belligerence. "He says I'm determined to make everybody like me."

"No, no, that's not fair." Dr. Fraser was clearly in no mood to scold his daughter, preferring to take any blame that was being meted out on his own head. "I dare say you're no different from most of your contemporaries who were sent to the same sort of school and college as you were. You were educated to believe that the world was your oyster."

"Don't you really believe in higher education for women, Father?" Maggie asked so seriously that her father greeted her question with a guffaw. "I don't think that Mother does," Maggie countered in self-defense.

"Yes, your mother is one of the lucky ones who is satisfied 'to do her duty in that state of life unto which it shall please God to call her.' She has never felt the itch that seems to trouble you and your generation."

"But it's *not* just my generation! I can think of ever so many women not of my generation whom you've admired and who certainly weren't just *housewives*." Maggie spat out the term of opprobrium with disgust. Suddenly she recalled an apparition that had transformed the Brimmer Street dining room one afternoon when she and Roger as children were eating their supper; she could still hear a magic voice and remember a large hat and a general sense that the mysterious lady who was the possessor of both must belong to a race of goddesses who existed in a realm quite removed from any that she, Maggie Fraser, had so far even glimpsed. Now, pressing her point with her father further home, she said, "You always liked Ethel Barrymore."

Her father laughed again. "I've adored her! *And* Madame Curie, *and* Ruth Draper, *and* Alice Hamilton at the Harvard Medical School. The remarkable woman—the woman of achievement—has a power to attract a man that is all her own. But I've never admired one that has achieved distinction at the expense of . . . well, whatever the quality is that makes her, above all, a woman."

"Maybe it's just because you don't know any other woman columnists that you take such a dim view. I wonder if you'd have felt differently if I'd been an actress." Maggie felt she must wring from him some sort of endorsement, however reluctant, of the course she had taken.

"If you'd been a real actress you would have had a real talent, and you would have had to serve your talent with humility and hard work. I have an unpleasant feeling that your present job is the other way around."

"I don't know why you seem determined to take such a gloomy view, Father. I'm happy! I have everything I have always wanted." Quickly she added with sudden soberness, "Of course I won't be *really* happy until I get Priscilla with me."

"Yes—Priscilla," her father said gravely. "There's the rub."

Maggie suddenly felt she must square herself with her father, explain motives and actions that she had never explained before. "I never would have asked Dexter for a divorce in the first place if I hadn't been sure I could have had Priscilla with me. Who would ever imagine anything as horrible as what Ma Brad did? And then, on top of it, Spaff moving in like that. I never meant to hurt Priscilla."

Dr. Fraser looked at his child a moment before handing her the palliative she was so clearly asking from him. "Of course you didn't," he said at last, "and yet, though that may explain what happened, Mag, it doesn't altogether excuse it. It has always seemed to me that there's one unwritten commandment which is the most important of the lot: 'Know thy neighbor as thyself.' Perhaps you haven't given enough time to knowing yourself *or* to trying to imagine what it is that makes other people tick. You have rather a habit, Mag, of hurling yourself at life."

"Well, Priscilla seems to be doing all right at Cornell, and loves her work, so perhaps I haven't done too much harm," Maggie said cheerfully, as though she were offering sufficient refutation of the charges. "It's beyond me how any child of mine can find entertainment in courses in animal husbandry and the physiology of domestic animals, but *chacun à son gout*!" she added.

Although Maggie had hardly been pleased with Priscilla's desire to fit herself to "do something with animals," still she derived solid satisfaction from the knowledge that she was, at Ithaca, at least, at a safe distance from the Bradfield orbit.

Dr. Fraser, appearing to feel that he had perhaps probed too deeply into a past it was too late to remedy, changed the subject by asking affably, "Speaking of Spaff, I suppose you've heard that she and Dexter are moving to New York in a few weeks?"

"What do you *mean*?" Color flooded into Maggie's face. "Whatever for? What are they going to *do*?" Her voice rose.

"Dexter's been offered—it's a question of having been drafted really—a big job at the Memorial Hospital. He's to work on the differential effects of the various components of X-ray. He had no choice in the matter. It was one of those things a man simply can't turn down."

"Oh." Maggie was more upset, clearly, than her father had imagined possible as she said again, "Oh," in a voice of unmistakable pain.

"You don't *mind*, Maggie, surely? After such a long time, it's surely nothing to you?"

"No. No, of course not. But—oh, I don't know. I just *think* of Dexter in Boston. I can't see him in New York at all! Especially with Spaff."

"There you go. Be careful," Dr. Fraser said chaffingly. "Your idea of Dexter and the actual Dexter himself may be two very different human beings. Personally, I see no reason at all why Dexter Bradfield shouldn't fit perfectly into New York and take up a good deal of room in it besides. He's too big a fellow to keep down. You mark my words."

Maggie had so little desire to mark them that her father mercifully produced the most delectable red herring he could think of. "I want to hear more about this column of yours, Maggie. Tell me, is it something that might lead on to bigger and better things?"

"Well, believe it or not—" she laughed now, happy at the distraction—"Mr. Prentiss is saying now that there's no reason I mightn't end up on the radio. Lots of the columnists do, you know. Wouldn't it be *fun*?"

Her father seemed prepared to take this cue for the rest of the evening: *fun* was to be the magic word. Wine and food were of his choosing; both did their share toward softening the rather harsh aspect that had frightened Maggie. Over an Upman cigar and brandy he said, chuckling, "Do you remember, Mag, when you were a little thing at the Brimmer School, you used to recite a poem about Columbus? How I used to laugh at your New England pronunciation of the refrain that you rolled out with such a tremolo: 'Sail awn! Sail awn and awn!' That's the way I see you. We haven't heard the last of you yet by a long shot!"

When her father left her at the Wrentham after midnight, and Maggie flung her arms around his neck at parting, she surprised herself as well as him by bursting into tears. "I don't know why I'm crying, Father. I knew nothing bad happens to doctors in wars—" she blew her nose—"but I'll miss you, even though I see you so seldom. Please take care of yourself. And thank you for a wonderful evening, and . . . just . . . thank you! You are my favorite man in the world!"

She kissed him again and turned and ran.

26

Six months later Maggie was to cry to herself, "It was premonition! It was premonition! I *knew* I was never going to see him again!"

Kitten had called her from Boston to tell her that Mrs. Fraser had received word that Dr. Fraser had died of a heart attack "somewhere in North Africa."

Maggie went on at once to Boston to be with her mother. Lying awake at night in the room that had once been hers and Roger's nursery, she felt as though she were abandoned alone in a deserted house. The very tables and chairs, the pictures on the walls, had ceased to hold any meaning for her. Without her father to serve as sounding board for the reverberations of her recent success, even that success seemed suddenly less worth striving for. She knew that she had been the apple of her father's eye; and without the loving, appraising twinkle in that eye there was no response that could ever again count for so much for her. For the first time in her life Maggie knew that she could not turn to her mother for comfort. The integer of her marriage erased, Mrs. Fraser had become a cipher in her own eyes. All she had been able to say to Maggie was "If one of us had to go first, it's better this way," and had covered her face in her hands.

In discussing the future the next day with her mother and Kitten, they decided among them that Mrs. Fraser would sell the Brimmer Street house and move, with the least possible furniture, into two rooms at the Hotel Vendome. Maggie, protesting that she *wished* she could help with all the dirty work involved in emptying out a big house, produced the unanswerable excuse of her own daily radio show about to go on the air. Kitten, with only the private commitment of five children to consider, did not question Maggie's assumption that "the show must go on" as the first and great commandment, regardless of any debatable merit of that show. Maggie, considering the fact that Kitten was still convalescent from her recent operation, asked her half a dozen times, "Do you really think you *should*, Kitten?" The answer was not "Somebody has to," but "Forget it, Maggie. I feel fine."

When Sweet Pea had suggested that a guest appearance for Maggie on Dorothy Dinwiddie's program might give her "Who's Fun" column a little more visibility Maggie accepted with pleasure. Mrs. Dinwiddie's "Coffee and Doughnuts," a half hour of interviews, chatter, and commercials, had been lapped up for a decade by the housewives of the Eastern seaboard. The outburst of letters that followed Maggie's appearance resulted in her being asked to appear again; and it was Mrs. Dinwiddie herself who sold to WABS the idea of Maggie's taking over her show while she herself went to Florida for two weeks' vacation. In her monthly column "Who's Fun" Maggie wrote, with all the breathlessness that Sweet Pea had urged upon her:

> Imagine my excitement to find myself on the air in place of the one and only Dorothy Dinwiddie! My interviewees have all been so co-operative, the sponsors so forgiving of my fluffing lines, and the technicians so helpful that I feel like an old pro! Listeners have written in fantastic letters, probably identifying themselves with the struggle of a fellow female to make good. I'm sure they're all dying to have Dorothy back at the old stand, doing business. It's probably the ham in me, but I hope she has such a wonderful holiday that she decides to prolong it indefinitely!

Mrs. Dinwiddie may or may not have made the decision herself, but when she returned from Florida she was told that "Coffee and Doughnuts" was to be no more. Purely coincidentally a new program, of much the same format, to be entitled "Who's Fun" (by special arrangement with *Fun* magazine), was to brighten the air waves of the Eastern seaboard, with Margot Masters as its star performer.

It was some time after Maggie had become firmly established as a radio personality that Paul Prentiss said to her one day, "You know, Margot, everything I thought about you the first night we met has come to pass, but I still don't think you're using all your assets."

"Such as?"

He looked at her again, as though wondering whether to advance farther. "Mrs. Bent. I notice you never mention her in your column. I admit you couldn't do a thing with her on the radio, but you haven't begun to get full value from her for *Fun*."

"But who wants to hear about Mrs. Bent? She's so stuffy! She does such dreary things—good works, committee meetings, discussion clubs. Believe it or not, she asked me to be *in* one!"

"You're a fool if you refused. Now there's the first assignment I'm giving you! You tell her you've changed your mind and want to be in the discussion club. This should have great snob appeal. Report to me after you're in!"

Within a few days Maggie was carrying out orders. After all, now that she was proving herself in the commercial world and some inner longing assuaged thereby, it was satisfactory to know that the other world, the world she so lightly called stuffy and yet, ironically enough, on whose importance Paul Prentiss and other Park Avenue colleagues put so high a value, was still there, and her own. It was her natural heritage. She did not have to beat against any closed bars, or stand, wistful and unknown, yearning on the outside looking in. With an almost haughty assurance she told herself that now was the moment to acknowledge this world, too, as part of her domain. In Sweet Pea's opinion it represented an important asset; and Maggie, streamlining herself for success more and more every day, was learning not only to count but to use assets.

Ostensibly to talk over certain aspects of the Green Lady, with which she was still concerned, she went to lunch with her older friend.

Over their demitasses she plunged in. "Now that Ray is away, I'm able to do more things that *I* like. If you'd still like to have me in your discussion club I'd love to join." A promise of dimples flickered, tentative and disarming, ready to deepen on signal.

The signal did not come. The dimples were hastily remanded. Mrs. Bent, ordinarily a facile chairman of the board, was having trouble. "Oh, Maggie dear! Oh!" she said again rather helplessly, distress in each syllable. "I'm afraid that now . . . I mean really it's more on your own account than anything because I'm afraid it would only be awkward for you, but the truth is that . . . er . . . Caroline—" She could not go on.

It was Maggie's turn to say "Oh!" She said it loud and roundly. "Oh! Mrs. Bent, please don't give it another thought! If Spaff is in your club, that settles it. There certainly wouldn't be room for me, too." She attempted a worldly laugh. But as Mrs. Bent's ears were more kindly than worldly, the laugh had a rasp to it.

Maggie did not have to spell out to Sweet Pea the snub she had received. With instinctive alacrity he offered the prompt restorative of flattery. "I hear on every side that your show is going great guns. Is it true that two new sponsors have bought time just in the last week?"

"Well, yes, it is." Maggie smiled, only too pleased with his method of consolation.

Margot Masters, the columnist, had been all very well, but Margot Masters, with a radio show of her own, cut an even more important figure. By the spring of '45, out of uniform, Maggie began to affect the habit of wearing no hat. Her golden blond (Trulite, No. 106½) hair shone as bright as the heavy costume jewelry that clanked at her wrists, neck, and ears. Her harlequin-shaped glasses, their frames varying from day to day in a range of colors, had become a badge of recognition to that small segment of the metropolis which calls itself "everyone in New York." She wore them not only on the streets, in restaurants and shops, but in the studio as well. They seemed as much an emblem of her new professional status as her first wrist watch and the capacious calf satchel that swung over one shoulder.

Insulated from all other distractions, Maggie found her hours in the studio the happiest she had ever spent anywhere in her life. Here, under the huge studio clock, she bowed in final fealty to the power she had served all her life. Time was king. *Tick, tick, tick*—each second was gold to her who clutched and clung to it like a miser. When her allotted half hour each morning had gone and she was off the air, her exclamation, given as never before, was "Where has the time gone!"

Each morning when she came into the studio there was the same atmosphere of expectancy, at least to herself if not to the porters busy emptying out ash trays filled during the preceding hour. First, she would remove her heavy bracelets so that their clanking would not be picked up by the microphone. Then, on schedule, would come that last unending minute during which she moistened her lips sixty times, sipped from a glass of water and tried to steady her shaking script. The great minute hand whose lumbering progress she followed glassy-eyed had reached its destination: there, through the glass partition, the director, Jack Zuratti, lifted his hand and suddenly pointed an accusing finger at her head. "Who's Fun" was *on the air*!

Gradually, like coming out of ether, her head would clear to absorb the mellifluous words of Merle Marvyn, the announcer.

> At this time, ladies and gentlemen, the makers of Noblesse—the stationery that makes you feel as *sure* as a coat-of-arms—once again bring you the glamorous boss lady of "Who's Fun." Today she is presenting to you the Noblesse Informal, that little folding card which is designed especially for the message gracious, whether it say "thank you," "deepest sympathy," or "cocktails five to seven—R.S.V.P." Because fun and fun people are as natural to Margot Masters as the right stationer is to the fastidious hostess, I am going to ask her to introduce our special guest of the day. Here she is, patreecian as the Beacon Hill she comes from, as informal as the Café Society where she shines as a truly representative personality of our time—Margot Masters!

And there she was—"on," thrilled as she had been the day before, thrilled as she would be again tomorrow to be meeting somebody new and sharing her thrill with her own public. Here, in this medium, Maggie's voice, always her single most powerful asset and charm, served her as photogenic features can serve a screen actress. There was a quality in the very timbre in which she would say to her guest "It's *sheer heaven* to have you with us this morning!" that could set tingling responsive reflexes in her listeners. The heart of the possessor of such a voice, they told themselves, must be as big as the world. To draw out a celebrity, to chuckle cozily, to *tchk, tchk* sympathetically—all came so naturally to Maggie that she used to confess to Sweet Pea, "I really feel immoral for being paid to do something I just *adore*!" If she received, in exchange, from the "personality" of the day the recognition of her own existence as Somebody, that, too, she just adored. For the first time in her life she felt that she knew who she was and, looking at the creature her public had created, she appeared to find it good. If there was hollowness behind the façade, then hollowness served as the perfect reverberator to send back to each egotist that Maggie interviewed—if he were not an egotist, why would he be there at all?—only flattering echoes of his own self-esteem. It was hard to tell where flatterer and flattered changed role in this ritual that beguiled the listening housewives. What sustenance in turn these hungry sheep absorbed it would be impossible to tell. The badinage was sprinkled with the use of whole names. ("Good morning, John Franklyn. It certainly is wonderful to have the star of a new Broadway hit in our studio this morning." "Good morning, Margot Masters, it certainly is a big thrill for me to be here." "Thank you, John Franklyn." "Thank *you,* Margot Masters.") Thank you for nothing? If any one of the housewives—like the little boy who saw that the emperor was not wearing new clothes but was stark naked—felt that this web of interchange was spun from a vacuum, all she had to do was to switch the dial. Maggie herself was isolated in her charmed circle of make-believe, and make-believed, that named itself Fame.

She enjoyed finding her desk piled high with letters from her unseen listeners. Many of them commended her for what she was doing, but even more asked her for advice. "What would you suggest that I do with a daughter who is determined to go on the stage?" "My sister-in-law is coming to stay, but she just hates cards. What sort of party could I ask my neighbors to?" There were even the solicitous ones: "You sounded to me today as though you had a nasty cold, dear. Have you ever tried just the old-fashioned remedy of . . ." There was as well a mound of correspondence from agents—agents of the publishers of a new book whose author might be persuaded to appear as a guest on Margot Masters' "Who's Fun" in the spirit of public service; agents of a Hollywood movie star, passing through New York, who felt a sense of personal responsibility about the bad publicity the motion-picture industry had been getting and in a spirit of fair play might be persuaded, etc., etc. There were as well presents from sponsors—hair shampoos, furniture polishes, detergents, soft drinks, and face creams.

Maggie telephoned Milton long distance with increasing frequency. "Tell me truthfully," she would say to Kitten, "how did the program go, *really*?" The fact that she knew the answer in advance only made her count increasingly on hearing it. "It was splendid, Maggie! It's uncanny how your voice comes over, with so much warmth and laughter in it. It's just like having you right here in our living room!"

When peace came to the Pacific in the summer of '45 and Ray told Maggie that it looked as though it might still be months before he got home, she wrote back, "Maybe it's just as well that you shouldn't be on hand right now. I want to knock your eye out, when you do get back, and naturally I still have a lot to learn." She could tell him proudly, however, that, in addition to her basic salary of $500 a week from the station, Ed Walch, the head of the station's advertising department, had been so successful in selling her to his salesmen that they, in turn, had sold the five spots possible for commercials in her half hour for $10 a week each, bringing in a total of $750 additional to her. "It's been fantastic how helpful some of *your* old contacts have been," she wrote. "Two of the sponsors were sold time by D.D.D. and T. ex-colleagues of yours."

Maggie, seemingly without effort, had mastered the art of speaking her commercials in as excited and natural a tone as that in which she described the Broadway opening of the night before. "I went to the most perfect party after the show, and I couldn't help noticing how beautifully *groomed* my hostess was. I knew at once that she must be one of the thousands of smart women who every day are making the acquaintance of Ssh! Have you ever stopped to realize that you, too, can be Ssh! sure?" She had learned not to lose her stride if Jack Zuratti, from the other side of the pane of glass where he sat with the engineer, held up a paper saying NOT SO NEAR MIKE or DON'T FORGET NEW COMMERCIAL. She enjoyed the semaphore code of wigwag with hands and fingers, each gesture conveying its own commandment: fists rolling over each other in mid-air—*speed it up*; pantomime of pulling taffy—*pull it out*; slashing of a throat—*chop it off*. She glowed with the sense of being a *pro*. Maggie had her own secretary—Dot Toulmin, a strapping corn-fed blonde with one blue eye and one brown, fresh out of Barnard and Katie Gibbs. She had "her" writer, who wrote the lead-ins and the sign-offs and had wit enough to know what to leave to her spontaneous gift for ad-libbing. The same writer did most of Maggie's leg work, rounding up "personalities," covering "events," conducting "pre-interviews"—anything that might serve as grist to Margot Masters' mill. But it was Maggie herself, at the weekly staff meetings, consisting of the "Who's Fun" staff and the head of the WABS program department, who contributed more new ideas and suggestions than all the others put together. The verdict was unanimous: Margot Masters was a natural. "Who's Fun" had proved to be a sleeper.

She wrote again to Ray, "Morrie Baum—I've told you about him, he's the head of our program department—wants me to meet some of the heads of ABS who are in town, from the San Francisco, Chicago and Los Angeles stations. What would you think of a wife who may be pulling down anywhere from $1,500 to $2,000 a week for broadcasting coast to coast! It could happen here!"

Ray wrote back, "May an ex-advertising husband, whose only claim to fame is that of an idea man, make the suggestion that your program, as you describe it, sounds too strictly Broadway? After all, peace has come at last to a suffering world. Wouldn't you be smart to work in more political figures, even some of international stature? It would help to put you yourself on a wider stage, Margot. My suggestion is: broaden your base, widen your scope." The letter was no sooner read than the idea was Maggie's and popped out, fetchingly fresh and spontaneous, at the next staff meeting. In due order a member of Eden's staff, returning from San Francisco, a representative of Luxembourg, and an Indian disciple of Gandhi's were scheduled to appear. By this time Margot Masters had two writers working on her scripts. As she disarmingly admitted, "I just wouldn't know enough, out of my own head, what to ask people like that."

The fact was that the correspondence between Maggie and Ray flowed smoothly along on parallel lines. Maggie learned to do quick and judicious skipping of passages that described his feelings about Japan, though she came to sharp attention when he said, "Peace or no peace, I may be here in Tokyo Bay for many more months to come."

"Oh, dear!" she wrote back. "How disappointing! I'm crazy for you to hear the show and give me your honest opinion of it."

Maggie enjoyed not only sending bulletins of her prowess to Ray, but, in addition to her telephone talks with Kitten, she kept her mother and Priscilla informed of her triumphs. Nini's adulation was only to be expected, but Maggie was particularly gratified when even Mrs. Bent offered her the reassurance she craved: "We're so proud, dear, to know a real *star*!"

The world through which Maggie moved parted to make way for her on sight. She was a public figure and gloried in it. Margot Masters had become the very epitome of the woman Maggie Fraser had longed to be.

27

WHEN MAGGIE wrote Ray that, thanks to a legacy from her father, she was thinking of buying a brownstone house in the East Nineties he wrote back, "Please don't do anything drastic till I get home. I too have a legacy to spend, darling, so wait and let me tell you face to face of a dream that I hope to make reality for us both."

Maggie was sorry that she had not met Ray's mother before her sudden death. Ray had written her about it weeks after it occurred, telling her there was nothing she could do. She had looked forward to the scene of reconciliation that he had prophesied; now it would never take place. One consolation, however, was that she and Ray, from now on, since a last-minute change in the old lady's will, were inheriting what amounted to a very large fortune.

Maggie in her newly won independence, however, was in no mood for caution or postponement. She wrote back, jubilant, "Don't scold me—but we own a house! After all, darling, if it's a mistake, this one is on my own money, and Paul Prentiss says it's a very good *investment,* that I'll be able to dispose of easily, though I'm sure I'm never going to want to, and when you see it you won't want to either! The furniture from Brimmer Street (Roger and Kitten don't want any of it in their modern house, and Mother wants only a few pieces in her hotel) will be perfect for it."

It was only a few weeks after the familiar tables and chairs, pictures and books had been delivered that Maggie was called to the telephone at the studio immediately following one of her morning's programs. She heard a voice so familiar—as familiar as her own—that it brought a catch to her throat.

"Roger! Where did you *come* from? Where *are* you?" she was able to bring out.

"In New York, thank God. I just arrived. Naturally, I want to get back to Kitten and the kids as soon as I can, but I've talked to them on the telephone and told them I'd wait over a couple of hours if I can see you. I have to lunch with one of my Army friends, but I can come along afterward. How are you fixed?"

Maggie was ahead of him that afternoon at the new house which she had insisted he could not leave town without seeing. She opened the door in answer to his ring and, before he was across the threshold, flung her arms around his neck. Then she held him off at arm's length. "You look so well! You look wonderful!" she exclaimed rapturously. It was true that the habitual lines of strain and fatigue on the face of the hard-worked young architect trying to support five boys and a wife was replaced on the features of the Army major by a look of health and general well-being. He held his well-set head higher than before. Though the hair had receded somewhat at the temples, his dark, deep-set eyes were glowing.

Maggie led him into the living room, half crying, half laughing. "I still can't believe it! I just wasn't expecting you. Kitten said it still might be months before you'd get back."

He was looking about him, recognizing familiar Brimmer Street landmarks. "This certainly looks like home," he said, standing before his father's shabby old Morris chair.

Suddenly, and quite as much to her own surprise as to Roger's, Maggie burst into tears. "I can't help it!" she gulped as she reached for a handkerchief. "Seeing you again makes me think of F-f-father!"

Roger's own eyes filled. Almost gruffly he said, "Sure it does. But Father certainly wouldn't approve of any carrying on. It was a wonderful way to go. I've talked to some of the fellows who were with him the morning he died. They said he was cracking jokes and never seemed in better spirits. Gee, there's the library sofa." He had carried them over the painful moment, and in another minute Maggie was pointing out plans for the disposal of other pieces, which were still heaped in corners of the room, under dust covers, along with packing cases of books and barrels of china exuding excelsior. The room was cool and dry in contrast to the damp summer heat outdoors, and smelled not unpleasantly of moth balls. They walked about together, exclaiming over joint recognitions.

"There's the rocking chair that always used to be in the nursery," said Roger, kicking it affectionately with a toe.

"I thought I'd put it in Priscilla's room here."

"Is she with you already, Mag? I didn't know."

"No, not actually. She's at summer school now, but she's mine. She's chosen *me*."

"You sound like the witch in *Rapunzel*."

"I *feel* like it! I can't wait to get my hands on her and lock her safely away from the Bradfields—forever!"

"You forget they're still my in-laws."

"You can have them." Maggie plopped onto the old, faded rose velvet sofa. Her face grew serious and her voice softened. "I hope you're going to find Kitten looking well, Roger. She seems fine," she threw out ineffectually.

"She certainly does in her letters. Father wrote so encouragingly about the outlook that the only way to live is to assume everything's going to be O.K."

"I'm *sure* it will be. It's just *got* to be." Maggie with brisk decision closed the subject. Brightly opening another, she asked, "I suppose you've heard that Spaff and Dexter have come to New York to live? Isn't that *some*thing?"

"Something for whom? For them or for you?" was the rather unsatisfactory retort.

It glanced off Maggie. "Can't you just *see* Spaff, throwing her weight around as wife of the Great Man? Believe it or not, she's already been taken into one of Mrs. Bent's too utterly utter little clubs."

It was Roger's turn to confront Maggie with a bland façade of his own. "I've always liked Spaff," he said. "When do you expect Ray back?" he asked with a cheer that did not conceal the fact that he had forgotten the existence of Maggie's present husband until this moment.

"Soon, I hope. He was one of the unlucky ones, like you, to be kept on to mop up afterward."

"It should be much nicer for you when he gets back—settling into the new house and all," Roger said rather lamely, just not adding, *or won't it?*

"Oh, yes, I can hardly wait." Without pausing to draw breath, Maggie hurried on. "What do you think, Roger, of my being famous? I am, you know!"

"I suppose it's radio that has put you where you want to be?"

"Yes, and my column."

"All the same, if it doesn't seem too blunt a question, what are you famous *for*?"

Maggie laughed. "You make me think of Father, talking about stopping to think what a man is a success *at*. I suppose families always say things like that! I'm famous because—because—" The only way around the question was another disarming laugh. "I know so many famous people!"

"O.K. You win."

Roger looked at his sister. Her hair was shining with surely a brighter gold than it had ever shone before—perhaps because of the bright mustard-colored print dress she was wearing and a heavy gold choker about her neck. The color on her cheeks was so high that a brother, instead of thinking, *How becoming!* asked himself rather, *I wonder if Maggie's got high blood pressure?* He was aware, too, of a stronger perfume in her presence—the positive smell, he supposed, of success.

"Well, it's what you always wanted," he said without emotion.

Maggie hesitated, unsure whether a brother's barb was hidden somewhere in the simple declarative statement. She was, however, in no mood for feeling touchy.

"Yes," she proclaimed boldly, "though I'd given up, years ago, ever thinking I'd get there. I was sure Ray was going to be the famous one."

Roger, rejecting pursuit of this line of thought, chose another fork in the road. "What's this career of yours going to do to your marriage, Maggie?" he asked.

"*Do* to it?" The question appeared to amaze her. "Why should it do anything? I'm sure Ray'll be thrilled. After all, he had a lot to do with radio himself at one time."

"I wouldn't say, offhand, that that would ensure his pleasure in his wife's picking it up where he laid it down."

"I know he'll be terribly interested, once he gets an idea of the picture firsthand. Right now, in some of his letters, he's talking about not wanting to live in New York when he gets back, but lots of men getting out of the service feel the same way. I mean they seem to feel they want to start life over again." Maggie airily quoted some article she had skimmed—was it in *The Reader's Digest*?

"But if he feels like that, have you thought, Maggie, of doing what he wants?"

His sister blinked at the question. "But I can't, Roger. I'm *professional*! My leaving New York is out of the question. Ray will see it my way when he gets home. I know he will." Maggie spoke with a lofty assurance from heights far above the plodding pedestrian who, after all, was going back to pick up a pretty limited little existence on Milton Hill.

Roger, back on his native soil only a matter of hours, feeling no stomach for delivering a lecture to his headstrong sister, said affably, "Well, as long as you're happy, that's all that matters. After all the *Sturm und Drang* of the divorce, in a way it seems a bit cockeyed to see you settling into a house that might as well be on Brimmer Street, filled with all the musty old furniture that I should have supposed would remind you of a world you've tried to get away from. I mean, you seem to have gone after things the hard way. I hope you and Ray are happy at the end of the road."

Maggie felt a sudden sensation of relief. How pleasant this was! Roger's judgment of her, like a third uninvited presence between them, was refreshingly absent today. They were talking as they had used to talk. He seemed concerned with her happiness as he had used to be concerned, not with reading her a lecture. Perhaps it was the very lessening of tension between them that made it hard for her to answer his question directly. She wanted him to carry away only a bright picture of her life. Letting the word *happy* drop, she parried, "You always used to tell me that I was bossy. Probably I am. And probably the American man simply doesn't like a bossy wife!" She observed with self-satisfaction how skillfully she had referred to the genus *American man* without directly implicating Ray.

"I'd say what you need, Maggie," Roger was going on, "is a light hand on the reins, with a firm hand on the bridle. Perhaps you think you're happy when you get the bit between your teeth, but I doubt if you really are."

"I don't think I've been very bright about knowing what I want—really," Maggie brought out abruptly.

Roger affably picked up the comment. "That's because you probably want different things. I've thought sometimes that your two marriages were expressing two sides of yourself. One part of you craved someone strong and solid, a man of formidable accomplishments and weight, like Father, but you also wanted someone quick and talented and adaptable, with a change of pace—perhaps even a little worldly—"

"Also like Father!" Maggie quickly interpolated.

"They don't grow like him on every tree. I guess there's an awful lot of luck in most marriages."

"You've certainly had luck in yours."

"I don't call what I've had 'luck.'" Roger, not trying to expatiate or attempt an approximation of the riches he had possessed, got to his feet, as though in answer to an audible voice of home. "I must run,

Mag. I'd forgotten how far uptown you are in the Nineties. I haven't much time to catch my train."

Maggie followed him to the door. "Give Kitten loads of love."

His hand was on the door, but Maggie stopped for one more almost pleading word. "And, Roger, you will listen to me on the radio, won't you? I know the morning is a bad time for most men. Even though I'm only the housewives' delight, I'm dying to know what you think of me, how I sound."

"Oh, I'll listen all right." Afraid, perhaps, that he had been more harsh than he had intended, he added, "It's swell, Mag, you've made the grade."

"And it's wonderful you're home, Roger!" she could answer with deep feeling.

"It's wonderful for me, I can tell you," he said, turning to her, his face already lit by the light of the goal he could not now wait to reach.

28

When Maggie went to Morris Baum, the head of the program department at the studio, in the spring of '46, saying, "I've had news about my husband in the Pacific," her face was so long that, as an employer who prided himself on being human with the best of them, he was preparing to offer condolences. She went on, however, to explain, "He's getting out of the service."

"Is this bad?" asked Morris.

"He wants me to meet him in Hawaii for two weeks' terminal leave, and I don't know how I'm ever going to make him understand that I just can't leave my show."

"Who says you can't?" Morrie asked unexpectedly. "It's the sort of thing your listeners would love—war wife rushing out to meet husband getting out of service. We'll record you on tape before you go, to fill your spot when you're away. Out there you'll pick up enough material to keep you talking for a month after you get home."

Fun magazine viewed the trip the same way. "It'll give you terrific material for your column," Paul Prentiss said, "and in addition I'll commission you to do an article on postwar Hawaii. We'll send a photographer to meet you out there."

It was only from an altitude of nine thousand feet above the Pacific that Maggie had time in which to read carefully what Ray himself had written her about his own feelings at their approaching reunion. She read:

Lying here at anchor in Tokyo Bay, during the last year, I've had more time for a sort of super self-analysis than I indulged in even during my night watches at sea. Maybe, too, being exposed to the beauty of Japan has played its share. Are you aware of "the subtle use of the useless"? If you could see, as I have seen, men walking along a Tokyo street and stopping to bow before a flowering fruit tree perhaps you could feel for yourself what it is I'm driving at. When I talk of the "useless" I don't mean anything to do with the kind of lazy bum I've been all my life. I'm even willing to face now—and it's not a very pleasant process—that if I had been a bit more mature at the time, I mightn't have crabbed so much at Alice's inadequacies when probably I was only trying to cover up my own. She thought she was marrying a budding genius, and, to do her credit, would have been willing for the sake of my writing to go anywhere to get away from "it all," if I'd had the guts to face it. When she plugged for the suburbs and good schools for the children, it was only in protest against the values of the advertising world. So when I got good and fed up with the result of my own action—or rather inaction—I decided to run out on the whole damn mess. And who do I run with? No, not just you, darling. Me. Myself. I came along too.

And you're probably asking yourself what all this has to do with you and me. It has only this: I feel as though I were a different man from what I once was, and feeling so, *I don't intend to go back to the sort of life I was leading before the war.* It's queer how every friend I have in the Navy feels the same way. If they were stockbrokers before, they want to be poets now; if they were poets, they want to be arctic explorers. Hold your hat. How do you feel about farmers—gentlemen or otherwise? Because a farmer I am determined to be. And thanks to Mother's inheritance—God bless her—not only do we eat, darling, but we eat what we want to—and when and where. Me, I should like, above all things, to return to the rolling acres of Missouri. I see us on a high bluff above the Mississippi. When you see that countryside you'll love it, and I'm damned sure Priscilla will too. There will be animals enough and to spare who will be bellowing, grunting, and whinnying for her ministrations. You've worked hard on your wartime stopgap of this radio wingding, but I'm sure if you're half the gal I think you are, you'll be glad to call it a day and settle back into some of the more primitive pleasures. I dare say your friend Prentiss is right and you won't find it too hard to unload the New York house. . . .

It's all ahead of us, Margot darling. I guess maybe my frame of reference has changed since Skipper's death. I ought to have my head examined if it hasn't. Anyhow, the world no longer seems flat to me, but—if you will excuse my being corny or wet—I've had glimmerings of another dimension where we might learn to live—and I mean *live*—with depth in ourselves and delight in each other. Let's you and me make a fresh start. (Parenthetically a lot of my friends are planning to make their fresh start with a new gal.) Not me. I want to make mine with you, Margot. We've a lot of emotional capital invested in each other. And where could there be a better place to begin than the Halekulani? Remember, darling? This is where we came in. . . .

And so, on schedule, indeed ahead of Ray himself, Maggie found herself once more on the veranda of the same little cottage at the Halekulani Inn at Honolulu, at the shore's edge, under the same low-leaning palm tree where they had spent the first week of their honeymoon. Just before sunset she looked up to see her husband coming toward her. Her first feeling was: He looks younger. How attractive he is! And then she was in his arms, held close. She could feel his tears on her neck as he kissed her, as though he could not have enough of her. With a sense of something close to confusion she was disturbed by his ardor. There were moments of closer intimacy to follow when she was almost frightened. Here was a strange lover. What had become of the faintly middle-aged husband she was prepared—indeed, adjusted—to meet?

The next few days were happy for Maggie. She enjoyed walking into the dining room with Ray, taking pride in the air of easy authority with which he wore his campaign ribbons and battle stars and the snap of assurance with which he returned salutes on the Main Street. They had cocktails at the Royal Hawaiian, and as they danced together to "It's Been A Long, Long Time," she knew they made an attractive couple, the embodiment of a happy reunion of lovers separated by years of war. For three days they did nothing more ambitious than lie on the sand—Ray very tanned and twenty pounds thinner, in tropical yellow and green shorts. Maggie, in a black bathing suit, afraid of the effect of the hot sun on her new golden hair tint, and aware of new little lines around her eyes and the drying effect of the sun on the creases across her throat, kept on a huge beach hat and, of course, dark glasses.

Lying on the beach the third day of their reunion, Maggie suddenly sat bolt upright and spoke very clearly. "You know really we can't keep this up indefinitely. Tomorrow we must get organized about my interviews and drive around the island to see what there is to be seen."

Ray rolled over on one side, his face away from Maggie.

"Did you hear what I said?" she asked.

"Yes, I heard. I don't approve of your use of the pronoun *we*."

"Well," she said, blinking her eyes into the setting sun over the slow-rolling waves, "what we're doing now may be *magnifique, mais ce n'est pas la guerre*."

He rolled over on his other side so that he might face her. "*C'est magnifique parceque ce n'est pas la guerre*. That's enough for me."

He kissed the hollow of her arm, but Maggie withdrew. She did not care for oblique or muted references to any experience in which she had not shared. In fact, she prided herself on the almost clinical tact she had displayed in *not* asking Ray to talk about the war, thus handing herself carte blanche to chatter on about the relative merits of commercial radio sponsors. (She was operating on the same principle when she told herself that if she didn't even recognize by so much as mentioning it Ray's crazy scheme of farming in Missouri he would probably "come round" by himself.)

Ray went on. "If you have to make our days in the islands into a business trip, that's up to you, Mag, but when you begin to talk about getting organized you can count me out."

So for the next three days Maggie dedicated herself to running people down, drawing people out, and writing people up. With photographer and car—courtesy of *Fun* magazine—she toured the island of Oahu from one end to the other. She stood on the blustery Nuuanu Pali to feel the sharp sprinkles of rain rushing up rather than down to lash against her cheeks. She drove around Kahuku Point through the fine tropical plantations of Wailalua. She came home late each afternoon to find Ray with one or more water-color sketches to his credit, perhaps still preoccupied with adding a finishing touch. Forgetting how lovable she had found his predilection for "dabbling" on their first honeymoon, she was aware now of a definite sensation of irritation, almost snapping as she exclaimed, "Heavens! Are you still doing *that*? Haven't you moved since I left you?"

"No. Should I have?" he asked, squinting at the outline of Diamond Head, his head cocked to one side.

"I suppose not, so long as you don't have any work that you have to do." The underlining of *you* was ever so slight, but detectable all the same.

Ray was too happy and at ease to be so easily baited. "Cheer up, honey," he said. That evening he took her to dine in a Japanese restaurant. While their dinner was being prepared they explored the garden behind the house, crossing a little bridge which spanned a tiny pond filled with goldfish. "Just like Mother's willow-pattern plates!" Maggie exclaimed. "It's all so quiet and small and fragile I can't believe we're on American soil."

Then, in stocking feet, squatting on cushions before the low table before them, they settled down in earnest to enjoy Maggie's first taste of an Oriental meal. Sitting close to Ray, she could feel the warm sweet sake tingle through her. She felt a sudden thrill in her proximity to Ray in such a setting. As the pretty "loyal American" Japanese girl, dressed in a kimono and slippers, pattered in and out of the room, Maggie pressed closer to him and with a teasing smile said, "She really is a perfect little Yum-Yum. You couldn't have seen anything more fascinating than that in Japan."

"I saw plenty that was Yum-Yum in Japan," Ray answered.

Maggie turned her face fully toward his, letting her smile play over him. "Darling, did you see anything so fascinating as to be irresistible?"

For a moment Ray teetered over the precipice of the temptation to tell Maggie the truth. He thought of Masu at the Green Lantern. What words were there to convey to his wife all that this girl had meant to him, coming into his life after the numberless years of faithfully observed vows in two marriages? There had been several weeks of struggle with himself before he clearly and deliberately made the decision to take the physical experience that was offered—something, he told himself, that would help to see him through a stretch of loneliness and could be forgotten the moment his face was turned toward home. But how much more than the fullest sensual gratification he had ever known had the months with Masu given him! He knew that it was to her that he owed not only his sense of youth recovered but, ironically enough, his hope that in his marriage he still might find the poetry he had somehow lost sight of along the way. Masu had become part of him, secretly, deeply, and forever. It was no sense of sin or guilt that prompted him not to speak her name now. Even Maggie would have to see that the interlude had not hurt her in any way. Rather it was because he knew that he could never forget Masu, with her gentleness and grace, her gaiety and mystery, that Ray had no wish to brighten an ineffaceable image by attempting to re-create it in words.

He could answer Maggie's question, "Did you see anything so fascinating as to be irresistible?" with a conscious tingle of power. "What do you think?" he asked, moving closer and taking her hand. "I don't know how come that you and I have sort of fluffed things in our marriage up to now. From here on out, things are going to be different, honey, just you wait and see." He smiled suddenly, using radio scripture to plead his suit. "Once we get out of New York, Life will be Beautiful."

Maggie, with masterly self-control and deliberation, simply injected into her voice some of the sweetness of the sake that was warming her. "That's why I can't wait to show you the new house, darling. You won't know you're in New York! It's like Boston—or St. Louis!" she added in a burst of sudden indulgence. "None of the hanky-panky of doormen and elevator men, but our own front door, and Mother's and Father's nice, rather shabby things. Paul Prentiss says my living room is one of the most original in New York. He wants it photographed for *Fun*."

"Isn't all this rather academic, Maggie? We're going farm-hunting in Missouri. Remember?"

The blunt, bluff Maggie who, as a bride in Hollywood, believed that her new husband was bound to bring her happiness as long as she just got him organized was gone. No longer vulnerable through the flesh (in fact, faintly resistant to what now seemed importunate demands), she had achieved the power of detachment necessary to the practice of subterfuge. Because she had hardened, she was able to answer softly, "Of course I remember. But I wanted to ask you what you would say to spending just this summer somewhere near New York? For one thing, it will be good for Priscilla to have a real holiday, and for another—you see, my radio contract runs to the first of September."

"Oh. You hadn't told me."

"Haven't I? Well, it does, and naturally it would simply ruin me if I tried to break it."

He took his hand away from Maggie's where it had been lying. "Maggie, look here," he said. "You don't mean to go *on* with this radio thing, do you? You realize there's no need for you to work any more."

"It isn't a question of need," she answered rather stiffly before turning to attack. "Don't you approve of women working?"

"Sure, I approve, Lucy Stone. I approve of a real bona-fide job. But certainly you know as well as I that what you're doing is a lot of crap."

Her cheeks flamed hot and her voice rose. "How can you, an advertising man, call it 'crap'? You lived off it most of your life!"

"And so who has a better right to speak? I would have made a hell of a better job of my life if I'd had the guts years ago to stand up and call it all the pack of cards it is. It's been too easy, for a laugh, to dish out the corny 'testimonials' nobody believes from phony doctors in smocks, phony 'socialites'—"

She interrupted him. "I take it that means me?"

"Come on, don't let's get personal." His voice suddenly softened as he shifted his attack abruptly. "Or rather what I mean is, do let's get personal—about you and me. Margot, you want our marriage to come first, don't you? And you know as well as I do that once you start in playing Our Lady of the Air Waves our marriage is going to be a washout—all over again."

At that moment a heaping dish of sukiyaki was put before her, and Maggie could cry, "Look, darling! You're going to have to show me how to eat with chopsticks!" just in time to extricate herself from a conversation she had no desire to pursue further.

Three months later Ray was the owner of a farm. To this extent, his heart's desire was realized. Like all such desires, however, it was cut down to specifications. The farm, instead of comprising several hundred acres of Missouri's rolling fields, high above the Mississippi, consisted of forty flat acres, some twenty of which, leased to a local farmer, were dedicated to the growing of potatoes, edged by sand dunes, on the south shore of Long Island. He named his farm Little Mo.

It was Maggie's fast thinking and fast talking that sold him the idea he would never have had for himself. "The real-estate agent says we're crazy to think of renting when there's such an opportunity for buying. Such a bargain comes into the market only once every twenty-five years. I think you'd be a fool not to snap at it, because . . . well, just think—it gives you everything you want, and without having to go poking off to the Middle West to look for it."

"I can't forget that I once vowed never to set foot on Long Island again. It does seem a bit ironic to end up just where I started."

"Don't be silly. It isn't where you started at all. It's miles away and quite different, and so far as that goes, how about me? I always thought I never wanted to look at eel grass again, or feel a blustery southwest wind, but then it will make Priscilla feel so at home—and Priscilla must be happy no matter who else isn't!"

Ray seemed entirely disposed to let Maggie's daughter become the focus for their joint attention. A week end spent with Sister, now the mother of two small children, in a crowded apartment in West Philadelphia had left him resolved not to repeat the experience. He had been so uncomfortable on a "studio couch" in the living room, and found the proximity of his grandchildren so nervously wearing, that he decided to settle for sending Sister a fat check each month. The little boy was named Skipper. When the kid was able to talk and walk, Ray would want to get to know him.

The fact that Alice was living in a small apartment in Philadelphia to be near Sister did not make the week end any easier for Ray. She deliberately kept away during his visit, although once Sister called her to ask for the address of a sitter she had promised to find. The mere crackle of the receiver that Sister held to her ear sent Ray stalking out of the apartment to take a walk by himself in the rain through the monotonous streets. He and Alice were grandparents of those two same children. From things Sister let drop, Alice saw eye to eye with him about matters of bringing up. Obviously they would have a lot to say to each other on the subject if they ever got together.

Ray returned to Maggie so determined not to discuss his family that he laid himself out to be particularly affable about Priscilla.

The day Priscilla moved in at Little Mo—the choice in favor of her mother publicly made for all the world to see—was the happiest day Maggie could remember.

Dressing for dinner on her daughter's first night at home, Maggie asked Ray, "Don't you think she's pretty?"

"I don't know what you call *pretty*, exactly. I'm just so stunned to see how she's grown, or filled out, or whatever the hell it is that kids do when they stop being kids and suddenly become female. Remember, I haven't seen her since the day we were married, when she was . . . what—ten or eleven years old?"

At dinner Maggie ordered a bottle of champagne. Ray proposed the first toast, lifting his glass toward Priscilla. "Here's looking at you, Priscilla!" he said. "Welcome aboard!"

She was dressed in white, her pale-yellow hair brushed smooth back from her forehead, curling into a page-boy bob behind; her round light-blue eyes gleamed their happiness. "Thank you!" she answered. "I can't believe I'm really here."

"*I* can, darling!—" Maggie's voice had a break in it—"because it never fails—when I'm determined that something wonderful is bound to happen, then it just *must* come true!"

The talk was lively and rippled along without effort. Ray teased Priscilla, asking if she was going to miss exams and having to make a nine-o'clock lecture instead of sleeping an extra hour.

"Ray, be serious. Don't tease Priscilla. Of *course* she's glad to take the whole summer off for a complete vacation and not even think of getting a job until we move into town in the fall."

"But, Mummy, I wanted to speak to you about that. I'm sure there must be kennels, or a vet, here where I could work part time—even if I'm not paid for it. I don't want just to sit around doing nothing."

"Oh *no*, darling! Not your first summer out of college! You must get to know some of the young people in the neighborhood. I've been planning a party for you!" she said a little too enthusiastically.

"What kind of a party?"

"Now don't look at me so suspiciously." Maggie just stopped herself from saying, "like a Bradfield." Instead she said, "An evening party, maybe even with dancing, just so that people around will know you've come to stay."

"Oh, Mummy, please!" There was a knot of visible pain on Priscilla's forehead. "I'm all right the way I am, and I just like to fool around, and swim, or sail by myself, or be with you or Ray," she added with the precipitousness of suddenly remembered manners. "Please don't give a party for me! I don't want to meet anyone new!"

Ray spoke as though Maggie were not in the room. "I'd take it as a favor if you'd take that little knockabout of mine out sometimes, Priscilla. It's like a horse that needs exercise. I hate to have her just sitting at her moorings. If it wouldn't spoil your fun, maybe you'd let me come with you sometimes. I won't intrude on your thoughts by talking. In fact I don't like people who talk on the sea."

"Or off it?" Maggie asked. Although she smiled, there was a definite ring in her voice that caused both her husband and daughter to look up sharply.

"*You* are an exception, darling," Ray said with mock gallantry. "And besides, you get paid for your talking. I wish someone would pay Priscilla and me for just—" he hesitated before bringing out the two ugly words—"shutting up. Don't you, Priscilla?" he asked affably, as though to remove any possible sting from the intention behind his words.

Maggie looked from one to the other, with something like fear discernible on her features, but she did not retort. She decided to remain silent—for once.

29

MAGGIE HAD said to Priscilla the day she moved in to Little Mo, "If you can just manage to keep yourself amused through the summer, darling, life will really get going for you in town next winter. Just you wait and see! And I know you understand that I wouldn't *think* of leaving you alone so much this first summer except for my national hookup. I just *have* to make good on it. You do see, don't you, lamb, that I just can't help myself?"

So with her usual inclination to believe that people would stay put on the particular square of her own personal checkerboard until she was ready to pick them up and move them again, Maggie felt entirely unencumbered to fling herself into the battle of making Margot Masters a household word across the nation. There was no sacrifice too great if it would help to achieve that end. Her life's goal was within her grasp; she had already made a name, but she was determined to make a still bigger one. Priscilla was there, close at hand, to be enjoyed fully by and by. Priscilla would wait.

While waiting, Priscilla found, in due course, a part-time job as assistant to a veterinarian near Bridgehampton. He was a graduate of New York State Veterinary College and seemed disposed to treat Priscilla as more than a professional addition to his life. Maggie, watching her go off with him to the movies on several evenings, though vaguely disturbed, was still gratified to see that her child appeared to be enjoying herself. At her mother's insistence she came home for an early lunch with Ray every day so that together they could listen to the "Who's Fun" program. Maggie's first question to them both every evening when she got home just in time for dinner (she was gone in the morning before they were up) was "Well, how did it go?"

The assumption was blandly made that neither could possibly have had anything more interesting to do during the day than listen to her radio program. Yet, as a sort of sideline hobby, she rather enjoyed making the officious motions of a solicitous wife. With a good deal of bustle she managed to arrange a study for Ray in which he might do his writing. To her, however, "writing" was an occupation as easy to pick up or lay aside as the beads running along the side of a baby's play pen. If he had the temerity to say, "I actually got two thousand words on paper this morning," she would exclaim, "But, darling, how *wonderful*!" in much the tone of voice she would have used to a small toddler who had shoved all his beads from one end of his bar to the other. To push her show of interest and encouragement even farther, she asked him one day, "What are you writing *about*, dear?"

Obviously reluctant to expose to the glare of Maggie's regard tender shoots still pushing their slow way through the shadows, Ray was able to say only, "Well, I'm really fussing around with half an idea—that's all it is, so far. It wouldn't amount to more than a collection of short stories—not even stories, either, so much as impressions of my time in Japan. I'd like to show how the conquering American stays on to be conquered by the land he is just beginning to understand and to love."

"Oh" was Maggie's only response. She had imagined, at the most, a blood-and-thunder war novel in the works, at the least a debunking satire on Navy regimentation. Now it was obvious that Ray was engaged in no more than a sort of interim doodling to fill up time that he would otherwise have to kill. There wasn't enough meat in what he had told her to warrant so much as the purchase of her customary collaborational notebook.

Her husband's activities, having thus shrunk in her eyes, Maggie found the next step easy. "Ray, I wish you'd come into the studio with me. I'd like you to meet Morrie Baum and get your slant on the whole setup."

The crack of the familiar whip brought him immediately to heel; the play pen was deserted. The very next day he was sitting in Morrie's office going over the mail sent in from all over the country to the "Who's Fun" program.

After dinner that night, sitting out on the terrace of Little Mo, Maggie said to Ray, "Well, I've been waiting to hear what you think. Have you any ideas for the show?"

"God help me, I have. Ideas, I can't help having."

Feeling no inclination to loiter in the purlieus of a discussion of Ray's personality, Maggie sharpened her focus as she asked crisply, "Well, what are they?"

"I was wondering how it would be if you were to drop the routine of having a famous person to interview every day and instead have somebody totally *un*famous."

"But that's the exact opposite of what people want! You said yourself, get bigger and better celebrities, not just Broadway ones, and your advice was so good that now I'm on a national hookup!"

"I know. But now I begin to wonder. I feel a certain wistfulness in some of the letters from your listeners. They would somehow like to get in on the act a little more. They feel it's all a shade snooty or highhat."

"Do you mean that people write in letters saying they *don't* like the show?" Maggie asked, her eyes so wide that she elicited an abrupt and rather harsh laugh from Ray.

"Listen, Margot, have you honestly been believing that the whole human race belongs to your fan club?"

"Why, no, of course I haven't. Don't be silly." She could feel herself blush. "Morrie only shows me such *nice* letters. Everybody sounds so friendly."

"And Morrie's quite right. If you faltered for a moment in your belief in yourself you'd be sunk at the dock."

"Well, then, what would you suggest?" Maggie asked much more meekly.

"Let me kick it around with the program department a little. We might come up with something. Maybe what I'm talking about should be another show entirely. Could be."

"Really?" Maggie leaned forward hungrily. "I never even *dreamed* of two radio shows!"

"Why not? There's no question that the personality you project in public conveys a lot of warmth. I have a hunch that members of your audience would like all those nice sunlamp rays turned on themselves, not just on some big shot who's in the blaze of publicity anyway."

If there was any sting intended in her husband's partitioning off an area where she was capable of demonstrating warmth apart from her private life, Maggie's flesh was inured against feeling it.

"Ed Walch came up with another idea in discussing advertising for the show," Ray went on, "which may have something to it. He asked my advice about who might do an article on you for one of the big women's magazines."

Maggie leaned forward eagerly, her eyes flashing. "An *article*? How exciting!"

"It's a question of 'building the name,' as Ed puts it, on as many fronts as possible."

"I think it's a very sensible idea." Maggie nodded her head sagely. "Who did you suggest?"

"Before I could come up with anything he made a suggestion himself. Me." Ray's eyebrows shot up with the corners of his mouth. "What do you say?"

"Why . . . why . . ." Maggie faltered, unsure.

"Ed says there'd be a big appeal in a story of the famous wife told by her husband—the whole thing to have a sort of off-the-record flavor. As a matter of fact, when I was sitting right there in his office he called one of the editors of *Every Woman's Home Magazine*, who seems to be a buddy, and he snapped at it."

"Ray, how marvelous!" Maggie was won over in an instant. "When do we start? Would you like an appointment for an interview?" she asked, giggling at her own joke.

"No, thanks. And there's one request I must make. I can't do the thing at all, Margot, if you're going to peek over my shoulder. I'll ask you for facts and background as I need them, but I must have carte blanche, and you'll have to wait to see it in print. Fair enough?"

"Oh, yes, certainly! I couldn't understand more."

"It oughtn't to take me too long. I'll go at it in the evenings, when I'm through my own writing."

In a few days he was at work, and within the week he had found time to present her with a scrapbook, on which he had painted in his best Gothic script, FAN FARE. "I promise you, honey, nothing will go into it but the nice letters. We'll keep it like a big box of candy you can dive into and stuff yourself on whenever you feel your system craves more sugar content."

It was a golden summer for Maggie; her sky was bright. There was, to be sure, a slight cloud of anxiety about Kitten, but no bigger than a man's hand. Since Ray's return and his evening on-the-spot reports of her morning's radio program, Maggie had telephoned less often to Milton. When she did call, one Sunday evening, she was shocked to have Kitten tell her that she was going into the hospital the next day for some "tests." She spoke so casually of "a little trouble with my back and some queer pains down my legs—nothing the least bit serious, but a nuisance" that Maggie allowed herself to be convinced that there was nothing to worry about. When she spoke to Roger, after what he told her had proved to be an operation, he was bluff and businesslike, saying merely, "It seemed to be a very slight affair and we expect her home in a day or two." Since this report was all that Maggie could glean from either Roger or Kitten herself, she accepted it at face value, because she wanted to.

To offset the slight undercurrent of worry, moreover, there was exciting news that a book of poems by Kitten, published in the spring, had been awarded a prize by the New England Poetry Society. In the citation her manner was welcomed for being as fresh and elliptic as a

Japanese *hokku*, and her matter as indigenous to New England as Robert Frost's. Maggie, who instinctively rejected the thought of measuring dear, faithful stay-at-home Kitten in terms of "success," was delighted that "something nice" had happened to her. "She certainly deserves it," she said to Roger, not appraising the talent but the prosy life that needed brightening.

Near at hand, Maggie's horizon was clear and cloudless. The drive back from New York to Little Mo in the late afternoon (the better half of their German couple acted as her chauffeur by day), knowing that Priscilla, as well as Ray, was waiting for her, gave her the heady sense of having everything she could want in life.

Maggie attempted to wrest from Ray at intervals an acknowledgment that he was glad he had bought a farm on Long Island instead of Missouri. At first he would answer, "It's too soon to say. But don't forget, I'm reserving the right to sell the place, and still think we may wind up on the banks of the Mississippi."

The next phase was to answer, "I'm *here*, Mag. Isn't that enough for you?"

It was not long, however, before Maggie could consider the case closed when he answered her question, "Sure. It was a swell idea."

Ray's outward appearance began, if ever so subtly, to show a turn in the tide. Both mental and physical outlines began, very gently, to blur. Gone was the lean, firm, clear-eyed, clear-skinned, almost young man who had received his honorable discharge from the Navy. There was a short time after his home-coming during which Ray drank nothing stronger than beer; then, without knowing quite how or when it had happened, he and Maggie were having martinis every night before dinner. One night Maggie said, "I don't know why, but your study is the coziest room in the house. Let's have drinks there." She started to whoosh a pile of papers to one side to make room for the tray put down by white-coated Hans. Priscilla cried out, "Oh, Mummy, don't! That's Ray's writing!"

"You mean the article?" The hand stopped motionless in mid-air.

"No, his *own* writing that he was working on this afternoon."

The papers were shoved aside as Ray shrugged his shoulders and smiled at his stepdaughter. "Your mother is a force of nature, Priscilla," he said. "The sooner we both learn to bow before the storm the better."

From then on Ray's study became Maggie's GHQ. The telephone she had promised him he would not have stole across the threshold on a long extension wire from the hall so that Maggie was able to lean back on the sofa, with her feet on a settee before her, and transact business with New York while Ray and Priscilla maintained a respectful silence. Ray never referred to the words he had written from Tokyo—those words which had spelled out his high resolve for leading life in a new dimension. Whatever compromises or appeasement he made was the fruit of a struggle without benefit of witnesses. If he might have claimed that pressures from without were too much for him, perhaps there was an even greater pressure within, urging peace at any price. He did not, however, have to explain himself to anybody but himself.

If Maggie could say with satisfaction to her friends, "I have the most perfect couple. Hans and Rosa get on beautifully," she could also say, "Ray and Priscilla seem made for each other. They have so much in common." She did not have to underline the fact that the "so much" was herself. Blandly thinking of them as disciples of the same idol, she could not suspect that they might be joint conspirators. There was, however, an occasional stirring of uneasiness. Once when Maggie said to Ray at dinner, "Ray, do come in town with me tomorrow. Morrie's going great guns trying to sell your new idea and I do want you to check on some of the gimmicks he's talking about," Ray had answered with a shameless lack of enthusiasm, "Make it next week."

"No, it's got to be tomorrow. I want to get it in the works at once," she answered with an imperiousness that was more frightening for being unconscious of itself.

"But, Mummy—" Priscilla looked unhappily from one to the other—"Ray was just saying that if he could have three more uninterrupted days—he's working so hard on the piece about you in the evenings—he'd really have his first story—"

"Priscilla!" For an instant temper blazed in Maggie's eyes. It seemed as though her next words must be "hold your tongue" or at least, "speak when you are spoken to." She melted as suddenly, however, as she had frozen. Putting her hand out, palm up, on the dining-room table, she invited Priscilla's handclasp. "Listen, my precious baby," she said, "you're used to taking care of little pussies and puppies. Don't forget Ray has two legs, not four. Ray's my responsibility, not yours, and *I* know it's very good for any writer not to get stuck in a rut. It's *good* for Ray to come into town—when I ask him. Now I want to hear what both of you did this afternoon."

When Priscilla told her they had had a sail in the *Bonhomme Richard II* (seventeen feet, water line), Maggie answered "How *lovely*!" in her play-pen voice. Both children had been rapped lovingly over the knuckles and were back at their beads.

In secret conclave with Ray she discussed her beautiful and mysterious child. "You see so much of Priscilla, Ray, can you get anything *out* of her? You don't really think she could do anything so stupid as to marry that young vet, do you?"

"If she thought she loved him I'm sure she would" was the disturbing answer, phlegmatically delivered.

"It's all very well for you to be so calm!" Maggie snapped. "You wouldn't take it that way if she were your child. Once I get her into New York this winter I'm determined to knock all this nonsense about being a female vet out of her head. If she likes animals so much, why doesn't she draw them or sculpt them? She's got quite a nice talent for painting, actually." Maggie warmed to the subject. "If she went to art school she'd meet young people who would be really attractive. I can sort of imagine Priscilla married to a clever artist some day, can't you?"

"I don't want to imagine Priscilla as anything, Maggie, but what she wants to be herself. Why don't you leave it up to her? After all, she is free, white, and twenty-one."

When she heard the front door close after midnight, on an evening Priscilla had been again to the movies, Maggie bustled out of her bed and bedroom, fastening her dressing gown as she padded into Priscilla's bedroom to be on hand to greet her as she came in.

"Did you have fun, dear?" she asked with too much enthusiasm. "Is Tom good company for an evening?"

"He's all right."

"Maybe it's none of my business—" Maggie chuckled cozily as she sat down on the edge of the bed—"but *I* like Bob Rufus, whom you took as crew in the last Yacht Club race. I hear on all sides that he's a remarkable young man. He ought to be. I knew his mother at college. I thought he looked frightfully attractive!"

"He's all right," said Priscilla, wiggling out of her dress as she pulled it over her head.

"Is that the way you feel about them all, darling—just 'all right'? Well, some day someone will come along who will be much more than 'all right'!" Maggie could not determine what progress she was making; Priscilla's back was turned as she rummaged in her top bureau drawer. Maggie went brightly on. "Have you had *twinges* yet, dear, about anybody? I know when I was your age I was forever having mad crushes on somebody!"

"No," Priscilla answered her own image in the mirror, as she rather fiercely tugged at the roots of her back hair before committing them to large curlers. Maggie, however, noticed that the back of her ears turned red in spite of her monosyllable of denial.

Back in her own bedroom, she reported this phenomenon to Ray.

"Listen, Margot," he said, "I know you're tickled pink to have Priscilla with you at last. But don't go overboard."

"But I want so terribly for her to confide in me! I can't bear to think of all those years when I was away from her, of her being without a mother to talk to!"

"Or to talk to her?" Ray's smile flickered only for an instant. "But don't forget that just the biological accident of one human being's giving birth to another still does not guarantee their intimacy. Intimacy has to grow slowly—particularly with a child as sensitive as Priscilla. Don't force things, Margot."

As Maggie could assure Priscilla that she knew just what Ray was like because she had been married to him so long, so she could assure Ray, "Priscilla still is my daughter, dear. And whatever you may think, we are very close and very congenial."

Maggie was not long in carrying out the threat she had made of filling the house with people for Ray's sake. She began by asking the Deacons for the week end.

On the Friday evening of their arrival Nini broke the news to Maggie that she and Dick were leaving New York permanently. "Dick is really a chronic invalid," she said with no attempt to conceal her disgust. "The doctor says he simply can't stand the pace of New York. He's retiring from business altogether."

There was none of the same sense of stricken loss that Maggie had felt years before when Nini told her she was leaving Boston. Today there was an upsurge of relief in knowing that she was to be rid of her. It was as natural for Maggie to rejoice in a friend's good fortune as it was to expect that friend to rejoice in her own. She had become, therefore, increasingly ill at ease in Nini's company. The truth was that every party Maggie was invited to and Nini not, every new celebrity that Maggie met and Nini not, and every personal or public recognition that was accorded Maggie caused Nini not simply a vague malaise but also a compulsion to deliver well-aimed darts designed to hurt her friend. The struggle of concealing her own triumphs was beginning to be too much for Maggie; she was a success, and it was impossible to conceal the fact from Nini. She was thankful, therefore, that the cause of such incessant strain was to be removed.

When Nini told her she was leaving New York, she cried out with far too much emotion, "Oh, dear! How *awful*!" The exclamation rang so hollow that she covered it quickly with the practical query, "Where are you going, Nini?"

"Santa Barbara, and I couldn't be more delighted," Nini answered promptly. "Everybody's agreed that the war has simply ruined New

York. I can't tell you how many people we know who say they simply can't put up with it another day. It's all become so second-rate. In Santa Barbara we'll have a divine house, and we're not far from San Francisco, which everyone knows is the only *really* cosmopolitan city left in this country."

Dick himself looked like an old man. Talking with Maggie, he admitted, "I suppose I'll like it when I get there, but I've always had a hunch I wouldn't care for the West. Frankly, it sounds a bit crude to me. Then I don't know when I'll ever see my children, living 'way off there. I've always had in the back of my mind that I'd rather like to end my days somewhere in New England." Yet, even as he wistfully repeated his old watchword, he pressed bravely on. "But Nini's the sort of gal that likes to be in the swim."

Nini's last bit of handiwork was an attempt to reduce Ray to the level to which she herself had reduced Dick.

In front of both the Masters she said, squinting out at the waves of the Atlantic Ocean, "Isn't it funny the way life works out? Here we are going to live in the West, and you both might be still living there yourselves if Maggie hadn't written me from Hollywood, asking us to look around for a job in the East for Ray."

The moment of silence that followed throbbed with Maggie's first spurt of blind temper against Nini. *What a mean, low-down, dirty—* she could easily have hit her across the face. She did not dare to look at Ray. Suddenly he was speaking. She listened, incredulous, as he spoke with perfect calm. "You're right. Things do turn out in the damnedest way."

Magnanimous? Or so ironic as to border on sadistic? Maggie could not guess. Least of all could she envisage the possibility that her husband spoke out of a vast reservoir of indifference to his own fate that had filled, drop by drop, over the years. She did not recognize the features of unconditional surrender.

The quartet sat a moment longer without words. They might all have been absorbed in watching the execution of a piece of sky writing, performed for their benefit, as silently, letter by letter, unfurling across the spaces of memory, the pattern of their respective marriages took shape. There unrolled, first, each marriage as it existed in and for itself, and then, like a feat of fancy figure skating, came the intricate interweaving—crossing, parting, reuniting, parting again—of the two marriages together. For a second the whole design hung across the vault of recognized experience, final, completed, before it silently dissolved back into the emptiness out of which it had come. Of the quartet it was Maggie alone who could feel that life had treated her as richly as she had always known it must.

30

On Saturday evening Maggie gave a dinner for the Deacons. She had discussed with Ray the suitability of inviting the Roy Jorgens from the other side of the island. Jorgens was one of several interested potential sponsors in the new show that Ray was working on for Maggie at WABS.

"Do you think it would be terribly crude for me to ask him with other guests, just as though he were a friend?" she asked.

"Listen, kid," was Ray's answer, "you can forget that word if you're in the game you've chosen. Shoot the works. He'll probably love it."

The choice of the evening was a particularly happy one, as Priscilla had accepted an invitation to go to a Yacht Club dance with the Rufus boy from next door. It was his parents who were first to arrive at the Masters'. Maggie had known Mrs. Rufus as Frannie Wainwright at Vassar and was not surprised that she was still considered "a lovely person." As Frannie Rufus crossed the flagstone terrace in her high-heeled yellow-linen evening slippers, Maggie noticed how natural her permanent looked, and how brand-new her shoes; her spotless pale-blue cashmere sweater, appliquéd with seashells hanging from her shoulders, buttoned only at the top button, was as conventionally right as the smooth tan that made the perfect setting for her diamond-and-sapphire bracelets and her strand of large (real) pearls.

Jimmy Rufus, also tanned, his hair still sleek from the water of his own swimming pool, followed in the rear. The very cut of his navy-blue blazer, tight and snug across the midriff, suggested that on its inner side, somewhere about the heart, lay a fat checkbook.

Within a quarter of an hour the Jorgens joined the party, and Maggie was wishing they had never been invited. Mrs. Jorgens was a handsome Swedish woman; a mouthful of beautiful teeth, a good figure poured into a tight-fitting white silk-jersey dress, and heavy scent proclaimed her, to Maggie, as ex-model or show girl. To exhibit her dress to advantage and to smile seemed to be the extent of her social accomplishments. Fred Jorgens, for his part, appeared long ago to have decided to let his power and glory speak for him, using himself only those monosyllables essential to his own care and feeding. He did not make the hour-and-a-half wait for the Andy De Fronzos from Sag Harbor pass any more quickly. Every fifteen minutes of the ninety Maggie spoke up clearly to say, "You know I've never seen either of these people. They're friends of a Navy friend of Ray's. I refuse to wait more than ten minutes more for them. Ray, do shake up another martini for everybody. Our tongues are in our vest pockets."

This was one of those evenings for Maggie when gin seemed to fire rather than soothe her mounting bad temper. The De Fronzos themselves, though causing pain, were visibly feeling none when they finally put in an appearance. The gin they had already consumed seemed merely to have blurred the edge of such compunction as they might have felt for keeping a dinner party waiting for them. Neither put up the slightest resistance when Ray greeted them with an outstretched cocktail shaker before they could get to Maggie.

Mrs. De Fronzo, saying, "Just a litty-bitty one," held her glass under the shaker till Ray filled it to the brim.

Maggie, beside herself, plucked Ray by the sleeve, murmuring, "Hans will *leave*, Ray, if we keep them waiting any longer in the kitchen."

Ray, in a sudden spurt of awakened masculinity or a rather swaggering mood of rebellion, said loud enough so that everyone, including Hans, could hear, "I'm writing an article about my Margot in which

I have given a touching account of how her servants would not be paid to work for anybody else. This is the perfect opportunity to put their doglike devotion to the test," and replenished his own glass.

Maggie was left without an answer and with leisure in which to contemplate the new arrivals.

Andy De Fronzo was known to the entire region of Beach Hampton as the most famous of the nonobjective painters whose works hung on the walls of the Beach Hampton Modern Art Gallery. One look at his wife, on Maggie's part at least, proclaimed that the choice of his most recent mate had been prompted by an urge which was non-nonobjective. Kay De Fronzo affirmed, as directly as a simple declarative sentence, female sexuality. She wore a low-cut tight black jersey sweater and a red cotton skirt. Her thick, wiry black hair fell to her shoulders. One would not have been surprised by the clack of a castanet in her smooth olive-skinned hand or by a red rose held between her teeth. She was strikingly beautiful and gave the impression of being, at the same time, strikingly bad. Her upper lip was short and straight, her lower lip full and pouting; her smooth, succulently moist lipstick succeeded in making her mouth appear to be the only feature in her face.

Her entrance hit the assemblage with as much impact as though a wildcat had been let out of a cage. Among her fellow females there was an instinctive ruffling of the fur and flexing of the claws; the tomcats lashed their tails, circling closer to the new arrival as they glared at one another.

She shook hands in a perfunctory way with Maggie as her hostess, and then turned immediately back to Ray, lifting her glass to touch his own. "I can't tell you how thrilled I am to meet you," she said. "*The Joneses* is one of my very favorite books of all time."

Maggie, hearing the last words, felt the pang known to every wife who sees the crude trap of flattery set for her husband, and steels herself for the thud which will presently follow when he falls into it.

At the table, the couples divided themselves into conversational tête-à-têtes as they were intended to do. Maggie noticed with a certain irritation that Ray was turned so far around in his chair to face Mrs. De Fronzo that he gave Frannie Rufus a view of his back.

It was not until the ice cream was served that Frannie Rufus made one last stalwart stand to attract the attention of her literary host. "I've just been reading Isherwood's *Portrait of a Family*," she said. "Which do *you* think, Mr. Masters, is the most important poet—Isherwood, Spender, or Auden?"

Maggie knew that Ray had been reading the same Isherwood. She sighed gratefully, thinking that at last he had it in his power to make amends for his bad manners. She heard him say, instead, rather gruffly, "I don't consider myself qualified to discuss poetry."

"Why, Ray, how can you say such a thing?" Maggie could not stop herself from saying. "You know you used to write poetry yourself!" She sucked the raspberry ice cream off the end of her spoon and pointed it toward him as she turned to Jimmy Rufus. "He wrote fifty sonnets when he was at Princeton!" she exclaimed.

Ray's face dropped as he looked, appalled, at his wife. For a moment he could find nothing to say. Then gruffly he brought out, "Maybe I didn't tell you they were love sonnets to a girl I was mad about at the time."

"No, you didn't," Maggie answered rather meekly.

"Her name was Alice."

Nobody being able to think of anything to say, Maggie shoved back her chair. "Shall we have coffee on the terrace?" she asked.

Hoping that her guests would go home sooner if she did not separate the sexes, Maggie led Mr. Jorgens out to the waiting hammock. The others followed, sinking into deck chairs—all except Ray and Kay De Fronzo.

One hour passed like two. Maggie could see into the dimly lighted living room where Ray had taken up his position at the piano in the corner, Kay seating herself beside him on the bench. Their two brandy glasses sat side by side on the piano as intimately as they were sitting before it. She watched, disgusted with herself for doing so, as Kay moved close, her thighs pressing against Ray's. When she leaned across him for her brandy glass her hair hung loose against his cheek. As he played, Maggie could see his face turned completely toward Kay's so that their lips, even their lashes, were very nearly touching. She could see that when his mouth was still and he was no longer speaking or gently singing, his eyes served as accompaniment to the music he let speak for him. "'*If I Loved You . . .*'" he began. Presently Maggie watched Kay get up to carry both their glasses across the hall to the library, where the liquor was kept in the folding bar, and return to Ray, both glasses replenished.

"Yes," Maggie said to Mr. Jorgens, and "No" and "Oh, really?" But when she saw Kay a half hour later get up again, again carrying two empty glasses, and, a second later, heard the music come to an abrupt stop with a discordant bang as Ray got up to follow, she remained in her seat by a herculean act of the will only a few moments. Then, murmuring, "Excuse me while I go see about more drinks," she hurried into the house and, as fast as her feet would carry her, to the door of the library. As she could not run the risk of being seen walking tiptoe down her own hallway, the clicking of her heels on the hardwood floor inevitably announced her approach. When she crossed the threshold Ray was stooping over the bar, rattling bottles about in a hollow attempt at busyness. Kay was scrutinizing her face in the mirror of her powder compact.

"Anything I can do for you, darling?" Ray asked in the bluff, genial tone of the host who hopes his party is being a great success.

"Yes. Before you come back into the living room, wipe that lipstick off your mouth."

Maggie's heels clicked now in the other direction as she returned to rejoin her guests on the terrace.

She never knew how the next hour passed. But suddenly she and Ray were alone in the living room, even the Deacons vanishing upstairs the minute the last car had left (both the Rufuses calling brightly out into the night, "Thank you *so* much! A wonderful evening!").

Maggie and Ray stood confronting each other. Neither made a move to sit down. It was as though each knew there was a scene to be played out.

Maggie opened it. "Well," she said, the ruffle of drums announcing more to follow, "do you consider that your behavior this evening was very amusing?"

"I don't think I thought about it much one way or the other. I don't know, either, what you mean by 'my behavior.' I don't recall having fallen flat on my face or having insulted any of our guests."

Maggie attacked her target with one bold, brash shot. "Are you in love with that woman?" she asked.

"Maggie, be your age." Ray opened a cigarette box and deliberately lighted a cigarette, as though to shift gears into slower motion. "I never saw her before this evening."

"She certainly made a dead set for you."

Letting the smoke curl slowly from his nostrils, he said, "I shouldn't have thought you would have cared."

"I do care—to have such a sordid, cheap exhibition go on under my nose, and right in front of Frannie Wainwright, too! It was humiliating!"

"What in blazes has Frannie Rufus to do with the price of eggs?"

"You wouldn't understand. Everything about her has always been so perfect, even at college. I'm sure Jim Rufus would rather be found dead than humiliate his wife in public that way."

"I'd prefer not to be asked to imagine what would or would not humiliate Jim Rufus. It humiliates me, if you want to know, that I haven't got a more entertaining neighbor to ask to spend an evening."

"Well, will you admit that that Kay De Fronzo is about the cheapest—" Maggie groped wildly for a word— "piece of goods that you've ever seen?"

"She's one swell-looking gal. Will you admit that?"

"You ought to be mortified, Ray! A man of your age! She's years younger than you. I hope you realize that. It made you look such a fool!"

"So I enjoy myself for a couple of hours with a gal who is a bit free and easy. Have I built her up as anything else? Would you prefer that I told you that I do know, somewhere, a girl for whom I could count the world well lost?"

The recurring image of Masu flickered before him. How crass, how stupid could this woman he had married be, yapping away at a mere ripple on the surface and missing entirely the deep, desolating gulf of estrangement he could feel inexorably widening between them?

"You realize you're trying to stir up a tempest in a teapot, Margot. Kay De Fronzo is not of the slightest importance to me."

"And I should say that I can't be of much importance." Maggie's tone became lofty as she went on. "Frankly, it seems strange to me, Ray, that, feeling as you so obviously do, you could ever have agreed to write an article about me for a magazine."

"You certainly don't think that every adman has to be sold on the commodity before he can write sales copy? Who are you kidding?"

"Oh, so I'm a commodity, am I?" Her voice trembled with anger.

"What else? You have to be sold, honey, just the same as you have to sell. What else, in heaven's name, do you think a radio program like yours is *for*?" Ray stopped suddenly, seeing the look of incomprehension on his wife's features. "Hell, Margot, we're not talking public relations."

"I couldn't agree with you more. You were saying that Kay De Fronzo is of no importance to you, and I am asking you, is our marriage of any importance to you?"

Ray suddenly turned dead serious before her; the words that had gone before were forgotten as half-good-natured sparring. His face looked suddenly stripped. "You ask me that. Is it of any importance to *you,* Margot?" he rapped out.

"What are you talking about?"

"I'm talking about the woman I came home from the war to find. You know damn well that I wanted nothing so much as a marriage that had meaning to it—and what is waiting for me? A female that's so neatly and efficiently zippered up that not only does she not want this husband—if you ask me, she doesn't want any husband."

"That's not true!"

"Would to God it weren't! I would have given my soul a few months back to find things . . . well, different. We're here such a hell of a short time, Margot. Something decent—why be ashamed to say it? something beautiful—between a man and woman is just about the best thing that can happen in a lifetime. And what do I find? A female that has turned into a slick operator—and an operator in an empty world, where every value is a surface value. I'm asking *you*, Maggie, which one of us has been the first to show that our marriage comes—I was going to say second, but perhaps it would be fairer to say *last*—that it comes after everything else?"

"Don't be absurd! Ambition is nothing to be ashamed of. As far as that goes, I'd like to know what's happened to yours along the way. I thought you had it when I married you. How do you think it makes me feel when I come home after a day of hard work—and I'm not ashamed, I can tell you, to pull down a good salary for doing a professional job—to come home and find you slopping about with a paint-box or maybe playing with your Victorian trade cards, like a child! Dexter's fussing with his moths used to drive me crazy, but at least it was scientific!"

"And whose fault is it that I'm left to slop about?"

"Listen to me, Ray Masters—" Maggie's voice was growing shrill—"I refuse to be blamed for *your* weakness and *your* laziness. I think *I* deserve a little pity!" Her voice trembled. "Have you ever stopped to think that maybe I wouldn't even want a career of my own if I had a husband who could interest and excite me—yes, maybe even dominate me? You're so damned supercilious, standing there trying to lay all the blame for our failure on me."

"You used the word *failure*, Maggie, not I."

"I'd like to know what else you'd call it," she spat out bitterly. "But I can tell you one thing—you're not going to get away with that cheap trick in *this* marriage. Don't forget, my name's not Alice!"

"I've been talking more or less about Alice this evening, as it happens," Ray said with infuriating detachment.

"I'm sure you have. I'm sure you must have been describing the dear sweet girl who inspired you to write poetry. So far as I can make out, you're turning quite moony about Alice in your old age. Perhaps you even wish you had never left such a paragon, especially in exchange for a wife that you seem to think—"

Ray put up his hand abruptly to stop her. "What's that?" he said.

They both stood rigidly still, listening over their pounding hearts. Outside in the hall there was the sound of a sort of strangled gulp, dry and hard, and then the sound of footsteps racing up the stairs.

They both went out into the hall in time to see Priscilla's retreating back. Her shoulders were stooped over, as though she were about to be sick. The next minute the door of her room banged shut behind her.

31

PRISCILLA HAD not come out of her room the next morning by the time Maggie had to leave for New York. Just after her show she was told at the studio that her daughter wanted to speak to her on the telephone. When Maggie heard her first words, sounding very faint and faraway out on Long Island, her heart turned over.

"Mummy, I wanted to ask you if it would be all right if I came in town to meet Daddy and go back to spend one night, or maybe two, with them in Greenwich?"

"Why do you want to go, dear?" Maggie managed to ask fairly affably. Her heart was pounding as she said to herself, *She's going back to them.*

There was an embarrassed pause. "Aunt Spaff called me this morning. She wanted to tell me some news about Daddy."

"Not bad news?" Maggie was too alarmed to notice that this was the first time she and Priscilla had mentioned Dexter to each other.

"No, no, wonderful news. He and Aunt Spaff are going to Stockholm next week. Daddy's been awarded some marvelous prize for his research in physics. Something about calibrating radioactivity. Naturally I don't understand it. But Aunt Spaff says that next to the Nobel Prize it's the highest honor he can have in his field. Isn't it exciting? He'll be world-famous."

Maggie was aware of an unaccountable impulse to cry. She also felt vaguely cheated. Fame and Dexter just didn't seem to go together.

It was very confusing, although, come to think of it, wasn't this just what her father had predicted years ago?

She was able to say with convincing warmth, "Of course you must go to Greenwich to see him, and be sure to give him congratulations from me, won't you, baby?"

Every evening that week Ray contrived to be out, getting back just in time for dinner when Maggie returned from the city. As he thus avoided their normal cocktail hour together, she assumed that he must be getting martinis elsewhere. The line Maggie had decided to take toward him was rather a high and grand one. She made it a point to forget the words he had spoken to her, obviously under the influence of alcohol. Unaware that she was, in panic, enveloping herself in a hastily stitched garment of self-esteem, she flung herself into playing the role of the wife who . . . forgives; in fact, she was ready to forgive her husband as she would forgive a badly behaved, silly adolescent.

It was easier still for her to expunge from her memory the words they had exchanged when, a few days later, Ray handed her the proof of the first installment of the serialized biography for *Every Woman's Home Magazine*. "Here," he said. "I've been able to wangle this to give you a look, along with the rough sketch the art department is planning for the cover."

Maggie snatched it from him and for several breathless minutes held it in her hands, drinking in, in hushed and rapturous reverence, the enlarged, highly flattered commercial rendering of her own face. The hair shone golder than buttercups, the eyes were bluer than forget-me-nots, the lips redder than American Beauty roses, and the skin was as free of pores and lines as the average gardenia petal. Under it she read, MY MARGOT, *Intimate Story of a Fabulous Woman Told As Only a Husband Can Tell it*. MY MARGOT . . . there she was. The whole long, restless search to find herself seemed for Maggie miraculously consummated. Here at last, face to face, she could confront the glittering, successful woman she had always longed to be. The worshiper who looked and marveled was aware of a longing, almost physical in its passionate intensity, to *feel* that she, Maggie, and this projection of her dreams were the same person. She seemed to be straining, in answer to a magnetic pull, to inject herself bodily into the manuscript she held in her hands. A faint, barely recognized shiver of doubt, bordering on fear, stirred somewhere within her. Feverishly she set to turning the pages of proof.

"Look!" she cried. "That snapshot of Roger and me at Northeast! Oh, and *look*! Father in his First World War uniform—the snapshot Mother always had on her bureau! Oh, Ray, doesn't it look *nice*?" Her eyes were starting out of her head, straining to digest the contents of the pages at a gulp.

"First Installment—'Love at First Sight,' " she read. "Oh, I like that. Where did it happen?" she asked without humor. "At Nini's in Boston, or on Eleuthera?"

"Eleuthera. Natch. Don't you think it's *much* more romantic? You were there because your parents were worried about a nasty cough you had picked up overworking in the Boston slums."

"Oh," Maggie answered vaguely. "What do you say about our divorces?"

"Our *what*? Be your age. In *Every Woman's Home*, we meet, we love—both unencumbered. I hope you'll like what I've said about your father. And about the Victorian Boston you were rebelling against."

"Oh, I'm *sure* I will!" Maggie hardly looked up, her eyes darting back and forth across the pages, until she suddenly asked, "What are the next installments going to be about?"

"The second—'My Husband's Career Is My Career'—tells how you helped me in Hollywood and how you plugged to get me a better job back in New York." Maggie was nodding hearty agreement. "And the third is 'War Wife'—the terrific job you did creating A.O.E.O. and the Green Lady—and in the fourth and last I tell about coming home to find you famous. I haven't decided on the title for it yet."

"Oh, Ray!" Maggie's voice was pulsating with warmth. "I think it's just *wonderful*! I'm sure it will do lots of good!"

As he closed the door behind him, to leave her as enthralled as a child with the toy of her dreams, Ray confided to the empty hallway, "Christ! She believes her own publicity!"

Late Saturday afternoon, when Priscilla got home, Maggie, out on the terrace, was holding the well-thumbed pages in her lap, caressing them as she might a priceless fur pelt. The sound of Priscilla's footsteps jerked her back, away from the world she had been enjoying, to face up to the unpleasantness she had decided to tackle, head on.

When she heard Priscilla's voice call, "Mummy?" she answered in as noncommittal a tone as she could manage, "Yes, darling, come out here. It's delicious and cool."

Priscilla opened the door and stepped out into the sunset. She was wearing a simple white-silk dress with a yellow sweater thrown over her shoulders. Maggie thought, *She's turning into a real beauty before our eyes.*

"Sit down, dear," she said in a voice full of promise, as she slipped the magazine back of a cushion. Priscilla sat down. Maggie lighted a cigarette, inhaled it deeply, and then, head on, flung herself into what had to be said. "I've been so anxious to talk to you all week, darling. I do hope that you weren't too much upset by . . . er . . . what you heard the other night, I'm sorry you were in the house when Ray had too much to drink. In all the years I've been married to him I've never seen him like that, in spite of what your Grandmother Bradfield may say to you."

"Grandma?" Priscilla looked confused. "Grandma never mentioned Ray to me."

"Well, you may as well know it now as later. The reason she fought so hard against your coming to live with me years ago was that she had some absurd notion that he was an alcoholic."

"Poor Ray," Priscilla sighed.

"Why do you say *poor*?" Maggie's voice sharpened. "He's leading exactly the life he chooses to lead."

"I know. But he can't be really happy, or he wouldn't have—what happened wouldn't have happened."

"Well, it won't again. The only trouble with Ray right now is that he's demoralized. I suppose most men are when they get out of the service."

"All Ray needs, Mummy, is a chance to get back to his own work again. I'm sure once he begins writing he'll be all right."

"Listen, darling, don't be naïve. I was, for years. Face it. Ray's not going to write another book—anyway, nothing that will be a success like *The Joneses.*"

"That's a terrible thing to say! How do you *know* he's not until he's had a chance? He's made a lot of notes, and I think some of them are marvelous."

"Oh. Has he shown them to you?"

"A few, yes. I know, of course, that I'm no judge, but I think he has a wonderful idea. I think he should have time, and quiet, and . . . well, sort of be allowed to digest everything he's seen and felt."

"Listen, lovey—" Maggie resorted to a favorite childhood pet name—"literary criticism is hardly up your alley. Don't feel you have to start looking after Ray. I've been married to him now for a great many years, and I've learned a lot about him in that time. He's like a great many other men—a big bluff and a cry baby. If he gets too much sympathy it's weakening for him. He needs to be taken out of himself." She hesitated an instant before plunging into the disagreeable subject. "I'm sure the reason he had too much drink the other night is that fundamentally he has a guilty conscience about not working harder. I'm so sorry you heard the edges of anything so unpleasant as a scene between us."

"Don't worry, Mummy, please." Priscilla's whole face seemed to come apart; not only her eyes but every other feature seemed to be pleading with Maggie to probe this painful wound no further.

Maggie hurried on, crisp and efficient. "I'm sure that when we all get back to town Ray's life will be much more organized. Such a thing simply won't happen again."

Priscilla was watching her progress, intent and tense. It was her turn now to initiate a topic precipitately. "Mummy," she said, "speaking of going back to town, I've been wanting to talk to you about my plans."

"Your *plans*, child? What plans?"

The quickening of her mother's response in turn strengthened Priscilla's resolve. She walked boldly up to the cannon's mouth. "About the winter. Mummy, I've decided I don't want to live in New York."

"But, Priscilla! What do you mean? Everything's *fixed*!" Maggie reached wildly in as many directions as she could think of in an instant. "Your room has been done specially. You have at least three different wonderful openings to choose from. First, there's the one at that fascinating new pet shop—"

Priscilla, hurling herself across the march past of the delights in store for her, stopped Maggie short. "I know. I feel so badly that you should have gone to all that trouble."

Maggie's eyes suddenly narrowed. It was just what she had feared. Spaff. Foul play. She saw it all. Maggie did not attempt to make her voice friendly as she asked, "Have you decided that you would prefer to live with your father? Is that the reason for this sudden shift?"

"No, no."

"Then what *do* you want to do? You can't tell me you plan to spend the winter buried out here at Beach Hampton with that dim little vet? There can't be enough sick dogs to keep him busy, let alone an assistant."

"No, I don't want to stay here." Priscilla's brows knotted. "I—I'm going back to Far Fields." She knew now that the widest leap was made, and forced herself on. "I'm going to help Aunt Marsh raise her Shelties and work for that vet in Beverly I told you about."

Maggie's heart was racing. How was she to avert this disaster? She got up quietly and, picking up a light-blue flannel coat that was lying across the back of the wicker chair in which she had been sitting, said, "Come on down to the wharf with me. Let's watch the sunset from there."

"But, Mummy, it's no good to try to distract me. I know what—"

"Come on," said her mother authoritatively. She was already on the lawn. "I'm glad you've got your sweater. Come on, baby."

There was a note in her mother's voice that Priscilla knew it would be futile to try to ignore. She followed, to heel, along the path that led them down the sloping shore, sweet with bayberry bushes, to the wharf. At its end was a rickety wooden bench. There Maggie sat down and patted a place beside her.

They both, for a moment, let the beauty of the sea and sky come forward to meet them. The lapping of the waves against the piles of the wharf was the only sound.

Maggie picked up the conversation as though they had not put it down. "You say you are going. Is it all arranged?"

"Yes."

"Since when?"

"Well, when I left home" (the natural way Far Fields was referred to was not lost on Maggie) "Aunt Marsh told me if ever I changed my mind about wanting to live with . . . to live in New York she would be glad to have me back any time. I wrote her a few days ago that after Labor Day I'd come."

"Priscilla, do you mean you intend to go back to *stay*?" The long-drawn-out sound that she gave the word carried, implicit in it, the ultimate of the incredible. Priscilla looked at her mother, now really frightened. There were two spots of high color in her cheeks. Her eyes were blazing.

"Well . . ." Priscilla could find no exit from her misery but the delivery of the monosyllable "Yes."

"Tell me—" Maggie was obviously making a superhuman effort to keep the lid clamped on emotions that were at the explosion point—"has this anything to do with what you heard the other night?"

"Please don't ask me," Priscilla brought out too quickly, only to go on in the voice of rational kindness one uses in speaking to a headstrong child. "It wasn't just that, anyway. I've thought before, lots of times, that you were . . . well, sort of mean to Ray." Maggie let the horrid little word hang for an instant before her while she blinked at it, refusing to recognize its existence before recoiling sharply. She recoiled now in retreat but only that she might lash back in return. *How New England,* she thought, *how Bradfield, this tactless, unadorned little snippet of personal judgment, masquerading as total truth!*

"*Mean*? How 'mean,' Priscilla?"

"Well, I think he gets sort of depressed being alone so much, and that's half the reason he drinks, and I think someone should show more interest in his writing."

"Someone being me?"

"Oh, Mummy, please, don't question me so much! Don't make me say things! I just think that my living with you isn't a very good idea," she brought out lamely. Sudden tears welled up in Maggie's eyes. She was aware of being engulfed; the cry that came from her carried the authority of desolation.

"It would break my heart to let you go back! You don't know how I've *lived* for the day that you would come to me, that I could really and truly feel I had a daughter of my own!" She waited to regain control of herself before going on. "I wonder whether you're hitting back at me for what I did to you long ago?"

Priscilla's look of incredulous surprise stopped her mother short before she went on. "Oh, I don't say you'd do it consciously, but there could be a deep-seated resentment against me. Don't think *I've* forgotten that I hurt you once, long ago, when I left you behind—when you were still such a little girl. You do understand, now that you're grown up, Priscilla, that I didn't know it was going to happen that way until it was too late?"

"Yes, I understand, Mummy. Daddy used to try to explain to me that once you found I couldn't go with you it was too late for you to . . . change. You couldn't have played a dirty trick like that on Ray, once he'd left his wife." Gravely pursuing the labyrinth back to those never-to-be-spoken-of days, Priscilla said, "The funny thing is, sometimes I wonder if your going away didn't make me love you almost more than some other children love their mothers."

"Absence making the heart grow fonder?"

"Maybe." She smiled in the dusk. "Anyway you seemed as far away and beautiful and romantic as—" she saw her vision take form—"that star. Oh, Mummy—" Priscilla's voice quavered now—"I've lived for the day when I could be with *you.* I wanted a mother of my own just as much as you wanted a daughter."

There were tears now on Maggie's cheeks. "But then, darling, why . . . why . . . if we both want—"

The straight young figure beside her loomed implacable. "But if it just doesn't work, it's worse than not being together at all. Isn't that true, Mummy?"

"Priscilla, tell me. Is it because you don't want to be under the same roof with what looks to you like an unhappy marriage?"

"I didn't say *unhappy*, Mummy."

"Well, then, *unattractive*. Whatever it is, it's something you don't want to have anything to do with. Is that it?"

"Something like that, I guess. Maybe if I'd been with you all along it would have been different. But now I think I'm too grown up just to be a sort of a fly on the wall, without wanting to say things, do things—"

"You mean, take sides?"

"That's what I don't *want* to do! I just want to go home, Mummy. Please don't be hurt, or don't be angry, or don't even be too disappointed, and *please* don't make Ray feel it's his fault."

"Because it's mine?"

"I didn't *say* that, Mummy! Don't put words into my mouth! It's just that I don't want to be where there is—or where there isn't—well, a sort of a peaceful atmosphere. It's not just watching you and Ray that makes me uncomfortable. It's knowing I could never be the kind of daughter you want. If I went on living with you, you'd be bound to be disappointed with me in the end."

"Unless you were disappointed with me first?"

"I didn't *say* that! It's just that I don't *like* parties, I don't *want* to meet a whole lot of new people, especially celebrities. I *wouldn't* be ashamed to marry a vet. Maybe I'm too much like Aunt Marsh. If I am, I can't help it. I like Aunt Marsh."

"And I'm sure she likes you," Maggie said bitterly. "I suppose she's shown you her collection?"

"Of daggers? Oh, yes," came the limpid answer.

"*Daggers*! So that's it!"

"Oh, dear, I didn't mean to . . . I thought you knew," Priscilla quavered.

Her mother was no longer listening. "It doesn't matter whether I did or not. But I can tell you one thing. I'm not going to let you fall into the hands of that twisted, neurotic, frustrated old maid without fighting!" Priscilla was cowering now before her mother's onslaught. "Yes, you heard me—*fighting*! The way I ought to have fought years ago, except that I was too damned much of a lady with all you precious Bradfields. Well, I'm not going to be a lady this time. The only way to deal with people like the Bradfields is to give them some of their own back." She knew she was saying terrible, irrevocable words—words that could never be wiped out, never forgotten—but her battle was born of desperation. No weapon that could help her to slash, hack, gash her way out of this thicket of bland, stubborn stupidity was too crass or too cruel to use. She plunged on. "If you're too much of a little fool not to know what's good for you, then it's time somebody told you for a change. If you choose to go back to Far Fields, then I tell you, Priscilla, it's the end between you and me. The *end*! I give you up . . . as hopeless. I can have nothing more to do with you!"

At the words *I give you up* Priscilla crumpled over as though her mother's fist as well as her words had hit her in the solar plexus. The girl's face was twisted into a look of pain—the pain of suffering without the power of putting into words her sense of annihilating rejection.

"Don't! Mummy, don't! Please, stop it!" was all she was able, helplessly, to say.

"Then tell me you'll stay." Maggie's own voice broke. Her tirade stopped as suddenly as it had begun. The perspiration was running down her face; she could feel it cracking her pancake make-up as she could feel her dress damp across the back. Like a wrestler who has expended his last ounce of energy, she waited, breathing hard, to hear the verdict of an unseen referee.

It did not come. No sound passed between them for a full minute. Maggie was the first to break the silence. "Well, Priscilla? How about it?"

"I can't change my mind, Mummy." Although thin and clear with the freshness of youth, her voice carried the ring of an iron and thoroughly adult resolve.

Maggie, too, transposed her own key. She spoke quietly, as though it were she who was bearing rather than inflicting the wounds. "If I can't convince you myself, I'm going to ask Aunt Kitten to. It wouldn't be at all unnatural if you'd listen to her rather than me. I shall call her in Milton after dinner. Now, it's time we went back to the house. Ray will be wondering where we are."

Up along the same path, through the long grass, they walked. Neither mother nor daughter spoke again. The lights from the house were flooding the lawn when they reached the top of the bank. They stopped. Maggie, in sudden reaction against the violence that had swept her, with a cry opened her arms. "My baby!" This time she could not hide her sob, nor the tears which wet both their faces, as she crushed Priscilla against her heart.

It was Priscilla's turn to show a face of steel. She pulled herself free from her mother's grasp as she gulped out, "I'm sorry, Mummy. I'm not doing it on purpose," and bolted into the house.

After dinner, when Maggie got Milton on long distance, it was Roger who answered the telephone.

"I've got to speak to Kitten," she said in desperate tones, low enough to preclude being heard on the other side of her closed bedroom door.

"Kitten can't speak to you, Maggie," came the surprising answer in a voice quite as low and desperate as her own. "We're just waiting for the ambulance. Kitten's had a sudden hemorrhage. The doctor wants to get her right into the hospital."

The ground fell away under Maggie's feet. She sat down weakly.

"Oh, Roger!" was all she was able to say for a second, then, "Would you like me to come on? Tomorrow's Sunday, and I have no show."

"Do what you like," he said not unkindly. "I've got to go now, Mag." She heard the receiver click in her ear.

Maggie ran down the stairs to tell Ray the news she had heard.

"Come on," he said, "let's go. While you're throwing some things in a bag I'll call the airlines, then I'll drive you to LaGuardia."

As they shot over the roads, with Ray at the wheel, zigzagging through the obstacles of week-end traffic, Maggie relayed the gist of her conversation with Priscilla to him, and then opened up a rapid fire of farewell injunctions.

"I'll be back late tomorrow night, and can spend the night in town. Ray, you've *got* to talk Priscilla out of this hysterical idea. Kitten could have done it, but now you've got to. I simply can't stand losing her. It will ruin everything for me—everything. She likes you. You've got great influence with her. Tell her you need her. Tell her for *your* sake, if not for mine, she's got to stay with us. She can write her own ticket—job, friends, anything she wants. But don't *let* the Bradfields get her back. It would be too horrible!"

Maggie kissed him almost savagely, hurling her final exhortation at him as she did so. "I'm counting on you! Don't *let* them get her!"

32

THE NEXT day in Boston was what the Bradfields called a "squealer." The thermometer had shot up early in the morning to hover near the nineties, with humidity to match. Looking out of her window from the Ritz Hotel into the Public Garden, Maggie had the impression that the very treetops were buzzing with the heat.

Before eight she telephoned Roger in Milton. "What's the news?" she asked without any greeting.

His voice sounded queer and strained. He might have been dictating a telegram, Maggie thought, it was so impersonal. "It's not good. I'm just starting for the hospital now. There's going to be a consultation this morning to decide whether to operate or not. If they do, it wouldn't be till tomorrow or the next day."

"But, Roger—" Maggie was afraid to ask her question outright—"Have you known all along that something like this might happen? It seems so sudden. I mean I never knew—has it something to do with that trouble with her back?"

"Sure it has. It's all part of the same damned thing."

"But I thought the operation was so slight," she said almost argumentatively.

"It was. They cut the posterior nerve tracts—just to stop the pain in her back and legs."

He had not said the word. But Maggie knew there was nothing more to ask. She tried to say cheerfully, "Will I be able to see her? I want to so much, if I can," but her voice broke.

For an instant the veil behind which Roger seemed to have withdrawn was torn aside. He spoke in instant response, with the kindness Maggie was used to. "Since you've come all the way up, it certainly should be arranged. I'm trying to keep the boys away—anyway, for today. Mother's out here with them. Let's leave it that you'll turn up at the hospital at four this afternoon, unless I leave word at the hotel that there's some change. Phillips House, fifth floor."

"Couldn't we have lunch or something?" Maggie asked with a wistfulness she could not dissemble. "Aren't I going to see you at all?"

"I don't see how I can make lunch, Maggie. I'll want to be at the hospital as much as I can. Here's Mother. She wants to speak to you." Roger seemed glad of an excuse to detach himself, and Maggie heard a quavering, faint little voice.

"Darling, Maggie, is that you?"

"Yes, Mother, it is. Aren't I going to see you either?"

"I feel so badly, dear child, but I don't want to leave the boys here alone, and—"

"And I'm still not allowed to set foot on Bradfield property, even at a time like this?"

A little gasp of pain and shock came through the wires. "Maggie, dear, please don't put it like that. But since both Mr. and Mrs. Bradfield are naturally under a great strain, I'm sure you wouldn't—"

"Want to put them under any more." Maggie finished her mother's sentence for her. "All right, Mother, I won't trouble anyone."

They talked a few minutes more. Mrs. Fraser asked about Ray and Priscilla and how Maggie was arranging the furniture in her new house. Maggie asked about her mother's rooms in the Vendome and about how she was arranging *her* furniture. There was little more to say except "I'll call you after I've seen Kitten. Good-by, Mother."

Maggie had the hot Sunday, alone in Boston, to herself. She knew that there was no good to try to call any old friends. They would all be out of town; the boarded-up houses on Beacon Street had already told her that. A shower, desultory reading of magazines, lying on the bed under an electric fan with nothing on but a slip, a prolonged lunch in the large dining room overlooking the Public Garden—somehow the hours passed.

Maggie was at the hospital fifteen minutes before the appointed four o'clock. The nurse at the desk, on the floor to which she was directed, said, "Mr. Fraser left word nobody was to go into the room. If you're his sister, he asked you to wait."

So Maggie sat on a straight-backed chair in the corridor.

She became gradually aware of the smells of the arena where life-and-death battle was joined. Her eyes, conditioned by the glare of a lifetime of physical strength, could only blink in this half-light of illness and pain. Aside from her short stay on the cheerful maternity floor of the same hospital, she had always instinctively turned from all that went on in hospitals. She had made it clear to Dexter from the start that any whiff of iodine in the conversation bored her. Maybe she had just been frightened all the time. She had always closed her ears even to the mention of stockyards, insane asylums, or prisons. Such grisly institutions were better fled from. A hospital was just as bad. She admitted to herself that even her experience of death had not yet brought her face to face with this dreadful tussle. Her father had died far away, and she had never seen his grave; he seemed rather to have withdrawn than to have died.

She had nothing to read. Thrashing desperately about in her mind, she could not fix it on anything gay. She was forced to look at, listen to, and smell what was around her. Actually, had she but known it, the achievement of the particular institution in which she sat was remarkable in keeping distressing sights and sounds away from the casual visitor. The corridors, with the shiny linoleum floors, were spotless and offered quiet surfaces for the rubber soles of the nurses' white shoes as they moved quickly and quietly about their duties. One, carrying at arm's length an object covered by a white towel, whisked by her. Another supported a woman dressed in a dressing gown and bed slippers, with her hair in a pigtail, walking very slowly. Maggie noticed that her chest was asymmetrical. The nurse and patient were laughing and talking together. Suddenly a door opened to let out fumes of ether and the sound of violent retching before it was quickly closed, the dangling sign on the doorknob superfluously reading NO VISITORS. Down the hall, at the desk, a doctor in white, with a stethoscope around his neck, was reading charts. A light flashed on over the door of a room down the corridor. *What a touching and mute appeal for attention!* Maggie thought. How much less could a human being vent his own surcharged emotions on it than on an electric bell! It could not suggest any degrees of need—shrieking, *I am desperate!* or *This is an emergency!* Only there was the unspoken statement, unvarying in emphasis over each doorway: *I exist. I need help. Come.* Farther down the hall a nurse, carrying a vase of flowers, opened a door into one of the rooms, from which spilled out sounds of a laughing party. There was a "Sssh!" from somewhere, and the door closed. A husband and wife—they were that, obviously—stood with their heads close in conclave with a doctor. All their faces were grave, as they advanced, on tiptoe, to enter single file into another room.

What a tangled switchboard of human nerve ends! All the strands of love, anxiety, or duty—no matter how loosely they hung or how remote their source—were knotted here at one bedside.

Maggie was frightened, thinking of Kitten. She felt she had lost her already. Of all the divisions between man and man—rich and poor, black and white, east and west—it seemed as though none was so complete as that between the sick and the well. The living and the dead were closer.

And then, suddenly, coming down the corridor, having left a door of one of the sickrooms open behind her, was Aunt Katta. She wore no hat, so that her close-cropped hair gleamed white from a distance. *She's an old lady!* was Maggie's first thought. Her next: *Maybe she won't want to see me.* Maggie got up hurriedly, as though to disappear, but Aunt Katta was approaching her with deliberate intent. As she came forward Maggie saw, to her immeasurable relief, that her hand was outstretched in greeting. In an instant it held Maggie's in its hearty grip. "Hello, Magpie," she said as naturally as though they had parted the day before.

"Hello, Aunt Katta," Maggie answered without stopping to think she was using a title it was not her right to use. "I'm awfully glad to see you."

The strong old face was after all much the same, Maggie saw now on closer observation; it was only that the figure as a whole seemed to have dwindled. Her head was set farther forward on her shoulders, and the shoulders themselves were stooped. Maggie saw at once that she had been intensely affected by something that must just have happened inside the sickroom; there was a preternaturally bright glitter in her eyes, there were mottled patches on her skin, and the pulse of her neck fluttered. In a wave of unusual understanding for an emotion that was not her own, Maggie saw Aunt Katta's suffering by the light of its own peculiar poignancy—that of the old, whose usefulness, therefore whose life itself, is over, forced to witness helplessly the slipping away of a precious, still desperately needed, younger life.

The straight line of Aunt Katta's strong mouth did not tremble, nor did her voice waver as she said, "Kitten's tickled pink you're here. She's expecting you. It's all right to go in. But you'd better not stay more than ten minutes, Magpie."

"Where's Roger? Is he with her?"

"No. I came in to spell him for an hour while he went over to the office. He'll let himself in with his own key and pick up some papers he wanted. I made him go even though he didn't want to. I thought it would be good for him."

"But I've been here all day! I could have—I've been dying to—" Maggie started to speak, and finally asked merely, "Aren't I going to see him at all?"

"He said to tell you he'd try to run into the hotel before you leave, but if he didn't make it he was sure you'd understand. It's a hectic day for him. He's been on the transatlantic telephone with Spaff and Dexter. They're flying home tonight. Braddy's coming on from Minnesota tomorrow." For an instant her lip trembled, then she spoke in a level voice. "Roger doesn't want to talk to anybody, Magpie," she explained.

"Aunt Katta—" Maggie found she dared to ask this old woman what she had not dared to ask her own brother—"is it hopeless?"

Aunt Katta did not flinch in the face of the word. "I'm afraid so. They're going to operate tomorrow; they might be able to prolong her life a little by suturing, but nobody's fooled, least of all Kitten. I think she's hoping not to come through it. It would be so much the quickest way out."

"But how *long* has she been getting worse? Nobody told me!"

"They haven't told anybody. Of course they didn't have to tell those of us who were here to see the change for ourselves. She and Roger have faced it together since the day she had to go back into the hospital. She's talked to me—a little—for the first time today. There were things that had to be said to somebody. Things that were too hard to say even to Roger—perhaps especially to Roger. I don't think she'll talk now to anyone else. It only makes it harder for her." Maggie was crying, and couldn't seem to stop as Aunt Katta went on. "What we've all got to do is to make it as easy for Kitten herself as we can." The fact that Aunt Katta gave no recognition of Maggie's tears helped to bring her round and get hold of herself. She listened quietly as Aunt Katta went on. "Roger told her you had a free Sunday and decided to come up on the spur of the moment. You'll find Kitten perfectly natural. She's not in pain. They're keeping her under heavy sedation. You'll see her appearance is terribly changed, she's so thin. Since yesterday she's lost so much blood that her mouth is dry, and it's hard for her to talk. But she's coming up with transfusions. Her spirit is the same as ever. Now I mustn't keep you, or she'll be wondering where you are."

Maggie mopped her eyes and blew her nose. She had taken out a hand mirror to peer questioningly into it. The reflection that confronted her appeared not to tell her what she wanted to know. She appealed to Aunt Katta. "Do I look all right?"

"You look fine. You look very well, Magpie." The last comment was going to be Aunt Katta's only reference to the years that had flowed by since their last meeting.

"*You've* hardly changed at all, Aunt Katta," Maggie said, clinging, she hardly knew why, to the tie that could bind them together for another minute.

"Bosh. I can tell I'm getting old every morning when I have to sit down to put on my stockings" was the bluff reply.

There was nothing further to say. Maggie knew that Aunt Katta would not wish to be thanked for anything. So, with as much crispness as she could manage, she said, "Well, then, I'll go right in," and walked firmly down the hall.

She put her hand on the knob of the door that was ajar. On it was a sign reading NO FEEDING BY MOUTH AFTER MIDNIGHT.

She tiptoed into the room which was in half-light. Kitten was lying flat on her back, although the hospital bed had been cranked up to put her head high. She was wearing a blue-satin bed jacket; her hair was braided into two tiny pigtails with a piece of blue-satin ribbon at the end of each. Maggie noticed with a start that the hair, which was pulled back from her temples and which escaped in little curls, was gray.

"Maggie! This is the most wonderful surprise!" Kitten said through white lips, and smiled. It was hard for Maggie not to draw back at the sight of the smile; Kitten's teeth seemed to have grown perfectly enormous. *Like the wolf's in the story of Little Red Riding Hood,* Maggie thought, in spite of herself. What had happened? Looking again, Maggie saw that the explanation lay in the weight Kitten had lost. Her face was reduced to its skeletal essentials. Her little frame was a house of bone only, but bone still lighted by light burning within. The eyes, whose customary blue surely must have been in the mind of the donor of the bed jacket, were no longer blue but almost black, or was the illusion caused by the deep shadows beneath them? The thin little hands and arms were as white as the bedspread on which they lay, and were not Kitten's—not as Maggie had known Kitten's for nearly thirty years. They too were part of this strange little skeleton. Into one of the arms was stuck the end of a long piece of yellow plastic tubing, whose other end dangled from a tipped-up bottle hanging on what looked like a coat tree beside the bed. Is this what Aunt Katta meant when she had said "transfusions"? Maggie looked away.

"You talk, Maggie," whispered Kitten, "my mouth's so dry." She moved a piece of ice among the strange skull's teeth.

"Oh, what wonderful pictures of the boys!" Maggie exclaimed with false excitement, seeing a row of the full complement of five framed photographs—Rodg, Brad, Mac, Kim, and Button.

"Roger brought them in from Milton this morning. He said they'd be more restful than the boys themselves." The same dreadful smile.

"Isn't Button *adorable*!" Maggie heard herself almost gush in a bright party voice as she picked up the picture of the youngest. "Doesn't that toothless smile undo you? I hope he doesn't grow any second teeth for *ages*!" What was she saying? She hoped he would grow them overnight so that his mother might see them.

As she put the picture back on the bureau her eye fell on a hospital table in the corner of the room. It was already spread like a high altar, with the elements necessary for tomorrow's oblation—several metal basins, an ugly instrument terminating in a metal ball, an array of scissorlike weapons, some tiny glass cylinders containing coiled threads, together with rolls and rolls of bandage.

Kitten had said, "You talk." What, in Christ's name, could she *say*?

A faint voice came again from the bed. "How's Priscilla, Maggie?"

Maggie could have flung herself, weeping, on her knees, beseeching Kitten to perform one last transcendent deathbed miracle to save them all. But remembering Aunt Katta's words—"We must make it easy for Kitten herself"—she forced back the torrent of words that were choking her and said cheerfully, "Just fine. She's really had a grand summer. She's loved the work and looks wonderful. I honestly have moments of believing she's going to turn into a raving, tearing beauty. Wouldn't it be a joke for that little mouse?"

"She *is* a beauty," said Kitten. "Give her my love. And you, Maggie? Roger's going to get me a radio if they keep me on here much longer. I hardly ever miss one of your programs."

"*Really*?" Maggie brightened. Kitten had commanded *You talk*. Here was a subject to which there was no end. She drew breath and began. "Well, it really is thrilling how well it's been going. My fan mail has been growing by leaps and bounds, and all I think, breathe, and *eat* is radio! And as if that weren't enough, believe it or not, Ray is in the process of dreaming up another program for me. This would be in addition to the morning one. I think the format is an inspiration, and we hope to get it onto a national network, and in the evening—which of course would mean that at last I'd be in the really big time, and with money, my dear, that would make your eyes pop—I mean something like two thousand a week. Imagine *me*, who wouldn't be paid to keep my big mouth shut, actually being paid for 'doin' what comes natralee.' They all say this new idea would be terrific when television comes in, which it's bound to any day. So, brace yourself for it, I may soon be *seen* as well as *heard* from coast to coast. Isn't it *some*thing!"

In the back of her mind a childhood rhyme echoed: "By at a gallop he goes, and then Back at a gallop comes riding again!" She paused to take breath.

Kitten's lips moved to ask, "Ray? How is he?"

"Ray's fine! I've never seen him better. He's simply thrilled with being a country squire—that is, in his time off from acting as my agent!"

"And you? I mean really?"

"Me? You can see for yourself—all over the place!"

"Happy, Maggie?"

For one ghastly moment she faltered. Those huge eyes of Kitten's were watching her, so that she could almost feel herself change color under the scrutiny.

"You know *me*! Never so happy as when I have ten different irons in the fire, which I certainly have at the moment."

Maggie got up to go. Stooping before a bunch of tiny sweetheart roses on the bureau, she stopped to sniff them, saying, "Aren't they the most delicate, exquisite—"

"Aunt Katta," Kitten breathed softly.

Maggie buried her face in them quickly to hide the tears she could not keep out of her eyes. "She would!" she said.

How could she bring this nightmare to an end? Standing at the foot of the bed, she said, "I love your pigtails, Kitten. I didn't know you'd let your hair grow."

"When I was in the hospital, the second time, it got to be a nuisance keeping it trimmed, so I thought, why not let it grow?" Kitten pulled at one of the little pigtails with her bony fingers. "Do you remember, Maggie, when you chopped it off on your wedding day?"

"Yes!" Maggie laughed, grateful for the lifeline. "Except Mother knocked on the door, and told me Dexter was getting restless in the broom closet! Then Spaff had to finish the job and saved the day—as usual."

Maggie stopped suddenly. She realized that this was the first time she had been able to name Spaff without bitterness, since they had married the same man. Spaff, Kitten, Maggie—the Triumvirate, Vassar, '22—in their long white-dotted swisses, three tiny specks in the line of eager, happy girls carrying the Daisy Chain. Now it was only through Kitten, serving as link in the chain of memory, that Maggie and Spaff could resurrect the image of what each had once been to the other. With Kitten gone, they would lose not only the most precious of the trio, but each estranged friend must now die finally to the other. Spaff would flutter off into the oblivion that had long since claimed the petals of the very daisies themselves. There would be left only Mrs. Dexter Bradfield and Margot Masters, hardly on speaking terms.

Maggie heard herself suddenly saying, "Give my love to Spaff when you see her, Kitten."

One last message through the remaining intermediary to the receding image, so nearly out of sight. Maggie gulped at the lump in her throat and turned away abruptly to see the door open and Fig Newton walk into the room.

He was dressed in white, with the inevitable stethoscope about his neck. Kitten started to make an introduction, but Maggie's cry of "Fig!" interrupted her.

"Well, by Jimminy, if it isn't Maggie!" said Fig, and came forward to shake hands. "How's your good self, Maggie?"

He turned to his patient. "I haven't seen this fascinating lady since the days at Dunster when we used to crook an occasional festive elbow together!"

Maggie responded with the kind of laugh which was the equivalent of a nudge in the ribs. "How's Wig?" she asked.

Fig puckered his brows in tribute to the woman he had married. "Wig, Maggie, is doing a good job."

Maggie just refrained from saying, *By heck!* Instead she said, "Give her my best, please."

Fig crossed over to Kitten and picked up her limp little white claw. "I expect seeing Maggie has done you more good than any of us medicos, isn't that true?"

"I'm just leaving, so don't tell me I'm tiring the patient!" Maggie attempted a lighthearted laugh.

She moved toward the door, faltered, and then came close to the bedside.

"You haven't tired me, Maggie," said Kitten through her dry lips. "I've loved seeing you."

She held out her arms, and Maggie, stooping close, held her for an instant in her embrace. Neither could say good-by. It was Kitten who whispered, "Take care of yourself, Maggie."

"I will," gulped Maggie, and went quickly out the door without looking back.

33

MAGGIE ASKED her taxi driver to let her out on the corner of Arlington and Marlboro streets. She could not face the thought of returning to her hotel room just yet. There were dark clouds rolling across the sky, and the air was so heavy with heat and humidity that it must fall of its own weight into thunder and rain; even so, she felt that a few minutes on a bench in the Public Garden might help to cool and compose her spirits.

She found an unoccupied bench under a purple beech tree. Looking at a nearby stone fountain, she recognized it not as it appeared on this blistering August late afternoon, but remembered it as it was on an afternoon in November, with the first scattered snowflakes of the season blowing about in the biting wind. It was filled high with dead, crunchy brown leaves—so high that, if one were very small and very young, it would be quite safe to stand on the stone brink and shriek, "Watch *me*!" and then leap wildly into the leaves, as sure of a soft bed as though one had been jumping onto a feather mattress, and then lie on one's back kicking and giggling insanely, inhaling city dust and dirt which changed one's giggles into coughing.

The dry, hot dust of the paths spreading around her suddenly ceased to be dry but were wet and oozing with the first spring thaw in March. A row of nursemaids, like sad winter birds, huddled on a bench under the lee of a wall of cut-off spruce trees propped up as shelter against the north wind. They kept their woolen-gloved hands tucked into the sleeves of their coats, and stamped their galoshed feet up and down on the boardwalk to keep warm, calling to their charges to scramble back onto the safe dry plateau and get out of all that delicious mud underneath, in which it was such fun, with pail and shovel, to dig out genuine, wet, fresh, golden mud pies. Much of the mud attached itself in cakes to the heavy leggings she and Roger had worn. Before prezipper days the only means of ingress and egress was via their mother's ivory-handled buttonhook.

The larger adventures of childhood—roller skating and coasting—occurred in the larger arenas of the Esplanade and the Common. But here, in the Public Garden, was the very starting point, the sheltered womb, of one's very earliest memories. Maggie could remember the first time she had put on a pair of real skates, her ankles folding over at right angles as she staggered around the frozen Public Garden pond, the span between her chubby legs widening with each stagger. Here one pushed one's doll carriage up and down and, in the spring, when the paths were beautifully and freshly raked, one played hop-scotch or marbles or mumblety-peg or even bounced a rubber ball up and down on an elastic. Then there was the ineffable excitement of the first swan-boat ride. *This* time, the optical illusion made it seem sure that the brass masthead at the bow must surely hit the bridge as they went under, and then at the last minute came the always wonderful reprieve which brought shrieks of delighted gratitude and surprise, echoing under the bridge as they slid silently and surely under its cool, dark shadow.

On Sundays the Garden took on a more formal aspect, seeming to serve as a crossroads for one's elders. Unitarians, headed for the First Church at the corner of Marlboro and Berkeley or the Arlington Street Church at Arlington and Boylston, exchanged greetings with Episco-palians on their way to Emanuel or Trinity. Maggie held her mother's hand on these pilgrimages, and in her other hand she carried her own prayerbook with her name *Margaret Fraser* written in gold letters on the cover. The first day in spring—when she was allowed to wear socks, and a new straw hat with a wreath of flowers around its natural panama and a black velvet streamer down behind—was a fine occasion. Those were the Sunday mornings when, after church, it was fun to walk slowly down Commonwealth Avenue in the noon sunshine and *oh* and *ah* over the beauty of the magnolias coming into bloom. Her father used to walk across the Garden some Sundays to meet them on their way home. He loved to stand at the head of Marlboro Street and remind himself of the time he had walked home with Henry James after a lunch at the Saturday Club, and imitate James's deep, sad voice as, looking down at the uninterrupted row of brick houses and sidewalks, he had said, "One could hardly call Marlboro Street precisely passionate!" Those spring Sundays, even when she was living them, had a storybook quality to them—like Boutet de Monvel illustrations. The very flower gardens suddenly, without warning, burst into full and faultless bloom of tulips at the touch of the *Alice in Wonderland* gardeners, on their hands and knees, tending the beds.

But as spring went, so did the enchantment. First came the pansies to serve as transition, and then as they disappeared from the flower beds and the familiar dramatis personae of her own Boston trickled away, pink and green cacti, punctuated with hot red poker sticks of plants with no beauty or sweetness, sprouted, spelling out WELCOME SHRINERS or WELCOME LEGIONNAIRES.

Today, aware as she had never been aware before of all that time had washed away of her own personal world, she asked not only where had all those old familiar figures gone but where had gone the most familiar of them all—herself. Where was fun-loving, bossy, little Maggie Fraser? Was Margot Masters, known to thousands across the air waves of the nation, she? Was she the heartbroken friend who had stood inadequate at a deathbed? Was she the daughter, the disappointed wife, the desperate, frightened, rejected mother? How hard it was to know at what point in one's life one could most truly say, "This is I!" All Maggie knew now, sitting under the gathering clouds soon to break over her head, was that the faster she had chased after the vision of herself as accomplishing and accomplished, the farther the reality of a happy woman had receded.

In that wild gallop over the surface of her life that she had offered for Kitten's comfort on what was surely one of the last days of her life, what of depth, or weight, or beauty, had she been able to offer? *Of Heaven or Hell I have no power to sing* . . . A breathless chase, a sense of nervous laughter, a kaleidoscopic panorama of places and people. What was she more than *the idle singer of an empty day?*

There was good, darling little Kitten quietly and unostentatiously accepting death as she had accepted life. One acceptance seemed to flow naturally out of the other. Hard-hitting, fast-talking, unheeding Maggie drew in her breath sharply. She herself would be terrified to die—*just terrified*! she told herself. Perhaps part of the fear, she perceived in an icy chill of apprehension, lay in the knowledge that there wouldn't be anybody to care one way or the other. The heavy weight of heartbreak that she carried in her own breast for the loss of Kitten would be duplicated nowhere for her own. She was indispensable to nobody. Indispensable? It seemed that she was superfluous; else why had Kitten and Roger not shared with her the tragedy they had been facing for the last months? Was it because they cringed at the thought of her tactless, overbearing interference? What a wide radius of grief there would be for Kitten's loss, deeper and deeper as it approached the center! Maggie had in the past often confessed to being vaguely "depressed" by that upstanding brood of bland blond boys; perhaps she had resented the pull they exerted, drawing Kitten out of her own orbit and back to the level of primordial woman. Now she could only guess what their mother's loss would mean to her sons; what would be Roger's Maggie did not dare to let herself think. Almost frantically she surveyed the dramatis personae of her own life, searching for possible mourners for herself. Who would they be? Not Priscilla. No, not even Ray, who seemed, in the war, to have learned so well to do without her. She felt on fire to make somebody—quickly, quickly—love her as much . . . She stopped abruptly. To love her as much as Kitten did.

Maggie wondered helplessly whether there was some horrible monster, unseen only by herself, who guarded the stronghold of her personality—a monster so terrible that all those nearest to her recoiled when they approached. Only Kitten's clear, unwavering gaze looked beyond, around, or through this beast so that, snarling, he must put his tail between his legs and, lowering his eyes as they met Kitten's, go skulking away. Kitten alone could see past the aggression, the braggadocio, the swagger—if those were some of the features of the beast's face—of the public personality. Behind this face she looked, direct and lovingly, at Maggie Fraser. (Maggie could no longer count the love of her dear diminished little mother, who, since the shock of her husband's death, barely knew who it was that she continued to speak of as "my darling daughter.") Kitten, then, out of the whole world, was the only one left to love Maggie Fraser. With that source of loyal devotion expunged, only Margot Masters remained.

And what credentials had Margot Masters, in her own right as a human being, to offer that would guarantee her being an object worthy of love?

She could only hope that she still sported a certain panache. She herself would not have dignified it by the name of courage, but at least a certain vitality of spirit that would not easily admit defeat. That was all. Perhaps Kitten had meant more, even, than the words conveyed when she breathed, "Take care of yourself." Her *self*—where was it? What was it? Who was it? She had simply no idea.

She felt afresh in an aching anguish what the loss of Kitten would mean to her. The shreds of her own diffuse personality had found focus as well as refuge in the citadel of her understanding and love. She felt scattered as well as bereft. Kitten had stood so deeply planted, so firm, while she had been busy hurling herself into the chase after happiness. And yet—she could not blink the fact—nothing had turned out the way she was so sure it must.

But even now Maggie could not bring herself to regret that she had not accepted her role as a Bradfield. Her return to Boston, intensified by her glimpse of Fig Newton, only prompted her to stamp her foot at the place all over again. What was *wrong* with them? She knew that they were good, and true, and strong. Yes, she could go so far as to admit that Dexter had a streak of nobility in him. But they were so—so *bland*! They had no change of pace, no ear for the music to which the rest of the world marched. They didn't even seem to be interested to know that it existed. Her father used to laugh about their plain living and high thinking, but, damn it, they didn't know *how* to live high, and they didn't have the imagination to think low. Only Dexter's favorite word *blah* could describe them.

If Maggie felt uprooted from the soil of the Public Garden, as the pit whence she was digged, she was at least free from any sensations of remorse or regret such as she was sure poor Dick Deacon must have. She couldn't see that she had done anything "wrong" anywhere; she had never deliberately set out to hurt anybody. She had merely wanted —life! And she had not been afraid to struggle for it. *If at first you don't succeed, try, try again . . .* Well, she had tried, and she had—succeeded. She breathed the word to herself with a sudden sigh, a sigh as deep as though she had pronounced its opposite, as though she had—failed.

And now Priscilla was slipping from her grasp back into the very world that she, Maggie, had rejected. Before Maggie's eyes the image of Priscilla sharpened into the very symbol of her own success or failure. Repudiation at the hands of her daughter spelled out, for the world to see, a verdict on her own life. It had failed abysmally, at its very center. Not only would the disgrace carry the public stigma of failure, but Maggie knew that it was from Priscilla's heart alone, of all the human hearts left her, that she might most reasonably expect the assuagement of unquestioning love. If that heart was hardened, then indeed she was bereft. Maggie's fists tightened till the knuckles grew white. *I cannot lose her! I cannot lose her!*

If only Kitten had been well *she* would have stopped her! Yearning to lay the weight of her sorrow and quandry on Roger's shoulders, Maggie was still able to vow that she would keep this trouble to herself. The vow was taken simply and from the heart, with none of the motives hidden to herself that years before had prompted her to conceal her involvement with Ray until the last moment. For perhaps the first time in her life she restrained a natural impulse out of consideration for the feelings and demands of another life other than her own.

Well, then, more than ever, it simply all depended on Ray. He must stop Priscilla.

The very fact that he didn't, he couldn't care as much as Maggie herself made it perhaps more hopeful that his persuasive powers would be successful where her own had failed. It was a truism that young people never listened to advice from their parents. There was no question that Ray and Priscilla got on beautifully. He could point out to her the cruelty of the thing she was talking of doing, not only for the personal sorrow that it would be to Maggie but the cruelty of putting her mother in such a position before the world. How easy it would be for people to say, "You see, even her own daughter can't stand her." The world wouldn't understand the deep-seated reasons of character—preferring New England to New York, the country to the city, and all the rest of it. The world would simply interpret such a move as direct repudiation. Ray could explain these implications; the child was so hopelessly unsophisticated that it might be just as well to suggest to her that worldly comment could and would be cutting. Surely, *surely* she would listen to Ray. Maggie sighed with anticipatory relief. Very likely she had worked herself into a "state" for nothing. Very likely Ray had spoken to Priscilla already, and the day was won.

A shiver ran through her. Suddenly she perceived that Boston's summer miracle had pierced the blanket of heat; an east wind had sprung up. There was to be no thunderstorm, only a sharp shift in the direction of the wind and a plummeting downward of the thermometer. She could feel hope tingle through her.

And then a clear, cool voice within her—more frightening than the voice of panic, because it sounded so plausible, so rational—said, *And if the day is not won, what then? It is not New York as such that Priscilla's turning her back on, and you know it.*

And there, before her, was the truth that she had kept at arm's length since she had heard it the day before. Priscilla wasn't going back to Far Fields because she didn't like New York or its environs.

She was refusing to live under the same roof with her mother and her mother's husband. She had made the irritatingly smug accusation that Maggie was being "mean" to her husband. Really, what a *childish* thing to say! *Of course Priscilla's too young to understand that when a man is weak and lazy and . . . well, downright silly (because that's what he was the other evening), somebody's got to keep things going.* Maggie said the last words to herself rather vaguely, if self-righteously. *But, even so, if she's just too immature to understand, then what? If the sight of the marriage is just more than she can bear, all right then.* Maggie's pulses quickened, and she drew her breath sharply. All right then. Suppose Ray weren't there to be "mean" to? She looked this new thought squarely, almost impudently, in the face.

Suppose she and Ray were to be divorced?

And here was a new thought for company—almost terrifying company, but stimulating all the same. Maggie felt as though there were no lengths to which she would not go to hold onto her child, now that she had got her, after the wait of half a lifetime. If Priscilla could be spared witnessing whatever it was that made her unhappy about her mother's marriage (likely as not there would be an unconscious resentment on Dexter's behalf against any stepfather), if she could have her mother all to herself and life on her own terms, how much would Maggie herself mind, really mind, losing Ray?

She was aware again, in a sharp, uncomfortable twinge, that the worst price to pay would be what people would say. Roger used to tell her that she was *mangée par les autres.* Well, if she was, she couldn't help it. She'd simply *hate* knowing the conversation that would fill the air. "You can't tell me that when a woman fails a second time it doesn't mean there's not something wrong with *her*! And that shiny new inheritance of her husband's too. My, my, and she's no longer young." *Well, I just wouldn't care, I wouldn't let myself,* Maggie said to herself. *Old? Who says so? This new Golden Blond on my hair has made a big difference, and so has the hormone cream. And besides, with Priscilla with me, I'd have someone to stay young for.* The next uncomfortable thought she had for company was how much she'd miss Ray in her work. And then there was the prospect of the future—the future after Priscilla had married and she was left all alone. She remembered her mother having told her that you couldn't really say you loved people for themselves until you'd proved you could live without them. Well, Maggie knew that the prospect of even a day alone was terrifying. So there it was. She would feel the repercussions of a second divorce only through her fear of what the world would say, through her fear of trying to swing her job without help, and her fear of ultimate solitude. As for missing her husband for his own sake—she preferred not to complete the thought, telling herself merely, *If it means keeping Priscilla, certainly I'd face a divorce!* A quickening gust made her shiver again. Maggie stood up.

It was wonderfully clearing; the black threatening clouds were scudding away before the cleansing wind. In a few hours she would be in a plane; she would mount on wings like an eagle, a sensation she always thrilled to, streaking through that fresh, bright evening sky. Suddenly she could laugh at herself. *Leave me alone an hour—it just goes to prove!—and I'm able to work myself into conniption fits. After all, nothing bad has* happened. *And the chances are ten to one that Ray's been able to talk Priscilla round to a sensible point of view. Anything else would be too crazy.*

Maggie hugged herself against the lash of the wind. *Things are bound to get fixed up somehow,* she thought. The perennial optimist was already flexing her muscles: *everything's got to be all right!*

34

Maggie spent the night in town, and went directly to the studio the next morning without calling Ray from New York. She told herself that she wanted to keep her head clear for her show without the distraction of discussing personal affairs first. Actually somewhere in the pit of her diaphragm there was a hard core of fear; she felt she must postpone even the possibility of hearing bad news.

Once off the air she went into the outer office to find Ray waiting for her. He greeted her effusively. Could it be too effusively?

"You're in the big time, Margot! Jorgens is signing a fabulous contract. I just wanted to give you the word. Now I'm off to meet him and the lawyers."

"Tell me more!"

"No, I'm going to save the juicy details till we can sit down to it. Believe me, it's better than anything I could have dared to have hoped for you. Tell me first—" his voice softened—"how did you find Kitten?"

"Awful. I'll tell you later. Listen, Ray, I must know—"

He was sidling toward the door. At the threshold he stopped only to say, "Listen, honey, you won't want me to keep the lawyers waiting. We'll go over everything later. I'll pick you up at the house when I can make it and drive you out to Little Mo. O.K.?" And he was gone.

She had not mentioned Priscilla. And neither had he. It was six o'clock before Ray got to the house on Ninety-fourth Street. Maggie had had a session with the man who had come to install a dictaphone in the downstairs room which was being converted into her office. She hoped that Dot Toulmin would be satisfied; you could never tell with a secretary. Ray found Maggie, in the garden behind, lying stretched out on a canvas chair, her feet up. She was wearing a black Shantung-silk dress and black glasses; her bare arms were golden from concentrated weekend sunning. Her bright toenails, matching the red of her fingertips, were visible through seamless sheer stockings at the open toes of her sandals. Standing on the threshold of the basement dining room, before she had even heard his footsteps, Ray stopped to look at his wife. She appeared to be in a state of suspended animation, with one arm, arching over her head, tossed back above her. He could not see the expression of her eyes under the glasses. Were they closed? But there was a look about her mouth that told him not only that she was not asleep but that she was preoccupied. The sight of Maggie in a moment of stillness and solitude, perhaps even contemplation, had an almost mesmeric effect on Ray. He stood watching her quietly before he said, "Hi."

"Oh!" Her legs swooped off the chair onto the ground, and she was already half out of her chair. "You frightened me! I've been wondering where you were."

"I've had a brute of a day, but I told Rosa to have the kind of meal that could wait for us. I can tell you one thing: I'm not starting for the country without a martini. Will you join me?"

"I certainly will." She gave a tug to her skirt, kicked away the footrest and reached for a cigarette. "How did things go?"

"It's in the bag. It's really a swell setup, Margot. We're signing a thirteen-week contract for a national network half-hour show on a weekday night. You start at fifteen hundred, but we've got you an escalator clause, so that you'll be bound to be making two thousand a week, minimum, at the end of a year if the show clicks. Baum and Walch seem to feel it can't miss, and with television just around the corner the future possibilities for you are really terrific."

"I seem to be the last person to know what the program is really to be. Can you tell me?"

Ray drew up a chair opposite her. "Well, first, it's to be called 'If I Were You.' How do you like it? Naturally your name comes in, too: 'with Margot Masters.'"

A slow smile broke over Maggie's face. "My, Ray, you are smart," she said with warmth. "I like it very much. *Very* much."

He paused only long enough to acknowledge her pleasure with a nod, then drew breath. "This is the routine. Listeners are to send in their problems—universal, down-to-earth ones: 'My mother-in-law lives with me and interferes with the way I bring up my own children'; 'my son who is earning good money and lives at home has never suggested paying his father and me board'; 'my wife is jealous of my secretary'; 'I'm embarrassed to bring home my business friends because my wife acts as though they were beneath her.' The Jorgens Company gives a hundred dollars outright to any person whose problem is chosen. Then, before the show goes on the air, the studio audience will pick four people who admit they have the same problem and feel they could be of some help. Each of these four, who make up the panel with you, will get a hundred dollars. As M.C. your business is to get the story from the guest of the evening. It's the sort of thing you can do with both hands tied behind your back. Then you get advice from each member of the panel, winding it up with a piece of your own: 'If I Were You.'"

"And is that all?"

"Listen, I'm telling you. Three months later if the guy can come back on the show *with* the person who was causing his problem, or demonstrate how he has learned to live with it, thanks to the help he got on 'If I Were You,' he gets a thousand-dollar United States Saving Bond—at a cost of seven hundred and fifty to the sponsor. The Jorgens philosophy is that there is virtually no problem that is not improved by a little spare cash. But before he is allowed to appear on the show he first has to be screened by the three Jorgens judges, showing that his claim of a cure is really on the up-and-up. The judges will be a rabbi, a priest, or a Protestant clergyman—picked from the Jorgens stable—one personal-relations counselor, also on the Jorgens payroll, and—don't drop dead—*you.*"

"Me?"

"Why not? Your fans love you already as one of these fabulous dames who know how to bring out the best in people."

Maggie shot him a quick, sharp glance, suspicious of a concealed "crack." There appearing to be none, she allowed herself the indulgence of expanding with delight at the picture he had painted. It was simply thrilling!

"On the program it's you who will get the story from the person who has licked his problem, just as it was you who got it from him before he had licked it. They're all hopped up about it at WABS—say it's got everything: listener identification, continuity, and the hope of hitting the jackpot. So, Margot Masters, you're on!"

"I love the idea!" Maggie exclaimed. "I'll be a panelist, won't I?"

"If it makes you any happier to have a handle to your name, I guess that would be it. Oh, and incidentally, they rubbed my ego the right way at ABS by suggesting that I be producer of the show, but I said nothing doing."

"Oh, Ray! Why? I think it would be a marvelous idea!"

He smiled. "Thanks. No, I think I'm happy just to serve as general over-all personal representative for you, Margot. You're going to need one from here on in. Aside from your column and two radio shows, there'll be more and more testimonials, guest appearances, articles that will need someone to negotiate contracts for. I've been thinking, and figure we should probably have ourselves an office. Something like 'Margot Masters Productions' in bold-face type, and then, in litty-bitty letters in the lower right-hand corner, 'Raymond Masters, Personal Representative.' Nice?"

It was not until they were settled into Ray's Packard convertible (he told her that the Jorgens Company was planning to present her with a Jorgens Juggernaut, so that this might be her last drive in a car of any other make for a long, long time) that Maggie opened her mouth to ask the question that had been choking in her throat. Before she could speak, however, almost as though he were offering her a quick snort of brandy to serve as stimulant and restorative in helping her to meet the blow he knew that he must strike, Ray spoke with more heartiness than he intended. "Oh, and here we've been so busy talking about 'If I Were You' that I haven't had a chance to tell you how hopped up *Every Woman's Home* is about 'My Margot.' I polished off the last installment over the week end. I couldn't sleep too well Saturday night, and sat down and just batted it off at a sitting, changing it from what the magazine has seen, because I figure with this new show you'll be a much bigger national figure by the time it comes out. I drew on my imagination a little to describe what a day of yours will be like when you're doing both 'Who's Fun' and 'If I Were You.' I did it just the way I thought you'd like it done, Maggie, and I hope you'll be pleased." He ended rather lamely. It did not escape Maggie that he called her by the name he had not used for years, perhaps as a term of very special endearment—or consolation?

"Ray, have you talked to Priscilla?" There. She had spoken the words she had been afraid to speak all day.

"Yes, I've talked with her." Perhaps he was as relieved as she that they were facing it at last. His eyes were on the road before him; Maggie could not guess what thoughts were behind his rather fixed stare.

"Well, what did she say? Please tell me you could do something with her."

"She'd already made up her mind, Margot. Nobody could have done anything with her. It's no use trying to stop her."

"But you *tried*, didn't you?"

The car gave a sudden little jump, almost as though of its own volition, in sharp response to the intensity of the question posed.

"O.K. Since you ask point-blank, I didn't."

"You *didn't*? What do you *mean*, you didn't?" Maggie, recoiling, squared her shoulders against the monster at her side. Like a snake preparing to strike, she took an instant in which to gauge the measure of her opponent before lashing out. "I told you to, Ray! I gave you *explicit instructions* just before I got on the plane."

"Well, I'm sorry, but I disobeyed those instructions."

"Then you've simply ruined everything! Priscilla likes you. You have an enormous influence with her. You could have done something with her if you'd wanted to. Why, Ray, *why*? Don't you *want* Priscilla to live with us?"

"You know damned well I love having her around. She's a swell kid. Priscilla's all right. I'm going to miss her. But she's thin-skinned, Margot. She's not like—" he hesitated only a fraction of an instant—"us. She just doesn't belong in our picture, and she's smart enough to know it."

"I don't know what you mean by 'picture.' I'm her mother, don't forget."

"She doesn't forget it, you may be sure of that. By picture, I mean the frame we offer her—our lives, our marriage, everything about our setup. It just isn't her dish, that's all. She doesn't understand it, and it makes her unhappy."

Maggie was angrier than she could remember ever having been. "Do I take it," she asked in a trembling voice, "that not only did you not try to persuade Priscilla to stay, but you actually encouraged her to leave us?"

Ray was slumped down in his seat, hangdog in the very way he pretended to be studying the road before him. "Well, in a manner of speaking, yes."

"But you just *said*! You just said you liked having her with us."

"Yes, and I also just said that I thought that we were not her dish. I told her, Margot, what I really believe, though I hate to have to say it, that in my opinion she'd do better away from the two of us. It's not a pleasant thought, I admit."

"Do I gather that we represent this source of contamination because of my being so 'mean' to you?"

He gave an excuse for a laugh. "Hell, no. It's much more complex than that."

Maggie sat for a few minutes without speaking. Then she asked, "Is Priscilla at home today? Will she be there when we get back?"

"She's gone, Margot."

"Gone! What do you mean? *Where?*"

"She's gone direct to her Aunt Marsh in Dunster. She left this morning."

"Didn't she even want to say good-by?"

"She felt, Margot—and I must say I agreed with the kid—that one more scene wouldn't make it easier for anybody concerned. I told her to scram, and I would speak her piece for her."

"I only hope it was *her* piece and not yours."

"It was. Believe me."

"I can't *stand* it!" Maggie's voice rose so that people in the next car might have heard her. "She just can't *do* such a thing! I won't allow it! I'll call Marsh. I *can't* lose her!"

"I'm afraid you have, Margot," Ray said quietly. He stole a quick look at her. There was something about the way her nostrils were dilated and her mouth closed that said, *Touch me not*. He waited for her to make the next move.

She made it with the suddenness of a pounce. "Ray, what would you say to our being divorced?"

This time, as though it were a sensitive partner in an unpredictable dance, the car slowed down. "For Christ's sake, Margot, why?"

"You must see why. If the sight of us, our marriage, is so upsetting to Priscilla—she has told me in so many words that I am 'mean' to you and that she doesn't like it—then I . . . I care more about keeping her with me than anything in the world."

"Do you mean it, Margot?" He was looking at her, incredulous. As Maggie confronted him, prepared to hurl defiance, she was first confounded and then, more gradually, disturbed by an unmistakable trickle of something clearly recognizable as relief flooding his features. Even his very shoulders seemed to droop in an easing of tension so that he looked suddenly five years younger before her eyes as he asked, "Wouldn't you really mind a divorce?"

She stiffened, suddenly alerted as she clearly detected an edge of something approaching pleasure in his voice. To her own surprise she rapped out, "Would you?"

"Well . . . that is . . ." She saw him like a man afraid of a trap about to spring beneath his feet, treading warily. "If a marriage doesn't go—I mean to say if the mainspring has more or less gone on the blink—why, then instead of tinkering with it, sometimes it's more sensible, more really adult to call it quits, with no ill will, especially when there aren't so many years ahead for—"

He faltered and stopped as Maggie demanded, "For what?"

"For happiness," he said, suddenly bold.

"I take it, then, that you can think of other ways in which you could be happy."

"Ever so many" came out too quickly—so quickly that Maggie asked, "Such as?" in a tone more menacing than any she had yet used.

"Oh, nothing special."

"Or nobody special?"

"Certainly not." It was Ray's turn for severity. "I mean just—oh, a chance to sweeten up some of the better things of life that have turned sour. Look here, Margot," he said abruptly, "this conversation wasn't my idea. It was you who first said the word *divorce*. It sort of took me by surprise that you'd been thinking on those lines. That's all. I'd never thought of it as a possibility that you would consider."

"And now that you know I would, you rather like the idea? You feel it would solve things for you? You've certainly made it clear that I have not made the kind of wife you wanted." This wasn't turning out at all the way she had envisaged. How had they got into this inextricable tangle anyway? Priscilla! There was the Ariadne's thread that would pull her out.

"I don't say that for myself it's what I'd choose, the way I gather you would," she heard herself saying rather primly. "It's not what I'd choose at all, as it happens. But I'd go through with it if it meant my keeping Priscilla with me."

For the first time Ray's face softened. There was a crack of compassionate feeling as he answered her. "Margot, be your age, my dear. It's not just you and I that make Priscilla unhappy. It's—"

"It's my raking you over the coals that does her in? Well, all right. You seemed to enjoy retailing your woes to that bitch who came to dinner the other night. Well, I'm taking you up on it. You say I don't want a husband. I take that to mean you don't want me for a wife. O.K. If you want out, the door is wide open. All you have to do is step outside."

"Listen, Margot, let's not talk about divorce just now. We're talking about Priscilla. Remember? Our being divorced wouldn't solve anything for her."

"But why *not*? I—I'd give up my job! I mean it. I'd give up everything, I'd do anything to give her what she wants. Maybe she'd like to travel," Maggie said a little tentatively, and then added in stouter tones, "Yes, we could travel together if she doesn't like either New York or Long Island."

"Margot, *dear*. Travel where? Just round and round the world? Kids Priscilla's age want to prove themselves. They want more from life than just being distracted. Besides, it wouldn't distract her. She'd be wretched."

"You mean she'd be unhappy all alone with me? With her own mother?"

Ray refused to answer the direct attack. "Listen, you just haven't thought the thing out, that's all. Priscilla's the most tenderhearted little creature alive. Do you really think she would be, could be, happy watching you go through the divorce mill a second time because of something she had said? You know her as well as I do, Margot. Better. You know damned well she couldn't sleep one night feeling she'd been responsible for the crack-up of your marriage."

Suddenly all her daydreaming vanished under the searchlight of Ray's appraisal. He was perfectly right, and by being so had proved that he knew Priscilla better than her own mother knew her. Awareness of the irony goaded Maggie back to the offense. "You didn't answer my question. Do I gather that you don't think that Priscilla would be happy living with me, by myself?"

"Do you?" asked Ray of the windshield before him.

Maggie's answer was a sound that was nearly a groan. It brought Ray's head around, for an instant, to look at her. "Face it, Margot. How does she fit into the life you've made for yourself? 'Celebrities' mean nothing to her, or publicity, or any of the social rat race either, and . . . Wait a minute—let me finish." He lifted one hand off the wheel to stop her as she opened her mouth to speak. "And even if you say now you'd give it all up for her, what would you have to give her instead? You can't impose the weight of your sacrifice on her shoulders. It's more than she should be asked to carry. She can't spend twenty-four hours of every day of her life feeling you breathing down her back, saying, 'I've given up everything for you. You only are my life.' It would be hell for the kid. She's got to be allowed to develop in the way her own instinct tells her is best for her. That's what I've told her, Margot. I couldn't tell her anything else. And you, for better or worse, you have developed in the way *you've* chosen. About the two most cruel words in the English language are *too late*, but I'm afraid they cover it. The two ways just won't jell. You might as well face it. It's tough. Very tough. But there it is. *La vie.*"

The unconscious look of pain on her face was reprimand enough to his futile reach for a light touch. For the first time he saw just the way she would look when she was ten years older. There was a furrow between her eyebrows, and lines running down, not up, from the corners of her mouth. Her nose looked hawklike, her eyes set. Today her expression was tragic, but he saw that some day it would be merely discontented.

Ray, prompted by the desire to see something else written across the features he knew so well, said gently, "If you're worrying about Priscilla, Margot, forget it. Let her go."

"How can I let her go—back to the Bradfields?"

"I hope you're damned sure, Margot, that your wanting so to hold onto the child isn't prompted by your own feelings of pride. Isn't it that you'll be damned to hell before you see your ex-in-laws come out on top in this hassle that has gone on so long?"

Maggie opened her mouth to speak and then, remarkably for her, closed it. With unusual self-control she said, "Of course there's some of that in my feelings. It would be silly to pretend that there isn't. But it just makes me sick, for Priscilla's sake, to see her brought up by a sex-starved New England spinster. I don't want her turning into some kind of recluse."

"You haven't such faith in her as I have, then. She may be taking the long way round, but she's fundamentally too healthy not to beat her way out. Priscilla's got a lot of guts." Ray hesitated before adding with half a smile, "If she didn't she wouldn't be standing up to you, Margot. She'll find her own little place in the sun all right. You see if she doesn't."

"If you knew Far Fields you could hardly call it a 'place in the sun'" was Maggie's frosty reply.

35

THE CAR quickened its speed. Neither Ray nor Maggie spoke for several minutes. Priscilla and her self-sufficient, neatly arranged little future seemed left behind in their wake.

But what of Priscilla's mother? Maggie asked herself. The desolation engulfing her and the fear for her own future clutched at her throat.

She spoke in a strained voice that sounded unnatural to her own ears as she brought out at last, hesitantly and—for her—almost abjectly, "Ray, do you *really* want a divorce? You were talking that way, weren't you, because I hurt your feelings?"

Ray opened his mouth to speak, and then, abruptly, shut it. "Very likely," he answered in a monotone. Then, as though forcing himself on to a brightness he did not feel, he threw out the sop. "Anyway, I don't want a divorce, Maggie."

"Why don't you?" she asked in the same small voice.

"A fair question." The tacit recognition between them that there was no question of his saying *Because I love you*, showed how far they had traveled. "Well," he said, "let's see." He might have been surveying a familiar piece of property, appraising its assets and liabilities. Almost affably he said at last, "Perhaps it isn't the most chivalrous thing in the world for a husband to say to a wife, but since we're facing facts, let's face it that I'm used to you."

"Ray, *really*! Of all the—"

"I know. But if I weren't used to you we would have come apart at the seams long ago. Don't forget it's you who've got me beautifully conditioned to the kind of life you've made. You yanked me out of California back to New York, you got me to give up my job in radio to go back into advertising, you put your foot down on Missouri, and settled me back on Long Island where I always swore I'd never set foot again. Our whole marriage has been lived on your terms, Margot. It's a little late at this stage of the game to expect me to stand on my own feet."

She was glaring at him now. Under the white heat of her scorn his words came to a standstill.

"You—you *coward*!" she flung at him at last.

"You mean you would have preferred the kind of husband with guts enough to leave you?"

"Yes!" she hurled at him.

She found herself reaching abruptly for the unaccustomed weapon of sarcasm. "Considering the things you said to me the other night, maybe it's not too late for you to find somebody else." She put her elbow on the door and cupped her face in her hand, as though to give herself up completely to enjoying the beauty of the countryside which was whishing toward them out of the gathering dusk.

"Not now." He almost had said *Not again*. "Oh, hell, let's face it. I'm not ever going to do anything in a big way—love, or writing, or even—"

"Even what?" she asked crisply without turning her face.

"Even suffering," he said. "I've had it." He went on, more for his own edification than hers. "Once you've been on the top of the heap—emotionally, physically, creatively, every other way—all you can expect is rather drearily to slide down the other side. Cheer up, Cuthbert, we'll soon be dead," Ray said with a stab at his old gaiety. "We may have a good life in the meantime."

"I don't know what a good life is any more" was Maggie's answer.

"Who does?" Ray stooped forward to apply his cigarette to the lighter on the dashboard. With the deep indraft of tobacco into his lungs he inhaled the knowledge, pervading his whole being, that his capitulation was complete and irrevocable. There would never come again such a moment, such a lifting of hope. Only as the door of the cage had swung enticingly and all-unexpectedly open had he allowed himself keenly to become aware of how every nerve in his body ached for reprieve from his captivity. But as it snapped shut again, he knew that unless it were to be a reprieve indeed—falling, through no act of volition on his own part, by the grace of God, on his unworthy head—he would never now lift his own hand to open it. What he had said to Maggie he believed; habit and cowardice both held him.

What he had not said—what he had not, perhaps, fully admitted to himself—was that he was imprisoned by pity, too. He knew that the self-deceived, frightened woman at his side, who must see herself triumphant or perish, would spit the word *pity* derisively back into his face. But the fact remained that he simply would not have the heart, any more than the stomach, to leave her to the fate that she had brought on her own head. Pity, in the end, was the strongest of all the ties that held him in bondage.

Another draft of his cigarette and he settled down to the serious business of driving. With city traffic well behind them, he stepped firmly on the gas, and the car quickened its rush through the night, cooler and damper with every mile.

Maggie settled well down on her spine, resting her head back against the leather seat. The wind yanked at her hair, pulling it straight out so that it tugged at her scalp, showing a telltale drab at the line where the gold began. Without sound, as effortlessly as though she had pulled out a stopper, her tears began to flow. They streamed, they poured down her cheeks, a few of them drying in the sharp wind as they fell. If Ray saw, he gave no sign. She did not cry to attract his attention, or, as she had often cried in the past, with the storming of a spoiled child. She pulled out a handkerchief to mop her dress, to blow her nose; somehow it seemed to tap the reservoir, and more tears gushed from her eyes. She wept silently, deeply, in total desolation. She felt her very being drained and washed away. She would have liked to be able to comfort herself by saying, *This is the price one must pay for having lived too hard*. But fear gripped her suddenly that she had not lived at all. Surely the knowledge that she was not loved by any human being spelled her death sentence. Her only daughter had repudiated her, and her husband remained married to her merely because he didn't have the gumption to leave. So far as gumption went, for her part, she did not throw him out because she knew that he could be of use to her and because she was afraid of what might become of her without him.

She felt Ray's hand on her knee. "Don't take it too hard, Mag. We'll manage."

His voice was kind. She felt comforted and aware that, strangely enough, Ray himself seemed to understand and condone the full fury of her bitterness against him. He knew what it was that she had expected from him when she married him. He understood that she had been cheated. What she did not understand was that the compassion in his voice was addressed to a woman whose life had broken to pieces in her hands and who did not know the reason why.

Ray let her cry on. Lacking himself the relief of even an outlet of temper, he could only suffer his own private hell, comfortless. The imagination that made him capable of understanding Maggie's disgust lighted for him the lights and shades of the vision that had betrayed him—far subtler than Maggie's paradise of posterlike bright and blinding colors. He could not have named that vision he had once believed in for himself. Poetry? Beauty? They were concomitants of the whole, but not the whole itself. He had seen it with Masu. Years ago, when they were young, although it hurt him unbearably to say it, he had seen it with Alice. Maggie, blind to its very existence, could have no conceivable idea what it was that Ray had lost.

The sobs gradually began to diminish in violence, like receding rolls of thunder. "All that you need, kid, is a good stiff drink and some shut-eye. We'll give you a couple of nembies." (It was their pet name for Maggie's favorite sleeping pill.) "After all you've been through in the last forty-eight hours it's not surprising you're dead beat. As a special surprise I've got something for bedtime reading that I think, that I hope you're going to enjoy."

Over the summer Ray's habit of reading to Maggie before she fell asleep had gradually become set. At first she had pleaded that her mind was so obsessed with "Who's Fun"—both on the air and in the preparation of her column—a half hour of a little detective fiction would serve as a sedative. No matter how harassed Ray himself might be with the business details he had been taking on in her behalf or work of his own, no matter how much he might want to read to himself for his own relaxation or pleasure, he would hear from the adjacent twin bed, the moment Maggie had snuggled down into it, "All ready." Recently he had been obliged to increase the dose: he was reading aloud from an hour to an hour and a half every night.

When, in due course, he heard his cue tonight, it came to him in such a muffled voice that he barely recognized it. "All ready," it said. "What are you going to read to me?"

Out of the open bathroom door, on wreaths of steam, floated the soft scent of the bath oil that had just sweetened Maggie's bath. On the pale aquamarine wall-to-wall carpeting a maribou-trimmed pink-satin dressing gown lay slumped. On the table between the beds was a glass of water with the sleeping capsules beside it, to be popped into her mouth as the reading drew to a close. The aquamarine mother-of-pearl radio-alarm clock was set for six-thirty the next morning. Getting into town for an early program took some doing from such a distant corner of Long Island. Another radio, this one a stronger receiving set, was also on the bedside table. Ray and Maggie were likely to entertain themselves, when they were preparing for the night, by tuning in on a Washington station and listening to a recorded playback of the "Who's Fun" program she had done in New York that morning. Tonight Ray had snapped it on, to hear Maggie's bright voice blaring out full volume before he could turn it down, "The guest we have in the studio this morning is one of my favorite people in the whole wide world, because I simply *live* by her wonderful cookbook! I have a feeling this is going to be my Red Letter Day!"

"Turn it off," Maggie had snapped from her dressing table without turning her head.

"Oh, I thought you might want to hear how Claudine's French accent comes over."

"Well, I don't." Maggie had not spoken again before getting into bed.

Now Ray snapped on the single beam of light inset into the headboard above his head; a growing bald spot suddenly gleamed under its beam. The eyes and forehead of the figure in the other bed were covered with a rubber bandeau, as was the chin. He knew that under the bandeau had gone a generous lathering of hormone cream. The back of the head showed a cherry-colored ribbon, tied across it to keep the wave in her hair set through the night.

Ray looked at the back of the woman in the next bed, hunched up and motionless under the bedclothes. He surveyed it as he might the mutilated victim of some physical smashup. The truth that Maggie had had to swallow had indeed been a knockout dose. *Has she regained consciousness? What can I do to bring her around?* Ray asked himself. He knew only that he could not bear this silence, this immobility so unlike the Margot of every day. Aware that he had within his grasp the only possible restorative, he reached for it. He must let her put her lips to a refreshing draft. All he could do for her, in his and her own helplessness, was to offer her the image of the self that she must believe in or die.

He picked up a sheaf of papers, held them at arm's length and then with a rueful shake of the head remembered the newly acquired tortoise-shell spectacles on the table beside him. He placed them on his nose.

"I thought you might like to hear the last installment of 'My Margot,'" he said. "I rewrote it as a surprise for you. I really put my heart's blood in it. I call it 'Success at Last.'"

"O.K." Again in a voice he would not have known.

"'How could I realize,'" he began, "'that right on the beach at

Waikiki, I was going to meet a new Margot and that this woman was my wife?' "

He read on, describing the successful life that he found his wife had built up for herself during his absence in the war. He told of the countless fans that Margot Masters reached (he was writing as though "If I Were You" was already an established program), her full days that still were never too full to give heed to a letter from a stranger, to someone who might need her help or advice.

Occasionally Ray shot a glance at the motionless back. If he could have prayed, his prayer would have been, *Please, God, let her take it for real.* If only the depth of his compassion could bring to pass the miracle that would transmute the tinsel into gold! He thought, after five minutes, that perhaps the shoulders seemed less tense; the soothing draft was beginning to take effect. An arm was thrown out from under the bedclothes and lay relaxed on the pink crepe-de-Chine blanket cover. On her hand was the heavy wedding ring, the badge of the second marriage characteristic of the Masters' vintage. He read on. Now he was telling about the surprise Maggie had for him in the discovery of their farm, Little Mo. Their Fun House, she called it—filled with Fun People over week ends and, when they had it to themselves, the perfect setting for their Fun Marriage. Because that is what he was privileged to have with this fabulous woman. . . .

He read:

> "So there it is—the story of our Fun Marriage. From the day I fell in love with Margot at first sight, I knew that I was in the presence of a terrific gal. Perhaps the fact that Margot and I have not had children has thrown us more closely together than is customary with most husbands and wives."

He shot another glance at Maggie. From the very position of her head, flung back on the pillow, he could see that he was winning his audience. Ray watched his wife's features, first with hope and then with satisfaction as the lips slowly turned up at the corners. Mission accomplished. The drug of flattery, skillfully administered, was working, as presently the nembutal would work too. The expression on Maggie's face spelled euphoria.

Now, as he neared the close of his article, Ray could allow himself the indulgence of reading for himself alone, as he had written, for himself. To whom else could he speak—ever?

He read:

"Naturally there are moments too intimate for a husband to speak of to others. Remember Browning's writing about the two sides of *his* famous wife—his Elizabeth—the world's side and his own? That's the way I feel about my Margot when I hear her over the air, along with the rest of the listening public:

"'Ah, but that's the world's side, there's the wonder,
There they see you, praise you, think they know you.
There, in turn, I stand with them and praise you. . . .'

"When the broadcast is over and the fans have left the studio, 'when I glide from out them, cross a step or two of dubious twilight, come out on the other side,' and we're home together at Little Mo, then I know that out of all the millions who may wonder what this fabulously successful woman is really like, I'm the only guy who knows. Then it is that I realize most deeply that her life is mine and mine is hers.

"Of this I cannot write. Like Browning, only can I 'hush and bless myself with silence.' "

ABOUT THE AUTHOR

THE SUCCESS *is Helen Howe's fourth novel.* The Whole Heart, We Happy Few, *and* The Circle of the Day *preceded it. Miss Howe is known not only as a novelist but as a monologist. She has appeared in her one-woman show of original character sketches in New York and London theaters and supper clubs, as well as in recitals throughout the United States. She belongs to a distinguished literary family: her father is M. A. DeWolfe Howe, editor and Pulitzer prize-winning biographer; one of her brothers is Quincy Howe, historian and news analyst; and the other is Mark DeWolfe Howe, writer, and professor at the Harvard Law School. Miss Howe grew up and was educated in and near Boston, spent three years in Hollywood, and at present lives in New York City during the months that she has to be away from her home in Somesville, Maine. She is married to Reginald Allen, business administrator of the Metropolitan Opera.*